Here Lie
All the Boys
Who Broke
My Heart

Here Lie All the Boys Who Broke My Heart

A NOVEL

EMMA SIMMERMAN

An Imprint of HarperCollins*Publishers*

hc.com

FIRST EDITION

Interior text design by Diahann Sturge-Campbell

Blood spatter © AbuSafyan/Stock.Adobe.com
Tombstone illustration © Andrew L/Stock.Adobe.com

Library of Congress Cataloging-in-Publication Data has been applied for.

ISBN 978-0-06-345976-2

Printed in the United States of America

25 26 27 28 29 LBC 5 4 3 2 1

To the girl I was at twenty-one—it all worked out in the end

Here Lie
All the Boys
Who Broke
My Heart

PROLOGUE

How do you fix a broken heart? If you ask Google, it's going to give you a list of dos and don'ts such as: avoid contact, get rid of personal objects and mementos, find a new source of happiness. If you ask my best friends, they'll tell you to get absolutely plastered and hook up with his friends. So, it's different for everyone, I think. There is no right or wrong way to heal. I myself have a different approach. When someone breaks my heart, I get out my journal and a bottle of wine and I write him a eulogy.

I know how that sounds—weird, creepy, unhinged, all of the above—but it's not like anyone sees it but me. It's my closure and my therapy, because if you break my heart then you are dead to me. Fictionally. So imagine my surprise when all the boys who broke my heart started dying.

Literally.

CHAPTER 1

August

It's the start of my senior year at Pembroke College—a new beginning. If my life were a Netflix limited series, this would be the first episode. I can picture it as the scene opens to a small apartment bathroom. The lights are off, but the midday sun shines through the windows, illuminating the space just enough to see my hand pop into the frame, like a zombie breaking free of graveyard dirt. I grab on to the sink, hoisting myself up off the ground. The camera zooms in as I look up into the mirror at the mess staring back at me. I pull what looks like a straw wrapper from my tangled hair. My shirt from last night is half off. One fake eyelash still on, the other glued to my cheek. I sigh at my appearance and stumble from the bathroom, but the camera is still focused on that spot, and the title of the show appears on the screen in my absence, in big, bold letters. I wonder what it would say. Maybe something like "Hot Mess," or "Redeemable?" with a question mark that slaps onto the end of the word at the last second. The audience would wonder how I got here. They would form their initial opinions of this character in front of them, and they might not like me.

Right now I don't even like me.

I pull myself from my thoughts as I tiptoe across the hall of the two-bedroom off-campus apartment, squinting against the offensive morning light, and I peek in at my bed, wanting it to be empty.

Short, light brown hair is lying atop the pillow next to mine. Slow, deep breaths rise and fall under my comforter. Shit. I step into my room, over jeans and shirts, the clothes from last night tossed about in a hurry. I can barely even remember if we . . . I let the thought trail off unfinished, unwanted as I pick up the black leather wallet on my nightstand and open it up. Nick Crane, age twenty-one, six two, brown hair, blue eyes, from Boston. Hm. Not bad. I study the ID a moment longer when he begins to stir, turning toward me. I quickly shut the wallet and set it down as he opens his eyes groggily and smiles up at me.

"Hey," he says.

He's cute, and I'm wondering how I've never seen him around before, considering we're the same age. Pembroke is a big school, but it's not that big. And by the time you're a senior, you either know or at least recognize just about everyone in your year. His lazy grin makes my stomach feel sour when I remember that I don't remember how we got here.

"Hate to do this to you but I have to go to work, so I need you to leave."

I don't really have to work today; in fact I specifically requested off for this whole weekend, but it's nicer than just telling him to get out for no reason. I start rummaging around my dresser, pulling out what I would wear to work if I was really going. The first weekend of the semester, also known as Welcome Weekend, is usually a three-day, nonstop party. Everyone is back from the summer, all tan and glowing, and the weather is still warm. Every house has people drinking on the lawn, every bar is packed full. I bet my friends are already up and out again, wondering where I am.

His smile fades as he looks around, then props himself up on his elbows. "What time is it?"

"Like two in the afternoon."

"Damn." He sits up fully now. "Do you want to grab some lunch before you go? Or even just a coffee?"

I find in these situations it's best to just be curt. "No."

The last thing I want to do is nurse a hangover in broad daylight with someone whose ID I had to check five minutes ago, like I'm the bouncer of my own bedroom.

"Oh, okay." He gathers his clothes from my floor and starts to put on his jeans from last night. "Well, maybe we could grab a drink sometime?"

He stands up, his white T-shirt still in his hand. I imagine us casually getting a drink together. He would have to remind me of his name, I would have more than one drink, and we would wake up here again.

"Maybe," I say, but I don't mean it.

I walk him to the door, stepping over the clutter of boxes I still have to unpack that are scattered throughout the small space. I trip over a box overflowing with the same books I bring to school every year, cursing to myself when my shin collides with the corner of *Little Women*, sending the stack toppling over. I give a silent apology to Louisa May Alcott and the March sisters as the hardcover hits the ground. He turns at the noise, and I lean casually on the kitchen counter, pretending I didn't just fall into it. I watch his eyes drift over to the empty wine bottles and take-out containers. Knowing I have to get all this cleaned up before my cousin Adrienne moves in tomorrow makes my head throb. I wrap my arms around myself, counting the slow, nauseating seconds until I can lie back down.

He steps out of my apartment onto the wooden platform before the stairs. "Can I have your number at least?" The look on his face almost makes me give it to him out of pity.

Almost.

"No, goodbye, Nate, it was fun."

"It's Nick—"

"Okay, bye-bye, now." I shut the door without another word.

I pull my curtains closed and get into bed. I can't help but feel a little disappointed in myself for falling back into this pattern so easily. Senior year was supposed to be different; I was supposed to have it under control, but here I am struggling to put together my memories of last night like an old puzzle that's missing pieces.

When I finally pick up my phone, I find that I have fifteen missed calls from my mom and younger sister, Claire. We are not the type of family that talks daily—sometimes I don't even speak to my mom weekly. They were just here on Thursday moving me into this apartment with my stepdad, Don, and youngest sister, Sofie, so what could they possibly need me for not even a full two days later? Dread forms in the pit of my stomach as I think maybe I did something last night that would warrant these calls. I quickly go through my messages and my profiles, covering all bases before replying to them.

I text them to say that I'm at work and am just now checking my phone. A chat bubble immediately pops up from Claire but goes away, then my phone is ringing again. I let it ring a few times while I look at her caller ID photo. It's a candid picture of her mid-laugh, which I can hear in my head when I look at it. Her hazel eyes crinkle at the corners, where freckled cheeks form an innocent smile. We don't look alike. We don't act anything alike either, at least not anymore. Claire used to always copy everything I did. If my favorite color was purple, so was hers. If I declared that I hated broccoli, so did she. But then I was old enough to wear makeup and get highlights in my hair, and she wasn't. Thus set the trajectory for the big personality divide. Golden-child Claire, and Sloane, the child sent from Satan himself to ruin my mother's life.

I hit decline on the call and begin typing.

> I said I'm at work and you can text me whatever it is.

I find that a little white lie here and there is better than having to tell my family that I'm severely hungover, especially after last year's events. I consider myself lucky that Adrienne isn't here yet to witness me in this state, since I'm sure my mom has her on Sloane patrol. That was one of her conditions for letting me finish out at Pembroke: moving in with my honors-college, fashion-major, has-her-life-together cousin. Adrienne spent all of last summer in New York City interning at Valentino, and I spent mine doing one hundred hours of community service. We are not the same.

Another text bubble from my sister. I watch the little dots that indicate she's typing. But then they go away. My phone is ringing again, this time from my mom. I decline her call as well. Claire's face pops up again, and instead of nostalgia, I'm just feeling annoyed. I answer the phone ready to bite her head off.

"Someone better be dead for you guys to be blowing me up like this," I snap at her.

There's a long pause on the other end of the line. "Um, well . . ." she says quietly.

I abruptly sit up in bed, which does nothing helpful for my head. "Wait," I say, lowering my voice. "Is someone actually dead?"

Hearing Jonah's name come from the other end of the phone makes my ears ring. A time-stopping, head-throbbing ringing that nearly drowns out the rest of what she says.

Claire fills in the blanks for me on how my high school ex-boyfriend died last night in a horrific car accident. My hand trembles as it hovers over my mouth and all I can say back is *oh*. The two of us sit in shared silence and I know if she were here right now she'd rest her head on my shoulder to comfort me; I'd then rest my head atop hers. The room tilts as I lean into the phone, wishing this were the case.

"I'm sorry," she whispers when I don't say anything more. "Are you okay?"

"Yeah. Just . . ." Shocked? Confused? I have more questions though I know she can't answer them.

"Yeah," she breathes. And I know she gets it without me having to say it.

When I hang up with Claire, I sit with my knees pulled into my chest, willing myself to cry, but no tears come. I start to think maybe I should feel bad for not crying, but in a way, he was dead to me already. I wrote a eulogy for him and everything.

I get a text from my mom. She's given up on trying to call me now that I got the news.

> Are you ok?

> Yeah I'm fine.

I get back up out of bed and dig through my backpack. Another text comes in from her.

> Are you sure you're at work? Claire said you sound like you just woke up. It's almost 3 pm on a Saturday. Sloane, if I find out you've been out partying all weekend you will be coming back home.

I roll my eyes at that. A third message comes through.

> You promised you wouldn't get into trouble this year, don't make me regret letting you go back.

I want to respond in all caps, I GET IT, but I don't, it's not worth the fight. I find my leather journal at the very bottom of my backpack. I bring it into bed with me and open it up to the first page, the first eulogy, Jonah's.

For anyone who doesn't know me, I am Jonah's girlfriend of three years. Or was his girlfriend. Because our beloved Jonah was taken from us too soon, in a fiery plane crash over the Atlantic. It just blew up, no survivors, so tragic. Jonah had always wanted to see the world. So much so that one day he just got up and left for the other side of it with hardly a goodbye to spare. Literally, he texted his goodbye to me. Had he just stayed here with me like he promised, this wouldn't have happened. Had he just followed through with our plans, he'd still be here. So, Jonah, now it is my turn to say goodbye, and I'll do it in person and not through text because I'm not a coward. I wish you could've seen the world, but now all you are seeing is the bottom of the ocean. I hope it was worth it.

There it is, my first post-breakup eulogy. I was absolutely devastated when we broke up, because you always think your first love will last forever. And we had a plan. We would go to Pembroke together, where I would be an English major and he would study medicine. We'd make a bunch of new friends, but we'd never grow apart. We'd move into a one-bedroom apartment together in junior year and get a puppy named Rocky, after Jonah's favorite movie. On graduation day we would toss our caps into the sky, all hopeful for the future, and as they tumbled back down, I would look over and see Jonah on one knee, with a ring in his hand.

Three days before freshman year started, I got a text from him saying that he was sorry but he wouldn't be joining me at PC; he was taking a gap year to backpack through Europe. He said he'd always love me and cherish the time we had together. I swear I've never cried so hard in my life. I begged my mom not to make me go to Pembroke without him, but thankfully one of us had a brain and I ended up here anyway. I unfollowed him on all social media platforms—I couldn't bear to see him living his life without me. I deleted every picture and video of him I ever took, and I did not keep in touch; in fact I've seen him only once since we ended things, at a bar back home over winter break two years ago. He gave me a nod and a smile, and I returned the gesture. A small agreement that we both ended up exactly where we needed to be. Jonah had stayed overseas after his gap year to attend a university in Scotland, and I stayed here in Massachusetts. It was like we never even happened.

The only proof of a relationship is right here in this fake eulogy.

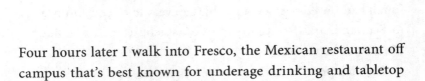

CHAPTER 2

Four hours later I walk into Fresco, the Mexican restaurant off campus that's best known for underage drinking and tabletop dancing, and slide into the booth with Annica and Danielle.

Annica greets me with an annoyed look; I'm late and they've been waiting. She flips her long auburn hair over a shoulder and slides a jumbo margarita my way from across the table. "Since I knew you'd be late."

I take it, grimacing slightly as the glass slides over what looks like a footprint. "Oh, you just know me so well."

"It was nine seventy-five," she says. That's Annica Labrant for you, wealthiest one in our friend group but if you owe her a dollar, she will never let you forget it. Maybe that's how her family stays rich.

"How about I buy you two Long Islands tonight and we call it even?" I suggest.

"But those are only four dollars," she retorts.

Ridiculous, I think to myself as I let out a sigh. I pull out my phone to send her the money.

I met Annica on our very first day of college in Writing I, and we did not hit it off. Her sharp brown eyes were almost always narrowed, sizing up the competition, and her mouth in a perpetual frown. But once you break through that tough, bitchy exterior, she's actually a great friend. The kind that wakes up in the middle of the night to come get you from the campus jail, no questions asked.

Danielle Montgomery, the third to our trio, drains the rest of her margarita and sets it down with a thud. "You have some catching up to do, Sloane." She clinks her glass to mine, a silent *drink up.*

I take a long sip: half lime margarita, half sangria. My favorite, and I know Annica ordered it. She's always good at that, remembering details.

My stomach turns when the icy liquid hits, in part from still being hungover, but also from the random guilt that comes over me when I think of Jonah. I tried to sleep it off after I got the news, but he was all I could see when I closed my eyes. What if he had left for the airport just a few minutes later? What if he was going just a little bit slower? Would it have made a difference? Or was it fated to happen? Somehow it just doesn't feel fair that I get to be here drinking margaritas with my friends and he won't see his ever again.

"Hello, earth to Sloane." Annica waves her hand in front of my face.

"What? Sorry, I zoned out."

"I said what happened to you last night? One minute you were at the bar and the next you were gone."

"Yeah," Dani chimes in. "We looked for you everywhere. You didn't say you were leaving. I was worried." Dani is always worried about something or someone. She's been the designated mother of our friend group since the first night we all got drunk together freshman year.

"Oh, yeah, I ended up bringing this guy back with me, I think Nate or Nick, whatever his name is . . ." I trail off, taking a long swig from the straw. They both look at me expectantly, waiting for details. But the details won't matter, because he wasn't Wesley McCavern.

When I don't give any Annica says, "Well?"

"Don't leave us in suspense! How was it?" Dani asks. We aren't a shy group; we'll usually dish out the most intimate details of our escapades even in a public restaurant. Nothing is off-limits.

"Honestly I don't remember. I think I blacked out." I rest my head on my hand with a sigh.

Annica only blinks before diving into her night. "Well, I went home with that hockey player I was telling you guys about yesterday—"

"Is something wrong?" Dani asks me, ignoring Annica, who is now glaring at her for interrupting. "You seem . . . down."

"I'm just hungover," I say, swirling my straw around. I debate not saying anything about Jonah, but if I can't shake this slump later, the two of them will know for sure that something else is up. "And my high school ex-boyfriend died last night, so that has me feeling, well, I don't know, kind of sad, I guess."

My friends are silent. Annica puts her hand atop mine with a frown. One table over, a birthday song breaks out in Spanish as the waiters crown the birthday boy with a sombrero. Disco lights flash around the room and music blares on the speakers. The whole restaurant is celebrating life and we're talking about death with three jumbo margaritas in our hands. It feels ridiculous. So much so that I can't help but laugh at the timing. Then I can't stop laughing, even after the music cuts out. My friends look at me with concern, which makes it worse. I don't know if it's the lack of sleep or the fact that I now have another buzz on top of the hangover, but I feel delirious.

"Are you having some sort of manic episode right now?" Annica asks, pulling her hand from mine. I can't stop laughing to even reply. Annica looks at Dani. "Is she?"

Dani shrugs. "How would I know?"

"You're a nursing major," Annica says back.

When my laughing subsides, I wipe the tears that have formed and chug the rest of my drink, making my throat feel frozen and tight.

Dani leans in, one reassuring hand on my back. "Are you okay?"

I wave them off. "I'm fine."

"Are you sure?" Annica asks, not convinced. "If you're not up for going out again tonight we can just hang out at our apartment and watch a movie or something?"

Our apartment, meaning hers and Dani's, and no longer mine. Again, one of the conditions of being allowed to come back meant moving out of our shared apartment and moving in with "a better influence," as my mother put it.

"Guys, really, it's fine. It's our last Welcome Weekend—we aren't sitting inside." I force a smile, but I can tell I'm not selling it.

Annica signals the waiter to bring another round before turning back to me. "Does your mom know you're going out this weekend?"

Dani follows with "I hope not. I don't want her to hate us more than she already does."

"Okay, first, she doesn't hate you two. Second, I am twenty-one years old. I can do whatever I want."

"Except sleep with a married professor and get a DUI," Annica quips. Dani shoots her a look. "What? Too soon?"

Three more jumbo margaritas are set down in front of us, and we each take one. I ignore Annica's not-funny joke. "Those are last year's mistakes. This is a new year, a new me." I raise my glass. "To being seniors."

THE THREE OF us walk down College Street as the sun begins to set over campus. I trail behind the two of them, tipsy from our dinner at Fresco and thinking of Jonah. The long road is lined with trees still green from the summer and houses that are in serious need of upkeep. Faded Greek letters mark porches with string lights hanging haphazardly from the balconies, and groups of underclassmen stumble about with large backpacks sagging from the missing weight of warm beers they were surely full of this morning. Red cups and empty seltzer cans are scattered throughout every yard as the daytime revelry continues into the night.

"You know, I'm gonna miss this place next year," Dani says before pinning up her short brown hair into a claw clip.

As if on cue, a barefoot, half-naked man with a beer box on his head runs past us on the sidewalk, nearly crashing into Annica.

"Are you sure?" Annica steps out of the way, her face contorted in disgust.

Dani laughs. "I just can't believe this is the last first pregame of the year with the boys. I think I'll miss them the most."

"Gee, thanks," Annica says.

The boys—Charlie, Sam, Jake, Asher, and Wesley—have been

our friends since freshman year. Annica went to a private high school with Wesley and Asher in a ritzy town just outside of Boston, and we quickly fell in with their group.

"Is Wes going to be here tonight?" I ask, my heart skipping a beat in my chest at the thought.

Annica glances at me from over her shoulder and arches a brow. "Why do you ask?"

The look on her face makes me wish I didn't. Annica has one rule for any girl she introduces to Wes: Do not sleep with him. She made a big fuss about it freshman year, saying her high school best friend did and when it didn't end well, they were no longer welcome to hang out with his group. Wesley is the leader type; if we were to be on the outs with him, we'd be on the outs with all of them. Part of me always thought it was because *she* liked him, but another part knows it's because these friendships mean the world, and not just to her.

"You said last night that he might not come in until Sunday, that's all." Though that's not why I'm asking, my question is answered as we approach their house.

Wesley McCavern is sitting on the porch railing, one leg dangling over the side with a beer in his hand and a backward cap on. I watch him as we walk up the sidewalk. He pushes up the sleeves of his PC sweatshirt and laughs at something Charlie says. Suddenly my mind is transported back to when we were eighteen and I walked up to this very same house, and he sat on that very same railing. He smiled at me then, and for a moment I forgot about Jonah, who had just broken up with me.

"There they are!" Charlie yells from the doorway. "Charlie's Angels have arrived." His nickname for the three of us.

This time Wes doesn't smile when he sees me; in fact he quickly averts his eyes. But all the same, I find myself forgetting about Jonah, even if just for a moment.

Charlie greets us first, bringing each of us in for a big bear hug, holding on to Dani for a bit longer than me and Annica. He asks us how our summers were and listens intently as we tell him. I've always had a soft spot for Charlie, as he's easily the nicest out of the five of them. Always checking to make sure we get home okay and a good person to spark up a deep conversation with. He was raised in a house with four sisters and it shows.

Sam follows behind, quieter, with his hands in the pockets of his black jeans. He gives us soft side hugs and hardly makes any eye contact, but we're used to it by now. Then Wesley stands, and he puts both arms around Annica and Dani, roughing up Annica's hair in the way that a brother would, which she absolutely hates. The two girls remove his arms from around their shoulders, moving on to the rest of the gang, and leaving Wesley and me alone.

"Hey," he says, opening his arms when I do for the most awkward hug of the century. My left arm goes up when his right does, causing one of us to have to change direction, making for a strange fumbling situation. Anyone watching might think we just met. Like we haven't known each other for years. Like we didn't sleep together this past summer.

I catch a whiff of his cologne in our short embrace. I always thought he smelled like detergent and rain. Like fresh laundry during a summer storm. It's usually a comforting scent, but now it makes my heart ache. His eyes are cast down at our feet when we separate, and I look toward the door, where my friends are talking to Asher and Jake. Annica quickly looks away, like she had witnessed this whole interaction.

"So how are you?" I ask to break the silence.

He takes a deep breath and answers on the exhale, "Yeah, uh, good. You?"

"I'm fine."

Wes nods, taking a sip of his beer and looking off to the side, where the setting sun casts a golden glow over his face. I could get lost in the way the light shimmers in his green eyes, but I snap myself out of it. This conversation has run its course.

"I'm going to grab a drink." I give him a tight smile and step around him, but he catches my wrist. Gently, like a whisper.

"We should talk later." He doesn't say about what; he doesn't have to.

It's about last summer, it has to be. I walk through their house imagining one specific scenario of this conversation: It plays out in my head like a movie scene. At the end of the night, everyone will be gone, and he'll catch me as I'm leaving the party. Small droplets of warm late-summer rain will fall around us and he'll tell me he hasn't stopped thinking about me, and damn it all to hell, let's just be together. We'll kiss as the rain comes down harder around us, like something out of a Nicholas Sparks novel.

A stray Ping-Pong ball hits me in the side of the head as I make my way through the living room, pulling me from my daydream. This is not *The Notebook*, this is college. I toss it back to the table where Dani and Annica are already in a game of beer pong. I keep down the hall toward the kitchen. The floorboards creak beneath me and my shoes stick to the ground with each step. Cream-colored paint chips from the walls, which are lined with mismatched couches and random pieces of furniture. It's obvious a group of boys has been living here for three years.

I grab a seltzer from the fridge and almost run into Asher when I turn around. He clicks his tongue and wags a finger at me as he leans on the wall. "Sloane Sawyer, you naughty girl." He crosses his tan arms and sports a smug smile, looking as though he just caught me doing something I shouldn't have.

"Asher." I give him a tight-lipped smile. "If this is about last year, everyone's over it by now." The boys loved to tease me about both the affair and the DUI. I let them make their jokes and waited for the next big thing to steal their attention.

"I saw you this summer," he says, eyebrows rising up to his sandy-blond curls that brush over his forehead. Wesley and Asher have the same light green eyes, being that they're cousins. And I wonder how it's possible to melt when I look into one pair and boil at the other.

"You all saw me this summer. I came back here for Jake's birthday party, remember?" I edge around him to walk back to the living room.

"I saw you after the party, and I saw whose bedroom you walked out of in the morning." That stops me dead in my tracks, and I turn again to face him. "You and Wesley. Interesting."

I walk back toward him, bringing the conversation down to a whisper. "I think you've just had too much to drink, Asher. You don't know what you're talking about."

He looks down at my unopened drink. "Maybe you just haven't had enough." He pops the top of the can. "Loosen up, Sawyer, it's a party," he says with a smile as he tips the can to my lips and puts a hand on the door to the backyard.

"Wait," I call out before he leaves. "Who all knows?"

He taps a finger to his mouth, pretending to think about it. "I think just me. For now." He gives me a wicked smirk. He thinks this is funny.

"Asher," I say through clenched teeth. "Please keep this to yourself."

He leans back against the door. "What's in it for me?"

"What is it that you want?" I bite out, not able to fully believe he would require anything from me just to keep a secret. But it's Asher after all.

He doesn't even need time to think about it. "Free drinks at the wine bar you work at, anytime I come in."

I gape at him. "I can't just make those free. I'd have to pay for them myself."

"Do you think Annica knows about what happened? Or Marissa?" I can't hide the flicker of my expression when he says it. "Oh, you didn't know her and Wes are back together?"

"Fine," I grit out. "Free drinks." He doesn't venture out of Pembroke anyway, so I likely won't have to give him free anything, but Asher was always the biggest asshole of the group for seemingly no reason, so he just might.

When Asher walks out the back door, I stand there alone in the kitchen, taking a breath. Wes is back together with Marissa Wilder. Of course. Of course! We've been friends since freshman year, why would that change just because of one drunken hookup? My mind switches back to Jonah as another stab of guilt pierces my gut. He hasn't been dead a full twenty-four hours and I'm already worrying about someone else. But Wes is in my mind like a song you just discovered and love. You play it over and over again until you're tired of it. It's been four years and I'm still not tired of it. I bring the seltzer to my mouth and start to chug. Then grab another.

THE PARTY FIZZLES out around midnight, when most people leave for the bars or other house parties. Annica left an hour ago for the hockey house and Dani is now wanting to head to the bars as well.

"You ready?" she asks, grabbing her purse and pulling the strap over her shoulder. I glance around the party, now thinning out, and catch Wesley's eyes. He tilts his head toward the stairs. To his room.

"Uh, no. I might go home. I'm just not feeling it tonight." It isn't a complete lie.

Dani gives me a sympathetic frown. "Okay." She rubs my shoulder. "Text me if you need anything." I watch as Charlie places a hand to her back to guide her out, and I wonder if anyone will ever love me like Charlie secretly loves Dani, with longing stares and light touches. He's her fallback. Her casual hookup whenever she's lonely. I can only hope for his sake that one day she gives him a real chance.

Jake and Sam follow the two of them out the door and that leaves just me and Wes. And Asher. At the base of the stairs with my hand on the railing, I look around the living room before going up. The last thing I need is Asher catching me leaving Wesley's room a second time. I wonder what I'd owe him then. He's nowhere in sight, so I climb the rickety wood staircase, then walk down the hall and into the last room on the left. Wesley's room.

It looks the same as it always has. Just a bed, no bed frame, a dresser with a TV on it, and that stupid high school flag he won't get rid of. "Wow, I love what you've done with the place," I joke, pretending to admire it.

"I actually added a new flag. You didn't even notice." He points to a small American flag in a mug on his nightstand.

"Wow, so patriotic, a real nationalist." It's easy to joke with him after a few drinks. Easy to pretend we're back to normal.

He starts to take off his sweatshirt, and his T-shirt underneath comes up in the process, briefly showing off his bare abdomen and chest, and I catch myself staring before he pulls the T-shirt back down and throws the sweatshirt into a hamper.

"Jake spilled a beer all over me," he says, ruffling his dark wavy hair and setting his hat on the dresser. "You'd think this kid would know how to hold his alcohol by now."

I clear my throat and look away from his toned arms, and his hands, the same ones that touched me and— God, get it together, Sloane. "So you wanted to talk?"

He crosses the room and sits on his bed. "Yeah." He looks down at his hands, then up at me still standing here. "You can sit if you want." He motions to the bed, but when I look at it all I can think about is last summer. I slowly take a seat, careful to create distance between us.

"I feel kind of weird about it, with what happened," he says finally.

I take a breath, wiping my sweating palms on my jeans. "Weird?"

"Yeah, we were both so drunk I almost feel like I took advantage of you or something."

"You didn't take advantage of me. I wanted the same thing," I say quickly, not wanting him to spend another fraction of a second thinking I didn't want this. That I didn't want *him*.

He nods before saying, "I think about it a lot."

My heart is beating so fast, it feels like it might leap out of my chest. "I do too," I admit, albeit a little too enthusiastically. Suddenly his next words seem like the most important ones I'll ever hear and all I can do is take in a breath, one almost too fragile to hold.

"And that's why I think it can't happen again," he says. "We're better as friends, and I just don't want that to go away."

I blink, as the feeling of electric anticipation turns into the sharp sting of loss, even though nothing tangible was taken from me. We are just as we once were. We are friends.

"Okay, yeah," I say, because I don't know what else to say. I could tell him what I really want to say. I could tell him that I think about him all the time. Even before what we did last summer. That all the alcohol and all the other guys are just a distraction. But instead, I lie. "I agree."

Friends. I can do the friend thing; we've been doing the friend thing. So why does it hurt so bad to hear him say it?

He clears his throat. "I'm sorry about your ex. Annica told us what happened."

"It's fine, I'm fine," I say, a little too clipped. I don't want to talk about Jonah, not with Wes. I stand from the bed. "If that's all you wanted to talk about . . ." I trail off.

"Are you . . . coming to the bars?" he asks, standing up with me.

"No, I think just home actually. I'm trying this new thing this year where I'm not a total disappointment." But the real reason is that I can't go out after this conversation and pretend to be happy. I can't drink and dance knowing I'm now the victim of unrequited feelings.

I tuck a loose strand of blond behind my ear. He tracks the movement. He told me this summer that he loves my hair, especially when it's down and long like it is now; he said it drives him crazy. He said that. Friends don't say those things to other friends.

His eyes meet mine again as his lips turn down. "You know, just because you made a few bad decisions doesn't make you a bad person."

I feel my eyebrows rise slightly. He pities me. Not only does he not want me, but he feels bad for me. And all I feel is embarrassment.

"Thanks, Wes, I'll see you," I say, leaving his room before this conversation can get any worse.

I TAKE OUT my journal when I get back to my apartment and flip to the last page. The one with Wesley's name, and nothing else. I didn't see or speak to him for the remainder of the summer, but the night after we slept together, I opened my journal and I wrote down his name. I didn't have anything else to add because I didn't feel brokenhearted over what happened, and I certainly didn't want him to be dead to me. I still don't. I sit with the pencil poised to write, but I pull it away. I consider ripping out the page entirely, but it's only the beginning of the year.

There's still plenty of time for him to break my heart.

CHAPTER 3

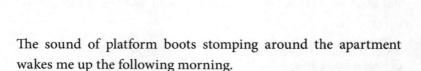

The sound of platform boots stomping around the apartment wakes me up the following morning.

My eyes are barely open when my phone begins to buzz with an incoming call from Adrienne. The click of her shoes comes to the doorway of my room and the buzzing ceases. "Oh! You're here," Adrienne says. "I thought you'd be out."

"No, I'm here." I start to sit up, yawning. I check my phone, thinking Wes would have texted or called last night. I half hoped there would be a long message waiting for me this morning about how he didn't mean what he said. But there is nothing.

Adrienne already has a full face of makeup on her olive-toned skin. Her long brown hair falls in waves over her black leather coat. "Can you be ready in twenty?" she asks, before going into her room.

"For what?" I call out after her.

She pops her head back into my room. "Jonah's calling hours. They're today. I told our moms I'd drive us both back to Cedar Falls. I have to grab some things from home anyway."

"Oh." I rub my eyes. "I didn't know you were going to that."

"He was my friend too." She frowns, then disappears from my room again.

"So TELL ME about your summer!" Adrienne says as we get on the highway westbound to our hometown. It's an hour drive to Cedar Falls.

"Oh, well there's not much to tell. My license was suspended, as you know—"

"Right, because you got arrested for drinking and driving," she says.

It's going to be a long hour.

"Yes," I say, flat toned. "So I lived at home and worked at that golf course down the street, since it was within walking distance. I did one hundred hours of community service and three months of therapy—that was a hoot. I went to some weekend course about why you shouldn't drink and drive. I had to go back to driving school because if your license expires while it's suspended you have to retake your driving test. So, that was my summer." Oh, and I slept with my best friend behind my other best friends' backs because it would be catastrophic to the dynamic of our group if they knew. But I didn't say that.

Adrienne was quiet, taking it all in. "Huh. Well, are you glad it's over?"

I rest my head on the window, watching the trees blur in the distance. "Very."

"Have you heard from that professor at all?"

I can't help but flinch at the mere mention of Professor Miles Holland. "No."

I regret drunkenly sharing that little tidbit with her last year.

Adrienne and I used to be close. In high school we were not only stepcousins after my mom married Don but best friends and neighbors. When we left for Pembroke, we started to drift apart. But you always have a soft spot for that one friend that you grew up with. After all, we were girls together.

When I told her about Miles at the end of last year, I made her promise not to tell anyone in the family. I could hardly deal with the disappointed looks they gave me over the DUI; I couldn't imagine what they'd say if they also knew I was a homewrecker. A life ruiner.

"Let's just talk about your summer."

I NEVER WANT to hear the word *Valentino* again as Adrienne pulls up to my house.

"I'll pick you back up at five?" she asks as I step out of the car.

"Yeah, that's fine." I shut the door and watch her back out and drive the ten seconds over to her house. Don and his family all built houses on the same sprawling expanse of land, with one long driveway to connect us. Nothing says family like a shared driveway.

My mom opens the door and envelops me in a hug. I hear her sniff me. "You smell like smoke and alcohol," she says, pulling away with a frown.

"Oh, lay off of her, will you, Iris?" My stepdad comes up behind her, hugging me next.

"Your sisters are upstairs," my mom says. "Go say hi. And take a shower before the calling hours please."

I roll my eyes when I'm out of view, trudging up the stairs to see the girls.

Claire is in her room reading a book. I round the corner of her large four-poster bed to see Sofie on the floor playing on her iPad.

"Oh, I didn't expect to see you in here, Sof," I say. Sofie looks up at me with her deep, dark eyes but doesn't say anything, just goes back to whatever is on the iPad. She looks so much like Don, with those strong Italian features. She was born with a full head of hair and a summer tan. Until then I never thought you could be jealous of a baby.

Claire sits up in bed, setting her book down. "She just comes in here to sit on the floor and watch TikTok sometimes."

"I see." I nudge Sofie with my foot. "What are you watching?"

"Makeup hauls," Sofie says, kicking her feet back and forth behind her.

"Makeup? You're only eleven," I say.

"For your information, I'll be twelve in six months."

"For your information, I knew that. Also for your information, twelve is still too young for makeup."

"No it's not," she argues.

"Yes it is," I argue back.

Sofie sits up from the ground. "Go back to school. You're annoying." She leaves Claire's room and slams the door.

"And that's how it's done." I smile at Claire.

She laughs. "You know I really don't mind her in here. She doesn't bother me." Though even if she did, I don't think Claire would say it.

"Should I call her back in and say you're going to let her play with your makeup, then?"

"Not that I own much of it, but no." Claire doesn't need to wear makeup; she is stunning enough without it.

I walk around her room, looking through her competitive dance medals and awards. "Did you start school yet?" I ask.

"Tomorrow, like you." Claire will be a junior this year at Cedar Falls High School.

"Excited?" I pick up the tiara she wore in last winter's *Nutcracker* production and place it on my head. "I bet you'll win homecoming queen this year," I say, turning to face her and giving a mock queen wave.

She walks over and takes the crown from my head, placing it back on her bookshelf with her other collectables. "Well, don't jinx it."

"I would never!"

"How have you been feeling?" she asks. "About Jonah."

Claire's life is pure and dreamy, like the ballet she does. I could never muck it up with my problems. The thought of her knowing every little dirty detail of my life makes me feel ashamed that I could ever let her down like that in the first place. So I don't get into my feelings or experiences with her. Big sisters give little sisters advice, not anxiety.

"I'm good, just here to pay my respects to his family and then I'll be back at school. What are you reading?" I change the subject.

"Oh, this?" She walks back to the bed and picks up the book. "It's so good. I'll give it to you when I'm done. It's about a world with dragons and magic, and a main character who loves both of these men, but they're brothers, so she has to choose."

"She doesn't have to choose; she can love them both," I joke. Claire only gives me a look. I run a finger across her dresser. "Well, I do love magical worlds that make me forget about this one," I mutter to myself.

"Just think, this time next year, this could be you publishing something like this." She holds up the book. "*New York Times* bestseller, that will be you, Sloane."

I can't help but smile when she says it. Claire and I have dreamed up fantasy worlds together since she was old enough to speak. We talk about characters like they're people we know. We love when they love, and we cry when they cry. We feel words on paper so deeply that they may as well be etched into our skin like a tattoo.

"I'll sure try," I say. And I would, for her.

"NERVOUS?" ADRIENNE ASKS as we stand in the receiving line at the funeral home.

"Yeah, a bit," I reply, with the inside of my cheek now raw from the nervous biting.

"Don't be, it's just John and Lisa." Jonah's parents. The way she says it gets under my skin. I know, I know them better than you do, I want to say.

Fresh tears come to his mother's eyes when she sees me. "Sloane?" she whispers, like she can't believe it's really me before her. I nod as I move in to hug her. "Thank you for coming. He really loved you."

I'm sure he did for a time. But only in the way that two high schoolers could love each other: blindly. When the relationship makes sense because he's the quarterback and you're a cheerleader. Would Jonah love me now? Probably not.

"I'm sorry for your loss," I say.

I hug his dad next and express my condolences. His absent-minded nodding makes me wonder if he's just shutting it all out. None of the faces in this line of people matter, because none are Jonah's.

I walk up to the casket, hands shaking, and look down at his face. He hasn't changed much over the years. He looks just as he once did when I'd find him fast asleep on the couch after football practice. The tears I had been holding at bay slide quietly down one after the other. The first boy I ever loved, and the first boy to ever break my heart.

"I forgave you a long time ago," I whisper.

BACK AT PEMBROKE, I can't help but feel a bit numb to it all. I show up to my only Monday class still in my pajamas, pick up my syllabus for Professional Editing, and go back home to lie in bed. Annica and Dani both call but I ignore them. I need one more day to mourn Jonah. I take my journal out and read through his eulogy again, cringing when I get to the end. It isn't right to keep this, not now, not after I told him I forgave him. I toss the journal in my schoolbag and get in the car. There's a park in Pembroke, just outside campus, with tall hills of green grass and a river that runs through it. From the tallest hill you can see the whole campus.

I lie down in the grass there, looking up at the blue sky. If there is a heaven, is Jonah there? Is his spirit floating around up in the clouds looking down at us? Or is it wandering the earth? Is he here right now lying next to me? I put a hand out beside me and run it over the grass. In the movie version of my life, there's a camera panning down above me. In my eyes I see him there, looking back at me, and my hand lies against his chest. But when the scene cuts back to camera view, it's just me, alone in the grass.

When I decide it's time, I take out the journal and rip out Jonah's page. I grab the lighter from my bag and hold them both out in front of me. With a stroke of my thumb, a small flame appears just under the eulogy. I bring them closer together until the paper begins to blacken above it, catching fire and spreading across the page. I hold it by the corner until the last of it turns to ash and blows away in the wind.

I RISE EARLY, feeling lighter than I did yesterday, like burning the eulogy removed an invisible weight from my heart. Tuesdays and Thursdays are when I have the bulk of my classes this semester, and even though it's syllabus week, I want to make a good impression today. I stand in my full-length bedroom mirror, smoothing down the beige blazer.

"You're going to ace all of your classes this year. You're not going to get into trouble. You won't let any boys get to you. You're going to write your first book. For Claire. For you." I write it down and tape it to my mirror. I read somewhere that writing down your goals helps you actually achieve them. I repeat the goals three times and by the end I kind of believe it.

I meet up with Annica for coffee across from the English building that houses most of our classes.

"I still can't believe they didn't make you retake Fiction Writing I this year," she says, grabbing her coffee from the counter. The sleeve of her beige blazer slides up her arm and I can't help but notice we're in almost the exact same outfit. She had asked me what I was wearing today, and I sent her a picture of my clothes laid out. Not expecting she'd put on the same thing.

I grab mine too. "You say that like you wish they did."

"Of course not. I'm just surprised." She sips her coffee before she adds, "You know I'd never make it through these classes without you."

We share an umbrella as we step out into the rain and walk

to our first class. It was a big deal when I went to the dean and revealed the affair I was having with Miles Holland. They debated having me retake his course, which would have put me behind on graduating. The other professors in the department read through my work to be sure it was satisfactory enough to move forward. In other words, making sure I wasn't trading sex for grades. Not that that was ever my intention in the first place.

"Do you think this Renner guy will be tough?" Annica asks, talking about our senior seminar professor. We're both English majors with minors in creative writing, and it's been nothing but somewhat friendly competition between us for three years.

"If he is, I guess I could just fuck him?" I joke, but she doesn't laugh.

Our class is full of the same group of kids from last year's Creative Writing I, with maybe one or two others that I don't recognize. I smile and nod at a few as we file in. Lochlan Renner is a short and stout older man with gray hair and bifocals. He clears his throat from his desk in the front of the classroom, adjusting his glasses as he gets ready to read off the list of names in his hand. We raise our hands in attendance as he rattles them off. When he gets to my name he pauses, getting a good look at me. Likely confirming that, yes, I am the girl whose work he had to review in order to move on to this course. He continues down the list.

"This is senior seminar," Renner says as he writes it in black marker on the board. "This is a two-semester course. We will read and analyze three books during this course and your midterm and final will be a short story that you will work on and submit at the end of the year. I will choose the best one to send to the Boston short-story competition. Any questions?"

CHAPTER 4

Tuesday nights are called Ladies Night at Water Street Tavern, one of the campus bars, where well drinks are all a dollar for girls. I stand at the busy bar with my debit card in one hand and my empty glass in the other. Wes and Marissa are at the other end of the square-shaped bar and from here I have the perfect view of her twirling her ash-blond ponytail through her fingers as she smiles up at him. Wes leans on the counter, his white quarter sleeve tightening on muscled arms. He turns to whisper something in her ear, exposing his cut jawline, and Marissa laughs. The grip on my glass tightens.

"Jealous?" Asher leans back on the bar beside me, his head cocked to the side.

I look over at him with a tight smile. "Jealous of what?"

He turns around and leans down, propping his elbows on the counter so that we're side by side. His bare arm brushes against mine and I tuck it closer to my side. "My cousin, over there with his girlfriend." The emphasized word is like a punch to the gut.

"Not at all."

"Then why are you standing here staring at them with a white-knuckled grip on your glass?"

I loosen my hold, flexing my fingers. "I'm just waiting for a drink."

Asher smirks, and it's hard to deny that he'd be just as attractive as Wes if he wasn't such a prick.

"I'm also seeing someone, so," I lie.

"Another professor?" he muses. "What does this one teach? Anatomy?"

I turn my gaze back to him. "Do you have a reason to be over here other than to be a dick?"

"I do, actually." He stands, and with our height difference I have to look up at him. "I'm conducting a little experiment."

"For fuck's sake," I say under my breath, rolling my eyes.

"Last night I asked Wes if he'd mind if I asked you out."

My eyes practically pop out of my head. "You did what?"

"And you know what he said?" Asher goes on. "'Why would I care?'" The words are another knife that strikes hard and true. "He doesn't know that I know what you two did. But you know what I think?" I only stare ahead, my teeth grinding together. "I think he would care." Asher leans down again, this time getting so close that his mouth practically touches my ear as he whispers, "Very much."

I lean away, giving him a hateful glare. "And your experiment is what exactly?"

He remains close enough to whisper, this time tucking a piece of my hair back, slowly tracing his fingers over the strands. "Working," he says, moving just his eyes to where Wes and Marissa still stand. Marissa is talking to the bartender, but Wes is staring right at us, his jaw clenched. He looks away when our eyes meet.

Asher walks away, no doubt feeling satisfied with whatever

fucked-up game he is playing, and I order two vodka sodas, both doubles, and both for me.

I walk back to the tables that our group occupies and take my seat in between Annica and Dani.

"What was Asher whispering to you about?" Annica asks when I sit down.

"Yeah, we were debating on coming up there to save you," Dani says.

"Nothing important, just his usual hateful bullshit." I look across the tables to where Asher sits still grinning. He winks at me and I gag internally. "He's so annoying. Why have we even tolerated him in this group for so long?"

Annica leans back in her chair. "Because he's Wesley's cousin and even though we don't like him, the boys do."

"And because he's hot," Dani adds. We both give her a look. "What? He is."

Annica scoffs. "Are you forgetting about the time we were walking to their house in the pouring rain and he drove past us honking his horn instead of giving us a ride?"

"Or when the PC gossip page posted my DUI mug shot, only to find out *he* was the one who sent it in," I add.

"Well, yeah, I didn't say he was nice to us; I just said he's not the worst thing to look at."

"Change of subject," I say. "How are your classes going this week, Dani?"

"While you guys are getting a syllabus week, my classes have all jumped right into the material. But I get to do clinicals this year and I am so excited. What about you guys?"

"Our only exciting class is senior seminar," Annica says.

"Yeah, our professor is having us all write a short story, and at the end of the year he submits the best one to Boston's short-story writing competition," I add.

Dani's face lights up. "Really? That would be so amazing for you guys!"

"Well, it would only be one of us." Annica looks at me and I see the competitive fire in her eyes.

"It could very well be neither of us," I say, trying to put it out.

Jake comes back to the tables with a tray of shots full of a clear liquid.

"What are these?" Sam asks, hesitant to take one.

"I have no idea," Jake says. He lives for chaos, and it shows. Sometimes I think Jake may be the only one in this friend group who makes more reckless decisions than I do.

Charlie picks one up and questions, "You don't know what kind of shots you ordered?"

"I told the bartender to surprise me." Jake beams. "Happy first Ladies Night of the year, bitches!"

We all take one. My eyes slide over to Wes, where he has Marissa on his lap. "Actually, give me two," I say, reaching across the table again.

In the low light of the bathroom at work, I don't look that hungover. With my hands gripping the sides of the porcelain sink I ask myself why I picked up a double the day after Ladies Night. Tuesday nights can get a little out of control due to the dollar drinks, but it's syllabus week—it's practically like a free week to get adjusted. I'm just getting adjusted, that's all.

The wine bar I work at, Cantine, is located in Bloomfield, the town next to Pembroke, a rich little suburb full of WASP moms married to lawyers and CEOs. The building sits in the quaint town square in between a Lululemon store and a vegan ice cream shop. Each shift I watch the stay-at-home moms walk around the square, going from shop to shop while their kids play in the grass square that the shopping area surrounds. Until they come in for happy hour, kids in tow, and order cheese plates and talk shit with their other rich friends about Lisa, whose husband lost his job and had to pull her son from private school to go to public school. The horror. But it's not the wine and cheese that brings them in; it's Tristan Brent.

When I walk out of the bathroom, I stop short of the bar, because there he is stocking the glasses. I run to the back of the kitchen where the schedule is, and sure enough, there is his name below mine.

"Fuck," I whisper to myself.

Tristan Brent is a shameless flirt. The twenty-two-year-old had been working at the wine bar all throughout college, and was the one to train me when I started working here last year. I would watch and learn as he greeted everyone with that side smile that held too-perfect teeth and created a too-perfect single dimple on his left cheek, his blue-gray eyes holding each stare in conversation. With light brown clean-cut hair, a finance degree, and a part-time gig as a firefighter, he was every WASP mom's wet dream. I used to laugh at the grown women who came in here and fell over him like schoolgirls but soon I, too, found myself struggling to find words when he looked at me. It wasn't long before he screwed me over and I had to kill him.

In my journal, obviously.

I decide to go back out and just pretend he's not there. He's standing behind the bar, arms crossed, leaning against the counter. I walk in and start rolling silverware, not sparing him a glance.

"I take it you're still mad at me," I hear him say. I don't give him the satisfaction of a response. "Over something I didn't do." I pick up a rag and start wiping down the bar. "Come on, Sloane, it's been months. I can't get a hold of you, because I'm assuming you blocked me. And you've purposely scheduled yourself to avoid working with me for the past six months."

I finally give in. "And there's a reason for all of that."

"I never made that bet."

The bet was one that he made with our two cooks, that he could get both me and Alaina, the other new waitress at the time, to sleep with him before his last shift, which was supposed to be at the end of the spring last year. But here he is, still working here.

"Honestly, Tristan, whatever. I just decided I don't even care anymore whether you did or didn't make the bet. Let's just move on." But that couldn't be further from the truth. Because I do care. So much so that you'd think my name was Sloane Vendetta Sawyer. I just couldn't let go of the past. But when I think of Jonah, and how I wish that I could've had just one last conversation with him . . . I am willing to try.

"Oh." He's taken aback by my sudden change of heart. "Okay, great. Let's get this shift started then, bar buddy."

Tristan opens the doors right at 11 a.m. and in walks Asher McCavern.

"Oh, you've got to be fucking kidding me," I mutter.

He takes a seat right in the middle of the bar. "I'd like a beer." He flashes an arrogant smile that makes me want to punch him.

"And I'd like you to leave," I say, putting my hands on my hips.

He remains seated and pulls his phone from his pocket. He types something in and then lays his phone on the bar. It rings Annica. I quickly grab it and hit the end call button.

"What kind of beer do you want?" I toss his phone back at him.

"What's on draft?" he asks.

It's a wine bar: The entire back wall of the room is lined with hundreds of bottles on shelves with a rolling ladder attached. Whenever I have to use it I think of that scene in *Beauty and the Beast* when Belle slides across the library on one. Except these aren't books—they're wine bottles—and I guess that makes me Beauty and the Bottles. Unless I'm hungover like today, then it's more like Bottles and the Beast.

I point beside me at the only three draft handles we have. "Use your eyes," I say.

He only huffs a laugh at my blatant rudeness. He chooses the IPA and I grab a glass to pour, purposely not a prechilled one because he doesn't deserve it. It's the little spiteful things.

"I actually came here to talk to you," he says.

"Our arrangement was free drinks, not conversation." I set his room-temp glass down in front of him.

"Fine, then I'll talk, you listen." He takes a long sip of the beer and sets it down, before casually running his hand through his hair in the same exact way that Wes does. "I think we can help each other out. You want Wes, and I want the family business."

I blink at him, confused. "How do these things even relate?"

"Our family's resort in Colorado is run by his dad, so naturally it goes to Wes, but he doesn't want it. I do. And I only get a shot if he passes on it." I know all about their fancy ski resort in

Vail. Their grandfather started the business and passed it down to his oldest son, Wesley's father, but he and Asher's father work together on it. Or so I thought.

"What does this have to do with me? And how do you know he doesn't want it, did he tell you that?"

"No, but I can tell. His dad wants him to move out there after graduation and run the day-to-day at the resort. Wesley hates it there but is too afraid to disappoint his dear old dad. That's where you come in. I can help you win him over, if you can convince him not to take the job."

"Why would you think he even wants me in the first place?"

"My experiment, remember? I suspected he'd be jealous. I just needed to confirm it."

"Then why would he say he just wants to be friends?"

Asher shrugs. "He likes his girls to be predictable, like Marissa. Cookie-cutter sorority girl with two brain cells, but her dad is on the board of trustees for the school and I hear she gives good head."

I roll my eyes.

"But you, Sawyer, are unpredictable. And so is whatever would come out of a relationship between the two of you. The whole dynamic of the group could implode, which, honestly, I would enjoy seeing."

"There is something wrong with you," I say. "And by 'unpredictable' you mean I'm not up to his standards, is that it?"

"Well, you sleep with married men and drink and drive. I don't think you'd be my aunt's first pick for her son, *but*"—he holds up a finger to silence me before I can even get started—"I can help with that."

"So that's how I'm going to win him over? By making him jealous? With you?" I laugh at how ridiculous that sounds. "Like anyone is going to believe that I'd ever date you."

"Ouch." He takes down the rest of the beer in a few gulps and sets the glass on the counter. "Just think about it," he says, before walking out of the bar.

I grab his empty glass and imagine Wes and me together. But do I want it if I have to scheme with Asher to get it?

CHAPTER 5

September

The trees on campus are slowly beginning to change color, and the air has a crispness in it today that has me sucking in a long breath, welcoming autumn. I meet Annica and Dani for coffee at our usual spot, the Bean. It's a quaint, family-owned coffee shop where the walls are lined with bookshelves and the furniture is all thrifted. The best part about it is seeing Annica's face flinch every time she sits on one of the used couches. "We have no idea where these have been," she sometimes says.

"What are you guys up to this weekend?" I ask when we're settled into our corner spot by the big bay window. Three weeks into the semester and we've decided to start coming here on Friday mornings to catch up on schoolwork together.

"I have to go back home to Connecticut for my little sister's dance competition tomorrow," Dani says. "My stepdad is picking me up today around three."

I open my laptop to look over my rough outline, which is due in four days. "Ugh, I do not envy you; those drag on forever."

It's uncanny how alike my and Dani's backgrounds are. When we talk about our childhoods, we're convinced we had the same one. Divorced parents, younger sisters, and moms that are essentially the same person. Annica can never relate. She's an only child who has never heard the word *no* from her happily married mom and dad.

"Well, I have a date tonight with Collin, but I'm not doing anything Saturday," Annica says. Collin, the hockey boy from the beginning of the semester, has been taking up most of Annica's time. I'm almost surprised to hear that she's available Saturday.

"What about you, Sloane?" Dani asks me.

"I have no idea, maybe writing?" As if the universe heard me trying to stay on track, my phone buzzes with a text.

> It's been weeks. Are we doing this or not?

Sent from a no-name phone number, but I know it's Asher. I've refused to taint my contact list and save his number for the past three years and I won't start now.

> Don't be dramatic, it's only been two weeks. And I don't know.

I've thought about Asher's offer, and I just don't know if I can do it. Even standing next to Asher feels wrong in the presence of Wes. Which is crazy considering he has a whole girlfriend. Asher starts to type but then it disappears. Ten minutes later I get another text.

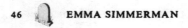

Come to Euros tonight for Power Hour.

It's just the guys, Marissa won't be there.

> If it's just supposed to be the
> guys then why would I go?

Wait, you're a girl?

> You're a dick.

I guess I'll finish the outline tomorrow.

I leave on the same jeans from earlier and put on a tight black long-sleeve. I grab my bag, ready to leave, when Ade comes out of her room.

"Where are you going?" she asks.

I slip my Converses on, holding on to the frame of the door. "Oh, um, just to Power Hour at Euros."

"What is that?"

"It's like a happy hour, but mostly guys go to it. I think it's just one-dollar beer for an hour and they, like, blast dad rock music in there. Honestly, I don't really know, I've never been." I wait for a moment, not sure if she'll say something else.

"Can I come with you?" she asks.

I blink, not sure if I heard correctly. "You want to go? To the dollar-beer-and-dad-rock hour?"

"Yeah, why not. We haven't been out together in so long. It'll be fun and I can be ready in like five minutes!" She goes into her room to start digging through her closet and I wait awkwardly by the door. She comes back out in exactly five minutes, in jeans and a white tank top, with a cream-colored sweater unbuttoned down the middle. The light colors make her skin tone look even more rich, and I just know the boys will have a field day with her.

We walk into Euros right at 8 p.m., and it's already packed with just about every guy on campus. Adrienne walks up to the bar as I see the group. I tell her to meet me over there before walking away.

"Hey, guys!" I say as I approach.

Sam, Jake, and Wes sit at a high-top table while Asher and Charlie play at the pool table beside them. The place smells like a mix of weed and flavored vape smoke. My eyes sting slightly when I blink.

"Sloane? Didn't think we'd see you here," Jake says.

"I'm surprised you can see anything at all," I say, waving the smoke away from my face. Adrienne walks over beside me, holding a bucket full of beer. I look down at it and ask, "Who is that for?"

"Us! Duh." She sets it on the table and the guys look at her wide-eyed. "Good to see you guys again, though I don't remember any of your names," she says to them.

Sam stands first and puts out his hand, which is shocking for the otherwise shy one of the group. "Sam," he says. "Nice to meet you again."

The others go around saying names, and I tell her that Asher and Charlie are the ones at the pool table. Adrienne's eyes linger on Charlie, with his tall frame and athletic build, and I don't blame her. He played basketball here until he tore his ACL sophomore year, but he still trains as if he's on the team. I don't bother telling her he's off-limits because, frankly, I don't think Dani would even bat an eye if another girl swooped in and snagged him. Though maybe that's exactly what she needs in order to commit.

I grab a beer from the bucket, even though I don't like the stuff, and Sam pulls up chairs for us at their table. I take the seat next to Wes. He gave me a nod when I walked over but he's been careful not to look my way since. The sleeves of his blue-and-white flannel are rolled up and I have to look away from the veins that pop out of his arms, leading down to his hands. Being this close to him makes me want to jump out of my skin. I want to grab him by the shoulders, shake him, and say, Just want me back, Wes! I just want you to want me back!

Sam and Jake are in silent competition to win over Adrienne, so I turn toward Wes. The swivel of the barstool makes it so my knees now touch his jeans, but he doesn't move them away.

"How is your semester so far?" I ask, desperate to speak to him, to hear his voice.

"It's tough, but it'll be fine. I feel like I live in the business building. How's yours?"

"Good," I say, thinking of what Asher said about me not being Wesley's mom's first choice. "Actually, it's great. I even have an internship possibly lined up for the summer." I don't, but I feel like it makes me sound like I have my shit together.

"Wow, good for you, Sloane." His eyes look me over and with a small smirk, he says, "I like your hair tonight." He holds my stare before taking a drink and it makes my insides flutter, because clearly, I'm not the only one still thinking about that night. Anyone else hearing that seemingly innocent compliment wouldn't know the implication, but I do.

"I heard it makes the boys crazy," I say back, and it was flirty of me, it was. But god, I can't help it.

He runs a hand through his hair as he looks away, a slight blush creeping up his cheeks. "You heard that, did you?" His voice now slightly husky.

I prop my head on my hand, tilting it slightly so that the blond pieces fall over my shoulder. "Yeah, but I can't remember where now. Hm. Who was it that told me that?" I pretend to think about it.

He sighs, and my gaze drifts over the curve of his jaw, down to the muscles of his neck. I want to commit every detail of him to memory, so I'll never forget.

"You're going to get me into trouble, Sloane." He leans in a little when he says it, and if I wasn't already sitting down, I would need to. I open my mouth to speak when I hear the most irritating, grating voice behind us.

"You guys want to play?" It's Asher, with two pool sticks in his hand, holding them out to us. I want to kick him for the interruption.

"Yes," Wes says as he stands. "I'm going to grab another beer first. You guys need anything?"

I grit my teeth and grab one of the cues from Asher, looking over to our beer bucket, but Adrienne, Sam, and Jake have already polished it off.

"I guess I do," I say. "But if you could get me a—"

"Vodka soda with a lime?" Wes finishes for me. I smile and nod. Behind him, Asher rolls his eyes.

We walk to the table as Charlie finishes reracking, and I ask if I can be the one to break it. I lean over the table, setting up the shot, when Asher grabs the cue stick from me.

"No," he says, facing away from Charlie. "You can't act like you're good at this."

"But I am good," I say. "My stepdad taught me."

"Well, tonight you're going to be bad at it. Botch the break and ask Wes to show you how to do it."

"And manipulate him? I told you I don't know if I want to do that."

"Just a few seconds ago you looked like you would do just about anything," he says with a knowing smirk. I sneer at him as Wes walks back over. "All right, Sawyer and Wes against me and Charlie," Asher says. "And Sloane wants to break the rack, so"—he gestures to the table—"have at it."

I walk to the middle of the table and get into position to hit the ball, but I consider Asher's tactic. I misalign the cue in my hands and strike, completely missing it.

With a sigh I stand. "I totally suck at this." I don't bother to look at Asher, who is laughing under his breath.

"Well, she's your teammate, Wes, you help her," Asher says, playing into our game. It seems to work as Wesley sets down his beer, and I feel a wash of shame over it. He walks over, positioning himself behind me to help me line up the shot, and it's like lightning when we touch, zapping away the guilt. I suck in a breath, and that's when we hear Jake say, "Marissa, hey!"

Wes backs away from me and I let out the breath I was holding, like a deflating balloon. "Asher, you show her. I'll be right back."

Asher walks over to me and blows out a breath. "Tough luck, kid." I roll my eyes and go to line up the shot again. "Ah, ah, ah," Asher says. "Wait until he gets back."

Marissa walks over to the pool table with Wes. Her heeled boots and full face of makeup make me feel underdressed even though we're at a dive bar.

"Okay, here, let me show you." Asher starts to move behind me.

"No, I'm good, I just remembered how to do it." I smile.

"No." He smiles back. "You didn't." He nods over at the two of them standing there. Marissa places a light kiss to Wesley's mouth, and I want to snap the cue stick in half. "Go back into the stance," he says.

I do, leaning down, pretending to be sloppy about it. I flinch at Asher's touch when he comes behind me and places his hands on my arms. He slowly slides his hands down to my hands and leans over me, pressing his body flush to mine. I pretend he's Wes. Especially when one of his hands moves to my waist.

"Now line up your body with the shot," he says into my ear. The hand on my waist slides up my stomach as he moves me over slightly. His fingers graze my bare skin as my shirt rises with the movement.

"Can you not?" I say, regarding the hand that's moving dangerously up my torso.

"I don't want to touch you either. Now shut up and flex your fingers."

I do it, and he positions the cue between them, drawing my dominant hand back toward the end of it, taking his sweet time.

"I think she gets it, Asher, just hit the fucking ball," Wesley's voice rings out from across the table.

I glance up to find him standing arms crossed and facing away from Marissa now, watching us. Asher huffs a laugh close to my ear at Wesley's annoyance before putting his hand over mine and breaking the rack. The force of it sends out a loud crack as the balls scatter around the table.

We both stand straight now, and I hold the cue stick vertical, the end of it resting on the ground. "Nice break," Asher says with a pat to my ass. I let the cue slide in between his legs before pushing the top end of it down toward the table. It comes up quick and hits him in the balls, not too hard, but hard enough. He lets out a pained *humph* and gives me a glare.

"Thanks for showing me," I say sweetly. "I think I got it now." I drag the cue stick to another part of the table to line up my next shot.

ADRIENNE AND I leave after that game and head back to our apartment.

When we're in the back of the Uber she says, "What's up with that blond kid? Are you seeing him?"

"Who?" I ask, staring down at my phone, thinking maybe Wes will text. Like if I stare at the screen long enough, I'll get a message telling me to come over.

"The one showing you how to play pool, which I know you already know how to do."

"Oh, Asher, no," I say. "He's not even a friend, more of a nuisance really."

"Oh, my bad, from where I was standing it just looked like you two were together."

That's the plan, I think to myself.

My phone buzzes from an incoming message and I hold my breath. But it isn't Wesley; it's my friend Ty.

Party tomorrow night at Phi Delt.

Let me know if you can make it! XOXO

CHAPTER 6

The three-story, brick-structured Phi Delta frat house vibrates with each pulse of the music coming from the building. Annica and I stare up at the flashing lights from the windows as we walk up to the door.

"I can't believe *this* is a frat house," I say, eager to get in. "Why do the ones at Pembroke all look like the next gust of wind might blow them over, but the ones here look like a government building?"

"How did we even get invited to this?" Annica asks. "I thought the twins hated you."

I finish putting my lip gloss on and check my hair on my phone camera. "It was three years ago. I wouldn't say they *hate* me, maybe just dislike. And besides, if anyone is still going to be pissed about what happened, it should be me."

A guy in khaki shorts and a polo stands at the double white-painted doors with his arms crossed. "Who do you know here?" he asks.

"Seriously?" Annica says, taking on her defensive stance. "What are you, like, sixteen?"

"What are you, like, thirty-five?" he says back.

"You little—"

Ty opens the door behind the boy, a red Solo cup already in hand, and smiles when she sees us. "Well, well, well, look who made it all the way to Boston. These are my friends, Cam; they can come in."

Annica sticks her tongue out at the freshman as we walk in. Definitely not something a thirty-five-year-old would do.

It was a two-hour drive east to get to Ivy Gate University, the rival school to Pembroke that Ty attends. Ty—short for Tyler—Thompson was one of the first friends I made at Cedar Falls when we moved there ten years ago after my mom remarried. With her big blue eyes and bubbly personality, she wins everyone over.

"Are you sure Ryan is okay with me being here?" I ask Ty.

She runs a manicured hand over her slicked-back long chestnut hair before she says, "Totally! Water under the bridge."

But I'm not entirely sure it will be. I haven't talked to Ryan and Colton Austi since freshman year, but things did not end on friendly terms. I cross my arms to stop my hands from shaking when I think about Ryan's eulogy in my journal. It's not like he didn't deserve one, but we had both wronged each other.

Past the foyer of the giant frat house, the party is in full swing. The thumping bass of the music, now ten times louder than it was outside, hits like a physical force. A kaleidoscope of lights flashes all around the room, making it look like an actual nightclub.

We enter the living room, where four long beer-pong and flip-cup tables sit in the center. A group of girls dances off to the side, under the lights, Ty's best friend Austin Reems among them, holding a Bud Light Platinum in one hand and UV Blue in the other. He meets us by the bar to make mixed drinks, his black-rimmed glasses askew and his smile wide as he brings me in for a hug. Upon closer inspection I can tell he's recently pierced his ears, and his shirt is one big collage of the lead singer of Panic! At The Disco.

"So I was just talking to Julie Hart, you know the one who works at the Dunkin' Donuts on campus—" Austin starts with Ty, stealing her attention long enough for me to make my drink of soda water and lime, no vodka. "And I told her maybe she needs to stop spending so many hours at Dunkin' and start dunkin' her hours in boys. And that's all I have to say about *that*." Austin takes a swig of the UV Blue and Ty clicks her tongue.

"How are you judging her for being single when you're also single!"

"Omg, like, you *know* I'm talking to someone. It's getting serious."

"Oh?" I ask. "Do tell us more."

Ty leans over to peer into my cup and frowns at the small amount of liquid inside. "Oh, honey, no need to be sparing with the alcohol—it's free!" She grabs a bottle of vodka, her gold jewelry clinking against the glass, and goes to pour some into my cup.

"No, that's okay," I say, stopping her. "I'm not trying to get too drunk."

"What?! That's not the Sloane I know!" She continues to pour, and this time I let her. Fine, just one strong drink to start.

There are people everywhere, and in the flashing lights you can hardly tell who is who. I start to think I may not even see the twins tonight. Ty leads us over to one of the tables where a new flip cup game is starting and declares that we're all in. She starts to introduce us but I don't pay attention to the names, because Ryan is also standing at the table.

He interrupts Ty and points at me. "What the hell is she doing here?"

My face goes slack and Annica's mouth drops open.

"I invited her!" Ty says. Ryan only glares at me before walking away from the table.

I turn to her, exasperated. "I thought you said water under the bridge!"

"Maybe the bridge is still in a little need of repair?" she says sheepishly, putting a hand on my shoulder. "He didn't say you had to leave, though. Just enjoy the party!"

I shake her off and follow Ryan to the kitchen, chugging my drink on the way there for liquid courage. I tighten my ponytail and nervously adjust my top.

"Hey," I say when we're both stopped by the alcohol.

"That wasn't an invitation for you to follow," Ryan says. "Or did you think I was Colton?" He rolls up the sleeve of his shirt before he digs around a cooler of ice for a cold beer. His black hair is cut short now, and I wonder if Colton's is too. They both used to wear it longer, and it made them look the same. But I guess that was the point.

"You're still spinning that story? That I was sleeping with your brother and not you?"

"Depends, do you still like to air out people's business on Instagram?" He crosses his arms, standing his ground.

"Do you think you didn't deserve it? You were cheating on your girlfriend with me, then called me— What was it again? An always wasted bitch?"

He steps toward me, raising his voice. "Then maybe you shouldn't have posted that I was a cheater all over the internet!"

"Maybe you shouldn't have cheated!"

"I didn't cheat! You weren't hooking up with me, remember? Oh wait, you probably don't! Don't think I haven't heard about you lately—you're still not very reliable. Or sober. You're just a sad little party girl with a shitty memory," he adds.

My face burns hot with rage. "You know what, I was going to come over here to make amends, but fuck you, Ryan." I turn to walk away but face him again, because I just need him to know. "For the record, I really liked you back then. You hurt me too."

"And you hurt Olivia, so I guess we're even." He pushes past me into the crowd, and I can feel my blood thrumming in my cheeks. Olivia, his girlfriend at the time, was a beautiful blonde on the Ivy Gate soccer team who I tracked down to tell her he was cheating. Sure, it was immature of me to post the screenshots, and yes, I regret that, but I was hurt. He was my first relationship after Jonah, and maybe I didn't love Ryan, but I loved the idea of him. I just didn't know the difference at the time.

I eye the bottle of vodka for a long moment before filling my cup halfway with it. Without any soda water or lime to cut the taste, I top it off with ice. It goes down like fire and settles in my stomach with a burn. I let the words and the feelings and the world spin by. Just for tonight.

Just for tonight.

THERE'S A LOUD banging noise coming from somewhere that makes me stir in my sleep. I open my heavy eyelids and don't recognize the room I'm in. I blink a few times, letting the spinning ceiling settle in my vision. I'm at the foot of a large bed. I groan and turn my head to see Annica, Ty, and Austin sprawled out on the bed with me, all in our clothes from last night. The light coming through the navy curtains tells me it's morning.

More banging comes from the other side of the door. "Open up this door—it's the police," a deep male voice says from the other side.

All of our heads pop up from the bed and we look at each other with one silent question. What the fuck are the police doing here? They usually come to break up a party while it's still going on, not the morning after. Ty gets up to unlock the door and two police officers are standing on the other side.

"Everyone downstairs, please."

When we're gathered at the bottom of the staircase, Ty is the one to speak up first. "What's going on?"

"We need to ask you all a few questions about last night before you leave. Officer Smith and I will speak with you each individually. Who wants to go first?"

None of us say anything, still unsure about what this is.

"We'll go right down the line, then." He points to Annica. "You first." She hesitantly follows the female officer to another part of the house for the supposed questioning, looking back at us with worried eyes.

"Can someone just tell us what is happening?" Ty tries again.

"There was a body found outside the building early this morning, identified as Ryan Austi. It seems he either fell or was pushed off the third-floor balcony."

WHEN IT'S MY turn to be questioned, I'm shaking like a leaf. I vaguely remember walking back to my friends after pouring myself a vodka on the rocks. We played flip cup. We went up to the third-floor balcony that overlooks the backyard . . . but what were we doing there?

Detective Grange is a tall man, handsome, and looks to be around forty years old. His brown eyes somehow match his skin tone perfectly. Focusing on his features is how I'm distracting myself from throwing up.

Detective Grange sits across from me and takes out a small notepad and pen. "So, Miss . . . ?"

"Sloane Sawyer."

"Sloane Sawyer." He pronounces every syllable as he writes it down. "Why don't you walk me through last night? What time did you get to the party?" His voice is deep, and slightly comforting. Like the people that narrate Animal Planet documentaries.

"Okay," I start. "Um, we got here around like ten p.m. We had some drinks, played drinking games . . ." I trail off because the rest is foggy.

"Did you see or speak to Ryan at all?"

"I said hi to him in the kitchen at one point." The kind of hi that sounds more like "fuck you," but he doesn't need to know that. Or does he?

"What did you do after you spoke to Ryan?"

"We played drinking games like I said, and at some point, we went up to the balcony—"

Grange looks up from his notepad. "What time was it when you walked out onto the balcony?"

"I—I honestly don't remember, but maybe like midnight?"

"Was Ryan out there with you?"

"There were a lot of people out there, but I don't specifically remember if any of them were him."

He continues to write. "And then what did you do?"

I close my eyes, trying to remember. What did we do? What did we do? I purse my lips, shaking my head. "We might have gone to bed after that."

"At what time?"

I come up blank. "I'm sorry, I just can't remember. I drank too much." The last part comes out as barely a whisper.

Detective Grange sighs and closes the notepad. "Thank you for your time, Miss Sawyer. Before you go, if I could just get your phone number and address in case we have any more questions throughout this investigation?"

"Okay, sure." I write them down, my hands still unsteady. Ty and Annica stand by the door with Austin, waiting for me.

"Let's get out of here," Ty says.

"Okay, what the hell just happened?" Annica says when we get onto the sidewalk.

I look over at the house as we walk away. "I feel sick," I say, taking deep, shaking breaths. "Did any of you see anything last night? Did he jump? Was he pushed?" I try to imagine the feeling of falling through the sky only to land on the hard ground. Did he die instantly? Or did he lie there in agony until his body gave up? I grimace at the thought.

Ty slowly shakes her head, tears welling up in her doe eyes. "He was so excited to graduate this year," she whispers. "There's just no way he would do that. It had to have been an accident."

"Did you talk to him again after you guys argued?" Annica asks me.

"I don't know. I can't remember anything after the balcony."

"When were you on the balcony?" Austin asks.

I look at him, confused. "Weren't we all?"

"No," Ty says. We're all quiet and I'm silently berating myself for getting that drunk. I try to think of every scenario of why I'd be on the balcony without my friends. And did I see Ryan again or even Colton?

"This is bad," I say, more to myself than anyone else.

"I'm sure it was just an accident," Annica says, rubbing my arm, trying to comfort me.

"I mean, it's not like any of us pushed him," Austin says. "I mean, you *didn't* push him, right?" I can tell he's joking, but I come off a little defensive in my reply.

"No, why would you even suggest that? I would never do that." I think of Ryan's eulogy sitting in my journal at home. "I would never do that."

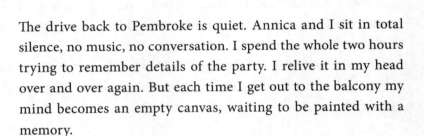

CHAPTER 7

The drive back to Pembroke is quiet. Annica and I sit in total silence, no music, no conversation. I spend the whole two hours trying to remember details of the party. I relive it in my head over and over again. But each time I get out to the balcony my mind becomes an empty canvas, waiting to be painted with a memory.

I drop Annica off and tell her to fill in Dani for me, though I regret it after I do, because I can only imagine the exaggerated version of this story she'll come up with. Finally going through my phone alone in my room, I hope there's something in here that will jog my memory but there are no posts, no texts, and no calls. The one time I wish I over-posted, and yet it's like I didn't even have a phone last night.

When I remember that I also wrote a eulogy for another now-dead person, I get out of bed to find the journal, intent on burning the whole thing. But it isn't in my bag. I figure it must be in my car from when I burned Jonah's page in the park weeks ago, and decide I'll burn it tomorrow, when it doesn't give me a headache to stand up. I lie back down and take deep breaths, waiting for sleep to take me.

It's dark when I open my eyes again. The hangover is gone but the reality of it being Sunday night and I still have homework to do sets in. My stomach growls viciously, reminding me I haven't eaten today. I go into our kitchen, but all the food in here is Ade's. In fact, the only thing that's mine is a bottle of merlot sitting on the counter next to the refrigerator. It stares back at me, daring me to pour a glass. Just one glass—it would help. The hair of the dog, or whatever they say . . . but I don't need it. I really don't.

I leave it there, untouched.

I have two discussion board posts to do, a quiz, and an outline to finish, but I pace around my room instead. I look at my goals taped to my mirror and say them again.

"You're going to ace all of your classes this year. You're not going to get into trouble. You won't let any boys get to you. You're going to write your first book." This time I don't feel as confident when I say them.

I text Ty and ask if she's heard anything else today about Ryan, and whether it was a suicide, an accident, or a murder. She says she hasn't, only that Phi Delt was put on probation for letting the party get out of hand. I order a pizza and get to work on my tasks. When I get down to the outline, I take a break. It feels impossible to pick something to write about when I know it matters. I have countless story ideas sitting in my notes app on my phone, and some I even started to write, but now none of them feel good enough. I still have tomorrow, I remind myself, and I almost shut my laptop but not before I get an email notification from a familiar address. MH55123@gmail.com sits unopened in my inbox, with no subject line, and I know that it's Miles Holland, the professor I had an affair with last year that ended with him being asked to resign. Hesitant, I click open.

Can we talk?

MH

No, Miles, we cannot. I delete it and close the laptop. Pure curiosity has me typing his name into the search bar of my phone a moment later. The first several results are for the book he wrote a few years ago. I click into the publisher's site to read his biography. His book *Shadows Over Stone Hollow* is at the very top. I never actually read it, but I know it's a mystery. That's his favorite genre. I scroll through his biography below it.

Miles Holland is an award-winning author, known for his bone-chilling words and captivating storytelling. Born and raised in New York, Holland is a graduate of Columbia, where his passion for literature grew. When he's not writing, Miles enjoys traveling with his wife, Kate, and his dog Moose.

Must be an outdated biography, because he no longer has a wife. Not after me, anyway. Another scroll toward the bottom brings up his photo, sending a queasiness to my gut. Ocean eyes stare back at me behind wire-rimmed glasses with a smirk that always looks as though he has a secret to tell. This must also be an old photo, one before the hints of laugh lines that have formed in the corners of his eyes, and the traces of gray at his temples. This Miles looks young, late twenties, I suspect. He's at least ten years older than this photo by now.

"Gross," I whisper to myself, and back out of the search. That's when the faculty page for Ivy Gate University catches my eye, showing that as of this year, that's where he's teaching. I sit up in bed, staring at the page. Holland and I were in the same city, on the same campus, last night, and I didn't even know it.

I decide to bypass the glass, as I uncork the merlot and drink right from the bottle.

My legs start to burn as I put the incline of the treadmill to ten. I text Ty again to ask if she's heard anything. It's noon on Monday: Her whole school must be talking about it by now. She replies to tell me they still don't know the cause. My phone buzzes again and I grab it immediately. It's a text from an unknown number, with nothing but a photo. I open it up to see a crinkled-up piece of paper with writing on it. I zoom in a little closer and gasp, causing my phone to fall out of my hands, hit the tread, and fly off onto the floor. I abruptly stop the machine and stand still for a moment, catching my breath, wondering if I just saw what I think I did. What looked like a copy of my journal, specifically the page about Ryan. I turn around to get my phone, but Asher is already there, picking it up from the floor. I snatch it from him before he has a chance to see the photo on the screen.

"I just came to talk to you about next steps," he says.

"What?"

"With Wes—"

"I don't have time for this right now, Asher." I step off the tread-mill and around him. He follows.

"Do you have time to deal with Marissa and Annica knowing your secret?"

I turn slowly. "I just had another one of my exes die over the weekend, you asshole." I watch his face fall, if only for a moment, and I feel smug knowing that he probably feels bad now. He doesn't say anything else, so I turn to leave. When I'm far from him I look back down at my phone, opening the text again, and this time there's a message below it.

I know you wrote this

I immediately feel lightheaded. I look at the eulogy again.

We are gathered here today to remember Ryan Austi, or is it Colton who died, hm, I'm always just such a "wasted bitch" I just can never tell them apart. I didn't know Ryan that long. Everything about our little tryst was short. Everything, if you know what I mean. Sadly, Ryan was killed while pretending to be Colton. It's something they did quite often and were rather good at. With an army of friends to back up their fake stories and identity swaps, they got away with it every time. Just not this time. Goodbye, Ryan. You might be missed by some, but not by me, since I'm always so drunk I'll probably just continue to mistake Colton as you. Through my unabashed drunkenness, you will live on forever. How unfortunate.

Oh, that is not a good look. Not at all.

> Who is this?

I stand there staring at the screen, waiting.

> They found this in his pocket. I told them it
> was you who wrote it. Is this why you pushed
> him? A grudge from three years ago?

This must be Colton. My hands are shaking so bad I can barely read the text. Why would a page from my journal be in Ryan's pocket the night he died? I run out of the gym to my car. I forgot to look for it this morning, but the journal has to be in here if it wasn't in my bag last night. I search my car but it isn't here. Did I leave it in the park? Did it fall out of my bag? The picture he sent is a copy of this page, like someone photocopied it. So not only is my journal out there somewhere but so are copies of its contents? I've never lost this journal, ever. And the only person I have ever shown this to was . . . well, it was Miles Holland.

> I don't know what you're talking
> about, I didn't write that

Can they even prove I wrote it? I guess with a handwriting analysis. Is that even a real thing they do or is that just in TV shows? I block the number and put my hands above my head. Slow breaths, eyes closed, trying to calm down. Okay, Sloane, focus.

Focus. I just have to retrace my steps from where I last had the journal. But that was also three weeks ago now.

I drive back to the park where I burned Jonah's entry and practically crawl around the entire hill on my hands and knees looking for the thing. It isn't here. I don't know why I expected it to be. I sit for a moment at the top of the hill. A chilly breeze rustles the trees below, sending the first falling leaves out into the wind.

How did Colton even get a photo of the eulogy? Shouldn't it be locked up in some, like, evidence cabinet or something? Unless they called him in to question him on it, which I'm sure they did. I bet they showed it to him and he read it and immediately knew it was me. If he told them that, then why hasn't Grange called me yet? And when he does, what the hell am I going to say? He could be at my door already; after all, I did give him my address. What if he's there right now with Adrienne?

I walk in the door fully prepared to see Grange sitting on our couch, waiting for me, but the apartment is empty. I tear apart my room looking for my journal, taking out every drawer, overturning every bag. It's not here. I finally sit on the ground surrounded by the mess and lean my throbbing head back against my bed. Jonah and now Ryan.

Jonah and Ryan, Jonah and Ryan, Jonah and Ryan. Their names run across my mind like a broken record.

CHAPTER 8

I walk into the Bean before Renner's class on Tuesday and almost do a double take when Detective Grange is standing at the register, ordering. What the hell is he doing here? Is he here for me? I should just leave. I should, but he starts to turn and I'm frozen.

"Miss Sawyer." His deep, velvety voice sounds shocked to see me. Maybe he isn't here for me after all. "I was just on my way to your apartment."

Okay, never mind.

"Oh."

"I wanted to have a follow-up conversation with you about last weekend's incident." He nods to the table in the corner by the window. Our table. "Can we sit?"

"I actually was on my way to class—"

"It won't take long," he says with a smile.

"Okay," I concede. "I'm going to grab a coffee really quick."

"Of course. I'll wait over there."

I debate running out of here but know that won't do me any good. I have about five minutes before I have to go over there to decide if I'll lie or tell the truth about the journal. I go through the pros and cons of each in my head. I get my coffee and nervously sip from the iced latte as I approach him. I hope he can't see my hands shaking. When I sit, he's staring out the window.

"This is a lovely campus," he says.

"It is," I agree.

Grange clears his throat. "But I am not here to talk about Pembroke." He digs through the briefcase he brought with him. "I'm here to talk about this." He lays a piece of paper on the table and pushes it toward me. It's Ryan's eulogy, the one I wrote. "Do you know what this is?"

He knows I know what that is, and I've made up my mind about my approach. "It's a copy of a page in my journal."

"You don't sound too surprised to see that I have it." He cocks his head to the side.

"Colton told me you had it—he knew I wrote it based on what it says. I expected you'd come see me about it."

"Hm." Grange considers for a moment, looking a bit annoyed that Colton said something to me before he could. That I had time to prepare. "Can you explain to me how this came to be in Ryan Austi's pocket the night he died?"

"I honestly don't know. I didn't give it to him if that's what you're asking."

Grange studies me. "You and Ryan were not friends, I take it?"

"We . . . had a disagreement three years ago. But we were both over it."

"You were?" he asks, glancing down at the page.

"Yes. I wrote that three years ago. I don't know how or why he had it and I—"

"I looked into you," he says. "History of substance abuse, arrested for drinking and driving, involved in an inappropriate student-teacher relationship last year."

How does he even know about that? "Are you accusing me of something?"

"Just pointing out that you have a history of making bad decisions. If you made another one at that party, I'll find out."

I visibly swallow at the threat, and he begins to pack up.

"I didn't give him that note, and I had nothing to do with his death, I swear."

Grange puts the note back into his briefcase and stands. "If you ever happen to remember anything else from that night, please give me a call." But what he really means is if I ever happen to want to confess, give him a call.

I purse my lips and nod, exhaling a shaky breath as he passes.

I'm FIFTEEN MINUTES late to Renner's class when I walk in. My classmates are all busy on their laptops, besides Annica, who is mouthing "Where were you?"

"Sloane," Renner says when he sees me sneaking in. "See me after class." Somehow his words are scarier than Grange's.

I open my outline for my short story. The one I never started. I watch the cursor blink on a blank document. It's just an outline, Sloane, it's just the bones. I type out the words: "Introduction, Rising Action, Climax, Falling Action, Conclusion."

My hands hover over my keyboard as my mind wanders back to my conversation with Grange. He knows there's something sketchy about the whole situation and his focus is entirely on me. I don't blame him. It *was* all too coincidental. I exit out of the outline and go into my email to pull up the one from Miles. He's now a professor at Ivy Gate, and he is the only person who knows about my journal. Is it possible that he would be the one to photocopy a page of it to give to Ryan Austi? But why? For revenge? I ruined his marriage and got him fired from Pembroke so he . . . what? Stole my journal to copy the pages and give them to my exes? Could he have been there at the party that night?

There's only one person that might know.

The class begins to pack up when senior seminar ends and I walk up to Renner's desk in the front of the class, preparing an excuse.

"Miss Sawyer."

"Hi, if this is about the outline, I'll have it to you by tonight. I'm sorry. I was having computer issues over the weekend and couldn't finish it during class." I figured that was better than saying I was so stressed out about almost being a murder suspect that I couldn't get it done.

"And the reason for being late today? Also computer issues?"

"No, just . . . running late."

"You know, I was on the board that decided to let you move forward in the writing program here." I nod, unsure of what to say. "Don't make me regret it." With that he goes back to his grading in a silent dismissal.

ANNICA IS OUTSIDE the classroom waiting for me. "Where were you?" she asks.

"I ran into that detective from the party; he had more questions for me."

"About what?"

Part of me does not want Annica and Dani to know the details of the journal. Honestly, the less people that know the better.

"Just going over the timeline of the night again."

"Oh," she says. "Will they call me too, do you think?"

I didn't think of the fact that they could call her again for questioning, maybe even about me and this journal entry.

Miss Labrant, has your best friend ever had any murdery tendencies that you're aware of?

"No," I say. "I don't think they will."

When I walk past the door to our world literature course, Annica stops short.

"Sloane, where are you going?"

"I'm not feeling good," I lie. "I'm going home to rest for a little bit." Another lie.

"Okay . . . will we see you later?" she asks.

"Um, maybe. Let me know if I miss anything important."

"Will do," she sighs, and heads into the lecture hall as I leave the building, but not to go home.

I SIT AT one of the long center tables in the Ivy Gate library, looking up at the vast collection of books that line the walls going up six floors. My foot nervously taps on the ground as I search for Cam, the freshman who stood outside the frat house front door all night watching everyone who went in. A girl two seats to my right gives me a pointed look at the sound my foot makes before giving me a "Shh!" I stop tapping and resort to biting my cheek.

Cam walks in ten minutes later, just like Ty said he would. He takes a seat three tables down and I walk over and sit across from him.

"Cam?" I say when he doesn't look up.

His brown eyes flick up to meet mine. "Yeah?"

"I'm Sloane," I introduce myself.

His eyes widen with recognition. "Oh, yeah, I remember you, you were at the party. Ty's friend."

"Yeah," I say, happy that he remembers me. If he remembers me, maybe he'll remember Miles. "I have a question for you about that night actually." I dig around in my bag for my phone to show him a picture.

"What the hell are you doing here?" I hear a voice from beside me. It's Colton Austi. "Cam, let's go."

"Wait, wait," I whisper. "I just want to talk to you guys about that night."

Colton crosses his arms and huffs in irritation. "You want to talk about how you murdered my brother?" He says it loud enough to earn a few looks from other students.

"I did not push Ryan," I bite out.

"But you wrote that note?"

"Yes, but—"

"Then it had to be you."

I sigh and pull up the photo of Miles. "Do you recognize this professor?" I ask him.

"No." His eyes remain on me.

"You didn't even look," I say. He makes an exaggerated show of looking before once again saying no. I show Cam next. "You were at the door all night. Did you see this man walk in?"

"I don't think so," Cam says. "He doesn't look familiar. Why?"

"Because he's the only person who knew about the journal that page came out of, and right now my journal is missing. I thought maybe—"

"I should post all over my social media that you're a murderer," Colton interrupts. He doesn't care about my explanation. His mind is already made up about me.

"Um, okay, well, that would be considered, like, libel or slander or something, because it's not true?"

"You did the same thing to Ryan."

"And I regret doing that, but what I said was true."

Colton grits his teeth, and nods at Cam again to follow him. "You won't get away with this," he says to me before walking away with Cam in tow.

I stay seated in the library trying to collect myself, wondering how I went from being a normal college senior to a murder suspect in one short month. The Netflix series about my life is now looking like one of those serial killer documentaries where my friends would all give interviews, saying things like "She just seemed so normal!"

I let my head hit the table with a thud.

"Shh!"

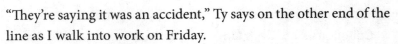

CHAPTER 9

"They're saying it was an accident," Ty says on the other end of the line as I walk into work on Friday.

"They? Who's they?" I ask.

"The school, the police, I don't know, just whoever makes these decisions. Someone came forward and said they thought they saw him walking along the railing or something for a dare, and they have no other evidence to go off." Ty is quiet for a moment. "Though Colton is going around saying some crazy shit . . . like that it was you."

I wonder if she knows about the note. If the whole campus does. "Me?" I feign shock.

"Yeah, but I think he's just looking for someone to blame. He's grieving, obviously."

"Right, obviously," I say, setting my bag down behind the bar just as Tristan walks in. "Ty, I have to go."

I greet Tristan with a welcoming smile, but I feel my lips twitch and he apprehensively returns it. "Just the person I wanted to see," I say.

He has on a Bloomfield Fire Department T-shirt and gray sweatpants. I'd be lying if I said it wasn't an attractive look. Especially the gray sweatpants, which I quickly avert my eyes from. Sometimes I wonder if I never found out about that idiotic bet if we would be together now. He sets his bag with his work clothes down by the bar, taking a seat before he has to go change.

"Not sure if that's a good or bad thing?"

"I just wanted to ask you something," I say, wiping down a glass.

"And what is it you wanted to ask?"

I try to think about how to phrase it: Have you received your eulogy lately? Just doesn't sound like something a sane person would say. "Have you gotten any strange notes recently?"

"Strange notes? Like what?"

Yeah, Sloane, like what? "Like, I don't know, strange. Anything you'd look at and be like, what the hell? You know?" But he does not know. I had a thought last night that maybe Ryan wasn't the only one to get a page from my journal. What if they all did? I had to know for sure.

"No? Have you?"

"Yeah," I lie, trying to think of a reason why I would ever ask this. "I think one of the regulars wrote a story about me and left it on my car after my last shift."

"What the hell?"

"Exactly! Yes, my reaction exactly. And in this story, I died. So I was curious to know if you got one too."

"No, but that's so creepy. You should tell Jess," he says, picking up his bag. Although Jess, our manager, would probably think it was funny.

"Right, I will. But just let me know if you ever get a note like that, will you?"

"Sure, Sloane, you will be the first to know."

I DECIDE TO surprise my friends out at the bars when I'm cut from Cantine early. But as I look around Ray's, our usual first stop, they aren't here. I text Annica and Dani while I sit at the bar to see if anyone shows.

"Solo drinking tonight?" a voice says from behind me. I don't need to turn around to know it's Wesley. He takes a seat beside me and orders a draft.

"Looks that way," I say, sitting up in my seat. When I turn around, I realize he's alone. Our group isn't with him. Marissa isn't with him. "Where is everyone?"

"Jake invited over some girls from Ivy Gate for a pregame but they're all so hammered I don't think they'll make it out. I think Annica and Dani are at the hockey house for a party. Did they not mention it?"

"I was working tonight but ended up getting off early. I just texted them," I say.

"So that's why you smell like french fries," Wes teases, and my cheeks turn pink. I didn't stop home to shower or change. I'm still in my jeans and the fitted white T-shirt I wore today, which, yes, now that I think about it, smells like fries.

"No Marissa tonight?" I ask, because I need to be prepared to get my feelings hurt these days.

"No, she's studying tonight. It's just me."

"Hm." Just him. I sip my vodka soda and try to quell the butterflies in my stomach over the idea of just me and Wes out tonight. Where that might lead.

"Hey, remember the end of sophomore year, and we were the only two out of the group to not have our fake IDs taken, so before the semester ended we tried to do the rounds and see if we could make it without getting caught?"

I laugh. "Yeah, and we only made it to three bars because you threw up and they kicked us out."

"What? No, we got kicked out because you thought you could dance on the table." He playfully nudges me and his touch is electric the way it sparks up my arm and I feel it everywhere.

"What's an elevated surface for if not dancing?" I say, taking a drink, trying not to cringe at the words that just left my mouth.

"Let's finish the rounds," he says. "Tonight. Just us."

The rounds he's referring to are the order of bars that are customary at Pembroke. Everyone knows you start at Ray's and finish at 157. There are five major ones you need to get to in a night; a lot of times we only make it to three.

"All five bars on a Friday night?"

"With the specialty drinks at each."

"You're on, McCavern."

And with that we cheers and chug our drinks, before ordering the Ray's specialty: a Long Island iced tea.

THE SECOND BAR, Loft, is a little hole-in-the-wall dive bar known for karaoke, barrels of peanuts, and some disgusting shot that no one knows exactly what it's made of. They put a trash can next to anyone brave enough to take it.

"We're doing the Grecian Urn," Wes announces as we walk in, aka the shot that no one knows what it's made of.

"Do you think we should finally ask what's in it? Now that we're seniors, I just feel like we should know," I say, trying to peer over the bartender's shoulder to watch what he's pouring in it.

Wesley reaches over to cover my eyes. "And ruin the mystery? No way. I want to die never knowing."

"Okay, fair." I laugh.

We're holding the shots in our hands, and I'm swirling it around with what must be a disgusted look on my face. I've done one only once in my time at Pembroke and I did in fact need the trash can they supplied.

"Time to man up, Sloane." Wes holds up the shot and I clink it with mine. Down the hatch, I guess. I hold my breath when I take it, anything to stunt the taste, which seems to work because it doesn't come back up.

"Ah." He sighs like he's refreshed. "So what are we going to sing?"

"Sing?" I repeat.

"Yeah, we're doing the rounds, so we have to do karaoke. I put our names in." He gives me a devious smile that makes me want to put my mouth on his like a magnet.

I look around the bar, which is already bustling with a crowd. I recognize a group of guys in the back who are in the Sig Chi fraternity. One of them being another ex-boyfriend of mine, Bryce Peterson. I let my eyes linger on him for a moment longer, wondering if I should go talk to him about the eulogy but . . . no, not tonight. Not while I have Wes all to myself. "Oh no no, I'm not singing." I shake my head. "No."

He leans in to whisper in my ear over the noise of the bar. "If you do this with me, then I'll owe you a favor. It can be whatever you want, and you can call it in whenever you want." Chills, instantly. If I said I wanted the favor to be sex, what would he say then? I open my mouth but our names are being called over the microphone on the small stage. "We're up," he says, grabbing my hand and pulling me to the front. Wes says something to the guy and he hands me a mic.

I recognize the sound of the keyboard as "Dancing Queen" begins to play. "It's your favorite, right?" Wes asks over the sound. If I didn't have to sing, I'd be speechless. "You requested it like five times at that one bar during spring break freshman year." Again, speechless.

He looks at me as it starts, ignoring the screen with the lyrics. He clearly doesn't need it: He somehow knows all the words.

"This song is, like, forever ingrained in my memory," he says in answer to the shock on my face. "Now, are you going to sing with me or what?"

We put on the best damn concert that I think Pembroke has ever seen, and I hope he can't tell that the blush on my face is from being so totally and completely enamored by him that it would consume me whole if I let it. But there's no time, as he's pulling me out of Loft for the next bar.

ZEPHYR, ONE OF our less-frequented bars, is on the top floor of a record store. It has a colorful, vibrant atmosphere with disco balls hanging from the ceiling and lava lamps on every surface. There are plush couches that surround a light-up dance floor and we both take a seat on one.

We're holding the featured lava lamp drinks in our hands, and Wes looks over at me. "You know, I actually really like this bar. I feel like we never go to it."

I look around, crinkling my nose. "Probably because these couches smell like mildew and the bartenders are all sixty-year-old men with porn staches."

Wes looks around like he's seeing this bar for the first time ever. "Well, great, now I can't unsee it." He puts his arm around the back part of the couch, almost around me. "So what are you doing after this?"

After this, as in tonight? Is he about to ask me to go home with him? "Um, I don't know, going home, I guess."

"I mean, like, after college, what are you going to do?"

My face falls because I realize this is the moment to ask him what he's going to do about the ski business. Asher would be on the edge of his seat right now if he were here. It makes me wonder if he is. If this whole night was somehow set up by him.

"You first," I say, turning on the couch to face him. My leg is now pressed up against his and I lean in closer.

"My dad wants me to take over the ski resort," he says, looking down at his drink.

"And you don't want to do that?"

"I don't know," he admits. "I'd have to move there and learn the ropes. I'm just not sure . . . if I want it." He looks up at me when he says it and then huffs a laugh. "That's the first time I've ever admitted that to anyone."

I give him a small, encouraging smile. "Then . . . what do you want?"

"I don't know. Part of me wants to do it because it's easy, but another part of me wants to make something of my own. Like a bed-and-breakfast by the beach, I don't know. Maybe that's a dumb idea." He looks away like he's embarrassed he said it.

"I think you should do whatever would make you happy." And that's no manipulation, just the truth.

"You know what would make me really happy?" he says, and I lean in, hooked on every syllable, because I want him to say *you, Sloane.* "Going to the next bar." He clinks his glass to mine and we finish our drinks.

WATER STREET TAVERN is a Pembroke-themed bar and home to all the biggest college game tailgates and watch parties. The music is always great and their specialty drink, the Wolverine, is guaranteed to put you on your ass. It's also home to the Ladies Night dollar drinks. We each get a Wolverine to start it off and a basket of chicken tenders to split.

We sit in a corner booth next to the dance floor. "Never have I everrrr," Wes starts.

I pick up a nugget and glare at him. "Oh, come on, what are we, freshmen?"

"Had to be in the next room listening to Annica having sex." He scrunches up his face in disgust as he says it.

I take a drink. "Thanks for putting that memory back into my head. My turn: Never have I ever had to retake a course because I forgot I signed up for it and failed it."

He raises his cup and takes a gulp. "Hm, never have I ever slept with a professor."

"Low blow." I take a sip. "Never have I ever had to have Charlie and Sam carry me home from the bar because I passed out. Take two drinks for that one actually," I say.

He does. "Never have I ever started talking to someone's cousin after sleeping with them," he counters. When I don't move, he says, "Well, aren't you going to drink?"

I don't understand the complete switch of the mood. When did it go from lighthearted to accusatory? "No, I am not. Because I'm not with Asher." He doesn't say anything, so I continue. If he wants to get personal, I can get personal. "Never have I ever continued to date someone when I had feelings for someone else."

We both stare at each other after I say it. My hands shake under the table as I wait for him to drink to it. To prove that I'm not wrong in this. He picks up his drink but pauses.

"Next bar." He gets up and heads to the door. I follow.

I CAN TELL we're both feeling the alcohol when we leave Water Street, and there's one stop left: 157, the closest thing to a nightclub that Pembroke has to offer.

"I hate this place," Wes says as we walk up to the door.

"Can't back out now," I say, handing the "bouncer" my ID. I use that term loosely because it's just other college kids standing at the door in all black with mini flashlights and earpieces. It's a college campus, it's not that deep.

The inside of the club is always dark as can be aside from the flashing strobes and large lit-up fish tanks that span the wall. There's one bottle service section in the back corner, which is always full, sometimes with our friends.

Wes orders us drinks: a vodka soda for me, a beer for him.

There's no specialty drink here. The only special thing about this place is that it's seen more blackouts than my hometown in a storm.

Wes takes a seat at the bar, clearly still reeling from our game of Never Have I Ever. But I'm not going to let him off the hook that easily. "Come on, let's dance!" I say over the music.

"There's no way!" Wes yells back.

"You owe me a favor. I'm calling it in!" I pull him to his feet as he chugs his drink and drag him to the middle of the dance floor. He's uncomfortable at first but song after song goes by and I have him jumping up and down, spinning me in circles. The lights are flashing all around us, the crowd moving with the same energy, and it's euphoric. I live for this feeling. Wes and I are in our own world just belting the words, laughing, pressed up against each other in the tight crowd, until he puts a hand on my face and pulls me in. His mouth crashes against mine and it feels like we're the only two people in this whole bar.

When Wes pulls away he looks at me with those beautiful green eyes and I think he's going to tell me to come home with him, and the yes is right on my lips.

"I have to go," he says over the music, and turns to leave. I catch his wrist.

"Wait, what? You're going?"

"I'm going home, Sloane, I—" He shakes his head. "I'm sorry." He pushes through the crowd and out the door, leaving me standing alone in the middle of the dance floor.

Without him there with me I start to feel hot and annoyed at the people all around me, shoving and spilling drinks. I go out to the back patio for some air. The late-September chill brings a cool relief to my skin and I feel the sweat on my hairline start to dry. I move to the back corner and find Asher leaning against the wall smoking a cigarette.

I scoff, going up to him. "I knew it. Have you been following us? Was this whole night some kind of setup?"

"Sloane?" he slurs, narrowing his eyes to see me. He's hammered.

"Well, since you're here, you might as well know I got you your answer, but I don't even know if you deserve to hear it." I wait for a reply, but he only takes another drag of the cigarette. I didn't know he smokes, I've never seen it, but he looks too gone for words. He looks like he's drinking to forget, not for fun. I sigh and walk away, back through the bar and toward the exit. I stop at the door, suddenly feeling kind of bad about leaving him out there. I should at least walk him back to the house. I make my way through all the people, out to the patio, but Asher is gone.

CHAPTER 10

October

The first week of October is always the Cedar Falls homecoming football game, and I've been looking forward to it all week. Anything to temporarily relieve me of thoughts of Jonah and Ryan . . . and Wes. I have a full car as we make the drive from Pembroke to Cedar Falls. I was able to convince my mother to let Annica and Dani come stay for the weekend, but I had to sweeten the deal. Asher and Charlie sit snug in the back seat with Dani in between them. Annica plays with the aux in the front seat. Wesley is back to avoiding me after our kiss last week, so when I put in the group message saying I had two extra seats if anyone wanted to come witness my sister become Cedar Falls royalty, I knew he wouldn't reply. I texted Asher separately asking him for this favor, knowing my mom would be too busy fussing over any boys I brought home to care about making backhanded comments to Annica and Dani. He agreed only because I still have the admission from Wesley about the business that he so desperately wants, and I said I'd tell him at the end of the weekend if he could stick it out in

Cedar Falls for two days. Charlie wanted to come because Dani was going and after that I had my four not-so-willing volunteers.

Of course, there's another reason I'm bringing them back here with me. There's another eulogy page I'm looking to track down.

"How much longer?" Asher asks from behind my seat. "Your driving is making me sick."

"Why did you invite him again?" Annica says from beside me.

"As a distraction," I say. Annica turns around to glare at Asher for no good reason, and he flips her off in return. "Can you two not?"

"I have to pee," Dani says.

I sigh. "I have a car full of children."

I CAN'T HELP but think of Jonah when I'm in town. Especially as the band and decorated cars go by with the homecoming court nominees atop them smiling and waving. I once sat on the back of one with my and Jonah's names written on the side. I tear up when Claire's car goes by and she has a big smile on her face. It's enough to take away the thoughts of Jonah for now. I look around at my friends and even Annica looks like she's having a decent time as she claps along to the fight song that the Cedar Falls High band plays. When all the cars have passed, we walk down the street behind them to the high school, where the parade stops.

"What are we doing after the game?" Dani asks.

"Yeah, what's the bar scene like over here?" Charlie says after.

"We have a dinner reservation in North Winwick at nine p.m.," I say.

I already made plans for after the game. I just didn't mention it so that no one could object. The next eulogy in my journal after Ryan's belongs to a man named Marco St. James. Marco recently opened up an Italian-style restaurant in North Winwick called St. James and we will be visiting the fine establishment this evening. Just because Tristan didn't receive a copy of his page doesn't mean the rest of them didn't. I just need to see that Marco is alive and well. Actually, I don't care if he's well, just alive.

"What's North Winwick?" Asher asks as we walk through the gate of the football field.

"It's a city just on the other side of Cedar Falls. We're one of the little towns that border it. Anything fun is in North Winwick," I explain.

Annica asks, "And what's the restaurant?"

"It's called St. James. Trust me, you'll love it."

"Sounds fancy," she says.

"Exactly."

People whisper as we walk through the aluminum bleachers, no doubt making comments about me and what I get up to at college. The people of this town thrive on drama so when I got arrested, it was enough fuel to light a wildfire of gossip. Sometimes I wonder if my mom and Don were more upset about the fact that I did it or that now the whole town talks about it.

My friends pick up on the stares and the whispering. Annica and Dani have been here with me before, so they know how it works.

"Sloane is like a local celebrity here." Annica smiles as she gives snotty waves to the gossipers. "They're obsessed with everything she does since it's so fucking dreadful and boring to live here."

"Annica," I scold, but can't help the twitch of my lips as they form a smile.

CHARLIE AND ASHER get really into the game, yelling at refs for bad calls and cheering on the boys. They mention at least ten times in the first half that they both used to play on their high school teams. When halftime rolls around it's time for the crowning. The band goes out onto the field, separating to make a walkway for the court. They start to play a slow song and the court begins to be announced from the booth above the bleachers. Don walks Claire out down the field and it reminds me to do a quick look around the bleachers. Our dad did not show. I wonder if Claire is trying to find him in the crowd. I stand up and whistle for her when they announce her and her activities in the school, which is a long list. She's the last one to walk and all five girls are now standing on the field next to their dads while last year's homecoming queen stands in the middle with this year's crown. The whole town is quiet as the drum roll starts. All I can hear is the pulse of my heartbeat in my ears, louder than the drum.

They announce Claire's name as the winner, and I swear I black out for a minute. I'm screaming and running down from the bleachers and onto the track with my mom and Sofie. I take a million pictures on my phone as they crown her homecoming queen and I wait not so patiently as they take photos on the field. When she walks toward the track, I run to pick her up and spin her around before our mom can even hug her. I don't care if she's embarrassed. I'm on an adrenaline high and I can't remember the last time I was so excited about anything.

When I walk back up into the bleachers, out of breath from screaming and laughing and jumping, my friends all stare at me wide-eyed.

"Wow," Charlie says. "Now I feel like I underreacted when my sister won homecoming queen last year."

"I thought we might have to call a priest for an exorcism the way you just jumped down the bleachers," Asher adds.

Annica laughs. "Tomorrow there will be a rumor that you did a line of coke before the game."

"Wow," I breathe, still reeling from the excitement, "let's go celebrate."

WE TRADE THE crowd and stadium lights for an intimate table with a single lit candle in the middle.

"Oh, you were right: This is fancy," Annica says with a content grin.

"Did you guys hear that?" I say. "Oh, never mind, it's just my wallet crying." I regret to say I did not look at the menu prices before coming here, but can you really put a price on your own sanity? I just need to lay eyes on Marco and I'll feel better.

The waiter approaches our table and I realize it's a guy I went to high school with. "Oh, Dalton, hey!" I say, standing up to hug him.

"Wow, hi, I haven't seen you in so long," he says. "How have you been?"

"Oh, you haven't heard?" Annica says. "She's been the worst."

"Don't listen to her." I laugh. "I'm jealous you work here. You must make great tips." I can't imagine how much money I'd make in a night if Cantine's prices were this high.

"Honestly, yeah, we've only been open for two weeks and my rent is already covered for this month," Dalton says. "Did you move home? I can put in a good word for you with the boss—he's super chill."

"Is he hot too?" Annica asks.

We ignore her.

"I didn't move home, no, but is he here by chance? The owner?" My heart thunders in my chest and I start to look around Dalton to see if I can spot him.

"Yeah, he is. He usually comes by each table after the meal to see how it went, so you can give your compliments then . . . and see what he looks like," he pointedly says to Annica. "Anyway, what can I get you guys to drink?"

THREE SEVENTEEN-DOLLAR COCKTAILS later, I thought seeing Marco in person would bring me some relief, but as Dalton leads him to our table I feel my palms start to sweat and my leg begins to bounce nervously. Marco has that same golden-hued skin tone Adrienne has, no matter the season. His wavy dark hair is slicked back, and with the scruff on his face he looks like a man in a cologne ad. Annica's mouth drops open slightly at the sight of him and I resist the urge to kick her under the table.

"How was everything this evening?" he asks. Marco looks us over, one at a time, as he says it. When his eyes land on me, there's not even a flicker of recognition in them. He either really doesn't remember me or is going to pretend not to. Suddenly I don't think I have the courage to ask about the note.

"It was *amazing*," Annica drawls.

"Yes, so good," Dani follows with emphasis.

The boys mumble a "good" and a "great," then they all turn to me, expecting me to chime in.

"I—" I don't have words. "I have to use the bathroom."

I quickly slide out of the booth and scurry off toward the restroom. Fuck, fuck, fuck. My friends rush in behind me.

"Are you okay? Are you sick?" Dani checks me over.

"I thought I'd be relieved to see him, but he doesn't even recognize me," I say.

Annica is confused. "Who? The chef?"

"Yes! Marco, I dated him the summer before sophomore year, remember?"

"*You* dated *him*?" Annica says. "The Italian god standing out there who looks like he just stepped out of a painting?"

"Yes," I say back, annoyed. "Why is that so hard to believe?"

"It's not, it's not," Dani says quickly. "He just also looks really old? Like not really old but, like, too old for us—you know what I mean."

"Accomplished," Annica says. "She means he looks too accomplished for you."

"Thanks," I say. "You guys really don't remember? I dated him all summer, his dad was in the NFL, and they had a second home in Italy?" I try to jog their memories, but they just look at me with blank stares. "He broke up with me at the end of the summer because he was actually *living* in Italy and never once mentioned that he was only home for the summer until the day before he was leaving?"

Still nothing.

"Super-Catholic guy who would ask me to take Plan B after each time we slept together even though we used condoms, and once put one in my parents' mailbox?"

"Oh my god, *him*?" they say in unison.

I roll my eyes. I'm glad we remember only the important things here. "Yes, him. And he doesn't even remember who I am. Did you see him just now? All 'How was everything?'" I say in a tone meant to be his. "I mean, who does he think he is?"

"The owner of this restaurant—" Dani says.

"Ugh, whatever," I cut her off. "Just tell the boys I started my period or something and text me when Marco goes away."

Annica leaves the bathroom, but Dani hangs back awhile longer. "Are you okay?" If Dani had a catchphrase, it would be that.

"I'm fine." I saw Marco, he's alive, he owns a restaurant. Whether or not he has the journal page in his possession, it no longer seems to matter.

She gives me a sad smile before leaving the bathroom, and I need another drink. I text my mom to say we ran into some old high school friends, and we'll be out late. She responds and tells me to stay out of trouble.

If only.

DALTON IS GETTING off work when we wrap up with dinner and invites us back to his place for a party. He lives right in downtown North Winwick, close to the small college that makes up half of the city. From the view of his living room window, I can see Marco's restaurant. I catch Dalton up on the real details of why I bolted from the table since he had to stand there and also awkwardly watch me run away.

"Oh, gross, he really doesn't seem like that kind of guy," Dalton says. "And he's thirty, so what was he doing with a nineteen-year-old while he was, what, twenty-eight?"

Asher opens his mouth, likely to make a professor joke, and I cut him a look that says *don't you dare*. "In his defense, I told him I was twenty-four at the time," I say.

"At least he comped our whole meal after you ran to the bathroom," Annica says. "He thought the food made you sick."

"Yeah," Charlie says. "Do any other exes of yours own restaurants? We can go try that again but order more this time."

"Aren't you guys listening? He didn't even recognize me! I was that insignificant in his life. Meanwhile I wrote a whole—" I cut myself off now.

Annica hears it of course. "Wrote a whole what?"

Dani talks over her. "With a face like his, he's probably dated half the planet, probably can't remember any girls at this point."

"Okay, I've heard enough," I say, pouring one shot, two shots, three shots' worth of vodka into a red Solo cup.

DALTON MANAGES TO fit more people into a one-bedroom campus apartment than I ever thought possible. Annica has been really hitting it off with him, and now they're partners in a beer pong game against Dani and Charlie. Asher is in the corner of the room whispering in the ear of a brunette, who laughs and bites her lip. I stand leaning on the kitchen island, looking through my phone. I want to talk to Wes. More than that I want to be friends again.

Part of me wishes we never did what we did last summer because then he might even be here right now. And we'd laugh and tease each other the way we used to, with that unspoken thing between us. I open Wes's contact and start typing.

> It's officially been a week since you kissed me in 157.

> I wish you wouldn't avoid me so we could talk about it.

> This weird thing between us. I just miss the way things used to be. I miss you—

"I wouldn't send that if I were you," Asher says, grabbing another beer from the fridge after peering over my shoulder. It makes me jump so hard that I drop my phone on the counter. I pick it up and delete the message I typed out. "Wes, Sam, and Jake are all at Ray's right now with Marissa's friends."

"Good to know." I go back to watching the beer pong game from the counter.

"You know, with your track record, I'm starting to think Wes is a little too young for you anyway," Asher says. "The restaurant owner, the professor . . ."

"It's better than what I can say for you. That girl you're cozying up to is in high school."

He scoffs. "No she's not—she goes to college with Dalton."

"Is that what she told you?" She could very well be in college. I don't know her; I just want to rattle Asher back, since he seems to love constantly doing it to me. I want to see his face fall with disappointment and replace his constant smug facade, just once. He looks back over at her, assessing. I raise my eyebrows at him. "Creep," I say, before taking a sip of my drink and peeling away from the counter toward the couch.

I DO MY fair share of drinking and even take a hit—and I do mean just one hit—of a community blunt before Asher snatches it right out of my hand.

"Do you think that's wise?" he asks, handing it to Charlie and plopping down on the leather couch beside me, putting an arm around the back. Dani glances over at us from the other couch, where she sits with Charlie.

I roll my eyes. "What are you, my keeper?"

Asher leans in. "I came on this stupid trip to your shantytown—now tell me what Wes said."

I sit with my arms crossed. If I turned my head toward him we'd be nose to nose. "It's not a shantytown, you jackass."

He breathes a laugh in my ear. "Just tell me what I want to know."

I turn to face him, thinking he'll back away, but he doesn't. "He doesn't want the resort. I'm sure if something better came along, he would take it. There, happy?" I can feel Dani's and Charlie's eyes on us, because I'm sure from where they're sitting it looks like we might kiss.

Asher smiles. "Ecstatic."

I turn my gaze back and watch Dani and Charlie quickly look away, pretending like they're watching the game of flip cup going on behind us.

"Now you have your answer and I did my part, so you can leave me alone," I say. He only leans in closer, lightly pressing his mouth to my neck, and I nearly jump out of my skin. "What the fuck are you doing?"

"My part," he says.

"He's not even here."

"Once again, he's not the only one we need to convince," he says, his eyes darting toward our friends.

I scoot away from him. "I changed my mind. I don't think I want to do this." I think about how I felt probing Wes for answers about his future. How wrong it felt knowing I was only asking for Asher.

"That's not what happened at Euros, Miss 'Ugh, I suck at this.'" He mimics me messing up the pool shot.

"Sloane, let's get next game!" Dani says, grabbing my hands and pulling me away from Asher. "Is he bothering you?" she asks when we're away from the couches.

"No," I say. "It's fine."

THE WEED AND the vodka start to mix together in my system, and I pass out senseless on Dalton's tiny black couch. The party roars on around me as I doze off.

The smell of smoke wakes me from my cross-faded sleep. Not weed or cigarette smoke, but something heavier, like a bonfire. It's still dark, aside from the glow of something orange that lights up the room. Dani is curled up on the recliner next to me, Charlie and Asher are on the floor, and everyone else is gone. I slowly peel myself from the leather to peer out the window, only to find Marco's restaurant up in flames.

I blink a few times, thinking maybe I smoked a laced blunt. Maybe it was some synthetic weed that makes you hallucinate. But when the fire still blazes bright before me I start to really panic.

I run over to Dani, shaking her furiously. "Dani, wake up, there's a fire." I nudge the boys with my feet. "There's a fire!" I say a little louder.

She startles awake. "What? A fire?" The boys both stir on the ground. Charlie only groans at the disturbance.

"Marco's restaurant, it's on fire!" She gets up this time, almost toppling over the boys, who are groggily propping themselves up and rubbing their eyes. I drag her by the hand to the window. "We need to call 911 or something!"

The boys come to the window, and I run over to Dalton's room, banging on the locked door. Annica opens it, wearing an oversized Wildcats T-shirt, my high school mascot. "What's wrong?" She squints at me through sleepy eyes.

"The restaurant is on fire. Wake up Dalton—we're going down there."

It seems someone already called 911 as two fire trucks and police arrive on the scene. Other nosy bystanders begin to crowd around the blaze at nearly four in the morning. The police start to roll caution tape around the perimeter, keeping everyone at a safe distance. We all just stand there in silence watching it burn. I'm waiting for the moment that Marco shows up with a devastated look on his face seeing his life's work up in flames, though I know his dad has enough money to build him five more restaurants by tomorrow. But Marco never arrives.

"Fuck, now I need to find a new job," Dalton mumbles.

"At least it burned down after your shift," I say. "Or you'd need more than a new job."

We watch them put out the rest of the fire. Marco must not know. He'll come to work in the morning and find nothing but the charred remains.

A firefighter comes from the rubble. "We got a body!"

Oh no.

My hand flies to my mouth as the six of us audibly gasp in unison. I glance all around the street. There's no parking lot for the restaurant, just street parking, and less than fifty feet away is an all-black Tesla, the same one that used to pick me up for dates two summers ago. Marco wasn't here to witness the fire because he was in it.

"I need to walk away for a minute," I tell my friends before heading in the direction of his car. I take deep breaths with my hands on top of my head as the shock of the fire starts to wear off and my hangover sets in. As I get closer to Marco's car I notice the folded white piece of paper under his windshield wiper. It can't be. Please, don't be, I think to myself as I take the paper from the windshield. When I unfold it, my fear is confirmed. It's another scanned copy of my journal entry, the one about Marco.

Today we are here to mourn the loss of not just Marco St. James but also the girl I was before I met him. Gone is the naive, sun-kissed girl lost in summer romance. That version of me was laid to rest with Marco, both suffocated by long, humid nights and lies. He was the type of guy mothers warn their daughters about. He was the monster under your bed—or rather, in it. Or on the couch. Or on the bar. You get the picture. But his

*death was not for nothing, no. For if he didn't take my old self
down with him, I may have fallen for another just like him.
And that is a fate worse than death.*

Arrivederci, you motherf—

"Sloane?" I hear Dani say, walking up behind me.

With shaking hands, I crumple it up and shove it into my coat
pocket. I frantically look all around me to see if there's someone
out there watching, waiting for me to find it. Was this even meant
for me to find? What the *fuck* is going on? My breathing is ragged
now, with my hands shaking uncontrollably.

"Are you okay?" she says.

"Yep, yes." I let out an unsteady breath.

"I know you didn't really like him but . . . what a horrible way
to go."

"Yes," I whisper, looking back over at the billowing smoke.
"Horrible."

"We should get out of here," she says.

We all walk to Dalton's apartment parking lot, where my car is,
after saying goodbye and getting our belongings from his apartment. The group is quiet as we all pile back into my car. I sit frozen
at the wheel. We're all thinking it but no one is saying it. This is my
third ex to die in less than two months.

"Do you . . . need one of us to drive?" Charlie asks from the
back seat.

I almost feel like I'm imagining it as a white Jeep Wrangler, the
same car Miles Holland drives, speeds past the lot.

"What?" I ask, distracted, but Asher is already at the driver's
side telling me to get in the back.

The fifteen minutes to my house drag on forever as music plays low in the background. I stare out the window completely zoned out, with my hand on the printed eulogy in my pocket. The slickness of my sweating palms starts to dampen the page. Asher parks the car and everyone starts to walk toward the house. I go around to my trunk to look for a pair of slippers or slides, realizing I only brought the heeled boots that I've been wearing since we got here yesterday. When I open my trunk my heart stops. A red gasoline container sits in the center of all the clothes, shoes, and other miscellaneous items that I've tossed back here over the years. I look around to see if anyone else caught a glimpse of what's in my trunk, but my friends have now congregated by the garage door, likely waiting for me before entering the house. I can only stare at the container. I know I didn't put this in here. I've never once kept a gasoline container in my trunk.

"Sloane, are you coming?" Annica asks. "We're waiting on you."

"Y-yeah," I stammer out, closing the trunk without grabbing the shoes.

I LIE DOWN in my old bed, staring up at the purple-painted ceiling. Jonah, Ryan, and now Marco. I repeat their names in my head like a grocery list. Jonah, Ryan, Marco, Jonah, Ryan, Marco. I go to turn on my side and the crunch of the paper in my pocket makes me flinch. Jonah's death felt like a cruel twist of fate. Ryan's felt like a bad coincidence. Marco's feels like a murder—I think of the red gasoline container in my trunk—and I'm the intended suspect.

CHAPTER 11

At least a dozen kids in Claire's class and their parents show up at our house for homecoming pictures. My friends hang out outside while I make small talk with the adults asking me about school and what I'll do when I graduate. It's an overwhelming amount of conversation for someone who is on the verge of a breakdown. I catch a few whispers here and there from some of the parents who saw the news about the fire.

"Did you see that new restaurant in North Winwick caught on fire last night?" one woman says.

"Yes! And I heard the owner was *inside* when it happened!" another woman says with her hand over her heart.

"I could see the smoke from my house!" one man says.

I can't hear another word about it, and I meet my friends outside. We sit in near silence watching a movie on the back patio but I'm staring at my car, afraid that if I look away the gas container might drive itself to the police station.

Eventually we call it a night; the boys go back to the basement while Dani and Annica share Claire's bed because she's sleeping at a friend's house after the dance. I lie there in the dark for at least an hour before getting up and quietly sneaking outside. The only rational thing I can think of is to get rid of this gas container; whether it was the one to start the fire or just some sick joke, I want it gone.

I take it to the edge of the woods behind my house, my feet crunching on the leaves in the yard with each step. I'm going to have to walk into the woods at least a few feet to toss this far enough but—

"What are you doing with that?" Asher's voice scares the shit out of me.

"Jesus Christ, Asher," I hiss. "What are you doing out here?"

"I was still out on the patio, couldn't sleep. Why are you walking into the woods with a container of gasoline? You don't seem like the kind of girl who starts forest fires for attention, Sawyer." Even in the dark I can sense the smug smirk on his face.

"It's empty. I'm just tossing it out. Trying to make room in my trunk." It's the best I can come up with when someone catches me trying to get rid of evidence in the middle of the night.

"So throw it away in the garbage can?" In the low light of the garage lamp I see him motion to the large trash bin that's outside the garage door. But I've gotten three hours of sleep since yesterday and I'm irritable.

"Will you just go inside and leave me alone?"

He's quiet for a minute, and I hear the crunch of the leaves under his feet as he walks toward me. "I do find it odd that here you are, trying to toss an empty gas container in the woods, the day after a fire burned down your ex-boyfriend's restaurant."

I open my mouth, then close it. The container shakes violently in my hands. I need to explain myself, but what do I even say?

Where do I start? "I'm going to tell you something, Asher, and you better promise me *on your life* that you will not repeat it."

Out of pure desperation I fill him in on my current predicament, down to every last detail. The journal entries, the conversation with Grange, how it very much feels like I'm being set up for a murder and I can't hide the panic and fear in my voice when I finally say it all aloud. It feels good to get it off my chest, but I can't help but wonder if he's the wrong person to tell.

"And how do you know I won't turn around and call this Detective Grange to tell him that you tossed an empty gas can into the woods and took the note from the crime scene?"

Wrong person, definitely the wrong person to tell. I throw the gas container at his chest so quick that he has no choice but to catch it.

"Because now your fingerprints are on the evidence, asshole."

I hear him huff a laugh. "Well played, Sawyer." He holds it up. "Let's toss out some evidence, then, shall we?" I can only blink at his willingness to go along with this plan. We walk into the woods together to dispose of the thing when he starts to talk again. "Now that I have another secret of yours to keep, I'm going to have to think of what I want in return."

WITH EACH DAY that passes I have a stronger and stronger urge to call up Detective Grange and tell him everything. I wonder if it would help me to get ahead of it, but then I probably shouldn't have gotten rid of the gas container and the copy of the eulogy, both of which are buried in a shallow grave in the woods behind my house. Asher hasn't said a word since Sunday, when we all came back to Pembroke and went our separate ways, but I've been sending him long-worded ramblings multiple times a day. I even tried calling him in the middle of the night last night when I couldn't sleep, but he didn't pick up. I start to feel paranoid that he did turn me in, but when I get back to campus late Wednesday night, Asher is in my room sprawled across my bed reading a book.

"How'd you get in here?" I demand.

He sits up casually. "Adrienne let me in. Where have you been? I've been waiting here for two hours. Adrienne said you only have one class on Wednesdays in the afternoon."

"Where was I? Where were you? I've been freaking out, texting and calling you for three days! I tell you that I think I'm being set up for murder and then you ghost me?"

He stands from my bed, putting the book on my nightstand and adjusting his hoodie. "You need to calm down. I've been doing research."

"Research? Research on what?" I feel like some crazy girlfriend needing to know exactly why he hasn't been replying to me. I almost want to ask if I can go through his phone.

"I've watched more *Criminal Minds* and serial killer documentaries in the past three days than I think some people do in a lifetime. I've also learned that the only crime you've really committed so far is destroying evidence, which will earn you a hefty fine, but no jail time. And that's assuming the container was even used for the fire. All three of these deaths could truly have been accidents and someone's playing a cruel prank on you."

"You're suggesting that Ryan and Marco both died accidentally, and someone just happened to be around with my printed journal pages to drop them off as a joke?"

Asher only crosses his arms. "You didn't answer my question: Where were you today?"

"I didn't answer because it's not your business."

"If you want my help, you'll have to make it my business."

"Fine. I was in North Winwick, looking around the restaurant to see if any more copies of the journal page were out there."

His hands fall to his sides. "You went to the scene of the crime? You never go back to the scene of the crime. You know who does? The criminal."

"Except I'm not a criminal!" I realize I'm yelling and Adrienne is in her room so I tone it down. "Which you know, because I told you everything."

"I actually don't know that. I'm just choosing to believe it." He walks over to the wall, making an effort to struggle stepping over all my clothes, books, and shoes, to my closet, where there used to be a shelf with books on it. In its place is a giant corkboard with printed names and red string.

I look from the board to him. "Asher, what the fuck."

"This is how they figure it out in the movies." He points around the board. "We have Jonah's, Ryan's, and Marco's names all up here. I didn't think you'd want to have to look at them every day so I didn't print their pictures. And the thing that ties them all together." His hand traces over the red string attached to each name and where it leads. "You." He printed my mug shot and pinned it below the names. "And as we get more suspects, we add them to the board."

"I can't have a fucking murder suspect board in my bedroom." I walk over to it and try to take it from the wall but it won't budge.

"It's screwed into the wall," he says.

I clench my jaw, unpinning my mug shot and crumpling it up in my hand. Underneath it is a polaroid of me that was clipped onto my string lights above my bed.

"Yeah, I thought you might do that." He smirks. "So, how many names are in this journal exactly and whose name is next?"

"No, we aren't playing detective. I need to just call Grange and tell him everything. I'll point the finger at Miles and, I don't know, they'll go after him instead of me."

"What solid proof do you have that Miles is behind it all? Because from where I'm standing, the only suspect in Ryan's and Marco's murders is you. Jonah was hit by a semitruck that flipped over the median, so we know that one was an accident." I don't bother asking how he knows the details of Jonah's death, as I'm sure it was part of his research. I think about my last conversation with Grange, when he brought up last year's events. He already doesn't trust me. If I go to him now and tell him about Miles, he'll wonder why I didn't mention him sooner.

"Well . . . I don't have proof, but I can try to get some." All I know is that Miles knows that my journal exists, and he has a reason to want revenge. But neither of those things would count as evidence.

"Back to my questions," he says. "Answer them."

I sit on the edge of my bed. "There are seven eulogies in the journal."

"So what's the next name?" he asks again.

I sigh and give in to this ridiculous detective charade.

"Bryce Peterson," I say.

"Peterson?" Asher scoffs and pauses before turning back to me.

"I think the world may be better off if we just let the professor get him. Who's after him?"

"Asher! This is fucking serious. What is wrong with you? People are *dying*. Wesley's name is in that journal—is that what you want? For Wes to die?" It hits me hard when I say it. Wesley's name is in the journal. I put my head in my hands. "Why is this happening to me?" I groan.

Asher continues, "Okay, then I guess we're about to be seeing a lot more of Bryce Peterson. I'm friends with some of his friends so we'll use that connection to keep an eye on him and hopefully catch the professor. Which is kind of a sick serial killer name if you think about it. The Professor."

I only stare at him. "This literally can't be my life. It just can't be."

"And in the meantime, we are going back to my original terms of the deal. You are going to get me that resort by any means necessary."

My mouth gapes open. "How can you even think about yourself in a time like this?"

"I'm thinking about my future, which is what you should be doing. Dani and Annica said you haven't gone to class all week. Don't fall apart on me now, Sawyer. I need Wes to want you. He needs to want you enough to stay here with you and leave Colorado to me."

I shake my head. "Fine, whatever." Because what is the alternative? I say no and he rats me out? His help has to be better than no help at all . . . right?

"I knew you'd see things my way," Asher says with a smile that makes me grit my teeth. "Now if you'll excuse me, I have a date."

"Who in their right mind would be dumb enough to date you?"
I grumble.

"No one as dumb as the people who dated *you*."

He has me there.

Asher leaves me alone in my bedroom, where I let out a long
sigh, looking at the suspect board. Was that really Miles's Jeep in
North Winwick last weekend? A twisted part of me hopes it was,
because if not, then who else could have done this?

My photo on the board stares back at me.

In both instances I've managed to be drunk enough to black
out and not remember the night. Is it possible that I would do
something like that? No, no, I can't even think like that. I can't go
down that road. I push that thought deep, deep down as I grab a
marker and paper and write "Miles Holland" in big letters, adding
it to the board. Then I look over at my goals taped on my mirror.
You're not going to get into trouble.

I cross out that line with the marker.

CHAPTER 12

Six days after the fire, a news article is posted saying the cause of the fire was a gas leak. It eases my worry just slightly knowing that I must have taken the only copy of the eulogy, and no one will be looking for evidence that points to arson. So now that's three supposed "accidents," two copies of my journal, and one seriously freaked-out Sloane. But the news comes just in time for Annica's twenty-second birthday. We're throwing her a surprise party at their apartment tonight and Dani is keeping her busy all day while I decorate the place with the boys. Charlie and Sam go out to pick up the cake, Jake is grabbing balloons, and that leaves Asher, Wesley, and me to be here alone cleaning up and taping streamers to the walls.

Wesley plays music while we work so that no one can acknowledge the weird silence between the three of us. Asher gives me looks every time we make eye contact, urging me to talk to Wes. At one point he stands beside me at the kitchen sink, and we speak in whispers while Wesley vacuums the living room in front of us.

"Miles wants me to meet him somewhere," I say, washing the

cups in the sink. He emailed me again the other day after I didn't respond.

"Good, where and when?"

I look up at him. "You think I should just do what he says and meet up with him? What if he really is the killer? What if he kills *me*?"

"Then this whole thing will be over, and I won't have to keep watching true crime documentaries."

I scoff. "You're horrible."

He leans down so he's close to my ear. "You haven't even seen horrible. And I don't see you talking to Wesley at all, when this is probably the best opportunity you're going to get."

"He won't even look at me," I say through nearly clenched teeth. "What am I supposed to do about that?"

Asher stands up again and looks past the kitchen island, where we're standing, at Wes and shrugs. "We make him look at you, then," he says.

"And how are you going to accomplish that?"

He smiles, and it's wicked. "By being horrible."

I hardly have time to question it before his hand juts out, grabbing me hard around the arm, his fingertips squeezing into my skin as he pulls me forcefully to him, and I drop the cup I was washing with a loud thud in the sink. My body slams into his and I suck in a breath at the pain.

"What the hell, Asher!" I try to shove him back.

The vacuum noise cuts out abruptly as it falls to the floor. "Asher!" Wesley barks out at him, storming over to us.

Asher gives me a small grin out of Wesley's view before whispering, "Now make nice." He lets me go and faces Wes in that devil-may-care way that he does.

"Don't fucking grab her like that, do you hear me?" Wes is standing so close to him that I realize they could almost be brothers when they're face-to-face.

Asher only pushes past Wes and heads to the door. Wesley runs a hand down his face as I rub my arm, still sore from Asher's grip.

"Can't you just pick someone else, Sloane? Anyone else but him?" His tone is pleading, and it makes me feel bad. I should say we're not together, I should reassure him of that at least, but I don't, because that is not the plan.

"I miss you." I don't mean for it to come out; it just does. It sounds desperate, but I guess I am. His eyes widen and I can see it was the wrong thing to say. I'm about to scare him off, so I recover. "Like as a friend. I miss being friends. We don't have to talk about last summer, or two weeks ago, just please stop avoiding me."

"I'm not . . . avoiding you. I'm just— I've been busy." We both know it's a lie. I'm trying to think of what to say next but he speaks again. "If you're going to get involved with my cousin, just be careful, okay? Asher is . . . he's just got a lot of personal issues." Whether he's talking about Asher's weird obsessive need to take over their family business or his total lack of regard for anyone's feelings, I want to tell him that I know about all of it.

"I am careful," I whisper. We're both quiet, staring out into the living room, and I'm silently scolding myself for having two weeks to come up with something to say to him and having nothing. But in my defense, I've been a little preoccupied.

"So do you think Annica is going to hate this whole thing?" he asks.

I smile, knowing that she probably will. Annica doesn't like to make a big deal of her birthday. She'd probably much rather go out for a low-key but very expensive dinner, which is actually the plan for tomorrow night. Charlie and Sam break up our moment when they walk in with the cake.

"Sorry it took so long. We weren't sure if we grabbed the right one," Sam says. He sets the white box on the counter, and runs a nervous hand through his black hair.

"How were you not sure? It should've been the only one at the bakery that said 'Happy Birthday, Annica' on it." But knowing Sam, he was likely too timid to ask the bakery to check and took whatever they handed him. And by the hint of powdered sugar left on the corner of Charlie's mouth, he was too busy sampling the pastries to care.

I lift the top of the box, revealing the circular cake with white frosting and blue writing in the middle that reads "Sorry I Backed into Your Car" with a frowny face.

I sigh. "Yeah, she's going to hate this whole thing."

DANI MAKES SURE Annica has a few drinks before arriving, so when we all jump out and say "surprise" Annica starts laughing. She laughs even harder at the cake, then hugs and thanks us each individually for the effort. I look over at Dani, wondering how many drinks she gave her.

Some of the hockey boys show up, followed by Marissa and her friends. Music plays from the TV while we all start to pregame for the bars. I can hear Marissa loudly bragging about her Tik-

Tok fame, if you can even call it that. She got 100K followers from posting her stupid sorority outfits during rush week and calls herself an influencer.

"So how'd it go?" Asher asks when we're alone on the couch.

"I had to beg him to stop avoiding me—he said he's just been busy. But I think we're good again," I say. I sneak a glance over at Wes, who is standing by Annica and Dani, but he's looking at me and Asher. He looks away when we make eye contact. "You didn't have to grab my arm so hard. I'm going to have a bruise."

He doesn't say sorry, because why would Asher ever say sorry. Instead he says, "Toughen up, buttercup," before standing and walking toward the door, where a whole host of people have just arrived.

Annica rushes over to me. "Why is all of Sigma Chi walking into my apartment right now?" I look over to see Asher bro-ing it up with one of the guys in the group, followed by Bryce Peterson.

"I invited them," I say, knowing she'll be a little less pissy if she thinks it was me and not Asher.

"Why? Are you seeing Bryce again? You know I don't judge you for your choices, Sloane, but I would judge you for this one."

I would have to lose a lot of brain cells before I'd ever go back to someone who not only called me another girl's name *twice* but gave me an STD and then told everyone he got it from me. Annica would be right to judge me for that one.

"No, I am not seeing him." Just stalking him. "Marissa's brother Hudson is in Sig Chi. I thought it would be nice to extend the invite. Since she's part of the group and all." The words are bitter on my tongue.

"Since when do you care about Marissa and being nice to her?

Just last week you said her voice was annoying and her hair looks fried from the bleach."

"Okay," I cut her off with a forced laugh. "Those were just observations. A general statement if you will. But if she's still sticking it out with Wes, then we should be friendly, right? And the Sig Chis are fun! Remember?"

"I remember how disgusting they were," she says, before turning her attention back toward the kitchen, where one of them is standing on top of the counter bonging a beer. "Hey! Get down from there!" Annica yells as she runs to the kitchen.

AROUND MIDNIGHT EVERYONE leaves the apartment party for the bars. Asher and I follow behind Bryce and his friends at a distance, with our own friends even farther back.

I sigh. "So this is it: We just follow Bryce around every day until someone tries to kill him? That's the best plan you could come up with?"

"Do you have a better tactic?" Asher asks.

"Yeah," I say. "We hurry up and get evidence on Miles."

Asher's mouth quirks up in a smile. "I was hoping you'd say that. Because you're meeting him at a coffee shop called Luna's on Ivy Gate's campus tomorrow."

I stop walking. "What?"

He turns to face me, walking backward down the sidewalk. "I emailed him back from your phone during the party."

"You *what*?" I follow after him.

"Don't worry, I'll be there in case he tries anything."

"That doesn't make me feel any better."

"I'm going to buy you a shot when we get to Ray's—you need to calm down."

"Don't tell me to calm down. You're not the one that has to somehow finish out senior year and catch a murderer at the same time."

"And try to win over Wes, don't forget that one."

"How can I when you remind me every two fucking seconds?"

"What are you two bickering about up here?" Jake says, throwing his arms around the two of us, and I realize I've never wanted to be Jake so badly. Never a care in the world, nor a thought behind those eyes.

"How many shots Sloane is going to do at the bar tonight," Asher says to Jake.

"It's zero," I say.

"Zero times ten." Jake bops my nose with his pointer finger.

"Jake, that's still zero," I say, wondering how he ever got into Pembroke in the first place.

I HALF-HEARTEDLY FOLLOW the group around from bar to bar, taking small sips of my drinks, determined to not let the alcohol get the best of me this time. Even though I want nothing more than to let my thoughts melt away for the night. Everything is standard until Bryce sneaks out of the side exit of the rooftop at Water Street. Asher is across the bar with Sam and I don't have time to get his attention, so I tell my friends I'll be right back and slip out the side door after him. Bryce takes the fire escape stairs down to the brick alleyway next to the bar and stops to pull out a vape. I'm crouched down on the landing, watching him, when Asher comes out after me.

"Did he come out here?" he asks.

"Yeah, he's down there." I point to the wall that Bryce is leaning on, smoking a vape pen and looking through his phone.

"What an idiot," Asher says. "Coming down to a dark alleyway in the middle of the night. This is, like, the perfect spot for a murder."

"You're doing too much 'research,'" I snap at him.

Bryce nods his head at someone who is approaching from the other end.

"Oh shit," I whisper. "Someone's here."

We're both crouched down on the landing waiting for the person to come into view. I recognize the clacking of the heeled boots before I see the short, definitely fried, blond hair. It's Marissa Wilder.

"What the hell?" I say. Asher shushes me. "Do you think she's cheating on Wes?" I can't deny the excitement in my voice when I say it. Asher shushes me a second time.

The two of them stand alone talking too quietly for us to hear, and so close together that I start to think that really is what's happening. If Marissa is seeing Bryce behind Wes's back, that'd be one less obstacle for me. She starts to dig around in her purse for something before pulling out a folded piece of white paper and handing it to Bryce. I grab Asher's arm.

"Do you see that?" I whisper. "That folded paper, that's what my journal page looked like on Marco's car."

Marissa Wilder. Marissa fucking Wilder.

Maybe she did find out about me and Wes and wants revenge.

"We don't know if that's what it is," he says back, but I'm already making my way down the fire escape, fueled on adrenaline. Asher tries to grab onto me but I'm out of reach.

They don't notice me coming until I'm practically standing in front of them. Marissa snatches back the paper from Bryce when she sees me.

"What are you guys doing out here?" I ask.

Bryce blows out a puff of smoke in my direction. "What's it to you?"

At the same time Marissa says, "We were just talking," her tone a bit defensive.

"Oh really? About this?" I grab the paper from Marissa before she has a second to react and start to unfold it, fully preparing for it to be my handwriting on the inside. But it's not; it's a list of what look like answers to a math test. "What the hell?" I say under my breath.

Marissa snatches it back at the same time Bryce says, "What the fuck, Sloane?"

I realize I made a huge mistake and I'm thankful it's too dark to see how red my face must be. "I'm sorry, I thought that was something else. Sorry," I say again, backing away.

Marissa stands with her arms crossed. "You better not tell anyone, Sloane. If I get in trouble for giving out test answers, I'll know it was you."

First of all, who the fuck passes off test answers behind a bar in the middle of the night? "I won't tell anyone," I say.

"Good," she says with a smirk, "because I don't think Wesley would be too happy with you if I got expelled."

I open my mouth to speak but Marissa turns to leave and Bryce follows. I walk back to Asher, who is now waiting at the bottom of the fire escape, on his phone looking bored.

"I take it you just made a complete ass out of yourself?" he says casually.

"It was test answers, she was giving him test answers," I say in disbelief.

"Yeah, she sells them," Asher says. "How do you think Jake passes classes?"

My eyes snap to him. "Why didn't you say that before I ran down there?!"

"I did make a small attempt at trying to stop you."

I rub at my temple and take a deep breath. "I'm too paranoid for this. I need a drink."

"No," Asher says. "You need to go home. You have to be on your A game tomorrow for the professor." He turns my shoulders and starts walking with me from the alley, toward the road.

"What about following Bryce?"

"If anything happens to him, you wouldn't be a suspect, because we just saw him alive and well with Marissa, and you're going home, where your roommate is and will be able to corroborate your alibi if you need it." I only stare at him, gritting my teeth. "Bryce will be fine," he adds.

I cross my arms, thinking about a drink. "You can't make me leave."

Asher looks back down at his phone. "Sure I can."

We stand at the end of the alley on Main Street as a black Honda pulls up. He shuffles me toward the car and opens the door. I know he's right, that I don't need to black out tonight just to give myself a break. But the thought of going home sober not knowing what will happen to Bryce and not having any type of plan for what I'm going to say to Miles Holland tomorrow makes a knot form in the pit of my stomach and I almost want to cling to Asher like a lifeline.

"I'll pick you up for Ivy Gate at ten a.m. tomorrow," Asher says from outside the car as I step in. I feel my breath shallow in my chest as the panic sets in. I'll never be able to sleep tonight.

"Wait," I say from the back seat before he shuts the door. Asher stands there waiting for me to say something. When I don't, he catches on.

"Oh, Sawyer," he says with fake pity. "Are you working up the courage to ask me to come home with you? Here, let me make it easy for you." Asher shuts the car door in my face and backs up, giving a small wave before making his way to the front entrance of the bar.

"Fucking asshole," I mutter to myself.

I WAS RIGHT: I can't fall asleep. I stand in front of the corkboard that's screwed into the wall. If it's here, I might as well use it. I print pictures of the deceased, pinning them under the names that Asher added. I tape sticky notes over them with details of their deaths and if they had a journal page and where it was found. Then I print a picture of Miles Holland and Ivy Gate and put those on the board, tying a red string from Ryan to Ivy Gate to Miles. I print a picture of a white Jeep, the kind Miles drives, and add another string from Marco to the Jeep I thought I saw. And just because I'm not completely convinced, I print a picture of Marissa and add it to the board with question marks. When I step back, it looks like an actual suspect board. And in the middle, with all lines connected, is my photo.

CHAPTER 13

It's an unusually warm day for mid-October and under normal circumstances I would be on my way to a pumpkin patch with Annica and Dani, a pumpkin spice latte in hand. But instead, I'm getting in the front seat of Asher's car to be taken to a potentially dangerous situation, no pumpkin spice latte in hand. Asher sits in the driver's seat in a T-shirt and jeans, sunglasses on, with one hand on the steering wheel. He looks like an album cover for a country music star who is borderline pop.

"Well?" I ask as soon as I get in the car. "Did anything happen to Bryce last night?"

Asher sighs. "He's dead."

My stomach hits my throat, like a ride that takes you to the top only to suddenly drop you a hundred feet. I stare at him wide-eyed. "You said he'd be fine!"

Asher lets out a laugh, his whole fake-solemn demeanor changing. "I'm just kidding, he's fine. Coincidentally enough I ran into him when I was picking this up. Here." He hands me a coffee cup and I just stare at him, mouth agape.

"You are such a—"

"Good person? For picking up a pumpkin spice latte for you this morning?" he interrupts. I have half a mind to take off the lid and dump it on him.

"Just drive the car," I say. He pulls out of my apartment complex and puts Luna's into the GPS.

"So what's your game plan? What are you going to say to him?" he asks. I lay awake all night last night playing the scenario over and over again in my head until I eventually fell asleep.

"I'm going to ask him what he wants and why he's doing this."

"And what if he plays it off like he doesn't know what you're talking about?"

"Then I'll change tactics." Though I don't know to what yet. My only definite plan is that I'm going to be secretly recording on my phone during the conversation. "What are you going to be doing the whole time?" I ask him.

"I'm going to be searching his car," he says confidently.

"You're going to break into his car? You don't even know what he drives."

He looks over at me. "That's why you're going to tell me."

"And when the car alarm starts going off?"

"Don't worry about that."

"It's a white Jeep Wrangler," I say. "And he puts the top down when it's warm out."

"Even better." He smiles.

NEARLY TWO HOURS later we pull into a small lot behind Luna's. It's an eccentric-looking café painted blue on the outside with flowers climbing up the walls. The back lot is small, with room for only a few cars, and sure enough Miles's Jeep is one of them. Asher parks across from it and we both get out of the car. He stretches his arms and legs and I nervously wipe my sweaty palms on my jeans.

"You ready?" he asks.

I shake my head. "No."

We look over at the Jeep, which is entirely open in the warm weather, just as I predicted. Asher won't even have to break in. "Man, this is too easy," he says. "Call me if anything crazy happens in there so I know to get out of the car."

"Okay," I say, but it's barely above a whisper.

Asher opens his mouth to say something but closes it to give me a tight-lipped smile before turning toward the Jeep.

I walk up the small set of stairs before the back door to the coffee shop and take a few breaths before going in. "You can do this," I say to myself.

I open the door and am met with the overwhelming smell of coffee beans and fresh flowers. Large vases full of stems sit all around the shop, making it difficult to see much of anything. I take a few slow steps farther in, getting closer to the coffee bar in the center of the shop. Small wooden tables are placed around it, each full of people, but none of them are him. My heeled boots clack on the white tile floor as I keep walking to where you order. When I look to my left I see a black-wire spiral staircase leading to an upstairs of the shop, where more tables are lined against the wall, overlooking the downstairs. I peer up at the landing, and that's when I see him. Miles Holland sits at a small table for two, with a coffee mug in his left hand. He brings it to his lips for a sip as his right hand types over the keyboard of his laptop, the bright white screen reflecting off his glasses. He sets the coffee down and checks the time on his watch. I'm suddenly flooded with memories, particularly the bad ones, and I duck back beneath the cover of the landing so that he can't see me if he looks down. What am I doing? I can't do this. I take out my phone and start to email him back saying I have to cancel and send it without a second thought. I creep around the spiral stairs just slightly to see his face when he reads my email. He only sighs and shuts his laptop, starting to pack up.

Shit.

I make my way back out to the parking lot and yell for Asher. His head pops up from inside Miles's trunk.

"You can't be done already! I just started looking back here, and he's got so much shit to go through."

"I couldn't do it," I blurt out, going up to the car. "I couldn't talk to him. I emailed him saying I had to cancel and he started packing up, so get out of the car, come on." I gesture for him to get out urgently, but the back door to the coffee shop opens and I hear Miles's voice as he leaves the café. He's turned around talking to someone as he steps out the door. "Shit, shit, shit!" In a moment of pure idiocy, I hoist myself over the edge of the trunk and land right on top of Asher with a thud. Something sharp digs into my back as I land, and I hiss before Asher covers my mouth with his hand. We lie completely still, barely breathing as Miles's footsteps get closer to the car and walk around to the driver's side door. He gets in and starts up the Jeep and I finally lift my head from Asher's chest enough to look at him with panic in my eyes.

The Jeep shakes and rocks as it pulls out of the gravel lot. Miles puts music on loud enough to drown out anything going on back here and I take a look at the mess we've gotten ourselves into.

Asher wasn't kidding when he said there's a lot back here to go through. There's a folded-up dog crate behind me taking up most of the room, and also the culprit of what's digging into my back. Multiple duffel bags, papers, towels, and other junk are scattered all around us. There's no room for me to get off of Asher. I'm lying on top of him, with his hands tightly wrapped around me to keep me from sliding into the crate and making noise. But that's the last thing I'm thinking about as Miles is driving to god knows where.

"What the fuck are we going to do?" I whisper to Asher over the music.

"We could try jumping out at the next stoplight?" he suggests.

"Into oncoming traffic?" I say. "Not to mention he'll see that in the rearview mirror."

"Then I guess we better hope wherever he's going is a short ride."

I start to get a kink in my neck after five minutes of trying to not have to rest my head on his chest. I give in and lie back down, which sends my hair up into his face. I hear him sputter trying to remove it from his mouth. He brings a hand up and smooths my hair back out of both of our faces, and the gesture feels gentle and comforting. The first comforting touch I've felt in weeks and I close my eyes for a moment just listening to his quickened heart-beat.

"This playlist fucking sucks," Asher says after about fifteen minutes' worth of songs goes by, and it hits me then that this is the playlist I made for him last year.

"I made him this," I say, more so to myself, because I can't be-lieve he still listens to it.

"No wonder it sucks." Hearing Asher's annoying voice rumble

through his chest snaps me out of my thoughts of comfort and I start to look around the trunk for any other place to go so I don't have to be in this position. There's a tiny bit of room where I might be able to curl up into a ball above his head but that would require me dragging my entire body over his face and I am sure neither of us wants that.

He makes an uncomfortable noise as I'm moving around looking for another spot. "Will you stop with that?"

"I'm trying to find another spot to move to," I snap back at him.

"Trust me, I don't want to be in this position either." Miles takes a sharp turn, which has my body sliding up against Asher's and rocking back. He lets out another groan and shuts his eyes, and that's when I feel it.

"Oh my god, tell me that's not what I think it is," I say, looking at him, as I'm now positive that he's hard against me.

"What do you want from me? You've been straddling me for the past twenty minutes during a particularly aggressive car ride." He grits his teeth and takes a deep breath.

"That's all it takes? Men are disgusting." I shake my head. Miles takes another turn, not nearly as tight as the first time, but for some reason I let my body slide against his again. And why? I don't know. I tell myself it's because I like seeing him miserable.

His arms tighten around me to keep me in place. "You did that one on purpose," he says. I would never admit that I did, or how feeling him underneath me with arms around me so tight is making my mind go to mush.

I try to reel it in. Try to clear out the thoughts that are popping into my head about him. It's Asher, Sloane. It's the same guy who is helping you only to get what he wants. He doesn't actually care if you go to jail for murders you didn't commit. Just three hours ago he told you Bryce was dead just for a laugh. He's cruel.

Minutes later the car slows to a stop, and Miles puts it in park. I hold my breath again, worried he might come back here for one of these bags, but his footsteps echo off the pavement, getting farther and farther away. I peek up over the trunk to see him walking to the door of a brick town house and putting the key in.

"Okay, we're good." I push myself up and climb back over the trunk, careful to stay behind the Jeep just in case Miles decides to look out the window. Asher climbs out after me, any sign of embarrassment from our previous predicament wiped from his features. He's all business again, like that didn't just happen. "What now?" I ask.

"Is this where he lives?" He looks around at the row of whitewashed brick townhomes with black trims and doors.

"I'm assuming so—he just went into the town house on the far left."

"Good."

"Good?"

"Now we know which one he lives in for when we break in tonight."

"I'm sorry, what now?"

"We didn't come all the way out here for nothing," he says. "Come on, let's go get the car and we'll wait until tonight to come back."

WE WALK DOWN the street away from the town houses, back toward campus. The streets are flooded with students in Ivy Gate gear for their home football game today. It makes me want to join in on the fun.

"Wait, I know where we are," I say. "There's a bar a few blocks down that me and Ty used to go to. They do trivia and drunk bingo; we should stop in there."

Asher thinks about it. "I did want to watch this game . . . A few hours wouldn't hurt."

We walk into the busy Winchester Tavern and take seats at the bar with the other students getting ready to watch the game. The two of us look extremely out of place in our non–Ivy Gate clothing. I remember that we are supposed to go to dinner tonight with Annica for her birthday, so I text her and Dani that I came up to Ivy Gate to see Ty this morning and am having car troubles. Lie, lie, lie, it's all I do these days.

"So why did you chicken out?" Asher leans in to ask.

I scoff. "Because I'm under a lot of stress and you practically threw me into that situation. When I saw him I just froze, and I couldn't do it. I couldn't talk to him."

"What did this guy do that has you unable to face him? Well, other than possibly kill two people . . ."

I level a glare at him. "The whole situation with him, I think I'm just ashamed of it. I feel sick when I think of him."

"Then why'd you do it?"

"Do what?"

"Why'd you date him?"

"I need a drink before we get into that."

The game starts and the bartender finally makes her way over to us. She barely looks twenty-one, with long blond hair and a tight, low-cut T-shirt. I watch Asher's eyes flicker down to her chest and back up. Disgusting.

"So?" Asher says, shifting toward me, prompting my explanation when we both have drinks in hand.

"Honestly, you probably wouldn't understand," I say.

"Try me," he says back.

I try to think of Miles and what drew me to him. Why did I do it? Why did I?

"It was the way he looked at me," I start. I can see Asher roll his eyes from the corner of mine. "See, you don't get it."

"No, no, go on. It just sounds cliché, that's all."

The TVs in the bar drown out all sound with the game but I let out a breath and decide to continue. "Well, I had a lot of guys just screwing me over left and right, hence the journal, and Holland just looked at me differently. Like I wasn't a means to an end, or just some girl to sleep with; he looked at me like I was someone . . . worth knowing."

"And did this professor who looks at his students like they're worth knowing mention he had a wife? I think *that'd* be worth knowing."

"He did, on the first day of class actually."

"And you went ahead with it because?"

"Because it was a thrill. The thrill of wanting something that you can't have. But being so close to getting it. I swear you can get drunk on the feeling. I think I was."

"I think you were probably just regular drunk," Asher mutters while taking a sip.

"You clearly have never experienced that feeling." I wave down the bartender for another vodka soda.

"You're right, because there's never been anyone I couldn't have." He gives me that arrogant smirk, and his eyes trail back to the bartender.

"Maybe one day there will be."

"Doubt it."

"Well, it's exhilarating. Sitting in a room full of people every week knowing just the two of you know this thing. It's in the stares from across the room, and the brushes of skin when turning in an assignment, like a secret language that only you two speak."

"You're just romanticizing fucking your teacher."

"It *was* romantic. He loved me, and I'd never . . . had that kind of love before."

"But you didn't love him back?"

"I thought I did, but it started to become something else. Possessive, jealous, controlling. He needed to know where I was at all times, who I was with, what I was doing. And then the day he told me he was leaving his wife for me it felt like a wave washed over me and snapped me out of a trance. The whole thing felt wrong suddenly. Then his wife walked in one day while I was there. I saw her face and I just knew that this wasn't the first time. That there were other people before me that he found to be worth knowing, and it repulsed me. I wasn't the one; I was just one of many. She left him, and I tried to as well, but he was not going to let me go as easily. He would show up wherever I was, he would threaten to tell the dean about the relationship even if he got into trouble for it, he would say anything to get me to stick around. It got so bad that I went to the dean and told him myself just so he didn't have anything to threaten me with anymore. Miles resigned and I blocked him on everything. That night was when I went out and got a DUI.

I thought I was going to be in trouble with the university over the relationship even though he was more so at fault here than I was. It didn't feel like that then, but looking back on it . . . he was my professor. Maybe I should've known better, but he *definitely* knew better. But I said fuck it and just dug myself a deeper hole. I barely remember the night but I do remember sitting in the Pembroke jail cell, cold, in just a crop top and jeans, thinking, Yep, this is low, this is an all-time low for me." I take a long sip of my drink. "Now if I don't fix this fucking mess I might end up back in a cell."

"Probably not in a crop top and jeans though," he jokes.

"Do you ever take anything seriously?"

"Do you ever not?"

Ivy Gate scores the first touchdown of the game and the whole bar whoops and cheers, loud enough to put an end to our conversation.

THEY WIN THE game, and people are hammered. I realize I may be on my way to that state as well. When my head starts to feel heavy from the alcohol I rest it on my hand, watching Asher laugh with the guy on the barstool beside him. I notice the faint few freckles on his cheeks and how his hair seems to get darker in the fall, not the same shade of blond it was when we came back to school in August, almost a golden brown now. When he laughs, you can see all of his white teeth, and I note how his canine teeth are just a little bit pointy, and it reminds me of a vampire. When his lips come back together, I wonder if they're soft—

"Sloane?" He looks at me like he's waiting for an answer.

"What?" When I lift my head up the room spins a bit.

He hands me a water. "Chug that. Then we're going back to you-know-who's house to see if he's gone."

I take the water. "He's not Voldemort—you can say his name."

"Professor Miles Holland?" he says with a raised voice. My eyes go wide and I look around to see if anyone heard that. He laughs. "Thought so. Come on, Harry Potter, let's go."

THE AIR IS significantly cooler than it was this morning. A light breeze blows over me and it feels good on my skin. It also keeps the drunkenness at bay. We made sure to mix in water and food with our drinks over the past few hours but I still feel a good amount of buzzed. The happy, laughing kind. The flirting kind.

By some stroke of luck, the white Jeep Wrangler is not in the parking lot when we get back to the block of townhomes.

"Huh, he's not here. Well, that's lucky," I say.

"Not luck." Asher smiles. "I got his number from your blocked list and texted him anonymously pretending to be Ivy Gate's campus emergency line. I told him there was a string of break-ins in the faculty offices and that all staff should come down there immediately to report anything stolen." I just blink at him. I need to keep a better eye on my phone, clearly. "I don't know how much time we have here, so let's make it quick. I'm not trying to have another trunk situation."

The trunk. Somehow, I forgot about that until now. How his body felt pressed up against mine. "You wish you could have another trunk situation." I mumble it but it's loud enough for him to hear. He stops on the stairs up to the front door before just shaking his head and putting a key in the lock. "Wait, where'd you get a key to his house?"

He opens the door. "Found it in his gym bag in the trunk, figured it might be for his house." The entryway is dark, the only light coming from a small kitchen light at the end of the hall. The sound of pattering paws comes down wooden stairs to our left until Moose, the golden retriever, is standing in front of us wagging his tail.

"Hey, buddy," I say, bending down to pet him. Moose licks my face excitedly.

"Looks like the professor isn't the only one who misses you," Asher says. We walk farther into the house followed by Moose. There are books, papers, and clothes scattered on every surface. It makes me wonder if the only reason his old apartment was so clean was because of his wife. Asher looks around with his arms crossed. "This is worse than the trunk."

"Just start looking for my journal," I say. "It's small, brown, and made of leather with a string that ties it together."

Asher huffs a laugh. "Where'd you get that? The year 1700?"

I give a mock laugh back to him as I start to comb through papers on the coffee table. "Just look around. Like you said, wouldn't want another *trunk situation* if he comes back early."

"If he comes back early maybe we'll just have to do a murder ourselves," he says casually.

I look at him incredulously. "Do murder? It's not something you just *do* like homework. Hey, wanna go grab a bite to eat and do murder on the way home?" I say mockingly.

Asher laughs, looking through the papers on the kitchen island. "Or we could hide in one of his closets until he falls asleep. Pressed up against each other again, after drinking, who knows what would happen then."

It plays out in my head. We'd hear the door unlocking in the midst of our search, and we'd run into the kitchen pantry, which has barely enough room for two. Our hearts would beat wildly against each other as we watched Miles put his keys on the counter through the slats in the door. He'd go into the living room and put something on the TV and Asher's hands would start to roam idly over me. His thumb would brush over my bottom lip and—

"You're thinking about it, aren't you?" he teases.

I stand up abruptly, my cheeks reddening. "No."

In the low light I can see the white of his teeth when he smiles, goading me. "If you want to fuck me, Sloane, just say so. We can do it here in your ex's house."

My mouth opens and closes again at his boldness, but he's just playing games. Being an ass. "There's nothing down here. I'm going to look upstairs." I leave him in the kitchen and go up the stairs with Moose still trailing behind me. The landing opens to a small bathroom and a bedroom. Miles's room is a little tidier than downstairs and it smells like his cologne. It's nauseating. Suffocating. I start to pull open the drawers to his dresser and dig through them. Asher comes in saying there's nothing in the kitchen and starts to look through the closet, carelessly tossing things around. When I'm done rummaging through the last drawer I stand up and run into Asher with a Darth Vader helmet on.

He presses the button on the side that changes your voice as he says, "Sloane, I am your killer."

"Not funny." I push past him.

He takes the helmet off. "This thing is pretty cool. I feel like I saw someone wearing one like it last year for Halloween."

"You did," I say, starting to dig through the closet.

"Wait a minute," he says, connecting the dots. "That was the professor with you at the Halloween party last year?"

"Yep, wearing that exact helmet."

"Huh, funny. Wes ripped that guy apart for being weird as hell after you guys left. Said he asked if he could try out the voice changer and the guy refused to take the helmet off. Guess now we know why." I ignore him as I stand on my tiptoes trying to feel around the top shelf of the closet. "Can't believe you got this guy to go to a college house party with you and risk being seen."

"Don't worry, he was rewarded after the party for his bravery." I'm reaching for the lip of a box in the corner and I almost have it.

Asher puts the helmet back and comes up behind me to help. "What kind of reward?" he asks close to my ear just as I manage to tip the box, and its contents come falling down around us.

I turn and look up at him. "Use your imagination." I bend down to start grabbing what fell from the box and he does too.

"I don't have to. I remember exactly what kind of costume you were wearing that night, considering it was hardly anything at all—"

I gasp, cutting him off. "Oh my god." Everything in the box is . . . me. There are photos of me, tickets from shows we've seen, a paper menu from a diner we went to where I drew us as stick figures, copies of my schoolwork for his course, and a few paperback versions of books I annotated for him. We dig through the pile, Asher giving a quiet "What the fuck" while picking through the mementos.

"I've never even seen some of these photos." I hold one up of me shot from outside the window of the Bean. There's one of me talking to Annica in front of the English building, another of me in my car. "When the hell did he take these?"

"This is like some creepy shoebox shrine of you," Asher says, then clears his throat, handing a photo to me. It is me asleep on the bed, topless. I gasp and snatch the photo from him, ripping it up and putting it in my pocket. "I'll let you sort through the rest of those."

I scour through them looking for more nude photos and that's when I find a picture of my journal. No pictures of the contents inside of it but just of the leather journal sitting on the counter-top of his old apartment. Likely from the day I came back upset over Tristan and wrote his eulogy there. It was before Miles and I were really serious, and he was more curious about the journal than upset that I had been talking to someone else while messing around with him. I told him what it was and he asked to read it. If he took a picture of the outside, who's to say he didn't take more of what was inside.

Headlights shining through the bedroom window catch Asher's attention.

"That's him," he says. "Let's go. There's a back door in the kitchen."

I scramble to put everything back into the box aside from the photo of my journal. "We didn't find the journal, though—I don't have the evidence."

"We can come back. Come on." He pulls me up before I can toss the box back into the closet.

We rush down the stairs and to the back sliding door just as we hear the keys at the front door. I give Moose a goodbye pat on the head before closing the door behind us and running into the night with Asher.

CHAPTER 14

I wake on Sunday morning to an email from Miles asking if we can reschedule, saying he'll be out this way in two weeks if I'm available. I immediately feel sick about it when I think of the shoebox shrine for me in his closet. If we uncovered anything last night, it's that Miles is undoubtedly obsessed with me. Whether or not he's a murderer is still yet to be determined.

I get a text from Annica this morning saying we're having a mandatory weekend debrief at eleven at the Bean. It's 10:50. I pull on a sweater and lounge pants, brush my teeth, and leave for the cafe. Both of them are already in our usual spot when I arrive. I barely have time to sit down with my coffee when Annica begins to interrogate me.

She cocks her head to the side when I sit and asks, "Where were you all day yesterday?"

Her accusatory tone catches me off guard, but I look her in the eyes to lie to her face nonetheless. "I was up at Ivy Gate visiting Ty. I told you guys that yesterday." I sneak a glance over at Dani but she looks down at her coffee.

"Well, Ty posted that she was in New York City this weekend

with her mom. So what is the real reason you bailed on my birthday dinner?" Annica asks.

I didn't even think to check with Ty about what she was really doing. I open my mouth to say something, but nothing comes out. The two of them have no idea about the journal pages or Miles or the fact that I'm running around playing detective with Asher. But I know what I have to say.

"Fine, I was in Boston," I say. "With Asher."

Annica looks as though I slapped her. "With Asher?" Her eyes narrow at me like she still doesn't believe me.

"Yeah." I shrug, playing it off like it's no big deal. "If you don't believe me just ask him."

"Wait, so are you two, like, a thing now?" Dani asks.

"You blew off my birthday dinner for *Asher*?" Annica says again.

I realize if I have to lie, then I might as well go with the one we were already planning on telling. I just didn't think we'd get here so soon.

"We had it planned already; I just didn't tell you guys because . . . I was embarrassed." I think it'll earn me pity to say it and make her less pissed about me bailing, but it doesn't.

Annica shakes her head. "You should be." Dani smacks her arm. "What?"

"I think Sloane can like whoever she likes!" Dani smiles. "Maybe Asher is nice to her."

Hardly, I want to say.

"It was nothing serious, really. Just two friends out on a day trip to the city."

Dani smirks. "So like a date?"

"No," I say quickly. "Not a date. We're just, you know, feeling it out." It's gross to even say it. Now that the buzz of last night has long worn off, I don't want to *feel* anything out with him.

"Have you guys . . . ?" Dani wags her eyebrows at me.

I have to stop myself from saying "ew" before I answer with "No." But the question makes me think of the two of us in the trunk, and what he suggested in the dim light of Miles's empty town house.

"Well, when you do, let us know how it is—I'm curious."

Annica nearly gags. "Ugh, Danielle, gross."

"What? I've heard good things!" Dani says, and I almost want to ask her what she's heard exactly but Annica speaks first.

"I just hope you know what you're doing." Annica sighs. "This could get messy. It could potentially—"

"Ruin the friend group?" I finish for her. "Do you really think after this long the guys would abandon all of us over a relationship gone bad?"

"Well, let's not test it out." She gives me a look that means business. "Anyways, Pembroke's Halloween weekend is in two weeks so how about less feeling out Asher and more feeling out our costumes. Sloane, maybe you should go as a lobotomy patient, since you clearly need one."

I only sigh.

By the time we leave the Bean we've decided to be the girls from the nineties movie *Clueless*. I had to fight Annica to be Cher; it made sense since I'm the blonde here. She caved, saying she's only doing it because she feels bad that I have to put up with Asher.

I know I need to talk to him today so I make my way to the

boys' house next to let him know of our new relationship status. Charlie and Jake are in the living room watching football when I walk in. They don't even turn around to see who just came into the house. I could be anyone—a cop, a burglar, a murderer—but they don't even spare me a glance. Thank god they aren't in my journal; they would be goners. I walk upstairs and stop short at the bottom of the next set of stairs that leads to Asher's room in the attic. The door is ajar and through the crack comes the faint echo of keys on a piano. I put my ear closer to the door, drawn in by the sound. The melody is light and slow, perfect for a Sunday morning, and I just can't picture anything so pure and good coming from Asher's hands. Opening the door farther, I sit at the bottom of the stairs. I've heard Asher play the piano only one other time last year, when Dani and I were up here in Sam's room hanging out with him and Charlie. Sam said they always knew when Asher had a girl over because they'd hear him play on the keyboard he had in his room.

"And that actually works?" I laughed.

"Every time," Charlie said. "We know because not long after the music stops you'll start hearing the headboard smacking against the wall." The boys grinned at each other in the way boys do. Dani and I only crinkled our noses in disgust.

I close my eyes to listen as each strike of the keys seems to bounce down the stairs and land in my lap. The melody quickens and then slows again. I almost don't realize when it's over. I open my eyes and there is silence. I quickly but quietly rise from the stairs and shut the door behind me before I have to listen to what Charlie said would come next.

I join the boys in the living room and it isn't until halftime that Charlie looks over and realizes I'm there. Eventually Sam and Wes both come home and join us, but Asher is still upstairs. I ask them all questions about the football game because I never bothered to pay attention to it in high school and they love to mansplain it, so I indulge them.

After a handful of questions Wesley speaks up. "Weren't you a cheerleader?" he teases.

And when I finally ask a question that has him stumped, I say, "Weren't you a football player?" He smirks and lobs a pillow at me. I toss one back, and it hits him in the face.

"Oh, you're going to pay for that." Wes playfully pins me down. Sam and Charlie don't even glance our way.

A door shutting upstairs has Wes sitting back, until a petite girl with jet-black hair traipses down the stairs and out the door, without so much as a hello or goodbye to everyone in the living room. It takes everything in me to stand up in front of the guys, in front of Wes, and go upstairs to Asher's room right after another girl just left it. I knock twice from downstairs, and I hear him say, "Come up."

He's shirtless, digging around in his dresser across from his bed, when I get to the top of the stairs and I clear my throat to let him know I'm there. He looks over his shoulder, genuine shock on his face to see me in his bedroom. He puts a sweatshirt on and I try to block out the image from my brain of what he just got done doing with the small, raven-haired girl. Does he prefer girls with dark hair? Why am I even wondering?

"What's up?" he asks.

I walk around his room, marveling at how large it is compared to the other boys' rooms. It's carpeted and even has a private bathroom. I see the piano on the far side of the bedroom, below the one window. It isn't a little keyboard like I had imagined in my head, but more like an actual piano. A dark rosewood digital one, and all I want now is to witness him playing it.

"Just came to regroup, remember?"

"Right," he says. "You should've texted me. I would've come to you."

I sit down at the piano bench. "Why? So I wouldn't have to wait for a girl to leave before I can talk to you?"

Asher runs a hand through his hair. "Something like that."

I turn the piano on and mess around on the keys. Don bought Sofie a piano when she started taking lessons, so I'm not unfamiliar with it. I had taught myself some basic melodies but nothing as complex as what I had heard him play.

"Aren't you going to play something? I hear that's a thing you do when you have girls up here."

He huffs a laugh and walks over to the keyboard. "Girls I'm trying to sleep with, Sawyer. Not ones that I'm trying to catch a murderer with. Where'd you hear that anyway?"

"Your roommates." I hate that I feel disappointed that he won't play for me.

He crosses his arms and leans against the wall. "What else did they tell you?"

"That it works every time." I look up at him. "Though I find that hard to believe."

When I finish playing through everything I know, which isn't much, nor is it impressive, he says, "Who taught you those? A five-year-old?"

"An eleven-year-old actually," I say back, thinking of how sometimes Sofie would try to teach me the chords. I stare back up at him from the seat until he gives a resigned sigh and tells me to move over. I scoot to the edge of the seat so that he has more room and bite the inside of my cheeks to stop from smiling.

Asher places his hands over the keys and pauses, likely thinking of something to play. When his fingers begin to move, the sound is slow and melancholy. Not like what I heard a few hours ago, but the opposite. This one feels like rain, and loneliness, and it makes me ache for something, though I don't know what. When the melody picks up and his fingers move across the keyboard with ease, it sends chills all over my body. I'm thankful I'm wearing a sweater so that he can't see it. I watch him in awe; I have never seen someone play a piano like this before, and it's extraordinary, beautiful, and somehow so sad. And when he's done he looks over at me but I don't have any words, only the resolute understanding of why any girl would jump into his bed after witnessing that. He starts to give me that knowing smirk and I'm certain he can hear my thoughts. I take a breath and stand, needing to make space between us.

"See?" I say. "It doesn't work every time."

"Okay, Sloane," he says, still grinning. He turns himself around on the bench, leaning his elbows on his knees and looking up at me. "Let's regroup, then."

Still feeling a little flustered, I smooth out my top. "I mainly just came to tell you that Annica and Dani think we're full-on dating now."

"And why would they think that?"

"Probably because I told them that." He arches a brow at me and I continue on. "They were grilling me about where I was yesterday and I couldn't really tell them I was breaking into Miles Holland's house looking for my journal, so."

"So you told them we were on a date."

"Kind of, yeah."

"Okay, that's fine, I was thinking we needed to accelerate things anyway. Wesley clearly feels like he needs to protect you from me, so the more we're together the more he'll try to get between us."

"Right . . ." I say apprehensively, because I still don't feel great about lying to Wes, but I guess if we're going to lie to some of the group we might as well lie to them all. "Well, if we're going to be together now, you're going to have to stop bringing girls here. Go see them at their houses. The guys won't believe it if you have a parade of girls coming through here."

"Really? Because I think it'll piss off Wes even more if I have a— What was it? Parade of girls coming through here?" He laughs.

"Okay, well, *my* friends aren't going to buy it if you do that. They're going to think my standards are so low."

"Well, I mean—"

I glare at him. "Don't even say it."

He stands from the bench and walks toward me. "No boys over your place either then, Sawyer."

"I only want Wes. I've decided I'm not sleeping with anyone else until I have him."

When he's right in front of me he looks down at me. "You're sleeping with me, though." He grins again and I want to slap the smirk from his mouth.

"No, I'm not." I cross my arms.

"Well, my friends definitely aren't going to buy it if you say that," he says, mocking what I said first. "They'll start to think I *have* standards."

"Fine, we can say we're sleeping together."

Asher puts a hand over his heart. "I am honored to be added to that list, even if in name only." I roll my eyes. "So is it a big list?" He is such an ass, I can only scoff at his arrogance.

"Not as big as I'm sure yours is."

"Mine is rather big," he says with a playful smile, and I start to think he's no longer talking about the list of people he's slept with.

I flush and walk away, toward the middle of his room. "There's something else I came to talk about. Miles wants to reschedule for next weekend, in Pembroke."

"Okay, and?"

"*And* it's PC Halloween," I say. "It'll be a madhouse on campus: It would be the perfect time for him to get to Bryce. Everyone's in costume, there's fake blood everywhere—it's like a classic scary movie murder setup."

"Right, right, we'll just have to up the security on Peterson. And we should probably both be sober."

"Sober . . . Okay, I can do that." But could I?

He rubs his hands together. "All right, then let's get this son of a bitch."

CHAPTER 15

Josephine didn't know much, but she knew
her love for George could withstand a
battlefield, and would survive the scars of
this war . . .

I type into my outline. My protagonist, Josephine, is separated
from her lover, George, during a gruesome world war. Josephine
clings to the one way she knows that George is still alive, his letters. But one day they stop coming. Josephine does what any sane
woman would do and becomes a war reporter to travel to the front
lines in search of George and—

Come over

My phone buzzes with a text from Asher late on the Friday of
Halloween weekend while I'm trying to focus on my short story.
I stare at my phone screen considering, before getting out of bed
and heading to the boys' house. When I get to Asher's bedroom,
I'm surprised to find Sam standing there.

"Oh, hey, Sam."

Asher stands. "Sam was just telling me all about how Bryce is in some secret society on campus."

"A secret society?" I question. "I didn't even know Pembroke had one of those."

Asher rolls his eyes. "That's because it's a *secret*, genius."

I ignore him and turn back to Sam. "How do you know about this?"

Sam sighs. "Because I'm in it."

"And what's your secret society called?" I ask.

Sam looks at us apprehensively. "Do you guys promise not to laugh?"

"No," Asher replies.

"Yes," I say, shooting him a look.

"We're called the Knights of Pembroke."

Asher tries to hold in a laugh, and I purse my lips, trying to keep a neutral face. Sam rolls his eyes at us.

"I knew I shouldn't have even said it," he starts.

"No, no," I say. "That's a cool name. I like it. Um, where is it? Do you think you could take us there sometime?"

"Not exactly," Sam says. "It's under the campus and it's for members only."

"How do you become a member?" I ask. "Can we get Asher in?"

Asher scoffs. "I am not joining something called the fucking Knights of Pembroke." He looks at Sam, whose face is red. "No offense."

"You have to be a legacy," Sam says. "That, or everyone inducted can vote on a potential new member, but everyone has to agree in order for that person to get in."

"Then how can we get in?" I ask. "It's important that we . . . become friendly with Bryce."

Sam doesn't ask why, and I'm grateful. "Well, usually I wouldn't be able to get you in at all but . . . we are hosting a Halloween party tomorrow night at midnight. Any nonmembers have to be brought by a member and blindfolded, so you don't know the location."

"Great! Then we'll go with you. That's okay, right?"

"I guess so," Sam says hesitantly. "But just know it can get . . . weird down there."

"Weird how?" Asher asks.

"I guess you'll see for yourself," Sam says. "But it can only be you two. Don't tell Annica and Dani or the rest of the guys."

"Okay, deal," I say.

Asher sighs but agrees.

"So do you guys want me to bring the blindfolds, or do you want to bring your own?"

I WAKE UP early on Saturday to prepare for the day, not really knowing what to expect. Annica wants me at the apartment by four to take pictures before we go to the boys' house. My costume arrives in the mail right on time and when I open it I just know Annica is going to throw a fit. The yellow outfit was sold out everywhere, so I got the outfit that she's wearing on the movie cover. I go to the salon for a blowout at noon and come back to my place to start getting ready, but when I get back Adrienne is leaving with a packed duffel bag.

"Where are you going? I thought you were coming out with me tonight?" I ask her.

"Oh, I'm so sorry, Sloane, I'm going up to Ivy Gate tonight for their Halloween with that guy I'm kind of talking to. I thought I mentioned it yesterday but it must have slipped my mind."

"Oh, okay, no worries," I say. "Have fun, be safe."

"You too, Cousin!" When the door closes behind her I listen to her footsteps going down the stairs. Even though she's gone I tiptoe to her bedroom and sitting on her nightstand is her pack of Xanax that she sometimes takes for her anxiety. I stare at it for a while, wondering if she'll really notice if one or two are missing. Against my better judgment I quickly pop one from the packet and put it into the clutch purse I'm taking out with me tonight. I put on my tight red dress with the matching red heel, and the big, fluffy white feathered boa. The last touch is red lipstick, which I carefully apply before grabbing my purse and heading out the door.

I REALIZE THE heels were a poor choice when my feet start to ache only halfway to the house. I wish I didn't agree to be sober so I could numb the pain just a little bit. When we come up to the house there are already a ton of people outside drinking on the porch. Jake is outside finishing setting up a big blow-up spider in the yard. The boys always go all out with the outdoor decor. There are three other blown-up figures in the yard and a ton of large fake spiderwebs covering the porch. Jake pretends to hump the blow-up spider from the back as we approach, and the boys all laugh.

"Every year he thinks that's funny and every year it isn't," Annica says.

"Boys will be boys," I say.

Wes, Marissa, and Charlie are all on the porch. Wesley is in a fighter pilot costume with aviators on his face. Marissa is dressed as his female counterpart in a much sluttier-looking version of his costume.

Annica says so just we three can hear, "Couples costumes are so cringe." I laugh, but then Asher comes out of the house dressed in jeans and an Amnesty International T-shirt with a flannel over it.

Well, shit.

I can only hope Annica doesn't realize that he's dressed as Cher's love interest in the movie. But of course, she picks up on it.

"Why are you a part of our group costume?" she asks him when we walk up onto the porch. "Why is he a part of our group costume?" She looks at me now.

I put my hands up in defense. "I didn't tell him."

"Oh, I did," Dani says. "Sorry, I didn't think it would be a problem. I actually thought it would be cute!"

"Surprise," Asher says, grinning at me. I can't say it doesn't suit him. He looks like he belongs in the nineties, though he looks more like Paul Walker and less like Paul Rudd. And unfortunately, Walker is the Paul I always thought was cuter. "Here, got this for you." He hands me a seltzer, and I give him a look like *what about being sober?* But then I take a sip and it's water. He really dumped out a seltzer and filled it with water to keep up the charade. I glare at him.

Wes makes his way around to our group, looking slighted that we didn't greet him before his cousin. Marissa just stands behind him with her arms crossed, staring at me. I return the look. She's still on my suspect list, for now. I can see Wesley's eyes from under the aviator glasses as he looks at Asher before pulling me in for a hug.

"You look . . . really good, Sloane," he says a little too low for Marissa to hear, but loud enough for Asher.

"Red *is* my favorite color," Asher muses, putting a hand on my back to guide me inside and away from Wes.

"What the hell?" I say to him when we walk into the living room. "Why would you do that? He was flirting with me."

"You call that flirting?" he says back.

"Also, I don't want a seltzer with water in it. I can handle an actual drink."

"Fine, then go get one yourself." He walks past me to the backyard, where there's a bonfire going and double the amount of people. I grab an actual alcoholic beverage and go to rejoin my friends in the living room on one of the couches. A dry ice machine goes off in the corner of the room, making it smoky, but we can still see Marissa and Wes by the stairs looking like they're having an argument.

"Charlie said he thinks they're going to break up again," Dani says.

Annica crosses her arms. "I doubt it. He would tell me." She thinks he tells her everything.

"I don't know." Dani takes a drink. "Apparently, he slept with someone else while they were on a break last summer. Charlie said he doesn't know who it was but Wes hasn't been the same around Marissa since." I hold my breath, my heart beating rapidly in my chest, waiting to see Annica's response.

Annica's eyebrows shoot up. "What? I can't believe he didn't tell me about that—we tell each other everything."

"Looks like not everything," I mumble.

"Do you know who it was?" she asks me. "I bet Asher knows. You should ask him."

"Um, yeah, maybe. But if he didn't tell you, maybe there's a reason for it. Maybe we should just leave it alone."

Annica narrows her eyes. "He must be embarrassed about who-ever it was. Maybe she's not very pretty. Or maybe she's a major slut." She looks at us for reassurance.

Dani just nods along and I say, "Yeah, for sure. Probably both."

I have bigger things to worry about tonight than Annica's obses-sion with Wes and who he sleeps with. She claims to love him like a brother but if it is something more, I wish she'd just say it already. Just put it out in the open and spare us the group dynamic excuse.

A hypocritical thought coming from the girl who does in fact like him in that way and hasn't said anything.

I start to chug my drink and hope they don't notice my hands shaking as I do it. I go to the kitchen to grab another drink and peer out at the backyard, making sure Asher is occupied, but I don't see him. Looking back in the living room, I see Annica and Dani join in on some of the drinking games going on and I lean against the wall by the staircase, digging around my purse for the Xanax. I take it out and look at it between my thumb and finger for a while before bringing it to my mouth. A hand catches my wrist and I look over to find Asher standing there.

"What is that?" he asks.

"Aspirin," I lie.

He forcefully turns my wrist so he can see the blatant writing on the pill that says what it is, and then gives me a stern look. "Drop it."

"What are you guys talking about over here?" Wes cuts in, looking pointedly at Asher's grip on my wrist. Asher lets go and I quickly pop the pill into my mouth and wash it down with a drink.

"Sloane's poor decision-making," Asher grits out, looking at me.

"I'd say," Wes remarks, still looking at Asher heatedly.

Asher meets his gaze. "Do you have something you want to say, Wes?"

"No," he replies coolly.

"Then can I talk to Sloane in private?" Asher asks.

Wes gives me another pleading look before turning and walking away. I watch him go, and Asher turns my chin up to him, backing me up against the wall and closing in on me. "Go to the bathroom and throw up that pill," he says, with only seriousness in his voice.

"What? No." I jerk my head away from his grip.

He grabs me again, this time a bit harder, turning my face back to his. "Then stop drinking."

"I'll be fine," I say defiantly up at him.

"Sawyer, I'm not watching both you and Peterson tonight. I'm telling you now, I will leave you to deal with him yourself tonight if you get too fucked-up."

"That's not our deal," I say, and I can already feel my body starting to relax.

"You're right, our deal was that we both stay sober. Now you're about to be double fucked-up. Where did you even get that?"

"I needed it to relax, okay? You're the one constantly telling me to, so now I am. Don't be such a buzzkill."

Asher steps away from me with his hands raised. "Fine, do what you want. Don't forget we're meeting Sam by the founder statue ten minutes before midnight. And be coherent."

AT ELEVEN THIRTY I tell my friends that Asher and I have a party we have to stop at real quick. Annica scoffs in annoyance, saying a group costume means we need to be together as a group. But I'm three drinks and a Xanax deep, so I only smile and pat her on the head, blissfully uncaring.

Asher and I walk up to Sam, who stands at the base of the founder statue with his arms crossed, looking around. He hands us two masquerade-looking masks.

"Oh, cute," I say, putting mine on.

Asher just holds his and looks back at Sam. "No one is supposed to know who goes to these parties," Sam clarifies. Asher sighs and puts it on.

"And the blindfolds?" Asher asks.

"Just put your hands on my shoulders and close your eyes. I'll lead you in."

Sam starts to lead us, looking back occasionally to make sure our eyes are closed. I know that only because I'm squinting just enough to still see a little bit. He leads us to the back of one of the campus buildings, though I can't tell which one, and through a door, then down a set of stairs and a hallway until we're stopped under a stone archway. Sam unlocks the door, and it opens to darkness.

"There's going to be a lot of stairs," he says.

"Can I open my eyes to go down them?" I ask.

"In a minute," he says, leading us in and closing the door behind us. "Okay, go ahead."

I open my eyes fully to see stone stairs that descend in a spiral. Sam uses his phone light to guide us down. Five minutes later we're at the bottom. The staircase opens to a hallway, lit by torches. Armored knight uniforms stand before the stone, as if they're guarding the place. I grab the mask of one as we walk up and move it as if he speaks.

In my best British accent I make it say, "Welcome to the Knights of Pembroke secret socie—" Its arm juts up to grab my hand. "Ah!" I jump back to Asher.

Sam laughs. "Good one, Kane."

Kane laughs too, lifting the helmet. "I've been getting people with that all night."

I glare at him as we pass through the threshold. We enter a sitting room with plush red couches, and mahogany bookshelves lining the walls. A wet bar sits in the corner and a flat-screen tv hangs on the wall opposite.

"Where's the party?" Asher asks.

"Through here," Sam says, pulling down a red book on one of the shelves, causing the bookcase to open.

"Now that's cool," I say, thoroughly impressed.

A party is in full swing beyond the bookcase. Strobe lights flash all around the open space and it's crowded with people dancing.

"This literally looks like a dungeon," Asher says. It makes me wonder what this place was originally built for. What it was meant to keep down here . . .

I spot Bryce almost immediately, dressed in some kind of toga situation and mask, talking to two girls on a couch across the room.

"He's here!" I say. I would normally feel relieved, but since I haven't felt an ounce of stress all night, it's more of a statement.

"You guys hang out here for a minute," Sam says. "I'll be right back."

"Ooh, refreshments." I spot what looks like a fountain of alcohol. Grabbing one of the goblets set out on a table, I fill it with the liquid from the fountain, taking a sip. I don't recognize the taste. It's part punch, and part something else. Maybe black licorice? It's not bad, I determine, drinking the rest of what I poured and getting more.

"What is it?" Asher says, grabbing a cup for himself.

"Some kind of punch," I say. I take another gulp as Asher fills his cup and Sam comes back.

"Oh, I wouldn't drink that," Sam says to Asher, not seeing the cup in my hands or my squirrel cheeks holding in what I just drank. "It's like ninety percent absinthe, ten percent shrooms."

My eyes go wide as I swallow what was in my mouth. Asher's eyes look from me to my empty cup.

"Great," he says.

"Absinthe and shrooms?" I ask Sam. "Like the stuff that makes you hallucinate?"

"Yep. We always serve it. If you stick around until three or four a.m., shit will start getting real strange down here."

Asher looks worried, but I still feel like I'm floating on a cloud. One where nothing bad happens to me ever. And I love this cloud. I want to stay on this cloud forever.

"Oh my god, I love this song. Let's dance." I grab both of their arms.

"I don't dance," Asher says.

"You two have fun with that," says Sam. "Just keep the masks on." He disappears down another hallway off of the open stone room.

"I'll just sit and watch."

Asher takes a seat on one of the couches that surround the dance floor, but I don't care if he won't dance with me. Strobe lights flash and dry ice pumps smoke onto the floor as I spin around, moving my hands up my body, into the air, feeling carefree. I almost don't even remember why we're here. When I open my eyes, Asher is watching me dance. My head starts to feel fuzzy, my inhibitions at an all-time low as another masked man comes up behind me and pulls me to him. I almost shove him away, but when I glance back toward the couch, there's a girl talking to Asher. To hell with it, I think, as I dance with the stranger. When the song is over, I feel Asher's hand wrap around my arm.

"Bryce isn't in here anymore," Asher says.

I look all around to find that he's right. I took my eyes off him and he disappeared. Asher grabs my hand and leads me down the same dark hallway Sam disappeared through. There are doors all the way down the hall. Some are locked, some aren't. Asher opens one that contains glass cabinets of alcohol. Most of it absinthe. We pass more people in costume as we walk farther down the hall. When someone in a Darth Vader costume walks by, I turn my head to follow. Asher doesn't seem to notice. Am I imagining it? The person turns their head back to look at me, and it's the same voice-changing helmet that Miles has, I'm sure of it. I grab Asher's arm as he opens another door to a room hosting a full-blown orgy. We both stand there wide-eyed as men and women fornicate before us. I don't know if I'm hallucinating now, or if that's really Sam in the back of the room with two other men.

"Will you two be joining?" someone near the door says to us while a girl's head bobs up and down in his lap. The whole thing feels wrong to look at but I can't stop looking.

"Sorry." Asher closes the door. We take a moment to process before he clears his throat and we keep moving. I wanted to tell him something before that, but now I don't remember as we get to the end of the hall and there's another sitting room similar to the one we entered through. It's decked out in Halloween lights and cobwebs. There are more knights in armor and other relics inside.

"Oooh," I say, taking out my phone and recording around the room. "I love the dead birds they hung from the ceiling for this."

"Those are paper bats," Asher says, walking around the room. "And you can't post any of this. Sam will kill you."

But I don't listen to him as I film down the wall over what seems like hundreds of photos of the society since it originated in 1910. I walk past a curtain to a small room with only a little table covered in white powder. A bloody body impaled with a sword sits in a chair next to the table.

"This looks so real," I say, reaching out to touch the prop, but my arm feels like it's moving through molasses.

Asher comes in after me and gasps. "Sloane, don't touch it!" he yells, and I startle, dropping my phone. He pulls me back behind him. "Fuck."

The room spins around me—colors and shapes collide and separate. "What is it? Don't even try to tell me this is another paper bat."

"No, this is Bryce Peterson."

CHAPTER 16

"Bryce?" I ask, confused. That doesn't even look like Bryce, but then again the room is spinning.

"Get your phone. We're getting the fuck out of here." Asher ushers me away from the room. "And do not touch *anything*."

He shoves me from the room in a hurry, down the hall, back out to the dance floor, through the bookcase, and up the stairs. The knight that grabbed me, Kane, yells something to us about leaving. Asher tells him to fuck off. When we're back aboveground Asher paces back and forth.

"Fuck, fuck, fuck," he says, tossing his mask on the ground.

Everything blurs around me and a sharp pain forms in my stomach.

"I feel—" But I don't get the words out as I vomit into the bushes. Then again, and again. I hear Asher say "fuck" again. I'm on my hands and knees as my body heaves, until darkness takes over.

I WAKE WITH cold water hitting me in the face.

"I'm calling 911," I hear Adrienne say.

Adrienne? That can't be right. I look around and realize through the spinning that I'm in my bathtub.

"No," I manage to say. Asher shuts the water off.

"Then I'm calling your mom," Adrienne says to me.

"No, please," I say again. If I get sent to the hospital with Xanax, absinthe, and shrooms in my system, my mom will have me finishing my degree online from the comfort of her living room.

"I'll handle it," Asher tells her.

I don't hear Adrienne's reply as I fumble out of the tub to throw up in our toilet before passing out again.

I OPEN MY eyes slowly, feeling a splitting headache behind them, and a severe need for water. I'm in my bed. I turn over, and that's when I notice the IV in my arm. I follow the line up to see a saline bag hanging over my lamp.

"What the hell?" I whisper.

There's a long breath from my bedroom floor. "Now that I know you're alive," Asher says, "you owe me big-time."

I look down to see I'm still in last night's dress, with a bath towel wrapped around it. "What the hell happened?"

"Bryce is dead," he says.

"That wasn't funny the first time you said it and it's not funny now." I stare at him.

"It's not a joke." Asher is sitting up, pulling a paper from his pocket. It's my eulogy for Bryce, ripped through the middle and soaked red. You can barely tell what it says, but I'd know it anywhere.

Frat boys, sorority girls, and everyone else who tolerated Bryce Peterson's existence—today marks the end of an era. An era of late-night "you up?," other girls on his Snapchat, and getting into the best frat parties, which in the end meant more to me than he ever did. May we never forget the way he gave me an STD, told everyone I gave it to him, then blacklisted me and my friends from everywhere. Bryce leaves behind a superiority complex, the beer box taped over the broken bottom half of his door, and the audacity.

May he rest . . . somewhere very fucking far away.

"Oh my god."

"Someone ran a fucking sword through him at the party," Asher says. "I ripped this off of him before we left. I'm sure by now the police are all over it . . . but at least this won't be there."

"Oh my god."

"And you taking pills and drinking absinthe-spiked punch." He shakes his head. "Don't ever fucking do that to me again. I had to literally beg Adrienne not to call 911 because you kept going in and out of consciousness. Dani came over and hooked you up with an IV."

"I'm sorry," I say. In my defense, I didn't know the drinks had a hallucinogen in them, but I feel bad nonetheless.

He shakes his head. "Do you remember *anything* from last night? Did you see the Professor at all?"

I try to think. I remember the night like a slideshow. Moments in time that flip through my brain. I remember the pregame and walking into the society clubhouse. I remember dancing and looking at Asher on the couch. I remember seeing an orgy, and I remember . . .

"Wait a minute," I say, sitting up, looking in bed for my phone.

"Nightstand," Asher says. I grab it and open up my photos. I knew it. I was recording. I watch the video as we walk into the memorabilia room. I make a dumb comment about the paper bats hanging from the ceiling. "Tell me you did not get it on video," Asher says, getting up from the floor.

I fast-forward through the hundreds of photos I felt the need to record before I found Bryce. His head was rolled back, which is probably why I didn't recognize him at first, but it's definitely him, with a giant sword through his abdomen. The eulogy page stabbed onto him.

"What . . . in the medieval." I shake my head, unable to comprehend what I'm looking at. He was really stabbed with a sword. "We need to go to the police."

"Well, we can't now," Asher says. "Not only did we take more evidence from a crime scene, but you have a video on your phone that shows us there and then *leaving* without calling anyone. It looks like we did it."

"I'll just delete the video and we can . . . I don't know, we'll just pretend the note wasn't there?"

"You think just because you delete something from your phone that they can't get to it?" Asher paces around my room with his hands above his head. "I'm going home to shower and sleep. Don't do anything stupid." He leaves my room without a goodbye. He's pissed at me, and I deserve that.

Adrienne comes into my room after him, arms crossed, also

looking pissed at me. "Next time, I will tell your mom," she says before turning to leave, not even giving me a chance to apologize.

I lie back down, unhooking the IV from my arm, and watch the video again, looking for clues. I rewind myself walking behind the curtain a million times before deciding to watch the entire video. This time I even watch the photos, wondering if maybe I'll see something in the reflection of the glass. When I get to the end of the wall where the recent photos are, I pause it. This year's photo shows twelve students, four girls and eight boys, with the faculty member that oversees the club. I recognize Sam, Bryce, and . . . no fucking way. Marissa Wilder.

Was she there last night? Would she have left Wes out alone to go to this? If it was to frame me then maybe . . .

I rewind a smidge to see last year just out of curiosity and I nearly drop my phone on my face. Sitting up, I zoom into the black-and-white photo on the wall. I can see him standing in the back. Last year's faculty member to oversee the club was Miles Holland.

"IT COULD BE either one of them," I whisper to Asher. "Miles oversaw the club: He would know how to get down there. He said he'd be here this weekend. Or there's Marissa, who is *in* the club. What if they're in on it together?"

We walk to the vigil for Bryce in the campus square. A small platform has been set up in the middle and they pass out white taper candles to light as the sun goes down.

"We still can't go to the police," he says to me in hushed tones as our friends all gather around a spot in the grass. Annica and Danielle wrap a blanket around the three of us, putting an end to that conversation. The boys all stand behind us. I glance back at Sam. I wonder if he's in trouble. I'd imagine all the society members are.

Dean Mathers gets up onto the platform followed by Bryce's family. He looks just as I remember him when I sat in his office last spring and confessed about my affair with Miles. His features hold the same disappointed frown and wrinkles, now that his college is plagued by more scandal. He starts the vigil with a prayer, before going into Bryce's accomplishments and urging anyone to come forward with any information about the killer. I shoot a look at Asher but he only looks away. Mathers also mentions the grief counseling services on campus for anyone struggling to cope with the loss. I wonder what the grief counselor would say to me if I went in there.

Bryce's parents and siblings light their candles first before lighting the ones in the crowd around the platform. Soon the whole grassy square is lit by thousands of candles. A song plays, slow and somber. People cry in the crowd, Dani leans her head on my shoulder, and Annica squeezes my hand. When the vigil ends and people start to clear out, our group stays to chat a little longer with Marissa and her brother Hudson. I stare at her with narrowed eyes.

"It was obviously a crime of passion," Marissa says, and I swear when she says it she glances at me. Or am I imagining it?

"Maybe him and someone else were high and fucking around with swords and it just happened accidentally," Wes suggests.

"How do you accidentally stab someone with a sword?" Charlie counters.

"They were serving absinthe punch spiked with powdered shrooms," Hudson says. "Not to mention they found him by a table with cocaine on it. It definitely could have been unintentional."

"No, I like Marissa's 'crime of passion' idea," I say, looking at her. "I bet it was someone who was in this secret club with him." I feel Asher nudge me hard with his foot. "Someone who knows him well. Maybe they had a secret together."

"Well, you're the one who used to date him—maybe it was you," she says, crossing her arms, quick to fire accusations right back at me.

Our heated moment is interrupted by Jake's laugh. "Could you guys imagine Sloane putting a sword through Bryce? Can you even pick up a sword?" he asks me.

"Maybe she had help." Marissa looks at Annica and Dani.

"I'm sorry," Annica starts, "but are you accusing the three of us of murder?"

"All right, that's enough," Wes cuts in.

But I'm no longer listening as I catch a glimpse of a beige checkered peacoat walking down the path leading to the southern part of campus. A coat I distinctly remember Miles having.

I shrink back into the group until I'm outside the circle, peering down the path. They've changed topic and are all too engaged in conversation to see me creep away after the man. I walk at a fast pace, trying to catch up as he turns the corner on the path, going through the wind tunnel that is situated between two of our large stone buildings. He's walking fast, almost too fast for me to catch up. Another turn and I lose him as I run around the corner and find no one on the path. It's dark now and only the sporadic lampposts provide a faint glow of light. I turn back around and run into Asher.

"What are you doing?" he asks.

I turn back around, scanning the path, which splits into three. "I thought I saw him again." When I turn back to Asher, his lips are pursed. He thinks I'm losing it. I can see it in his eyes. "He's on this campus, I know he is."

Asher sighs. "Come on, I'll drive you home."

In the car my eyes fill with tears threatening to spill over. "We couldn't stop this from happening and now Bryce is dead." He doesn't say anything. "Why is someone doing this to me?" My voice cracks. "I don't know what to do."

"There's nothing connecting you to Bryce right now. No one knows we were there, and maybe like Wes said, they'll think it was some kind of drug-induced accident."

"What if there was another eulogy page down there? Then Grange could somehow get word, and he'll know it's me. Two deaths with two eulogies is no longer a coincidence." I wipe at the tears sliding down my cheeks.

"He works for Boston PD, which is two hours away. He would have nothing to do with this case."

"How do you know that, though?" Asher opens his mouth to reply. "And don't say 'crime documentaries.'" He closes it.

"You said there are seven names in the journal. Who is the next one?"

"Graham Monterra," I say.

"Hm, I don't recognize the name."

I stare blankly out the window. "He was a senior when we were sophomores. Fine art major."

"Yikes," Asher says. "Talk about wasting your money. Paying tuition to paint."

"He was really good actually . . . Just not to me." I sigh. "I have no idea where he is or what he's up to now."

"I'll do some digging and find out."

Asher pulls up to my apartment and I want him to stay, if only to not be alone, but I don't ask, and he doesn't offer. He just parks the car and waits for me to exit. He offers no words of reassurance, no comforting touches.

I get in bed and go through their names in my head, the lullaby that puts me to sleep these nights: Jonah, Ryan, Marco, and Bryce. Jonah, Ryan, Marco, and Bryce.

Wesley, Wesley, Wesley.

Asher.

IT RAINS HARD on the highway as I drive up to Ivy Gate. I have all the information from Ty about which building Holland teaches in, which office is his, and when his office hours are. I decided after the vigil last night that I would confront him and try to put an end to this mess. I pull up to the building and sit in the car for a moment, giving myself a mental pep talk. Do it for Jonah, for Ryan, for Marco, for Bryce. I fiddle nervously with my coat the whole walk up to his office. I can do this, I can do this. I'm just going to barge into his office and say . . . what?

The jig is up, Miles. No, no one talks like that. Maybe I'll say something like *I know exactly what you've been up to, Holland.* But that doesn't feel right either. I stop short upon seeing the name plaque next to the door, which is wide open. He has office hours for another hour still so of course it's open: He's expecting students. He's just not expecting me.

I take a breath and stroll in, deciding on not saying anything at all.

But he isn't here. I let out the breath I was holding. He isn't here, but these are his office hours—Ty confirmed it. Maybe he stepped out for a minute, maybe I should casually be in here waiting for him when he gets back. I sit at the edge of his desk, facing the door, for one minute, two, three. I imagine him walking in and the shock on his face when he sees me. Ten minutes pass and he still doesn't come back to his office.

I decide to start snooping around, mainly looking for my journal. I go through the books on his bookshelf and the drawers in his desk. No sign of it anywhere. When I tug on the middle drawer of the desk, it's locked.

"What are you hiding in here?" I say aloud. I feel around the bottom of the desk for a key or anything to unlock it but come up short. Frustrated, I walk over to his window to think and watch the dark clouds roll in, casting a shadow over the courtyard below. And that's when I see him. There's Miles Holland in the courtyard with another girl. She's turned away from me, a student of his, perhaps. I watch him tuck a piece of her hair behind her ear as he leans in to kiss her. Then he departs, likely coming back to his office. The girl turns to watch him leave, and it's Adrienne.

I jump back to avoid meeting her gaze, hitting the edge of Holland's desk, causing papers to litter the floor. Holland is the guy she's been driving up here to see? What the *fuck*, Adrienne. I gather up the papers quickly and toss them back on the desk, but one catches my eye. It's an invitation to a gallery opening in Boston the first weekend of January, exclusively showing works by Graham

Monterra. I catch glimpses of the campus art studio and the phantom smell of oil paint mixed with weed just from reading his name.

"Oh my god." Shaking, I take my phone from my pocket and take a picture of the invite on his desk. Why would he have this if he wasn't planning to go after Graham? I peer out the window to see they're both gone. He could be back up here any minute. I lose all the nerve I built up to come in here and now the thought of seeing him alone in his office scares the shit out of me. I bolt from the room and back to the parking lot without running into him. I get a text from Asher.

> I know where Graham is.

> > So do I.

I send him the photo of the gallery opening.

> Where did you find that?

> > On Miles Holland's desk

My phone immediately starts ringing with Asher's number on the ID.

"Asher, we have a problem," I say upon answering.

"Yeah, we do: You're at Ivy Gate without me. And on top of that, Sam said the police are asking for a list of every person that came to the Halloween party."

"Okay, then we have a few problems. Adrienne is seeing Holland. I just watched them kiss from his office window."

"Wait, what? Your roommate?"

"And cousin," I say. "It's fucked, Asher, fucked."

He sighs through the phone and I can imagine him running his hand through his hair like he does when he's stressed. "Well, did you talk to him?"

"Um, no, I was a little taken aback by my cousin betraying me to stick around and chat. But I went through his office and he had that gallery invite on his desk. He also has a locked drawer that I bet my journal is in." I look up at the stone building. "I should go back in there. I came all the way up here to face him."

"No," he says. "Just get out of there and we'll go back together."

"Sloane?" a familiar voice says from behind me, and I turn to see Austin Reems walking toward me. "I thought that was you."

"Austin, hey." I go back to the phone conversation. "Asher, I have to go."

"Sloane, don't—" I hang up.

Austin's pale face is pink in the chilly weather. "What are you doing up here?"

"Oh, I was just meeting with a professor," I say. "Probably going to head back to Pembroke."

"What? No! You should come out with me and Ty tonight. It's drunk bingo night at the Winchester. All of the old townies come in for it, so it's always me, Ty, and a bunch of knit-blanket-smelling grandmas that probably live in asbestos-filled attics. Sometimes there's even a fight."

"Between you and Ty?"

"No, usually Ty and the grandmas. You'll just have to come witness it for yourself."

It has been a while since I saw Ty. And maybe after a drink or two I'll get the courage to stay here until I talk to Miles. Maybe even go right to his town house. Asher would lose it. "Okay," I say. "I'm in . . . Also, what the hell is asbestos?"

Austin puts a puffy-coat arm around my shoulder. "What you do every day, sweetie. As best as you can."

"Get ready with me while I tell you about the gruesome murder that happened at Pembroke College," Marissa's voice rings out from my phone. I can't believe she's using his death for likes, and worse than that, it's working. This video has over a million views.

I frown to myself as I lie on Ty's couch, watching Marissa beat her face with foundation while she dishes out all the information regarding Bryce's murder. I painfully watch the entire five-minute video, hoping she might provide some new information. But the only thing I gathered from the video is that she wears too much makeup.

An email notification flashes on my screen. I pull the tab down over the video and my stomach drops at the message.

Were you in my office yesterday, Sloane? I would recognize your perfume anywhere. Vanilla and honey.

MH

I shudder. Yeah, I'm getting the *hell* out of Ivy Gate.

Last night after four sangria pitchers and two bingo wins, I found myself back in Ty's apartment with two plants. Asher called me again to make sure I didn't see Miles. I told him I won two plants at bingo, and named them Ernest Hemingvine and Oscar

Wildflower. I don't really remember what we talked about after that; in fact I think I fell asleep while on the phone with him. I can only hope I kept some of my other budding thoughts about him to myself.

I ignore the creepiness of the email as I angrily reply to Miles.

I know everything you've been up to. You won't get away with it.

I MAKE IT to Renner's class just in time to avoid another disappointed glare. The first drafts of our short stories are due before winter break and today is a peer review of what we have done so far. Renner pairs us off into groups of two and I'm thankful I don't end up with Annica. My peer reviewer is a girl named Sasha with blue hair and a lip ring.

"Mine's not totally fleshed out yet," I say, handing the pages to her. I had added on to the story. While on the front lines looking for George, Josephine begins to receive letters again. She writes back to George urging him to tell her where he is so she can find him. She comes across a medic who says he can help her, but his reasons are selfish and she doesn't fully trust him.

I haven't written the ending yet.

"That's okay—neither is mine," Sasha replies. I start to mark up her story, thoroughly impressed with the writing, and really loving the plot, when she interrupts me. "Who does she choose?" she asks.

Her question feels loud in a quiet room full of working students and startles me slightly, causing my pen to slip over a word. "I'm sorry?"

"Your story—who does she choose? The medic or the soldier?"

I look around for peering eyes and ears, specifically Annica's. "Probably the soldier." I lower my voice when I say it, and go back to writing.

"Why is she so mean to the medic who is helping her? She basically just met him. She doesn't even know him."

"Because the medic has his own agenda; he doesn't care about his cousin."

"They're cousins?" she asks, confused.

"No, I didn't mean to say that. I just meant the medic doesn't care about the soldier."

"It seems like he cares about the main character, though."

I sigh with annoyance. "He doesn't."

"That's not what it sounds like, especially when you wrote—"

"You don't know him," I interrupt, a little bit too abrasive.

"Okay . . . sorry," Sasha says. I sigh, feeling rattled and embarrassed for snapping at her like that. She starts to mark up my paper, and I go back to hers.

When I get back from class, Adrienne isn't here. Part of me is relieved, because I have no idea what to say to her. I thought about it on the entire ride back to Pembroke today, but all I could come up with was *How could you?* Unless she really doesn't know that he's the same professor I was seeing last year, but how could she not? I never showed her a picture but I told her his last name, and surely she could connect the dots. The longer I think about it, the more irritated I become. She has to know.

I go right to my room without even showering the stench of sangria and bar off from the night before and print Adrienne's picture and name. I add it to the suspect board with string tying her to Holland. And then I lock my bedroom door.

I can no longer trust her.

LATER THAT NIGHT we all meet up at the boys' house for some type of surprise that Wes claims to have. We come to find that it's a weekend away at his family's resort, all expenses paid. And the kicker? Marissa can't go that weekend.

"This is perfect," Asher says once we're alone in his bedroom. "This is the opportunity we needed."

"We need to talk about Miles and Adrienne," I tell him. "What am I going to do? What if she's helping him?"

He rubs his hands together, plotting. "With Marissa not going, this is perfect for ushering you into phase two."

I sit on his bed while he paces. "Asher, are you listening?" But he doesn't acknowledge it. I sigh, giving in. "What is phase two?"

"Phase two is where Wes finally gives in and realizes he wants to be with you. He'll dump Marissa, and you two can be together. Phase three will be where you ultimately have him in your clutches and you make sure he stays here with you after graduation to pursue some other venture."

I play with a strand of my hair, thinking about this double-edged sword in front of me. I want Wes to love me naturally, not because we tricked him into doing it. The further this goes along, the more wrong it feels, but if I tell Asher that, what does that mean for me and all my secrets? Are we close enough now that he would let me out of the deal without any repercussions? Are we close at all? I start to feel ridiculous for any and all of the conflicting little thoughts that pop into my head about him. We are not friends, we never were. Maybe I just need some distance to remind myself of that.

Before I can get up to leave, I hear Asher's door open, and someone comes up the stairs. Sam steps into the room with his hands on his hips and looks between the two of us.

"Why did you two want to see Bryce last weekend?" he asks in an accusatory tone. "Did you know something bad was going to happen to him?"

I look at Asher, unsure of what to say. So Asher replies, "We didn't say that."

Sam narrows his eyes at us from under shaggy black hair. "Yes, you did."

"No we didn't," Asher says again. "When did we say that?"

"When you asked me if you could get into the society. Are you really trying to convince me that you never said that?" He waits for an answer, but we don't give him one. He goes on, "I thought it was odd but wasn't going to ask. And then I remembered that Sloane used to date him. Is he not like the third or fourth ex-boyfriend of yours to die in a few short months?" he asks me. I can feel the blood drain from my face. "Look," Sam says. "The police are hounding all of us to give them a complete list of everyone who came to this party. I didn't tell them you two were there, but I need to know what is going on. Did one of you hurt Bryce?"

"Sam, no, of course not," I say. "But . . . you can't tell the police we were there either. I can't get in trouble this year with the police. My mom will pull me from Pembroke."

Sam purses his lips, likely debating whether or not he believes me. He's not one for arguments or confrontation, and I feel that we have him on our side until Asher opens his mouth.

"Did you enjoy the orgy?" Asher asks. My eyes snap to him, and I wonder if I heard him right. If he really just asked that.

Sam's face turns a crimson red. "What?"

"We saw you," Asher says. "In the back of the room, with all of those guys. That *could* stay between the three of us, if you never tell anyone we were there."

Sam grits his teeth. "That—that wasn't me."

Asher crosses his arms. "And we never said anything about Bryce."

Sam looks between the two of us, his mouth open like he may argue, but he closes it and turns on his heels to leave.

"Asher!" I reprimand him when the door shuts—no, slams—at the bottom of the stairs. "How could you do that to Sam!"

"Do you want to go to jail? Because once again, you look like a suspect, and the only thing keeping you from an orange jumpsuit is me. I didn't feel good about blackmailing Sam either but it had to be done."

I shake my head, walking to the door. "I have to go home."

"Back to Adrienne?" He raises a brow. Oh, so he was listening. I turn to look at him, but I don't have anything to say. "We're both so close to getting what we want," he says in a low voice.

CHAPTER 17

November

Bryce's case continues on like the weather in November, cold. Sam won't speak to me after Asher's outburst, so I rely on Marissa's TikTok for updates. Due to most people at the party being on a hallucinogen, and everyone wearing masks, the police can't identify everyone who was there. The members are being questioned relentlessly, or so Marissa says in her last video, titled: "Get ready with me to help the police catch the killer." Branding herself as some type of college detective hero.

"You're being a recluse," Asher says to me in my bedroom. He sits across from me on the floor in a hoodie and sweatpants, his hair messy from the hat he wore and his cheeks a little pink from the cold air. He isn't wrong. It's a Friday night, and I've committed my weekend to staring at the suspect board. In the past three weeks I've barely left my apartment, thinking that maybe everyone is better off if I just stay put. I let my social life, and more importantly my schoolwork, fall to the wayside. I glance at my goals list taped to the mirror. When I received an F on a test

Monday I crossed out the *ace all of your classes* line. "Everyone's questioning if we're even together at this point. I keep having to find girls to hang out with so I can lie and say I'm going to your apartment."

I roll my eyes. "Oh, poor you," I say in my best pity voice.

"My birthday is tomorrow," he says. "We're going out. You have to show up for that at least."

I bite my lip. "I don't know. It's risky."

"What is risky?" he asks.

I pull up the last few emails from Miles and hand him my phone. I watch him scroll through them.

I can explain if you'll meet me.

MH

I know where you have class, I could just drop by.

MH

Please answer me.

MH

I watch Asher's mouth slowly form a frown. "He sounds . . ."

"Unhinged?" I finish for him. "That's why I'm staying here, the one place where he can't find me."

"Can't find you? He's banging your roommate—you think he doesn't know where you guys live?"

"Adrienne would never bring him here; she's smarter than that."

"Have you talked to her yet about this?" he asks, handing my phone back to me.

"She's never here anymore," I say. It's true. If I leave for class, she's just getting back. When I come home, she's already gone again.

Asher shakes his head. "You can't let this get to you. I still need you, Sawyer."

"Asher," I start. I'm about to tell him I just don't have it in me to pursue Wesley right now. Not until this gets resolved. I don't even want to go on this trip.

"Sloane," he counters. "We know we have until the gallery opening before Miles makes his move on Graham. That's like weeks away. Please," he begs. "Please help me with this in the meantime. We made a deal."

I want him to leave, so I say okay, but I'm not sure if I mean it. The truth is I'm avoiding him, and Wes, and all of them, really. Knowing Wesley's name is at the end of the journal makes me feel like there's a ticking time bomb strapped to him. What's the point in trying to win him over if he may not be around to win over in the end? But then again, how do I protect him if I'm not there?

I GET TO Power Hour for Asher's birthday a little late and all my friends are already there sitting around two high-top tables. Asher sits on one end with a beer and a small blue-frosted cake in front of him.

"Hey, everyone," I say, approaching the tables with Asher's gift bag in hand.

"Sloane!" Charlie yells, throwing his hands up. "Where have you been!"

"Sorry, guys, I've been picking up a bunch of shifts to afford the ski trip."

Wes gives me a sympathetic look. "Sloane, I told you it's covered."

I shrug. "I know. I just don't want your parents to have to pay for the flight. I wanted to pay them back."

"His dad isn't going to take the money," Asher says to me, wrapping his arm around my waist and pulling me toward him.

"Your dad might," Wes says, before taking a sip of beer.

Asher leans over the table. "What was that?"

I don't understand the jab but I defuse Asher by holding up the small bag with his gift inside. "I brought you a present." I set it in his lap and leave his arms to hug Dani and Annica. Luckily Dani is swamped with schoolwork these days, and Annica is always with Collin, so neither of them has found it odd that I haven't been around much lately.

"Ooh, open it," Sam says. "Unless it's something indecent."

"In that case, definitely open it," Jake teases.

Asher looks in the bag and starts to laugh as he pulls out all fifteen seasons of *Criminal Minds* on DVD. He silently reads the note taped on the front that says "for my partner in solving crime."

"Thank you," he says to me from across the table, and I smile back at him. The rest of the group takes in the weird exchange.

Charlie breaks the silence. "That was the most awkward thank-you I've ever seen."

"Yeah, McCavern, go kiss your girlfriend for the gift," Jake adds on.

Girlfriend.

I know we told our friends we were dating but it's so weird to hear someone say it.

"Oh, no, that's okay," I say, ignoring the side look I get from Annica.

"You know what?" Asher smiles, digging his finger into the icing of his cake and smearing some onto his lips. "I should kiss my girlfriend." He gets up from the chair and comes toward me.

"Asher, don't you dare!" I try to run around the table but he's faster as he grabs me around the waist and manages to plant a kiss to my cheek, covering it in blue icing. I grab a napkin from the table to wipe it off and Asher pulls up another chair next to him.

Wes gets up from the table.

"Your lips are blue now," I say to Asher after he wipes away the icing on them.

He leans in a little so that our shoulders are touching. "Yours could be too." Then he gets even closer and, oh my god, he's going in for a kiss. In front of all our friends.

I pull away. "Later," I say, in case anyone is listening.

Asher doesn't pull away; he just leans in farther to whisper, "Speaking of later." His voice in my ear raises goose bumps on my arms. "I'm coming home with you."

My heart starts to beat wildly in my chest. Coming home with me? "For what?" I ask.

"There's a girl I'm seeing that lives in your complex. She also has a birthday gift for me, one that's a little less appropriate to give in front of my friends."

I turn my head toward his so that our noses are practically touching. "You want me to drop you off at another girl's place?" I say in a hushed, irritated tone.

The corner of his mouth upturns. "Unless you were planning on giving me this very particular gift—"

"I'll drop you off." I turn back toward the table, regretting coming here.

"Great." He smiles. "Could you grab me another beer?"

"You have a full one," I say, looking at the one on the table.

"Well, it's my birthday, and I would like another one." He nods toward the bar, and I turn to see Wes standing over there.

I give him a tight smile. "Of course, coming right up." I walk up to the bar and stand beside Wesley.

"Hey, stranger," he says. "Haven't seen you around. Are you doing okay?"

I huff a nervous laugh. "Uh, yeah, just working a lot and . . . school."

"Right." Wes nods before turning to me. "Well, I miss you."

I think of when I said that to him at Annica's party and he looked like I had told him I loved him. Maybe I should have. I should've just told him I'm in love with him and he'd either have to accept or deny it. The games would be over. But I didn't say it then, and I won't now. "You do?"

"Yeah," he says. "You know, as a friend."

"As a friend, right."

Wes leans in to talk over the music. "I'm super stoked you're coming on the trip. I think you'll love it," he says with a small smile that elicits one from me.

The bartender hands him his drink as Asher walks over.

"You ready to go?" he says to me.

"What? No, I just got here."

Wes looks at Asher and says, "Yeah, why don't you guys hang out a little longer?"

"Because Sloane has another birthday gift for me at home, one that would certainly get us kicked out if she gave it here." Asher winks at his cousin.

Wes clenches his jaw. "It seems like she'd rather stay here."

Asher steps closer to Wes. "No, it seems like *you* would rather her stay here."

"Okay, okay," I say. "It's fine, Wes, I— Yeah, I told Asher I had another gift at home. It's . . . it's not what you're thinking, though."

"It is," Asher says, being an ass. "Come on," he says to me, grabbing my hand and heading toward the door.

"Sloane." Wes catches my other hand. "Will you just . . . call me if you want to talk . . . about anything?"

"Um, yeah, sure." I give a small wave over my shoulder to my friends as we leave.

"YOU ARE ONE hundred percent *not* calling him." Asher leans back in the passenger seat, texting on his phone. Probably telling this girl he's on the way. "If he wants to talk, he can do it on the trip."

I roll my eyes.

"You're quiet tonight," he says. "Usually I can't get you to shut up."

"I'm annoyed that I have to drop you off at a booty call."

"She lives in your complex—you're basically just driving us back to your place. Like a girlfriend would do."

"Don't call me that." We pull into the parking lot, past rows and rows of the same-looking building before stopping at mine. "You can walk to hers."

"Moody Sloane." Asher tsks. "You know, I've missed that bitchy little attitude of yours this past month." I roll my eyes and we walk up onto the sidewalk, stopping at the landing to the stairs. "Thank you again for the gift. Now I don't have to illegally stream it."

"You're welcome," I say.

We both stand there facing each other for a moment in the brisk November night, our breath forming puffs of smoke in the air. His eyes roam over me and it feels like he's debating on hugging me or something. But then his mouth quirks up in that grin he does before he says something annoying.

"You sure you don't want to be the one to—"

"No." I turn to walk up my stairs and he stands there watching me go. "Happy birthday, asshole."

CHAPTER 18

Thanksgiving used to be my third-favorite holiday. My birthday being the first and Christmas being the second. But today, the last thing I want to do is go back to Cedar Falls to make small talk with the family when all I really want is to sit alone in my room and order takeout. Adrienne went home on Monday, but I still had class so I couldn't trap her in the car for an hour for an interrogation. I wonder if she did it on purpose.

The whole way home I practice smiling in the mirror, making sure it looks genuine and real. I rehearse the lines I'll say to my family at dinner.

"School is great! I can't believe I only have a semester left!

"I don't have a job lined up yet, but I have some promising interviews scheduled!

"Yes, I am still good friends with Dani and Annica. They're doing great; they say hi!

"I only look thin, frail, and lifeless because I'm being set up to go to prison forever and my life is crumbling around me!"

When my mom opens the door to see me standing there alone

her face falls. "Where's Asher?" She looks past me like maybe he's still getting out of the car.

"He has a family to spend the holidays with too, Mother."

"Oh." She frowns and looks me up and down. "Really, Sloane? You look like you just got out of bed."

I roll my eyes, walking past her into the mudroom. "That's because I did."

"I just can't believe you couldn't have at least brushed your hair. This is a holiday after all," she says, following behind me, before her whole demeanor changes as we walk out into the kitchen, where all of Don's family is seated around the table. "Look who's here!" she says excitedly, like she wasn't just berating me for how I look.

All my step-relatives get up to hug me and kiss me on the cheek, an Italian custom I had to quickly get used to. Lots of hugging and kissing. Adrienne is at the end of the table with a boy I don't recognize. She gives me a wide grin when we make eye contact and waves me over to her. Quite excited for someone who has spent the past three weeks avoiding me. Claire is at the kids table in the living room with Sofie, Vinnie, and some of our other younger cousins so I take my seat next to Adrienne and she introduces me to her supposed boyfriend, Paul.

"So nice to meet you, Paul. I feel like Adrienne is always up at Ivy Gate. I never even see her anymore. Like entire weekends, sometimes during the week. She must really like you."

Paul laughs nervously, glancing at Adrienne with a look that I swear is confusion. He must not see her that often, then. Because she's there seeing someone else.

"Well, I'm not *always* with Paul," she says. "I have class, and I work at that boutique downtown. Just busy."

"Right, busy."

Adrienne only shrugs and goes back to eating. But I hope she knows I'm onto her.

THE DINNER DRAGS on, and I find myself stuck making small talk with the rest of the family until I can leave. I even get to use some of my rehearsed lines. When Claire leaves with her boyfriend to go to his family's house, and Adrienne starts retelling about her summer in New York, I decide it's time to go. I told our dad I would stop by his house before going back to school and I plan on making that visit even shorter than this one. We only ever see him on holidays with his new family, and usually Claire and I just sit in silence while his wife, Eve, talks about her kids' accomplishments and our dad nods along, just as thrilled with these kids who aren't even his. While his own are sitting right in front of him. Today I'll endure it alone, since Claire is otherwise occupied, and it makes me wish I actually was dating Asher so I'd also have an excuse to go somewhere else.

Their white-picket-fence house smells like pumpkin pie and nutmeg when I walk in. Small kids I don't recognize run around the foyer playing a game. Must be Eve's side of the family.

"Hey, Sloane," Hallie, my stepsister and Eve's high-school-aged daughter, greets me from the kitchen counter as I make my way in. I like Hallie; she reminds me of myself when I was her age. Her younger brother, Cameron, sits on the kitchen stool across from her eating dessert. He looks over at me with whipped cream smeared in the corners of his mouth and gives me a nod.

"Hey, guys," I say.

"Your dad is in the living room," Hallie says, setting up her phone for a TikTok.

I walk over to the counter where bottles of wine sit half full and pour myself a hefty glass before going into the living room with the other adults. My dad smiles and stands to hug me when I walk in. He's tall and thin and has always looked young for his age. Once when I was in high school someone mistook him for my boyfriend at a carnival. We were both mortified, though I think he secretly liked that someone thought he was that young.

"Where's your sister?" he asks.

"Oh, she's with her boyfriend. She told me to tell you she's sorry that she couldn't make it."

He gives me a confused look. "Boyfriend? Since when?"

"Since like almost a year now." I say it with an edge in my voice because he would know that if he bothered to show up. "They were homecoming king and queen this year."

"Oh, right, yes, I texted her congratulations."

I turn to go to the couch, mumbling under my breath, "An in-person one would've been better."

I go to sit, but not before Eve comes from around the corner, rushing toward me. "Oh no, sweetie, no red wine on the couch, please!" I pause mid-sit and look around at her relatives who are sitting on the white couch with red wine. I almost think she's joking, but she continues, "That's just such a full glass is all." I blink at her as I lower myself onto the hardwood floor and take a long sip.

"You guys remember my daughter Sloane?" my dad says to the company on the couch. I know that they're Eve's family and

I definitely saw them at their wedding and maybe a time or two after that, but I can't name a single one of them.

"Oh yes, of course," a lady who looks a lot like Eve says. "You're the one that goes to Pembroke, right?"

I stop sipping to reply. "Yep."

"Do you like it there? That's where my son wants to go in the fall."

Next fall I will no longer be a student there, and that's another kind of sadness I'm not ready for. "Yes, I like it."

"A lot of partying," Eve says to the other woman with a hand covering her mouth from me, like I wasn't supposed to hear it, even though she said it loud enough for even Hallie to hear in the kitchen.

"I've heard that," says an older man standing by the fireplace.

"Poor Sloane had an incident with it last spring, called us in the middle of night because she got arrested." Eve frowns and the others gasp.

I give her an incredulous look. "Actually, I called my dad, not you." The room falls quiet. And it's true, I called him first. I thought maybe, just maybe, he might care enough to help me. But he only sighed, the long pause on the line dragging on and on, before telling me to call my mom. I wonder what he'd do if Hallie called him from jail. Would he drop everything to go and get her?

"I don't think this is an appropriate time to really discuss it, Sloane," my dad tries to cut in.

"Your wife brought it up!"

Eve throws up her hands in defense. "I was only trying to warn Collette of how dangerous it can be."

"Well, please, let me chime in, then." I look at the wide-eyed woman who must be Collette. "Not only is there excessive drinking, but the teachers sleep with their students, and just last month a kid died at a secret underground party by having a sword shoved through him. But you should totally send your son—he'll have a blast." I chug the rest of the wine and go to grab my keys from the kitchen island.

"Sloane!" My dad follows after me. "You are not going to just leave after chugging that!"

"Don't worry," I say, slipping on my shoes, "if I get arrested again, I'll call my mom." I slam the front door shut behind me, and he doesn't follow. Sometimes I wonder if I should write *him* a eulogy, but I think I'd need a bigger journal for that.

It's LATE BY the time I get back to Pembroke, and the route to get to my apartment from the highway always takes me past College Street, where the boys live. I almost miss the light on in the attic bedroom as I drive by.

Asher is home.

Don't do it, Sloane, don't do it.

I stop my car, put it in reverse, and turn down their street. I guess I'm doing it, if only out of curiosity. For once the front door is locked and I feel like this is a sign from the universe that I should just go back to my own apartment, but I knock anyway. Asher answers the door in plaid pajama pants and a sweatshirt, his hair messy and his eyes sleepy.

I realize I don't have anything to say. I don't even know why I stopped by. "I saw your light on. I just thought I'd come say hey . . ."

He steps aside and I walk into the otherwise empty house, no other boys in sight. "Why are you not with your family?" he asks.

"Why aren't you?"

"Touché."

I follow him up to his room. "I was there for a while at my mom's, then I went to my dad's. And at the end of the day I just realized I wanted to be alone, I guess."

"Oh, should I leave?" he jokes. "So you can be alone?"

What the hell am I doing? *What the hell am I doing?* "I should probably leave. I don't even know why I stopped over." I turn to go.

"So what do you want to drink?" he asks, walking over to the small cart by his dresser. "I have scotch or scotch."

I turn back around and sigh. "I guess scotch."

Asher puts a movie on and I sit on his bed with a glass of scotch. By far the weirdest Thanksgiving I have ever had.

"My dad is probably at some casino in Vegas, and my sister is with her boyfriend's family," he says finally.

I cough after sipping the drink he gave me. I've never had scotch and I don't think I ever will again. The liquid settles in my stomach with a familiar burn. "Where's your mom?"

"She's not around." He swirls the drink in his glass.

"Ah, divorced?" That would make sense and explain why Asher is the way he is.

"Dead," he says.

I nearly choke on my next sip. "Oh my god, I'm so sorry . . ." I wait for him to tell me he's kidding, but he doesn't. "How did I not know that? I feel like a bad person for not knowing that."

"Well, I don't really go around playing the 'dead mommy' card, but maybe I should. I wonder if that would win me some pity fucks. What do you think?"

I lean back on his headboard, shaking my head. "Your ability to make anything a joke is astounding."

"I probably should've mentioned that before the trip. Would've been really awkward if you had asked about her there."

I debate asking the next question, because it requires getting personal with Asher, the thing I've been trying to avoid lately, but my curiosity wins again. "What happened to her?"

"Cancer."

"I'm sorry."

He changes the subject. "Do you like the scotch?"

"No," I answer honestly.

That's one of the perks about hanging out alone with Asher: I don't have to lie to him, or be polite to him, or be anything I'm not. I'm not trying to impress him. He huffs a laugh, but I can't get over the fact that I didn't know his mom was gone. If we really were dating, I'd be the worst girlfriend on the planet.

"What's your middle name?" I ask.

"Why?"

"Because I'm realizing I know next to nothing personal about you. If I have to meet your family in two weeks, I should probably know more about you."

"Okay, fair. Collins is my middle name."

"Asher Collins McCavern." I test out his full name on my tongue, like a wine that you're trying for the first time. How you're supposed to swirl it around and smell it first. Though I usually just gulp it down. "I like that." He doesn't say anything in return. "Aren't you going to ask mine?"

"We're not hanging out with *your* family," he says. I shake my head again at his blatant crudeness. "Fine, what is yours?"

"Elizabeth."

"Sloane Elizabeth Sawyer." He says each name with a pause in between, and I don't think I've ever heard any man say my full name before. I'm not sure how I feel about it. Would I like it if it were Wes saying it? I make a mental note to find out.

"What's your favorite color?" I ask.

"Blue."

"Favorite movie?"

"The *Lord of the Rings* trilogy. They were my favorite books growing up."

"Interesting," I say.

"What, you didn't think I'd be into fantasy?"

"No, I didn't think you knew how to read."

He smirks. "If that's impressive, wait until you see how high I can count."

I laugh and continue with my line of questioning. "If you could have dinner with anyone in the world, who would it be?"

"This is a dumb question," he says.

I swirl around the scotch. "Just answer it. Mine would be Lana Del Rey, or no, no, wait, it would be—"

"Hans Zimmer," he says.

I shake my head, still thinking. "No, not him."

"No, that's mine," he says. "He's my favorite composer."

"Asher Collins!" I say, surprised. "You are such a nerd—I had no idea."

He shakes his head. "Okay, enough with these questions."

"But I'm just getting started! Just a few more." I can feel my cheeks getting hot from the drink as I manage to choke down the rest of what he poured me if only to get it over with. I'm surprised how it goes right to my head for such a small amount, and now I get why people drink this stuff.

"My family wouldn't think it's weird if you didn't know who in the world I'd have dinner with. In fact, the weirdest thing between us—" he starts but cuts himself off, also drinking the rest of his drink and setting it down on the nightstand beside him.

"Is what?" I ask.

He looks at me with his mouth in a hard line. "How awkward you are with intimacy."

My mouth drops open. "What? Me?" I am not awkward with intimacy; I am awkward with him. There is no manual on how to fake date someone to trick the guy that you really like into liking you.

"Yeah, you. You practically spaz any time I try to touch you in public."

I turn toward him, ready to argue. "Because we aren't really together. I don't want to be touched by you." I've said this before, but each time I say it, it feels less and less true.

"Well, that is less likely to happen if he thinks we're not together. Do you not notice how he looks at you when I'm near you? I think his head would explode if he actually saw us kiss."

"So what, what do you want from me? We're already telling everyone we're sleeping together. Should I cling on to you at all times too?"

"Is that what we're telling people? Because that's not what Annica and Danielle have been saying. You've been absent this entire month and Annica is blabbing on about our sex life that isn't really happening, questioning if we're even really together and accusing me of cheating on you. Though I will say that gets Wes pretty riled up, jumping down my throat about what he'd do to me if I hurt you. Then I have Dani offering me advice on how to be romantic. Honestly, it's been torture."

He's right, and now I feel flustered and overheated. "I just, I—"

"It's fine," he says, putting his hands behind his head and leaning back. "Just loosen up a little on the trip and try not to run away when I touch you."

I can feel my cheeks turning red. He's talking to me like I'm a prude, which I am most certainly not, but I'm also not the kind of person that can fake affection that isn't there.

"Then let's practice." I can feel my heartbeat in my ears at what I just suggested, and I half hope he shuts down the idea. But only half.

He only raises a brow. "What?"

"Yeah, let's practice. Maybe I'll feel more comfortable, and it'll look more natural, if we just . . . tried it out first."

"What exactly would you like to try?" The corner of his mouth turns up.

I take a breath and scoot in closer to him. "Well, I can move in closer, like this." I scooch down and lean a little toward him so that my arm is now against his. "And you can put one arm around me like this." I take his arm and put it around my shoulder before snuggling up to him and leaning my head on his shoulder. I'm sure it looks just as strange as it feels. He only lets out a long sigh. When we're this close I notice he smells like cinnamon and pine. It reminds me of Christmas.

"Is this helping you?" he asks after a moment.

"I mean, it might if you weren't so stiff." I squirm around under his arm, trying to get comfortable.

"I don't know what you want from me right now. This isn't what I thought you had in mind."

I sit up again with a sigh, scooting over so we are no longer touching. "What did you think I meant?"

He smirks. "Come back over here." I do what he says, moving in toward him. "Closer, Sawyer," he says quietly.

I'm nestled into him again, as his hand lifts my chin, sweetly this time, not in the rough way he grabbed me on Halloween. My breath catches in my throat when I realize what it is he wants to try. I try to calm myself down because it's just a kiss, Sloane, it's just a kiss. And it's a practice one at that. This is like eighth grade with Bobby Mathews behind the bleachers all over again, and somehow I'm just as nervous. I look up at him from under my lashes before he tilts my face toward his and gives me that usual snarky grin. He leans in slow, and my lips part ever so slightly and my eyes flutter closed. Then Asher Collins McCavern's lips are on mine.

And I was right, they are soft.

He tastes like scotch and spearmint gum as he deepens the kiss, and his hand moves back to my hair, where it settles, tangled in the long strands. But it doesn't last long, and he ends it by pulling away from me. And that was all I needed to confirm what I already thought. I'm in trouble.

"Not bad," he says, as our faces are still so close. "Anything else you want to try?" He smiles with those white teeth and I feel dizzy.

"I— No, that was good, fine actually, it was fine." I start to edge to the side of his bed. "I think we're all set for the trip, then."

"And here you go running away again," he says, leaning back against his headboard.

"I'm not running away." Though I certainly am, because if I stay I think we might end up practicing a lot more than a kiss. "I have stuff to do tonight."

"On Thanksgiving?"

"Yes, actually, I have . . . Black Friday shopping to do. For skiing stuff. Outfits for skiing and whatever else you need for . . . that."

"Okay." He smirks. "Just make sure they're tight. And get a bathing suit for the hot tub. A slutty one."

"Oh my god," I mutter, leaving his room.

"See you in two weeks, Sawyer," he calls out after me.

CHAPTER 19

December

I'm an anxious flier. I wasn't always: It's something I developed as I got older. As a kid I would laugh whenever we'd hit turbulence, but now, as we're getting ready to board a five-hour flight to Colorado, I wish I would've taken another Xanax from Adrienne.

"Here's everyone's boarding passes," Wes says. When he gets to me and Asher he looks at the passes again. "Oh, it looks like me and Sloane are sitting together. Sorry, Asher."

"Oh, well, that's okay," I say. "Asher is the row behind us."

"I can switch with you," Annica offers. "Dani can sit with Charlie. Then you can sit with Asher."

"I don't think we should be switching seats," Asher warns. "Sometimes in first class they check."

Annica gives him an odd look. "I have never seen that happen."

"Yeah, let's just keep these seats," Wes agrees.

I'm too busy tapping my foot and biting the insides of my cheeks to make a comment. We file onto the plane and Wes lets me have the window seat. I've never been in first class, so I fidget in the seat and nervously flip through the menu that is in the seat pocket in front of us. I have a date with a bottle of champagne the moment I see that flight attendant. I take a few deep breaths with my eyes closed while Wes is turned around talking to Sam, who's in the seat across the aisle.

"Don't worry," Asher says, standing over my seat, "if the plane goes down, it'll probably be a quick death." I open my eyes to his evil smile and I glare back at him. "Did you tell your family you love them just in case?"

"I hate you," I say back to him, and that's when I see our flight attendant. "Excuse me! Hi." The older woman smiles as she walks over to me. "I saw on the menu that you have bottles of champagne; I need one of those, please."

"Of course," she says. "We serve drinks right after takeoff so I'll bring that to you then." I smile at her wearily and groan to myself when she's gone.

"Champagne won't stop the plane from crashing," Asher says now from in between the seats.

"Stop. Talking."

The flight attendants come by, making sure seat belts are buckled, and begin going over safety procedures as the plane makes its way to the runway. I bounce my leg nervously and have moved on to chewing my lip now that my cheeks are raw. When the plane makes its last turn and the engines begin to roar I take another breath, and another. Wesley catches on and reaches for my hand. It helps, but only a little. He lets me squeeze it as hard as I want as the plane accelerates and lifts off into the sky.

Wes leans into me during takeoff. "Did you know flying is the safest way to travel? Even safer than driving." I open my eyes to look over at him and away from the window beside me as the plane rocks and shakes.

"Yeah?"

"Yeah." He smiles at me. "And there's a theory I read where you can imagine turbulence like the plane being in Jell-O. The Jell-O might move, but the plane is suspended within it, so it can't go up or down. Basically, turbulence can't cause a plane to fall from the sky."

"Did you learn all of this from being a fighter pilot for Halloween?" I joke.

"Yeah, something like that."

I try to focus on the softness in his gaze when he looks at me, or the way his one wave of dark hair separates from the rest and dusts his forehead, or how his hand feels in mine. Perfect, like it's meant to be there.

"If you could have dinner with one person in the world, who would it be?" I ask him as a distraction.

I hear Asher scoff from behind us. "Not this shit again," he grumbles.

ONLY WHEN WE'RE cruising at a high altitude and the seat belt signs go off do I let go of Wesley's hand. The flight attendant comes over immediately with a mini bottle of champagne for me.

"Oh," I say. "I think I need at least two more."

She smiles and nods.

"I didn't know you were so nervous to fly," Wes says, pouring my champagne into the little plastic cup for me.

"Yeah," I breathe.

"Why don't we put a movie on," he suggests, flipping through the options on the TVs in front of us. We settle on some beachy rom-com.

"I think he's living out your dream," I say when one of the main characters owns a beach house that he rents out.

"Forgot I told you about that," Wes mumbles, embarrassed. "Though that's a little small-scale. I don't want an Airbnb; I want an actual B and B that I can run."

"So like Lorelai from *Gilmore Girls*?"

"I don't know who that is, but sure, like her," he says.

"So do you have any ideas for where this bed-and-breakfast will be?"

"I do." He waits a moment before deciding to reveal more. He takes his phone out and goes into his photos. He pulls up a photo of his family's beach house in Nantucket. I've never been there but I've seen it on his Instagram.

"Your family's house?" I ask, confused.

"My dad wants to sell it; we don't use it enough. Ever since the night we talked about it I've been working on a business proposal to present to my dad to turn it into a hotel."

"Wow." I look back up at him, and I can see in his eyes that he's excited about this idea, and it makes me excited for him. "That sounds perfect for you, Wes."

"Yeah, Marissa hates the idea. She's already looking at houses for us to move to Colorado." He puts his phone away and goes back to the movie. I want to say that she's insane considering they've been together for less than a year. Bold of her to assume they'd be moving to a new state together after college. But Wes and I have been a couple for, well, never and I would move anywhere with him if he asked.

"Well, if my opinion matters at all, I think you should go for the beach house, if that's what you want."

"Your opinion always matters, Sloane."

ASHER CATCHES UP to me at baggage claim after our flight and throws an arm around my shoulder. I resist the urge to shake him off, because that is not what we practiced.

"*That sounds perfect for you, Wes.*" He mocks my voice in my ear with a laugh. "You really sold it, Sawyer. I could kiss you right now." My breath catches in my throat again at the thought of another kiss.

"I didn't sell anything," I say to him. "I meant what I said."

"Even better."

"Did I tell you I messaged Graham to—"

"No, no, no," he cuts me off. "We are on vacation this weekend. No talk of murder."

"That's another thing: Doesn't it feel wrong that we're just putting a pause on the whole thing? We should be home stalking Miles or Adrienne or even Marissa, because she's still on my list."

He stops walking and stands in front of me, whispering, "Sloane, everything will be okay for a weekend. We have proof that Miles isn't going after Graham until after the holidays. Just enjoy this trip."

"What if I can't?"

"Then use the money you saved up to buy yourself a plane ticket home. But good luck with your flight anxiety. They don't give you free champagne in economy." Asher pats my cheek before walking away.

THE MCCAVERNS SEND a driver to pick us all up from the airport. I don't say much on the thirty-five-minute drive to their grandparents' house, feeling tired from the champagne and long day of travel. Just this morning I was turning in my final draft to Renner and now I'm in Colorado. It doesn't even feel like the same day. As we pull up to the house the group gathers by the van windows to marvel at the home, oohing and aahing. I'm inclined to join them when we step out in front of the stunning three-story stone structure. Surrounded by snowcapped pine trees, the home exudes a warm glow of light from the large picture windows all around it. It's like we stepped out of Pembroke and into a Hallmark Christmas movie.

Wesley's mom greets us at the door, with a warm smile and eight cups of hot chocolate on a tray. She's a petite woman with long dark hair pulled back in a clip and deep brown eyes with laugh lines at their corners. She looks like she gives a good hug. And she does, as she pulls each of us in for one as a greeting.

"I'm sure you're all so tired from traveling. Wes, why don't you show everyone to their rooms? It's late so I'm about to head back to the resort with your father but you guys have a good night and I'll see you in the morning. Oh, and try to keep it down—your grandfather is already in bed."

"Got it. Good night, Mom." Wes gives his mom a kiss on the cheek, and I watch Asher as he turns away to walk toward the stairs. This is his family home too, after all; he doesn't need to be shown around.

We walk through the rest of the kitchen, which leads out to a grand living room area with plush leather couches, draped with fur blankets arranged before a tall stone fireplace. In the corner is a Christmas tree that almost touches the top of the high ceilings. It's a marvel in itself and I'm wondering how they even got this thing in here, let alone decorated it.

"This is the living room," Wes says as we walk through it. "Through that door is the dining room." He points to the right where there's an opening off the kitchen. "Down that hall is my grandfather's bedroom, the sauna, the study, and the door to get to the back patio." We start up the wide set of stairs that leads to the second floor. "Our rooms are all up here. There are five rooms, so a few of us will have to double up."

"Annica and I will stay together," Dani says.

I scoff at how quick they are to exclude me. "What about me?"

Annica gives me a look. "Are you not staying with Asher?"

"Oh, um, yeah, I am. I forgot."

Annica only levels a suspicious stare at me.

"His room is at the end of the hall," Wes says. "Since he didn't bother to wait for you to show you where it was."

I give everyone a nod goodnight as I make my way there. Wes has his own room, Annica and Dani go off to theirs, and Charlie, Sam, and Jake argue over who gets a room to themselves and who shares. I don't hear the decision when I enter Asher's room. He's already unpacking when I walk in. I look at the large king bed in the center of the room. I didn't even think about the fact that we'd be sharing a bed all weekend.

"Listen, I have to go to the resort tonight for business. Don't wait up for me," he says. "In fact, wait in Wesley's room."

I scoff as I drag my suitcase over to the other closet. The bedroom is huge and luxurious with stone floors and a fireplace in the corner. "What's at the resort? And why do you need to go over there so late?" I haven't checked the time but it has to be at least midnight.

"Just some things I want to check up on," he says, throwing on a jacket. "Get some sleep. Or don't." He winks before closing the door behind him. What does he expect me to do? Go into Wesley's room, strip down, and see what happens?

I start to unpack and put my clothes in the armoire. I think about leaving the room to hang out with Dani and Annica, but then they'll ask where Asher is, and wouldn't it seem weird if he left at midnight for the resort, and left his girlfriend here? Unsurprisingly the bathroom has a Jacuzzi tub and a rain shower, so I decide to take a warm bath before getting into bed, thinking about what Asher could possibly be there checking on. Maybe he wants to get a head start on the resort operations. Maybe he wants to prove to Wesley's dad that he wants it more.

When the clock hits 2 a.m. Asher is still not back. I debate texting him, but he said not to wait up. I close my eyes and go through my nightly routine: Jonah, Ryan, Marco, Bryce. Jonah, Ryan, Marco, Bryce. I count them like sheep.

I stir slightly when I feel Asher getting into bed. I glance at the alarm clock next to the bed and it reads 5 a.m. I close my eyes again to continue sleeping, thinking that he likely wasn't doing resort business at all.

At seven, Wes is waking everyone up. "Time to hit the slopes!" he yells down the hall, knocking on all the doors.

Asher gets up to shower and I take out my clothes for the day.

I bought an all-black ski outfit from some trendy website, and though it does look good on me, it's so tight I can barely move.

"I approve," Asher says, checking me out when he comes back from the bathroom. "Don't forget to layer up on socks."

I ignore his comment and go right into what's bothering me the most this morning. "How was the resort last night?"

He clears his throat. "It was fine."

"Great," I say, leaving the room and heading downstairs to where the group has started to congregate in the kitchen. Wesley's mom made a breakfast spread for all of us and the boys are already digging in.

The driver takes us over to the resort, which looks like a log cabin on steroids. Three large buildings surround an ice rink in the center. Behind it, towering over everything, are tall snowy hills. I can see little figures race down them from here.

The moment we hit the lobby, Jake beelines for the large mahogany bar in the center of the room.

"Let's have a drink before we do this," he suggests.

"Need some liquid courage?" Wes teases.

"To keep up with you and Asher on the black diamonds, yes," Sam agrees.

I assume that's a type of hill, but I ask anyway, "What's a black diamond?"

"The most dangerous hill," Annica says. "Probably not something five drunk idiot boys should be going down, but hey, why not." She crosses her arms in her white puffy snowsuit with fur trim. Dani has on a colorful one, something that somehow looks modern but retro at the same time. Jake orders a shot ski to start for the five of them and they line up to take it. The bartender is a girl that looks to be in her mid-twenties. She's got beautiful golden skin with ice-blue eyes and long dark hair. She brings the shot ski and winks at Asher.

"Did she just wink at your boyfriend?" Annica scoffs.

From behind the guys, I can't see what he may or may not have done back.

"Long night?" she says to him with a smirk. "You look tired." And then it dawns on me that *she* was the resort business.

"I think she might be flirting with him too," Dani whispers.

"Aren't you going to say something?" Annica asks me. "Do you want me to?"

The boys do their shot and all order a beer. Wes turns around to ask what we want. It's on the house, he says. I walk up beside Asher where he stands talking to the bartender away from the prying eyes and ears.

"Hi, I'm Sloane," I say to her. "I'm Asher's girlfriend."

Her smile disappears as her eyes go back to Asher.

Asher laughs uncomfortably. "It's an open relationship," he says to her with a shrug.

I glare up at him.

"I'm Brandy," the bartender says, still with a wary look in her eyes.

"Hi, Brandy, nice to meet you. Can I get a vodka soda and make it a double."

"Double vodka?" Asher asks, eyebrows raised. "And so early in the morning?"

Brandy turns to fetch the drinks, probably happy to be away from this conversation.

"Being a total dick?" I say back to him. "And so early in the morning?"

He looks down at me quizzically, then says with a laugh, "Are you jealous of Brandy?"

"Of course not," I spit back. "I just can't have you telling everyone we're in an open relationship. I mean, what if one of them heard you?"

"Then you could pretend to be upset about it and Wes would swoop in to save you. Maybe I should've said it a little louder." He looks over, considering. Brandy comes back with the drinks and I pick mine up, chug it, and set it right back down, holding back the gag at how much liquor was in it. "You good?" Asher asks, watching my face. "You happy with that decision you just made?"

"Ecstatic."

We head outside so Dani, Annica, and I can rent our skis. Also on the house. The boys get snowboards, Wes and Asher each having special ones that they keep here. I have never skied, but neither has Danielle, so we have lessons this morning on the bunny hill while the rest of them hit the adult side of the resort.

"Annica says it's pretty easy, so we'll be pros in no time," Dani says as we make our way to the small slopes, full of children. I watch them all flawlessly navigate the hill, and I think she must be right: If kids can do it, why can't we?

We eat our words, and the snow, as we fall over and over again. Jacques, our French instructor, grows more and more irritated with us by the hour and my body starts to ache from the effort.

"Maybe we should hit up the bar?" I suggest, since my double vodka soda has long since worn off.

"Yeah, fuck this." We hang out at the outside bar with other people our age. A DJ plays house music over the crowd and we settle in by one of the heat lamps.

"So what did you say to that bartender?" she asks.

"Oh, *Brandy*," I say. "I introduced myself as Asher's girlfriend and she scurried away." That's not exactly how it went down, but Dani would be shocked to know that apparently Asher and I are in an open relationship.

"Annica told me last night that she doesn't really think you guys are together. I don't know why she cares so much but it seems to really bother her for some reason."

I roll my eyes. "I wish she would just relax about the whole 'relationship in the friend group' thing. She doesn't even like Asher. If the two of us broke up it would not affect this group at all."

"I don't think it's that; it sounds like it's just about Asher in particular. She doesn't trust him."

"Do you?" I ask her.

She looks at me. "Do you?"

No. "Yeah, of course."

The house music grows louder around us until the DJ gets on the mic. "This next one goes out to Sloane, from her secret admirer," the DJ says, before playing a remix of "Murder on the Dancefloor."

My mouth hangs open as every worry I've decided to put to the side for this trip comes crashing into me.

"Secret admirer?" Dani says. "Is that Asher trying to be funny? Do you even like this song?"

I stand up, suddenly feeling dizzy, looking all around the outdoor bar and dance floor for Miles. Could he have followed me here this weekend? He did threaten to show up at school, so who's to say he isn't here?

When Annica and the boys come back from the more intense version of skiing/snowboarding, I grab Asher and pull him aside.

"I think Miles is here," I say in a panic.

He crosses his arms, his hunter-green jacket crinkling beneath them. His face is flushed from being outside for hours and indents from his goggles mark his face. "What did we just talk about in the airport yesterday?"

"The DJ got a request to play a song about *murder*, and said it was for me from my secret admirer. Who else would it be?"

"How do you know it wasn't for a different Sloane?"

"Oh, do you think there's more than one of us being set up?" He doesn't say anything. "That's why!"

He puts his hands on my shoulders. "Okay," he says. "Just—"

"Do not even tell me to relax or calm down," I say.

"It could've been one of the guys who requested that as a joke. Honestly, I bet it was Jake," Asher says. I mean . . . I guess that's possible, but my gut is telling me danger is lurking somewhere in these mountains. Asher can tell I'm still not convinced. "Okay, say Miles is here. Graham is in Boston right now, your guy Tristan is in Europe, and Wes is here with us at a resort with top-notch security. Same with my grandpa's house. I'm telling you, you don't have to worry."

"She doesn't have to worry about what?" Annica interrupts, looping her arm around mine, and Asher lets out a long sigh. She turns us away from Asher. "What's going on? Is it about the bartender? Because I'll throw a drink at her if you want me to."

I can't hide the twitch of my lips at the thought of Annica throwing a drink at Brandy, and for what? Technically she has done nothing to me. "No, no, it's fine. We worked it out."

"Are you sure? I'd really do it, you know. No one flirts with my best friend's . . . whatever Asher is to you, and gets away with it," she teases as we make our way toward the resort's steakhouse restaurant.

"I'm sure." I huff a laugh, wishing I could tell her that Brandy isn't the real threat here. Not by a long shot.

"Everything okay?" Wes asks when we sit down at the table with the rest of them.

"Yeah, she's fine," Asher answers for me. "Sloane just hit her head one too many times on the bunny hill."

I glare at him.

"We did fall down a lot," Dani says.

"You're feeling better now, though, aren't you?" Asher pointedly says to me with a hand on my knee.

"Yes," I lie.

CHAPTER 20

"Let's play Truth or Dare," Annica says, opening her drink. We're all seated in the large hot tub situated in the back of the house, where we have a picturesque view of the mountains.

I laugh. "I feel like we're too old for—"

"Charlie, truth or dare?" Jake says, cutting me off. I guess we're playing, then.

Charlie claps his hands together. "Oh, dare, for sure."

Jake looks around, thinking of a dare. "I dare you to dip your balls into the snow for five seconds."

"Or it's five shots of whiskey if you don't complete the dare," Annica adds. We're already off to an insane start. Five shots of whiskey if you don't want to do something? I'll be vomiting everywhere.

"Fuck," Charlie says, but he gets out of the hot tub and goes over to the snow-covered area that isn't part of the heated stone flooring. Facing away from us so we just see his ass, he drops his trunks and does a squat. I look away as he lets them drop and lets out a howl. The group cheers him on. Jake counts to five, very slowly, and when the time is up Charlie sprints back to the tub.

"All right." Charlie looks around at us for his victim. "Annica, since this was your dumb idea, truth or dare?"

"Truth," she says.

"If you could sleep with any of the boys in this hot tub, who would it be?"

"Sam." She says it quick before turning to me, preparing to ask me a question, but the group is stunned. It can't be just me that thought she'd say Wes. "Sloane, truth or dare?"

"Whoa, back up." Jake shakes his head like he's trying to comprehend her answer. "Sam? Why him?"

"Because ninety percent of the time you're a drunk idiot, and the other ten percent you're just an idiot," Annica tells Jake as she goes down the line. "Charlie and Dani are together."

"I wouldn't say *together*," Dani corrects her.

Annica continues. "Asher is one of the worst people I've ever met."

"Right back at you," he grumbles.

"Wes has been one of my best friends since we were kids—he's like a brother to me at this point. So, if I had to pick one of you it would be Sam. Happy? Now, Sloane, truth or dare?"

I feel like she only started this childish game to bait me into answering a question. She thinks I'll pick truth and there's clearly something she wants to know about me and Asher.

"Dare," I say with a smile.

She only smiles back, and I know I've chosen wrong. "I dare you to make out with Asher right here in front of all of us." I clench my jaw. I do not want to do that in front of Wes. Not at all. "Or you can do the five shots of whiskey. But it would be weird to choose that over your boyfriend."

My heart races as I look over at Asher, who sets down his drink. He's leaned back on one of the lounge seats in the hot tub, while I took the bench-style seat next to it. With Wes on the other side of me. I consider the whiskey. She never said what kind of whiskey, and I did see peach Crown in there, which might not be so bad. But the choice is made for me when Asher leans over and puts his hands on my waist, lifting me onto his lap so that I'm straddling him. The only thing between us is the fabric of our bathing suits. We practiced a kiss but we didn't practice making out and now I'm overthinking this. Should I go in leaning left or right? Is he going to use his tongue? Should I? How long should it last? We should've practiced this too.

I look into his eyes and they only have pure amusement in them. He raises an eyebrow as if to ask if I'm ready as one of his hands snakes up my back, the other gripping my backside, sliding me closer to him. I follow his lead, sliding my own hands up his chest and around his neck to pull him in. When his mouth is on mine it's not the same gentle kiss from two weeks ago; it's hungrier. Another kiss and my mouth parts for him. His hand on my ass grips me tighter, and his tongue slides over mine. Our mouths move faster, exploring, needing to taste each other, and I forget we're sitting in a hot tub with our friends. This time when he pulls me against him I moan into his mouth and we both pause, catching ourselves.

Well, shit.

"Okay, that's enough, thank you," Annica says with a hint of disappointment.

I take my hands from his hair and try to scoot back. Asher just repositions me so I'm still sitting on him but my back is on his chest. I clear my throat, trying to regain my bearings. I swear this hot tub is a million degrees. I sneak a glance at Wesley but he's leaning over the side on his phone.

"I'm going inside to call Marissa," Wes announces, getting up and leaving the hot tub.

"Um, Jake, truth or dare?" I say, a little breathless.

"Dare."

"I dare you to suck one of Annica's toes."

"Ew, what?!" she squeals. That'll teach her.

He does it and the rest of them continue to go around. I remember what we discussed about being too stiff so I lean my head back. I can feel Asher breathing and he whispers in my ear.

"Want to play a game called Nervous?"

"Never heard of it," I reply. I feel his hand on my thigh start to move inward.

"It's easy. I ask if you're nervous and you just say yes or no."

"Sounds like a dumb game." But then his hand starts to move, a few inches past my knee.

"Nervous?" he asks.

I guess we're playing his dumb game. "No."

The group is cheering on Dani doing push-ups in the snow as Asher continues to whisper to me. His hand stops halfway up my inner thigh. "Nervous?"

What is he doing? Where exactly does the Nervous game end? "No."

His fingers swirl around my inner thigh and land almost at the lining of my bathing suit. "Nervous?"

My legs instinctively open for him as if they have a mind of their own. "No." I breathe the word because there's nowhere else to go. His hand moves up and over my lower stomach, toying with the top lining of my bottoms; he puts two fingers in the seam and stops himself.

"Nervous?" I ask him. What. Am. I. Doing. And what is *he* doing? Our friends are still playing the game, no one is paying attention to us, and Wes is gone. There's no one to fool, just ourselves.

"I'm never nervous," he says into my ear as he slides his fingers down. I suck in a breath and I start to feel like I should yell *nervous, nervous, nervous!* That's when Sam asks Asher truth or dare and I grab his wrist under the water, snapping my legs shut.

"Whatever the hell you two are doing under the water, please wait until you get to the bedroom to finish it, ugh." Annica shields her eyes.

"Truth," Asher says, wrapping his arms around my middle.

"Have you slept with the bartender at the resort? The hot one with the big boobs," Sam clarifies, though we all know which one.

"I have," Asher answers matter-of-factly.

"Recently?" Sam asks. And I know Sam is asking out of spite. He's still mad at us. I hold my breath waiting for Asher's answer. I don't know why, because I know the answer. But I don't want to hear it.

Asher leans his head on my shoulder and puts his lips to my skin. "You only had one question, Sam."

He continues the trail of light kisses from my shoulder up to my neck, and even in the hot water it gives me goose bumps. When he reaches the nape of my neck my head lolls to the side, inviting him in for more, and god, what is happening right now? Every touch, every feeling of his lips on my skin, I feel like I need more of it . . . and it scares me. I mean, he just admitted to sleeping with another girl to everyone while holding me. Wouldn't a girlfriend be annoyed about that? But I'm not his girlfriend.

"I'm over this game," Annica says, getting up from the hot tub. "And I'm over watching whatever is happening in the corner." She waves her hand over at us, and if my face wasn't already flushed from the hot tub, I would blush. "Dani, let's go watch a movie," she says to Danielle, who gets up after her.

"Sloane, come join us after . . . that." Dani wags her eyebrows at us.

"You guys wanna play pool in the basement?" Jake asks the rest of the guys. Sam and Charlie get up with him, and then it's just me and Asher.

When we hear the door shut for the last time Asher says, "I don't think Annica will be bothering us anymore about whether or not we're together." Then he hoists me up, practically shoving me off him. My knee collides with the other seat and water splashes up into my face.

"Ow?" I say. "A simple 'Can you get up?' would have sufficed." But he's already getting out of the hot tub.

"I have more business at the resort tonight, so don't wait up."

It takes my brain a moment to catch up and come back to reality. The one where all of that was for show, and the way he was touching me is a lie. "Wait, what? You're leaving again? After I told you there's a potentially dangerous serial killer here?"

Asher points around the house. "Security cameras. Everywhere."

I scoff. "It's not even late. What am I supposed to tell everyone else?"

"Make something up. Say my dad wanted to meet me there or whatever." He grabs a towel and heads inside, leaving me alone in the hot tub, which now feels much, much colder.

Back in the house I can hear the clacking pool balls from the basement as I trudge down the hall and toward the stairs. Maybe I'll join Dani and Annica for their movie. Or maybe . . . Wesley's door is open just a crack as I stop before it.

"I know, I miss you too," I hear him say from inside and I roll my eyes. "Why would you even ask that? She's in Asher's room . . . Yes . . . No . . . I'm not having this conversation again, Ris."

I back away from his door and tiptoe to my room. So Marissa does have an idea about me and him, which means she would have a motive.

After a hot shower I get in the bed, too large for just one person, still wrapped in a towel and thinking about what happened in the hot tub. The way his hands gripped me, his mouth on my neck, his fingers dipping between my thighs. I wonder if we hadn't been stopped, would he have kept going? The thought alone makes my toes curl and I slide my own hand up my thigh the way he did to me, just to feel the sensation of it again. I close my eyes, imagining it's him until I get to the same place where he stopped. I can't do this to the thought of Asher, I just can't.

Instead I get up to join Dani and Annica for the movie, telling them Asher fell asleep early. Annica gives Dani a look when I say it, as if there's an inside joke that I'm not aware of. But that's not true, of course. I am so painfully aware of the joke. I *am* the joke.

THAT FAMILIAR SCENT of cinnamon and pine fills the room and I know without opening my eyes that Asher is back. I feel the bed move as he climbs in beside me, but my eyes are still heavy with sleep and the way he so carefully moves tells me it's probably still the middle of the night. So I let myself doze off again, savoring the warmth. I might even scoot a little closer.

When I start to wake on Saturday morning, I can feel his skin on mine and the way his chest rises and falls in his sleep. Somewhere in the night we've become almost chest to chest with his arm draped over me. I start to stir and he does too, his hand running down my side. It makes me wonder if he knows it's me beside him. Perhaps he thinks I'm Brandy. I don't wait around to find out as I get out of the bed, careful not to wake him.

A stream of light comes through the shades as I dress for the day. The boys are planning on going back to the resort for more snowboarding while Annica, Dani, and I go to the spa and shops. Tonight we have some nice dinner planned here at the house with the whole McCavern family. I grab the book I brought with me, intent on reading in front of one of the large windows with the view of the mountains, but when I come downstairs, I find I'm not alone. There's an elderly man with a cane sitting in a leather recliner by the fireplace. Asher and Wesley's grandfather. I almost pivot and go back upstairs but he turns to look at me.

"Charlotte?" he calls out to me, and I know that's one of Wes's older sisters. I continue down the stairs until I'm in view.

"My name is Sloane," I say, walking closer to him. "I'm Asher's . . . friend."

The old man looks me up and down, not in the creepy way men do, but in an eyes-narrowed, assessing way. "Hm," he says. "I hope my grandson treats you well." He looks to be in his late seventies if

I had to guess. Gray hair, but he still has a lot of it. And the same green eyes both of his grandsons inherited.

I smile, thinking of the way Wes comforted me on the flight here. "He does."

"There's a fresh pot of coffee on the counter if you want any." He waves a hand toward the kitchen.

I notice he doesn't have a cup. "Would you like some coffee too?" I offer.

"I would, though I'm not supposed to have the stuff these days . . . but I'm sure a little won't hurt."

"I won't tell if you don't." I smile at him and his lips turn up in return.

He points a frail finger at me. "I like you."

I pour us each a cup of coffee, mine with vanilla creamer and his with a splash of milk and two sugars, and sit in front of the fireplace with him while we drink it. I'm not usually nervous around strangers; in fact, I find that I'm pretty personable with most people. There's just something intimidating about being alone with the patriarch of the McCavern family. The man responsible for generating all of their wealth. I almost feel like I should start taking notes, write down everything he says.

He asks how I like the resort and I admit to him that it's been great but I don't know how to ski or snowboard. He says surely Asher must have taken the time yesterday to show me—after all, he used to teach lessons here when he was a teenager—but I didn't have the heart to tell him that the moment we stepped outside I didn't see Asher again for almost five hours. Not to mention wherever he goes at night.

Asher eventually comes down the stairs and joins us by the fireplace.

"Are you talking Sloane's ear off, Grandpa?"

"She was nice enough to come down here and sit with me," his grandpa says. "Lord knows my grandkids don't visit anymore."

"I literally live here with you when I'm not at school," Asher says, and that's news to me. Clearly I missed a few topics when I questioned him. "What's on your agenda for today, old man?"

"Preparing for tonight's dinner and driving Elaine crazy," he says. Assuming Elaine is the live-in nurse.

"Well, don't do that, or one of these days she might poison your meds," Asher jokes.

"If only," his grandfather says back. "Hey." He grabs onto Asher's hand with his own weathered pair and says, "This one's a keeper, so don't fuck it up."

We both laugh, and I feel bad lying to their grandfather. "I'll try not to," Asher says.

"And teach the poor girl how to ski before you leave, would you?"

Asher looks over at me, then back to his grandpa. "I'm trying," he lies. "She's a slow learner." I just shake my head. "Well, Sawyer, go get your tight little snowsuit on. It's early, so not a lot of people will be over there yet."

"What, now?" He has to know I had plans today with the girls.

"Yes, now. You'll be back by noon for the spa." He gives me a look that says *do it for my grandpa or I won't hear the end of it.*

I look between him and his grandpa and give a smile before getting up. "It was nice talking with you," I say. "I'll see you at dinner." He gives me a smile and I turn to go back to the room and put on that monstrosity of a snowsuit.

THE SUN IS bright this morning and the fresh snow glistens as Asher and I head out to the slopes.

"Did you have fun with Brandy last night?" I ask him.

"Do you really want to know the answer to that?" he says, looking down at me.

I look away. "Not really." I follow him as we walk past the bunny hills, toward the lifts. "Wait, where are we going? The bunny hills are over there."

"I know, but you practiced on those yesterday."

"And it didn't go well. I don't think I'm ready for a bigger hill."

"You'll be fine."

We get on a lift, and as it takes us up, up, up, my hands start to shake at the thought of going down one of these hills. I distract myself with the vast beauty of the empty mountain and the way the sunlight makes it glow.

"You probably shouldn't have talked to my grandfather," Asher says as we make our way to the top.

"Why? I was just trying to be nice."

"Because when our fake relationship is over he'll just be disappointed in me for dropping the ball."

I don't have any snarky remarks for that. "I'm sorry." He doesn't say anything else as he helps me off the lift and we're at the top of a very steep hill. "Oh my god, Asher, no."

"It's a blue square; it's intermediate."

"What makes you think I'm an intermediate skier on literally day two?"

"Because on day two you're with me." I half think he's going to set me up and give me a hard push down the mountain to see how it goes, but he stands in front of me. "Okay, show me what Jacques taught you yesterday." I stand with my feet hip-width apart and bend my knees slightly. "Okay, not terrible." He adjusts me slightly. "Ready?"

"No."

"Perfect." He puts my goggles down over my eyes and grabs my hands, pulling me to the edge. "Bend your knees. We're going to go down with me in front of you and you can practice just sliding and breaking. Did you learn that yesterday?"

"More like sliding and breaking my legs," I mutter. But he takes my hands, which are gripped around the poles, as we start down the hill.

"Bend your legs more," he says. I do and immediately lose my balance, falling on my ass. He continues to slide backward until he motions his skis into a backward V shape and comes to a halt. "This is going to be a long morning."

"This was your idea," I grumble, getting back up. He gets in front of me again, holding on to me as we slide down the mountain a little farther, him keeping his skis in that V motion and using his arms to hold me out in front of him, keeping us from going at a fast pace.

"Okay, I'm going to let go of your hands and you're going to balance," he says. He lets go and I use the poles and my weight to balance like Jacques taught us yesterday, but I pick up too much speed and crash into Asher. He holds on to me as he tries to bring us to a stop, but I lose my balance, once again landing on my ass as he lets go of me and moves out of the way. "It's okay, get up." We still have a long way to go to get down this hill.

After about five more times of falling and one time bringing him down with me, both of our patience is wearing thin.

"Okay, there you go," he says. "You're doing it!" This is the longest I've been able to stay upright, and Asher takes his skis out of the V formation to slide down backward ahead of me before turning to slide down next to me, and I realize there is nothing in front of me to slow me down now if I need it.

"Whoa." I start to pick up speed. "Okay, I want to slow down."

"Pizza," he says from beside me.

"Pizza?" I'm confused and panicking.

"Put the skis in a V, like a pizza!" He goes to show me the motion and I've been watching his backward V form all morning and it's the first thing that comes to mind, but that only sends me flying backward and spinning down the mountain. When I stop moving I lie in the snow, staring up at the sky, trying to catch my breath. My entire backside hurts from falling on it today and yesterday. Asher stops beside me and sighs. "I said pizza."

"I heard you."

"Then why didn't you do it?"

"Because this is my second time ever skiing and I don't know what I'm doing." I stay on the ground, afraid that if I get up I'll have to start again. My thighs are burning, and my feet are throbbing.

"If you would just listen to what I'm telling you to do, this would get done quicker. You're hardheaded and you never listen," he says, and it makes me feel like he's talking about more than just skiing.

I sit up. "I never listen? You're the one who is constantly pushing me into things I don't want to do, even when I say no."

"Because I'm trying to help you!"

"Help me? No, you're trying to help you! And you're so mean."

"Mean? What is this, third grade?"

"You are the biggest asshole I've ever met. I don't know why we're doing this at all. I never wanted this," I yell back.

"And you think I did?" he yells back at me, and now we're definitely not talking about skiing.

"It was your idea!" He doesn't say anything back. "I'm done. I don't want to do this anymore." I look down, realizing we're only halfway down this damn mountain.

"Don't want to do *what* anymore?" he asks.

I bite the inside of my cheeks.

"Just . . . help me get down the rest of the way so I can go to the spa." I sigh. He helps me up and I get back into position as he holds on to me the remainder of the way down. This time we manage to stay upright the entire time.

"Be ready for dinner by five," Asher says to me before walking back into the resort, leaving me standing out here alone.

"THAT WAS NICE of him to take you out for lessons," Dani says when the three of us are lying face down on three massage tables.

"Yeah, a real gentleman," I sarcastically mumble with my face in the small hole of the table. I needed this after today and yesterday. If it wasn't $200 an hour I'd book five more hours.

"We heard you talked to Vernon this morning," Annica chimes in.

Vernon? Was that someone at the resort? "Who?"

"Asher and Wesley's grandpa," Dani clarifies.

"Oh, yeah, we had coffee together."

"We heard: That's all he talked about this morning," Annica says.

"I think he likes me," I say.

"Asher has something good going for him, then."

I think about Asher's comment on the lift this morning, about disappointing his grandpa. I should've asked, so instead I ask Annica. "What do you mean?"

She scoffs in that snarky way she does when she can't believe we don't know something that she knows. "Has he not said anything to you about his dad? They had to, like, cut him off because he lost half a million of the resort money gambling. Now their grandpa pays for Asher's school and stuff and is apparently really hard on him. Worried he'll be like his dad. I don't blame him either—I'm sure he will be."

"He's not," I snap back. I don't even know why I feel the need to defend him when he's been nothing but rude to me for four years now, but I do.

"Isn't he? I mean, where do you think he's going every night? Yeah, our bathroom window faces the driveway. I saw him leave the past two nights and not come back."

My face grows red from under the table. "He's doing business at the resort." And I feel so stupid for having to give that as an answer when we all know what he's really doing.

"Is that what he's telling you? He's lying to you, Sloane. He can't be trusted."

Deep down I know Annica is looking out for me, that she's trying to warn me that the man she thinks I'm seeing is not being honest with me, and in any other situation I'd be grateful. But we aren't a couple, I know exactly what he's up to, and I can't do anything but defend him.

"I trust him," I say, and leave it at that.

The masseuse moves around the table and adjusts the towel to massage my neck. That's when something star-shaped falls from her pocket.

"Oh, you dropped something," I tell her. But when I get a better look I realize it's dollar bills crafted into a star. Like the money origami Miles used to do when he left me tips at Cantine.

"Whoops, fell out of my pocket," the girl says. "Sorry about that."

"Did you make that?" I ask.

"A customer this morning left it as a tip. He said he couldn't make a snowflake so a star would have to do. I thought it was cute either way."

I sit up. "Who was the customer? What was his name?"

"Um, sorry, but I can't give out that information. Can you lie back down so we can continue, please?"

"I'm getting lightheaded actually. I'm going to go." I get up from the table and rush out of there before my friends can protest.

CHAPTER 21

"I saw the money origami with my own eyes, Asher. He is here," I say as I dress for dinner in a short black silk dress that ties around the neck.

"So many people can make origami money," Asher says. He buttons up the white button-down and slips on a black blazer over top. I try not to look at him as we finish getting ready in the room, still mad about our ski lessons earlier.

"Oh really, like who? Who do you know that does that?"

"Okay, no one personally but"—he lets out a defeated breath and turns to me—"Sloane, please, I need this dinner to go well. Everyone in this house is safe tonight, and tomorrow morning we leave here. Just get through this dinner and tomorrow when we get back to Pembroke you can have a full-on panic attack over whether or not Miles was here, okay? I cannot have you going down there acting like I broke you out of a psych ward on our way here."

"You don't believe me," I say.

"Please," he says again, handing me his glass of scotch. "My dad is coming here tonight, and he's . . . very particular so I just need you to be good. No, I need you to be perfect. Okay? Can you just be that? Please."

The pleading tone that he's speaking to me with is unsettling to say the least and does nothing to quell my anxiety. But I take a few sips of his drink to calm myself down. Everyone is safe here, I repeat to myself.

"Fine."

ANNICA IS AT the bottom of the staircase posing for pictures that Dani takes of her. There are a few more people gathered in the living room that I don't recognize. Asher points to a tall brunette standing with a slim, ginger-haired man.

"That's Wesley's sister Marceline and her husband, Adam. And over there"—he motions to a younger-looking girl with a blond balayage, similar to mine—"that's Charlotte, his other sister."

"Is your sister here?" I remember him saying he had one on Thanksgiving.

"No, Kara really doesn't come around much."

"Asher, my boy!" A stocky and already drunk man with rosy cheeks approaches us as we make our way into the dining room, with his arms out wide. The man puts an arm around Asher and roughs up his hair with the other. Asher smooths it back out, annoyed.

"Sloane, this is my dad. Dad, this is Sloane."

"Call me Ben." The man smiles, holding out a hand. I take it.

"Nice to meet you," I say with a smile.

"How did my son manage to get his hands on a girl like you?" Ben teases, hitting Asher on the arm.

Wes approaches from behind Ben, clapping a hand to his shoulder. "We're all wondering the same thing, Uncle Ben." I laugh nervously as Asher grinds his teeth together. I see his jaw working behind his tight-lipped smile.

"Asher, why don't you go play something on the piano while everyone mingles before dinner. You know your grandpa loves that," his dad says, and gives him a look, one I can't decipher. Asher looks between the three of us apprehensively before heading toward the piano in the corner of the dining room.

"So, Sloane." Ben puts an arm around me, steering me away from Wes. I glance at him from over my shoulder as we walk away, and Wes gives me a reassuring nod. "You're the first girl Asher has ever brought home. I wonder why that is. I was starting to think he wasn't even interested in girls." The thought almost makes me laugh. He is certainly interested in girls, lots of them. He's so interested in girls that he simply couldn't pick just one to bring here, is what I want to say. But I just laugh along. "What's your family like, Sloane?"

"My family? Good, they're good people."

"Do they have money?"

The question throws me off guard. "Um, kind of, I mean, my stepdad does. Not like this, though." I don't know what kind of answer I'm supposed to give. I just hope that's the right one.

"So you want my son for his money, then?"

I stop abruptly. "What?! No, I would never—" I shake my head furiously.

"I'm just kidding," Ben says. "But you can never be too sure. Ah, Charlotte, my favorite niece." Asher's dad turns to talk to Wesley's sister without a formal ending to this conversation, but I take it as my cue to walk away. Asher is at the piano playing a slow melody and I come to sit at the bench with him.

"Your dad just asked me if I'm a gold digger," I say.

"That's rich coming from him." He sighs. "Just try to stay away from him. He's no doubt here looking for handouts."

"This is the song you played me," I say, when I recognize the melody.

"'Clair de Lune,'" he says. "It was my mom's favorite."

"Oh, I—"

"Dinner is ready, everyone!" Wesley's mom calls out, stifling our conversation and the sound of the piano. Everyone starts to file into the dining room to sit at the long table in the center and we get up from the bench to join them. Each seat holds a red placemat, with more silverware than I would think needed for a dinner, around a gold-trimmed plate with a fancy folded napkin adorned with holly. I take a seat next to Asher, with Danielle on the other side of me, and Asher's dad directly across. He gives me a wink as he sits down and I look away immediately.

A man stands at the end of the table, looking almost identical to Asher's dad but shorter and thinner. I recognize him from Wesley's photos: It's his dad.

"It's so great that we could have almost all of our family here this weekend, along with some new friends. And what better time than the fiftieth-anniversary week of the resort being open. It warms my heart that in just a few short months it'll be in the hands of my son and the legacy will continue—"

"And Asher's," Ben interrupts.

Wesley's dad cuts a look to Ben, his brother. "Well, I mean, if Wes decides to take him on as an employee, then I guess so, but seeing as I've managed to handle it on my own, I don't see any reason—"

"It is a family business, John." Ben stops him again. "Let's not be so quick to cut out family."

"Dad," Asher says, shaking his head.

"Don't interrupt me."

"You just interrupted Uncle John twice," he says back, and I kick him under the table as the room grows quiet. Everyone sips their drinks with their eyes down, trying to wish away the tension.

"So you're taking his side?" Ben asks Asher.

John clears his throat. "There are no sides, Ben. Let's just enjoy this dinner, shall we? Wes, do you want to add anything?"

Asher looks at Wes now. "Yes, Wesley, is there anything you want to add? About the business, or just your plans for after college?"

Wes stands and clears his throat. "Yes, actually there is."

I suck in a breath. Is he really going to do this now? Asher is practically on the edge of his seat.

Wes raises his glass of wine. "I am . . ." He looks around the room and stops when he sees his father's proud face. "I am excited for what the future holds. Cheers! To family," he says. The rest of the table raises their now almost empty glasses. I glance over at Asher, who remains unmoving; he does not raise a glass, he does not say cheers. Servers come around with soup and salads and idle chatter continues on both sides of the table.

"Asher, see me in the study after dinner," his father says as he swirls around one of the large gold rings on his fingers. His tone reminds me of a teacher asking a student to stay after class. And not in a good way. More like a *you just failed a test* kind of way.

Asher just sighs. A few seats down I watch Wesley's mom look like she might say something but then decide not to. I look down the table to see Annica looking at me with eyes that say *See? Told you.*

The main course of ham, potatoes, and a vegetable medley is served while Jake and Charlie regale the table with a long tale about how they lost Wes on last year's spring break trip to Cancún, which I did not attend because I couldn't afford it, but the story sounds very similar to *The Hangover*. Wes buries his red face in his hands as everyone chuckles, his own grandpa nearly choking on his food for how hard he laughs. When it's quiet again, Wesley's brother-in-law brings up the one thing I was hoping wouldn't come up.

"So what's going on at your school and that kid that was stabbed? Did they catch the guy who did it?"

I choke on my wine and begin to cough. Dani pats my back.

"No, not yet," Wes answers. "I don't know if they ever will either. They can't even nail down who was all there."

Sam shoots Asher and me a pointed look.

"What a shame," his mother says.

"Yeah, Marissa is pretty close to the case because she's in that club, and she said they have like no leads," Wes says.

No leads still? Somehow that brings me relief.

"Speaking of Marissa," Marceline says. "Where is she? I was hoping to witness a proposal this weekend."

Now it's Wesley's turn to nearly choke on his drink. A proposal?

Was Wes planning on proposing? Our friend group is silent, staring at him anxiously, awaiting an answer.

"Proposal?" Wes says, eyes wide. "That's . . . I haven't even—"

"That's way down the line," his father finishes for him. "He has more important things to focus on right now, Marceline."

"Well, that's not what you told me when I was about to graduate." She cocks her head to the side.

John looks flustered now. "It's different for you," he says.

"Why?" she shoots back.

"Who wants dessert?" Wesley's mom stands before John can answer.

DESSERT IS SALTED caramel gelato with a side of Jake begging Asher to play "Bohemian Rhapsody" on the piano for him and Charlie to sing to. I almost don't think he will, but Asher gets up followed by all the boys now as they gather around and drunkenly belt out the entire Queen song, the whole room laughing even harder than they were at the story.

Annica, Dani, and I cheer them on, which leads to the boys taking requests. Asher can play anything they throw at him. It's incredible to watch, really, and unfortunately very attractive to see him get lost in the music. Occasionally he'll glance up at me and smirk, and I have to look away to keep from blushing.

When Vernon retires for the night, the party is over. Wesley's parents and sisters are leaving, and the group decides to get back into the hot tub. Everyone but Asher, who follows his dad down the hall and to the right, to the study. I tiptoe down the hall after Asher and his dad until I stand in front of a small alcove with two large double doors. One has been left open just a crack. I shouldn't be spying on him and his dad, but the way Ben looked at him during dinner put a bad feeling in my gut.

The two of them are smoking cigars, drinking what looks like scotch. Asher sits on a long blue velvet couch in front of a fireplace. I can't see Ben, but I can hear him talking from somewhere in the room.

"What the fuck was that?" Ben says tersely. "You said he didn't even want this place."

"I did say that," Asher says casually.

"Is this a game to you? This is our inheritance."

"*My* inheritance," Asher corrects him.

Ben comes into view now behind Asher on the couch and drives the hot end of the cigar into Asher's neck. My hand flies up over my mouth.

"What the fuck." Asher swats the cigar away and it springs from Ben's hand onto the carpet.

"Great, now look what you did," Ben says, picking it back up. "The carpet is burned."

"Yeah, fuck my neck, right?" Asher stands and sets down his glass.

"You are going to find a way to get this business from your cousin, or so help me, god," his father threatens him with a pointed finger in his chest, before picking up Asher's glass and downing the rest of it. "If there's one thing my brother is right about it's that you two need to be less focused on your slut girlfriends and more focused on your futures."

"Don't fucking call her that," Asher spits back, and seems to brace himself for what he knows is coming next. Ben moves quickly and backhands him hard across the mouth, then grabs him by the collar, saying something inches from his face that I can't hear. His dad lets him go and tells him to get out of his sight. Asher strides toward the doors, and I don't leave quick enough, still frozen in shock.

"Enjoy the show?" he says as he brushes past me. I open my mouth to say something, but what is there to say? I follow down the hall as he trudges up the stairs and slams the door to our room. I can hear Dani laughing from outside in the hot tub where our friends are and I wonder if I should just go back out in my dress. But something nags me to follow him.

Asher is on the love seat in front of the fireplace in the bedroom, a new full glass of scotch in hand, looking just as he did in the study, but now with a bloody lip and burn mark on his neck. His hair is ruffled like he's been running his hands through it and his blazer is tossed on the ground, leaving just the white buttondown, wrinkled and stretched from where his dad grabbed him. He looks defeated and broken.

I shut the door behind me, but he doesn't look at me, and I don't know what to say. I slip off my heels and make my way to the couch, where I sit on the stone floor in front of him. He still doesn't look at me, just straight into the fire watching the flames crack and burn, so I lightly place a hand to his knee, and then rest my head against his thigh. I look up at him, and he looks away.

"Asher—" I start.

"Don't," he says, taking a sip of the auburn liquid in the glass.

So I don't.

We sit like that for a while until I get up to join him on the couch, sitting with one leg tucked in so I can face him. From this side I can see the small burn blister forming on his neck.

"Is he always like that?" I whisper to him.

He doesn't say anything, just stares unblinking into the flames.

Everything in me is saying to comfort him, but I don't know how. I think of Thanksgiving in his bedroom as I scoot closer to him, leaning in slow and gently pressing my lips to the burn. I wait for him to push me away, but he doesn't, he just sighs. So I press another light kiss to the side of his mouth, where his lip is cut. He still doesn't turn toward me, so I put a gentle finger to the other side of his jaw to turn him to me. He goes along with it. The look in his eyes breaks my heart a million times over and I want him to say something rude, I want him to give me that know-it-all smirk. Be an asshole, I think. Make a snide comment. Just don't be this.

I test the boundaries further when I lean in and bring my lips to his, soft, the way he kissed me in his bedroom. He lets me do it, but he doesn't kiss me back. Not at first. I hear him set his glass down on the side table, before he brings up both hands to wrap around my waist and pull me to him. And I guess I could blame this on alcohol. I could blame it on circumstance. Anything other than the truth.

Asher kisses me back now, like he did in the hot tub. Deeply, passionately. He leans back onto the couch and I crawl on top and swing one leg over him to grind my hips into his, eliciting an immediate reaction from him. He slides his hand up my backside, lifting the dress, as his other hand unties the silky fabric from around my neck. The dress falls down the front of me, exposing my chest. Asher kisses down my jaw and neck as I unbutton his shirt in a frenzy.

"This is wrong, isn't it," he says in between kisses.

"Yes," I breathe, but I hardly know what I'm agreeing to, and the yes sounds more like a moan. I think he likes the way it sounds because he lays me down, continuing the trail of his lips along my skin. His fingers trace my inner thigh, moving dangerously up, and I arch my back in a silent answer.

His breath is hot on my skin when he says, "We shouldn't be doing this."

"We—" But I don't finish the sentence as his mouth moves over my nipple and his fingers are pushing my underwear to the side. I suck in a breath. "We . . ." I try again but I don't even know what I'm saying. What did he say? Why are we even talking?

When he runs a finger through me I'm on fire and I hear him curse under his breath. He starts for the buttons on his pants and says again, "We shouldn't be doing this."

"Yes," I breathe again, because that's all I can manage in this state.

He stops moving. "Yes, we shouldn't be doing this?"

The sound of his voice, no longer heady but clearer, makes me focus. "No." I shake my head, trying to think of what the right answer to that question is.

"No?" He sits back and looks around like he just woke up from a dream.

"Wait," I say, sitting up too, but he's already moving to get up off the couch. I reach for him. "Asher—"

He catches me by the wrists. "No, I don't want your pity fuck or whatever this is." He gets up, his shirt now completely unbuttoned, showing his bare chest.

"It's not that at all. I—"

He grabs his jacket from the floor. "I have to go." To the resort. He doesn't have to say it; I already know.

"Asher, wait!" But he's already gone.

I feel a cold chill wash over me as a slight headache begins to form in my temple. What the *fuck* was that, Sloane. I put my head in my hands, trying to breathe, but with him gone, all the thoughts of Miles and murder drift back and the room begins to feel like it's closing in on me. I can feel my hands become wet with tears and I can't take another night in here alone. Before I know it I'm down the hall, knocking on the door.

"Sloane?" Wes says when he opens his bedroom door. His green eyes take in my tearstained cheeks and red running nose. "What's wrong?"

"Can I stay in here with you tonight?"

THERE ARE TWO knocks on the door in the morning, followed by Annica's voice. "Wes, your mom wants to know what time our flight is today." She lets herself in and I don't even have time to hide under the covers before she spots me and stops in the doorway. "Oh."

I jump up quickly, still in Wesley's T-shirt and no pants. "Annica," I start.

"You have got to be fucking kidding me," she says in a low voice.

"It's not what it looks like," I say, because it's not. Wes gave me one of his oversized shirts and let me cry until we fell asleep. But Annica is not in the mood for an explanation. She goes to turn around. "Annica, wait!" I follow her into the hall. "Nothing even happened!"

She whirls around to me. "You're in his bed, wearing his shirt, with no pants on. How could you even continue lying to my face right now?"

"Annica, seriously, nothing happened," Wes says, coming out into the hall after us.

Annica narrows her eyes, looking between the two of us before landing on me, and there's realization there. "You're the girl, aren't you?"

I shake my head, confused. "What?"

Dani and Jake have come out of their rooms now to see what's going on.

"The girl! The one him and Marissa are always fighting about, the one he slept with last summer. It's you, isn't it? And don't even fucking lie."

"Annica," Dani says, trying to calm her down.

Annica shakes her off, still looking at me. "Answer!"

"I—" I look around to the rest of our friends now gathered in the hall. "It was an accident. It was just one time."

Dani's mouth falls open as I hear one of the boys let out a low whistle.

"An accident? What, did you trip and fall into his bed, Sloane, what the fuck? How could you keep this from us, and then lie right to my face about it on Halloween!" Annica fumes. Asher groggily comes from his room to see what the commotion is, his split lip bruising over now. "Ah, perfect timing, here's your cheating boyfriend! I guess you two have that in common at least. Asher, do you not even care that she's sleeping with Wes?"

Asher only shrugs.

"Oh my god, *what* is going on in this group?" Annica throws her hands up, defeated.

I try to reach for her. "Annica, I'm sorry, okay—"

"No, don't touch me. We are not friends. Friends don't lie."

She turns on her heel and strides for her room, slamming the door. Dani gives me a sad smile, touching my arm, before following Annica to their room. I let out a long, shaky breath, trying to process what just happened. Asher turns to go back to the bedroom, and Wes grabs my hand, but I pull away, intent on going after Asher.

"This is all your fault," I say, storming after him.

He turns when we get into the room. "My fault?"

"Yes! I never would've gone in there last night if you would've just stayed here! Why couldn't you just stay here?"

He shakes his head. "Because this"—he motions between the two of us—"isn't the plan. We can't . . . be that way and I just . . . I needed to get out of here. I needed—"

"What, what is it that you needed?" I bite out.

"Someone else," he says quietly.

My arms go slack at my sides and my voice cracks. "Well, I needed *you*, Asher. My life is falling apart and you are the only person who knows it. I needed you." I can feel the tears streaming from my cheeks again as I so desperately cry over him, of all people.

He looks away like he doesn't want to watch me cry. "This is all going to work out, Sloane. Whatever just happened out there was for the best. Okay? Wes will probably have to break up with Marissa after this, we'll call off our fake thing too, and you'll have Wes. You want Wes, remember? You want Wes." I can't tell if he is trying to remind me or himself, as he keeps repeating it.

"I'm glad you have this all sorted out," I say bitterly through my tears.

"You saw what happens to me if I don't."

I clench my jaw and I think about his teary green eyes last night. And it all makes sense to me now. The way he is, and why he does the things he does. The way Wes is always watching him when he's near me. I thought it was jealousy but now I think it was partially out of fear that Asher would turn out to be like Ben. And god, I want to hate Asher so badly still, but I just can't.

I take a moment to calm down. "I will help you get what you want, but we can't do this anymore. I don't want your help and I don't want to be your fake girlfriend anymore."

"Fine," he says.

"Fine."

CHAPTER 22

January

January 2 comes faster than I expect, and I haven't heard from Miles since I suspected he was in Colorado when we were. I say goodbye to my family after being there all winter break, and hug Claire extra tight before packing up my car. It's a three-hour drive from Cedar Falls to Boston, where the art show will be held.

I've decided I am going to end this with Holland. This time I won't back out like I did twice before.

I know Asher prepaid for the hotel room downtown and can't get a refund if we cancel: He told me so when he booked it last month. Back when we planned to do this together. So when I get to the check-in counter I'm not surprised by how easy it is. That and the fact that the girl at the counter looks to be eighteen and too into the book she's reading to care about her job. She hands me the key for room 317 without asking for an ID or even a card for a security deposit. All she says is that they had to change the room to a single king suite and they'd refund the difference to the card on file. Not that it matters now that I'm doing this solo. I take my duffel bag and go to the third floor.

In the middle of my shower, a loud noise from the hotel room makes me pause. I shut the water off and remain still, listening. What if it's Holland? What if he tracked me here and now I'm alone in this room, with no one to help me? Another noise makes me jump. There's definitely someone out there. I slowly get out of the shower, wrapping a towel around me and securing it tight before grabbing the hotel-supplied hair dryer under the sink. It's better than nothing, I guess. Tiptoeing from the bathroom, I open the door slightly, holding the dryer above my head, ready to strike the intruder.

"I thought that was your bag on the bed," Asher says, standing in the middle of the room. I let out the breath I was holding, and the hair dryer falls to my side. "Were you . . . going to hit me with that?" He laughs.

"I thought you were Miles! What are you even doing here? I told you I don't want your help." I cross my arms to keep the towel up.

"I had a feeling you'd come here anyway and I came to make sure you don't do something stupid."

I can see his split lip has almost fully healed and the burn on his neck is now barely more than a faint pink mark. I want to tell him that I'm more likely to do something stupid with him here. His eyes make a trail down my body, wrapped in the towel, and I might as well be standing here naked.

"You have to leave," I tell him.

"I paid for this room, Sawyer. I'm not leaving. You can leave."

"That's not an option."

"Then I guess we're doing this together." He gives me a wry smile.

"Fine."

"Fine."

"But you're sleeping on the couch," I add.

"Already planned on it." He tosses his bag on the white pull-out couch and turns back to me. "Anything else, princess?"

I roll my eyes and stalk back into the bathroom to finish washing my hair. What the hell does he think he's doing coming here after what happened in Vail? I had planned to continue on the way we originally started, which is me pretending he doesn't exist and focusing on Wesley. But seeing his stupid face again makes me feel weird in ways I can't explain.

I dry my hair and dress in another black cocktail dress. When I come back out, he's dressed in a beige sweater and brown slacks. He looks . . . good. Dammit, he looks really good.

"Have you been talking to Wes?" he asks as he puts on his coat.

"Yes, he called a few times over break to see how I was doing." Something you didn't bother to do, I want to add. I bend down, trying to clasp my heels, but the dress is tight, and I struggle.

"Here," he says. "I'll get it." He bends down before me to clasp my heels, and I don't object. "What about your friends?"

"Annica isn't speaking to me," I say. She has blocked me actually. None of my calls and texts will go through to her. Dani says to give her time, and that she's just hurt over the lie, but knowing Annica, there is no amount of time that will fix what I did in her eyes. And as far as the lying goes, Wes and I hooking up is only the tip of the iceberg. If they knew the full extent of what I wasn't telling them, they would both block me.

Asher's hands brush over my ankles and he seems to linger down there a moment too long. "We need boundaries," I blurt out.

"Boundaries?" He stands and looks down at me now.

"Yes, no more touching or kissing or—"

"Licking or sucking," he finishes for me with a smirk.

"Asher," I warn, because he's not taking this seriously.

"I'm just teasing," he says, but we're still close enough that I can smell his cologne and it makes my heart beat faster.

"Whatever happened that night in Vail was just . . . an accident. We both had too much to drink and there's a lot at stake here." That's the lie I've been repeating to myself all December. But I need to hear it. I need the reminder. Because if Asher and I go all the way, I'm afraid there will be no going back.

Asher puts on his peacoat and picks up mine, holding it out for me to put my arms into. I step into it, and he leans into my ear from behind.

"I'll be on my best behavior." It sends chills down my arms.

I turn toward him so we're face-to-face. "Good."

"Great."

It's a twenty-minute taxi ride to the gallery. I squirm uncomfortably in my tight dress and take deep breaths in the back of the car. When the Uber stops in front of a square glass-paneled building, I step out and into a crowd. Graham managed to get a large gathering of people to come to this opening. It's no surprise; he was quite good in college. I'm sure he's only gotten better. We file in when they open the doors, and I'm already looking around for Miles.

Servers come around with champagne and I take two, downing one on the spot.

"Because that'll help," Asher mutters behind me, taking one for himself.

It doesn't take long, not long at all, as I spot Professor Miles Holland standing on the opposite side of the gallery. I stop abruptly, causing Asher to run into me and spill his champagne on himself. "Dammit, Sloane."

I spare only a second to glance back at him, but that is enough to lose sight of Miles. When I turn back around, he's gone.

"Sloane?" I look to my left to see Ty and Austin.

"Ty?" She looks like she belongs in an art gallery in her chic black plunging blazer and slacks with a small YSL bag slung over her shoulder. I hug her, and then Austin, who is also dressed the part of a patron of the arts. "What are you guys doing here?"

"We're here with this guy that Austin is seeing—oh, you *have* to meet him, he's dreamy." Ty clings on to my arm as she says it, nearly pressing her face to mine, never one for personal boundaries. "What are you doing here?"

"Oh, I'm here for, um . . ." Trying to come up with something that doesn't involve Graham or Holland.

"She's here indulging me and my love for art," Asher interrupts. Ty and Austin both look at him and Ty's smile widens.

"The situationship, I take it." She holds out a hand and he takes it. That's what I had told her he was that night we went out for drunk bingo. My situationship.

"The one and only," he says with a smirk.

But I'm standing there trying to comprehend the fact that here we all are, at the same gallery opening in Boston, with a murderer.

"Excuse me, I have to use the bathroom." I leave Asher there to answer the million questions that Ty and Austin will probably be asking right about now, the perfect distraction to get away from Asher and do what I came here to do.

I push through the crowd looking for Miles and grab another champagne flute from a tray, not bothering to even glance at the artwork on the walls. Graham is a realism painter, down to the very last detail. It's impressive, as long as you're not the subject. I make my way around one of the freestanding walls in the middle of the floor and nearly run into a man in forest-green corduroys and a navy coat. He looks at me with wide eyes behind gold-rimmed glasses.

"Holland," I say. And I'm not scared anymore. Not now, when we're in a crowded room and I've had three glasses of champagne in thirty minutes.

He takes his hands from his navy coat pockets like he wants to hug me, but pauses, knowing better. "Sloane, what are you doing here?"

"I need to talk to you."

Miles looks around, like he's looking for someone else. "I've been trying to talk to you for months, and you choose now? This . . . isn't a good time."

I ignore him, continuing like I rehearsed in my head. "I know what you're doing, and it needs to stop."

His eyebrows rise. "You know?"

I can't hide the shock on my face at his admittance. I mean, that's what that was, right? Am I recording on my phone? Shit,

I'm not recording on my phone! I dig through my purse for it as I continue. "Why are you doing it? Revenge? Are you really that pissed at me that you want to ruin my life?"

"Well, I wanted to ask your permission first. I'm not trying to ruin your life."

"My *permission*? You wanted to ask me first if you could *murder* all of my exes?"

His brows knit together at my accusation. "What?"

"I've already told the police about you, so you might as well turn yourself in, Miles. I won't let you get to Graham."

"I don't know what you're talking about, Sloane. Have you been drinking?"

"I know you have pictures of my journal in your closet. Who else would be doing all of this?" I throw my hands up in aggravation.

He shakes his head, provoked. "That was *you* who broke into my house?"

"I mean, how didn't you realize? You emailed me that you can recognize my perfume anywhere, didn't you?"

I feel someone come up behind me. "Ah, the Professor," Asher says.

Miles looks between us before saying to me, "How about we discuss this in private when you're thinking straight."

"Miles, you should—" A familiar female voice trails off as she rounds the corner. "Sloane?"

I cross my arms and give her a *caught you* smile. "Adrienne. Where's Paul?" I ask her.

"I—I was going to tell you after winter break," she stammers out.

"Let's leave." Miles puts his arm to her waist to lead her out. I try to grab onto his jacket but Asher catches my hand.

"You won't get away with it, any of it!" People turn to look at me, the crazy girl yelling in a gallery. "They're leaving—we need to follow him," I say to Asher.

"No." Asher hangs on to my wrist. "What did he say?"

"He . . ." But the conversation begins to float out of my mind like ashes from a fire. I try to grab onto the pieces. "I think he admitted to it, but then he was confused. And wanted my permission for something. Oh my god," I say. "I think he was talking about permission to date Adrienne."

"So . . . he wasn't talking about the murders?" Asher asks.

"I—I don't think so but it happened so fast. I did tell him the police are onto him."

"Let's hope that's enough for him to leave Graham alone until we can get a solid confession." I let out a long, shaky breath, feeling a headache coming on as the adrenaline leaves my system. Now also very unsure about whether or not Miles is the one behind it all. "Speaking of Graham," Asher says. "You're never going to guess who his guest is tonight." He ushers me around the wall and back into the crowd toward Ty, Austin, and . . . Graham.

"Sloane!" Austin waves us over. "This is the guy I'm seeing, Graham. This is his opening."

My mouth drops open as I take in Graham and Austin side by side. Graham's eyes widen when he sees me, just like Holland's. Surprises all around. He opens his mouth but I stick out my hand before he can say anything.

"Sloane Sawyer," I introduce myself. My hand is still shaking from my encounter with Miles.

Graham catches on and takes my hand. "Graham Monterra. It's nice to meet you."

"Your work is . . ." I look around, trying to find a word, any word. Just pick a word, Sloane. "Good." Good? I want to be a writer and the best I can come up with is *good*.

"You think so? Thanks. Someone once told me it was a collection of half-assed trash that would fail to evoke emotion from even the simplest of creatures and looks to be painted with all the sophistication of a toothbrush."

Now *that* was the best I could come up with. I'm surprised he remembers it word for word.

Austin's face scrunches up in disgust. "What raggedy jealous bitch said that to you?"

Graham only looks at me and I'm preparing to be outed for my words. "I can't remember," he says. "But at the time I think I deserved it. And I never got to tell that person that I was sorry."

I blink at him. "I'm sure whoever it was . . . would say that all is forgiven."

Graham gives a nod of understanding before someone is pulling him away for a sale. Ty and Austin go to the bar and Asher puts a well-placed hand on my waist to steer me away. I remove his hand.

"Boundaries," I remind him.

We walk around the gallery and my head spins with not only the conversation with Miles but the one with Graham.

"So how does it feel?" Asher asks.

But I don't know what he's referencing at this point. So I ask, "How does what feel?"

"Graham's into men now," he says. "Do you think it was sex with you that made him switch sides?"

I swat his arm, hard. "He's always been bi, you jerk."

Asher laughs. "So what happened, then? How did he end up in your journal?"

"You remember that big bonfire we had at the end of sophomore year?"

"Yeah . . ."

"We were burning one of his paintings."

Asher frowns. "Painting of what?"

"For Graham's senior show he showcased the human form. The naked human form. Mine and many others. Out on display for all to see."

Asher nearly chokes on his champagne. "You're telling me there was a painting of you naked and we burned it?"

"Yep. You couldn't see my face, but I knew it was me. I totally freaked out at the show. I didn't have enough money to buy it so I called Annica and Dani, and then Wes. The four of us scrounged up enough and I took it home that night and we lit it on fire."

"Huh," he says, considering. "What a shame. I bet that would be worth a lot of money someday."

"Well, it's not about the money; it's about my dignity," I say. "My virtue."

"Because you have plenty of that," he murmurs.

I resist the urge to hit him again. "Imagine someone taking a naked picture of you and posting it everywhere. How would that feel?"

"Feels like I'd become very popular." He smirks, and I get a flutter in my lower stomach at the thought of him naked.

"Well, I didn't like it. Not to mention there were like twenty other naked bodies in his opening, so I wasn't even special." I shake my head at the thought. I've never felt more exposed or embarrassed in my life. Which is saying a lot after dating Bryce.

"Hey, lovebirds." Ty comes up, interrupting. "We're all invited to Graham's after-party when the opening is over. I think me and Austin are going to leave now to grab a bite and freshen up, maybe change into something else. Want to come?"

I hesitantly look over at Asher. Miles is gone, but who's to say he won't come back? Though I guess there's not much he can do in a gallery full of people, and if he was smart he'd be hightailing it back to Ivy Gate right now.

"Okay," I say. "Yeah."

We pile into an Uber with Ty, Austin, and Graham's brother.

"This is Laken. He's catching a ride with us," Austin says. When the car pulls up Laken sits up front, which leaves us four for the back.

"And you didn't call an XL?" I ask.

"Just sit on your boyfriend's lap." Austin waves a hand like it's no big deal. Which for any other real couple it wouldn't be.

Asher puts me on his lap and I do my best to sit upright to not touch him any more than I have to, but in the city traffic, the car feels like it's not even moving. I give in and lean my back and head against his chest, and I hear him take in a long breath like he's savoring the scent of me. His hands around my waist tighten and I know we're both thinking of the hot tub and that damn Nervous game.

I debate asking Ty where she's staying tonight and if I can join her, but the way she and Graham's brother are getting on I feel she may already have someone sharing her bed.

We stop at a pizza place for an hour or so to eat.

"Where are you guys staying?" Ty asks me.

"The Four Seasons," I reply.

"Rub it in, why don't you," Austin says. "We're cramming four people into Graham's studio apartment. His stove is next to his bed. When he cooked for us this morning the bacon grease was literally hitting me in the face. It just wasn't what I meant when I said I wanted breakfast in bed."

"We have room for two more," I offer.

"No we don't," Asher says, giving me a look. I know that look.

"We do," I say again.

"I'm not opposed," Ty says. "We can stop at Graham's to change and go to the hotel to freshen up and pregame."

I smile. "Great idea."

Ty WHISTLES AT the room. "You're right, I think we could all fit in here. And then some." She heads for the bathroom and Austin goes to the minibar.

"Do you think they charge for this stuff?" Austin asks, opening the vodka.

Asher opens his mouth to say yes but only purses his lips and sighs. I go into the bedroom and Asher follows me in with his bag.

"I need to change," I say.

He digs through his bag and looks up at me. "Okay?"

"Boundaries, Asher, boundaries," I remind him again as I sit at the end of the bed trying to get the clasp of the heels. I hear Ty yell out that the Uber will be here in seven minutes. So much for a pregame, I think as I struggle with the heels. Asher comes around the bed with a sigh and kneels on the floor before me, working on the shoe.

Ty then yells out that they're going to the lobby.

Asher gets the first heel off, then works on unclasping the other. In my head this is romantic. In my head he takes his time. He slides off the heel, but his other hand stays on my leg, and his mouth presses slow kisses all the way up my leg until—

"What?" he asks, breaking me from the daydream, and I realize I am staring down at him.

"What? Nothing. Let's . . . We need to hurry." I stand, reaching up the back of the dress, trying to get at the zipper. "I can't get this."

"How do you manage to undress yourself when no one is around?" he says sarcastically as I turn around so he can get it. "It's stuck." He yanks on the unmoving zipper.

"Pull harder."

He gives it one hard pull and I hear a pop as the zipper breaks. "Well . . ." He trails off.

"Okay, no problem, I'll just . . . pull it up, then." I grab at the bottom hem and start to pull it up but it's tight and I realize halfway up that I can't get it over my chest and head without help. "Go get Ty," I say uncomfortably.

"She's probably in the Uber by now. I'll just do it," he says.

"I don't want you to do it," I argue back, because I don't have a bra on under this tight dress that I feel like I'm now suffocating in.

Asher stands back and crosses his arms. "I'm not calling her for this."

"Then I just won't go." I attempt to throw up my arms, but they're already stuck in an upward motion. He tries to hold back a laugh because we both know if he doesn't help me then I'm stuck like this.

"Stubborn," he mutters.

"Fine, just . . . make it quick. And don't look." I put my arms up straight so he can pull it the rest of the way over my head. He rips the dress from me, up and over my head in one swift move. I lose my balance, grabbing onto him for support, and he catches me around my bare back. He looks down and I bring up my other arm to cover my chest. His eyes darken and I suck in a breath.

In my head he kisses me then, and it takes me by surprise—but no, this isn't in my head, this is happening. He lets go of me, breaking the kiss, and grabs my phone from the bed, tossing it at me.

"Tell your friend we're not going."

"What?" I say, a little breathless. He doesn't need to repeat himself as he takes off his sweater. I fumble with my phone, texting Ty to head there without us and we'll meet them.

Asher kneels down in front of me again, digging his fingers into the waistline of my tights and rolling them down slowly. Ty only sends me back a winky face as Asher starts kissing up my thighs.

"Boundaries," I breathe, saying it more to myself than him.

"Then tell me to stop," he says, looking up at me. But *stop* suddenly feels like a word I never learned. I wouldn't know how to pronounce it if I tried. He takes my silence for what it is and stands again, starting to unbuckle his pants, staring at me. "I don't know what you've done to me." He takes the belt off, tossing it on the ground. "But I can't stop thinking about you. When I'm with another girl, I'm wishing they were you. I can't focus, I can barely sleep." His pants are off and I can see his erection bulging through his boxers and I'm practically panting. "And I don't even know why," he continues, "because all we do is fucking fight."

He backs me up to the bed before lifting me up and laying me down. He kisses me, hard, and my hips instinctively move up to meet his. I slide a hand down to palm him through his boxers and he moans in my mouth. He kisses down my body, his fingers roaming around my inner thighs, until he reaches my chest. He bites down on my nipple as he slides a finger through me, earning a cry from me at the mix of pleasure and pain, and I think I may be way in over my head with him. His mouth continues down, down, down, until his tongue replaces his fingers and he makes a noise like he's drinking water for the first time after being lost in the desert.

It doesn't take me long, not long at all, when his tongue is flicking over that sensitive bundle of nerves at my core. I see stars and I say his name over and over, as the orgasm rips through me. He doesn't let up until I go thoroughly limp beneath him. He crawls back up and I pull his mouth to mine. When we roll over so that he's on his back, he flinches.

"Ow, fuck," Asher curses, and sits upright, holding me on his lap. He pulls back the covers and there in the middle of the bed is a small black gun. We both stare at it, our breaths rising and falling in tandem. "Did you bring a gun here?" he says finally, bedroom eyes replaced with concern.

"No, did you?"

"No."

I suck in a breath. Graham.

CHAPTER 23

"We have to go back to the gallery." I spring off of him and start digging for clothes.

"Fuck," Asher hisses, getting off the bed. He puts on a hoodie and sweatpants and I shimmy into leggings and a T-shirt before grabbing my coat.

I try to get a hold of Ty and Austin during the taxi ride to the gallery, hoping and praying Graham made it to his after-party. But neither of them picks up.

Asher and I are dropped off at the front and I run to the entrance. Finding the doors unlocked, I push my way in, Asher behind me.

"Graham?" I call out for him. "Graham?"

There's no reply.

We walk through the empty gallery until I notice what looks like a hand from behind one of the freestanding walls. "Graham?" I run toward it and gasp with horror at the sight. Graham is slumped against the white wall, now splattered with blood, with a bullet hole in his chest. "No, no, no, no—" I kneel in front of him.

"Sloane." Asher tries to grab onto me but it's too late.

"Graham!" I pull him to me, trying to feel for a pulse. "Graham!" I yell again, and I might be crying now, I might be, but all I can focus on is the blood. It seeps from his shirt and his mouth. Graham gives a small raspy breath. "Oh my god, oh my god. Asher, call 911!"

"Sloane," he warns, his eyes trailing up to the painting above us, with my journal entry taped over top. The one for Graham.

"Call them! I don't care how this looks, call them! Just call someone!"

Asher pulls his phone from his coat pocket and dials 911.

"Graham, can you hear me? The ambulance is coming, help is coming." I rock back and forth, keeping my fingers on his wound as more blood leaks from his mouth and onto me. Asher walks around us. He talks to me but I don't hear it. I only hear Graham's labored breaths and the sirens getting louder and louder as they approach the gallery.

"Sloane," Asher warns again. "We need to leave now."

"He's still alive," I say. "He's still alive." I hold on to Graham like he'll die instantly if I let him go. But Asher begins to pry my hands from his body. Red lights flash throughout the gallery and Graham once again leans on the wall as Asher pulls me away.

"They're here," he says. "They'll take it from here." Asher hauls me up from the floor, ushering me to the back of the gallery and out the exit. The frigid January air is like a shock to my system as I breathe in frantic breaths, each one burning my throat and nose. We come out onto another street and Asher goes to call an Uber.

"No." I grab his phone from him and take off down the street to circle the building. I need to know what's happening. I run two buildings down before turning the corner onto the main street where the front of the gallery faces. There are two cop cars and an ambulance parked in front.

Asher comes up behind me and snatches his phone back. "Are you crazy? You are covered in his blood. We need to go."

When the stretcher gets rolled out the front door and toward the ambulance I expect to see Graham with an oxygen mask over his face, but instead it's a body bag. A sound somewhere between a choke and a sob escapes me as I turn and bury my face into Asher's hoodie.

Graham didn't make it. We were too late.

Asher takes off my coat and swaps it for his hoodie, tugging it over my head and telling me to keep my arms inside. The ones covered in blood. He grabs a taxi to take us back to the hotel and we don't speak on the way there.

In the hotel lobby, the same girl sits at the front desk reading her book.

"Excuse me," Asher says to her. She doesn't even look up. "Excuse me," he says louder.

She looks up and smiles at him. "Hi, sorry, how can I help you?"

"We're in room 317, and we were out for a while tonight. When we came back there was something left in our room. Did anyone go into the room while we were gone? Cleaning crew or . . . ?"

"Room 317? Oh, yeah, actually. A woman came in and said she was staying in the room, so I gave her a key."

"You what?" he says through clenched teeth.

"Yeah, I wrote down her name. Where is it . . . ?" She looks around the desk. "Oh, here. Uh, Kate Holland?"

Kate Holland.

"His ex-wife," I say, feeling like an idiot. Because this whole time I was so intent on Miles being the main suspect that I never even considered Kate. Kate has a motive, and probably hates me even more than all my suspects combined.

"There is no one else staying in the room," he snaps at her. "I should have you fired." The girl looks terrified then. "You're going to get us into a new room, immediately, now that a psychopath has our fucking room key, do you hear me?"

"Y-yes." She scrambles around the desk, checking availability. "I can move you to the fourth floor right now. I'll send someone for your bags—"

"No," Asher cuts her off. "We'll grab our own bags. Just give me the new room key."

She hands us the key to 408. "I—I'm sorry, she said your names and knew the room number. I just thought—"

Asher only huffs in irritation, pushing me along to the elevator.

"Kate Holland," I whisper, shaking my head.

We get into the room and I take off the hoodie, once again staring at the blood on my hands. It's my fault. It's my fault he's dead.

Asher puts the new key in my hand. "Go to the new room. I'll grab our stuff."

"What about the gun on the bed?"

"I'll wrap it in a towel and bring it with us."

"Bring it with us?!"

"I can't leave it in here!" He runs a hand through his hair, frustrated. "Go to the room."

I do what he says, mindlessly walking to room 408. I get into the elevator with another couple. They move close to the wall when they see me. Asher comes into the room a few minutes later and puts the towel with the gun on the table. And we stand there staring at it.

"We should've done something," I whisper.

"What could we have done?"

"The past two months we carried on like this wasn't happening: We stopped digging. We could've figured this out sooner but we went on that stupid fucking ski trip and now Graham is dead." Asher doesn't say anything, either because he thinks I'm right or because he's tired of arguing with me. The handgun sits unmoving on the table and it's hard to imagine something so small causing so much pain.

"I didn't have time to take the eulogy," he says after a while.

"Good," I reply, and head toward the bathroom, where I sit under the hot shower water watching streaks of red snake down the white porcelain tub. Even after I scrub my hands clean I still see Graham's blood everywhere.

ASHER IS ON the couch with a pillow and blanket when I finally come out of the shower. I go into the bedroom to put on the other oversized T-shirt I brought for bed. Thank god for overpacking. I don't text Ty or Austin about tonight. I wonder if they've heard by now. If they're still out with Laken, I'd imagine they have.

The bed is big and cold and I toss and turn in it, saying their names again, adding the newest addition. Jonah, Ryan, Marco, Bryce, Graham. Jonah, Ryan, Marco, Bryce, Graham. I sit up, looking out toward the couch.

"Asher?" I say into the darkness.

He's quiet for a moment and I think he may have fallen asleep already, but then he replies, "Yeah?"

"Will you sleep in the bed with me?"

"Yeah." I hear him move around on the couch, and the sound of his footsteps as he comes into the room. The bed moves and the familiar, now comforting scent of cinnamon and pine fills the space between us. "Are you . . . okay?" he asks after a while.

My face crumples but he won't see it in the dark. "No." And I've come to expect that every time I cry in front of him, he only awkwardly stands at a distance and waits for it to be over. So when he reaches out a hand to hold mine, I let him.

I OPEN MY eyes early Sunday morning and Asher's face is the first thing I see. I watch him sleep while his eyes flutter under long lashes, and I count the faded freckles over the bridge of his nose. I hope he's dreaming of something nice, something better than this. I carefully remove myself from the bed, slipping on my jeans and sweater from when I got here yesterday. I grab my duffel bag and put in the towel holding the gun, before I leave the hotel and drive straight to the Boston Police Department.

I look up at the tall brick-and-concrete building before me with "Boston Police Department" in big gray letters above the double doors. It's busy inside for a Sunday, but I suppose crime doesn't stop for the weekends. I walk up to a woman at the front desk who is stirring cream into a cup of coffee.

"Hi," I say nervously.

"How can I help you?" she asks, pouring in sugar next.

"I'm looking for Detective Grange," I say. "I'd like to speak with him. It's . . . important."

The woman still doesn't look up at me. "He's got a busy morning," she says.

"I have information on a murder," I blurt out, and she finally looks up from her coffee at me and clears her throat.

"Okay," she says. "I'll take you to his office." I adjust the duffel bag on my shoulder and follow her back through the station, past police officers chatting and drinking their morning coffees. The woman knocks on the door of Grange's office.

"Come in," that deep, comforting voice calls from behind the door. She opens the door and ushers me in. Grange looks up at me with a flicker of surprise. "Miss Sawyer, it seems I don't need to make the trip to Pembroke after all."

"Hi," I say, taking a seat in front of his desk. "I take it you were wanting to talk to me about last night?"

"And I take it you're here to tell me about it?"

I take a deep breath. "I'm here because I'm being framed for murder."

CHAPTER 24

"You are being framed for murder?" Grange repeats back to me.

"A few of them actually." I fidget in my seat and nervously pick at my nails. He raises an eyebrow in question. "The eulogy you found on Ryan . . . it wasn't the only one. There's a journal full of them. Someone is killing the boys in the journal and leaving the pages."

He doesn't hesitate as he slides over a bag that was sitting on the end of the desk. I hadn't even noticed it. Inside the bag is my journal page left at the gallery. It was taped over the painting above him, splattered red. I skim over the parts not covered in blood.

We are gathered here to remember Graham, which is coinci-dentally how much weed he smoked almost daily, who lived his life like his art: shitty and devoid of real human emotion. Imagine someone studying every inch of you, from the curve of your smile to the color of your bare skin. Now imagine them putting it all on a canvas and hanging it in a campus gallery like the Louvre but with nudes. Seriously, how was that even allowed—I feel like I need to speak with someone at the uni-

versity about this? Anyways, never listen to a man who calls you his muse, or considers watching cartoons high all day part of the "creative process." Graham, if you're with us now, just know I burned your stupid painting and I hope you used the money we paid for it to buy yourself some real talent. Though I know you spent it on drugs. You may be gone, but your memory, much like that painting, will haunt me literally forever.

I stop reading, holding back a fresh sob.

"Yeah," I breathe. "I wrote that."

"I assume you have more of an explanation for me this time?"

"I do."

Grange pulls out a pen, paper, and what looks like a recording device. "Let's start at the beginning, then, shall we?"

I START WITH Jonah, and how he was the first journal entry death I ever wrote, but that he died in a car accident, and I never heard about a journal page being found anywhere on him. Then Ryan, which Grange already knows about, emphasizing that I still do not know how he got the page, but that I no longer think he accidentally fell off that balcony. I then tell him about Marco, and his restaurant burning down the night I was there and how his journal entry was under the windshield wiper of his car. I left out the part about the gas container being buried in the woods behind my parents' house. The last thing I need is for police to show up there.

"And what did you do with the journal page you found there?"

"I threw it away . . ."

"You threw away evidence?"

It's technically buried in a hole with the gas container. "Yes . . ."

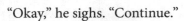

"Okay," he sighs. "Continue."

I tell him how the news called it a gas leak, but I was suspicious because of the note, and that the only person that even knew about the journal was my ex-boyfriend and ex-professor Miles Holland. I swore I saw his car the morning that we left North Winwick, and he's a professor now at Ivy Gate, where Ryan died, so it makes sense. Then I get to Bryce and how I basically stalked him trying to keep him safe. I thought I saw Miles's Darth Vader costume on Halloween, and he had emailed me saying he would be out by Pembroke that weekend. I tell Grange how Bryce died from being stabbed with a sword on Halloween, the page stabbed through as well.

"I heard about that," Grange says. "But I did not hear about any notes being found. Presumably because you took it?"

Technically Asher took it, but I won't bring Asher into this. "Yes."

I continue to tell him about how I went to Holland's office hours to try to get a confession, and that's where I found the gallery opening for Graham on his desk and I just knew it had to be him. So I went to the opening and saw Miles there. I spoke with him and he seemed to be confused about me calling him a murderer and stormed out.

"We left the gallery, went to get pizza, stopped at Graham's place for my friends to change their clothes, got back to the hotel, and that's when I found it," I say.

"Found what?" Grange asks.

I slide the duffel bag across the floor. "The gun that killed him. It was in my hotel room, under the covers. The girl at the front desk said she let a woman up to our room while we were gone, a woman named Kate Holland." Grange takes the duffel and care-fully pulls back the zipper, revealing the hotel towel. "We didn't want to touch it, so we wrapped it in a hotel towel."

"Who is 'we'?"

So much for keeping him out of it.

"Me and my friend Asher. We were on the bed . . . um, hang-ing out . . . when we found it. But I knew Graham was in trouble. That's why we went back to the gallery. And when we got there he was already shot, and the journal page was taped to the wall. We're the ones who called 911."

Grange looks from me to his notes, tapping his pen on the pad. "Let's start with Graham. What time did you leave the gallery opening?"

"It started at seven and I think we left around eight thirty, got to Slice around eight forty-five, stayed until ten eating and having drinks, then we got an Uber to Graham's, probably stayed there until ten thirty, but Asher and I didn't get out of the car, then went to the hotel around ten forty-five."

"I looked through the gallery footage all night and Graham was shot around ten thirty, but we couldn't see the shooter. I'll need the name of your driver that took you to his apartment and to the hotel so I can verify that you did not go back to the gallery at that time."

"Um, sure." I take out my phone and turn it back on, ignoring the influx of texts from Asher asking where the hell I went with the gun. I go to the app to find the driver. "His name was Brandon Jones—here is the ride info." I slide my phone to him.

Grange picks up the phone on his desk, putting it to his ear. "Carmen, can you bring me an evidence bag? And tell Wilson we need a warrant for the security footage at the Four Seasons Hotel downtown, as well as Slice, the restaurant . . . Yes . . . and we need to contact Uber support to get in touch with a driver . . . Brandon Jones, license plate HTW334. Thanks." He hangs up and opens a desk drawer, pulling out a pair of gloves.

"So . . . am I in trouble?" I ask.

"Yes," he says. "But how much trouble is yet to be determined." The woman from the front desk comes back in with an evidence bag for Grange, and with gloved hands he picks up the gun and drops it in. "I'm going to get this sent out to the lab and you're go-ing to move to another room for more questioning."

"But I've told you everything I know."

"I'd like to hear more about Miles Holland."

An officer escorts me to a small room with a table and two chairs, the kind of room where criminals go in TV shows for in-terrogation. Grange comes in thirty minutes later.

"Should I have a lawyer here?" I ask when he walks in. "This room makes it feel like I should have one."

"You're not under arrest," he says. "But if you would like a law-yer, we can get you one."

I know Asher would tell me to get one, he'd say I shouldn't have even come in here without one. But doesn't that just prove my in-nocence even more? That I came in here voluntarily to confess all of that? And Grange did say I'm not under arrest; he just wants to know about Miles. "What else do you want to know?"

I give Grange all the details on Miles and his wife, how our re-lationship started, how it ended, how he used to stalk me, threaten me, how I once found pictures of me in his closet, though I didn't say how recent that was or how I had to break into his town house for them. And last I tell him about the emails he's been sending lately and our conversation at the gallery. When it feels like an hour or two have passed, an officer comes in to steal Grange away for what feels like another hour.

"WELL, YOUR DRIVER confirmed you both were in the car the entire time he took you and your friends from Slice to Graham's to the hotel, and confirmed the time, which lines up with the shooting. We should have the security footage from the hotel and restaurant in a few hours."

"A few hours? But I've already been here for like three?"

"These things take time," he says. "But like I said before, you're not under arrest—you could leave at any time. But if you want to help us catch the person behind this, you'd better stay."

I think of the two names left in the journal, Tristan and Wesley. "Okay, I'll stay."

WE TALK ABOUT the two of them, and Grange assures me they'll be protected. We then go through the journal again from the beginning, this time in more detail. I give them a DNA sample. By the time they get the hotel and restaurant footage that verifies I was there when I say I was, and Grange finishes up his questions, it's past 7 p.m.

Asher must be freaking out right now.

"Wait, did you get the fingerprints for the gun?" I ask when he stands up, concluding our session.

"Some things take more time," he says. "Now, I have a lot of work to do, and you're free to go. For now," he adds.

"And you're going to look into Miles and Kate? And make sure nothing happens to Tristan and Wes?"

"Yes, we are going to do everything we can."

"Well, I can help you—"

"No, you need to stay far away from this. In fact, you should have little to no contact with the other two people in your journal if possible."

"That's . . . not possible," I say. "I work with Tristan and Wes is my . . . well, he's one of my best friends."

"Find a new job," Grange says. "And if the other one is really your best friend, then you'll listen to me when I say to stay away." He walks me to the front of the station and out the doors. "I'll be in touch," he says to me before I walk back to my car.

I CALL ASHER on my way back to campus. He picks up on the first ring.

"Where the *fuck* are you? I have been freaking the fuck out, Sloane. Where is the gun?"

"I took it to the police," I say. "I've been at the police station." He's quiet on the other end. "It's okay, I'm not in trouble. Well, I probably am for taking the journal pages, but I wasn't arrested for murder . . . yet . . . so that's a plus."

"Just get back to campus. I'm at your apartment," he says before hanging up.

ASHER IS SITTING at the bottom of the stairs that lead up to my and Adrienne's apartment door when I pull up. He stands when I get out of the car.

"I'm sorry I left this morning," I say, walking toward him. The falling snow covers his hair and his eyelashes.

"Why the hell would you go to the police without me?" He

barks the question at me like I'm a kid that needs scolding. I figure sitting out here for two hours and wondering where I was all day must have made him irrationally angry.

"The real question is: Why did I wait so long to do it?" I say back. "This is what I should've done from the start, Asher, don't you see that? If I would've just gone to Grange after Marco's fire, when I knew I was being set up, Bryce might still be here; so would Graham. People died because we tried to play detective and it didn't work! Their deaths are my fault! All of them are."

"That's not true."

"It is, it is true. And I'll have to make peace with that, but I won't let it happen to Tristan and Wes. It's all in the hands of the police now, like it should've been from the start."

"So, what? That's it?"

"What else is there? They can do more than we can. I won't put more people in danger."

When he doesn't say anything else, I turn to walk up the stairs.

"And what about this?" Asher says. I look back at him standing there, his hands slack at his sides.

"I don't even know what *this* is," I reply, knowing that the "this" is us.

He nods once, and takes a step back, then nods again before walking back to his car. I bite my lip to stop myself from telling him not to go. But the entire drive back to Pembroke gave me time to think and wonder if I would still feel this way about him had this never happened to me at all. It's like that syndrome where girls fall in love with their captors. He wasn't holding me captive physically, but mentally. I now feel like I need him. Somewhere along the way he's become some kind of emotional crutch as well as my psychological tormentor. Every rude remark paired with a smirk, every jab ending in a kiss, and even though it was all for show, it's the only thing that's been enough to distract me from the weight of it all. If he's gone, will it crush me?

Back in my apartment I set my bag in the bedroom and am met with my suspect board. It won't come off the wall so I take a small blanket and toss it over the board. I don't want to look at it anymore. It's someone else's problem now.

The second thing I notice is my goals taped to my mirror. Grabbing the marker, I cross out one of my last two goals.

You won't let any boys get to you.

It wasn't just Asher that got to me; it was all of them. The dead ones and the alive ones. There's knocking at my door that pulls me from my thoughts. Asher. He came back. I stand in front of the door, hesitant. If I open it will he swoop in, gathering me in his arms to finish what we started in the hotel?

I decide I need to know as I unlock the door, swinging it open to find Miles Holland standing there.

I try to shut the door but he puts his foot in to stop it from closing. "Wait! I just want to talk to you!" he shouts through the crack of the door.

"Well, I don't want to talk to *you!*" I push harder, but he manages to shove the door open. I back up away from the entry as he steps in, with a small briefcase in hand. It probably has a gun in it, or knives, or whatever he uses to kill people. Maybe it's my journal or its contents. "I told the police everything—they're probably already at your place," I say, mustering up some courage.

Miles looks around my place. "That's what you keep saying."

I realize my phone is in my bedroom. Maybe I could run for it and lock him out of my bedroom while I call 911. "What do you want? What's in the briefcase?"

"This is what I've wanted to talk to you about," he says, holding it up. "It's my next book. I want you to read it. You told me before that you wanted to be the subject of my next one; well, now you are." He holds the briefcase out to me. I did say that once, in a lame attempt to flirt. I never thought he'd take it seriously.

"Just get out of my apartment and I won't tell anyone you were here."

"Like how I haven't told anyone that you broke into my house?"

I turn and run down the hall for my room and he follows, getting in the door before I can close it behind me. I grab my phone from the bed but he rips it from my hand and tosses it into the hall. He stands by the door, blocking my way out.

"This isn't what you think. Don't panic," he says, trying to reassure me after chasing me to my room and throwing my phone into the hall. So reassuring. "I'm here because I love you."

"You're sleeping with my cousin," I say. "In fact, where is she right now? Did you kill her too?"

"Adrienne? No, I only reached out to her to get a better feel for your life. It was research for my story. She doesn't understand."

"So you're using her?"

But he's done talking about Adrienne. "I've been watching you. You've been miserable without me. Drinking too much, throwing yourself all over these boys. Adrienne says the blond one from the gallery makes you cry. I would never do that. He doesn't know you like I do. I can give you a better life than he can."

"Is that why you're killing my exes, then?"

"I'm not a killer, Sloane. I mean, look at me. Do you really think I could kill someone?" He motions up and down his body.

"Then you're having your wife do it for you," I say.

"My wife? Kate? I haven't talked to her since she walked out on me. It's you I want. Seeing you yesterday, hearing your voice, I just had to see you again. I needed to make things right. If you take me back I'll be better, I'll change. Just read the story I wrote—you'll know how much you mean to me." He comes closer until I'm backed up to my bed.

"I don't want to read your story. I want you to get out of my apartment, you fucking psychopath."

I try to push him away but he catches my wrist, bringing me close to him. "Maybe you just need a reminder," he says, grabbing the back of my head and pulling me in for a kiss. I try to yell and push and kick.

"Sloane?" I hear my name from the open front door.

"Asher!" I scream, and he comes running. Miles turns as Asher walks into my room, and hits Miles square in the jaw. He throws another punch, and Miles falls to the ground. But he doesn't stop there. Asher winds back over and over and I think he may actually kill him. It's years of pent-up rage at the hands of an abusive father. I wonder when he looks at Miles right now, is it really Ben that he's seeing? "Asher, that's enough! That's enough!" I put my hand on his shoulder for him to stop and he looks back at me long enough for Miles to get up, broken and bloody, and run out of the room. I grab Asher's arm before he can run out after him. "Just let him go," I say.

"Did he hurt you?"

"No," I say. "I have to call Grange." I push past Asher to get my phone in the hall. Grange doesn't answer so I leave a message saying Miles just forced his way into my apartment and assaulted me. Hopefully that's enough for them to arrest him and get a warrant to search his place.

Asher goes into the bathroom to wash his bloody knuckles and I stand in the doorway watching in silence.

"I'm staying over," he says. "And tomorrow we can go back to not speaking or whatever it is that you want."

I don't fight him on it as he takes up residence on our couch next to the front door. I go to my room and get into bed, but I can't fall asleep. I have a feeling neither of us can.

WHEN THERE'S A knock on the door the next morning, I hear Asher answer it.

Annica's voice booms from the hallway. "Well, you're not who we were expecting." Two sets of boots walk in.

"I thought you weren't talking to her right now?" Asher says.

"Oh, Sloane's going to talk today," Annica says. "She's going to do a lot of it."

I sit up in bed as I hear them coming down the hall.

Dani peeks her head into my bedroom door with an apprehensive "Hey."

Annica shoves past her into the room and tosses her phone at me. On it is a photo of me and Detective Grange outside the police station last night posted on PC's gossip page. The caption reads "PC's Sloane Sawyer seen being taken into custody by Boston PD for multiple murders."

"No, no, no." I shake my head as I read it, scrolling down to read the comments, and there is no shortage of them.

Elianna551: Isn't this the girl who screwed her professor and got him fired?

DukeFan40: Nah it's the girl who got a DUI for being over double the adult legal limit after leaving Sig Chi

Griffin_H: It's the same girl LOL looks like she still doesn't have her shit together

I'm gripping Annica's phone so hard it feels like I could shatter it in my palm.

"You have five minutes to explain to us what the fuck is going on." Annica crosses her arms.

CHAPTER 25

"Get ready with me while I tell you guys all about the suspected murderer on my campus. Her name is Sloane Sawyer," Marissa's voice echoes from my phone. Dani sent me the TikTok Marissa made about me and I watch it in silence while the three of us sit at our table at the Bean.

"That fucking bitch," I mutter. I bet she just couldn't wait to post that.

"She's probably just off the rails because Wes broke up with her after the ski trip, though I don't know if he told her why exactly," Dani says.

"It sounds like he told her." I hand Dani's phone back to her.

"Forget about that," Annica snaps. "Start explaining."

I tell them everything. Well, not *everything*, but almost.

I explain the murders and the journal pages, and I tell them that me and Asher being together was only because he caught me trying to throw out evidence, and that there was never a real relationship, hence why he's been "cheating" on me the whole time. I do not, however, mention that it was a two-sided deal, the other side being to manipulate Wesley into passing on the resort. I know

Annica too well, and she would rat me out to Wes in a heartbeat. I also admit to her that I've liked Wes for years, and this past summer really was not intentional—I never meant to hurt her or him or anyone.

"Wow," Dani says, wide-eyed, when I'm done explaining. "Why did you feel like you couldn't tell us any of this?"

I fiddle with the handle of the coffee mug, turning it this way and that. "I didn't want you guys to get hurt. People have died. I figured the less people involved the better."

Annica crosses her arms, glaring at me. "But you sought out Asher instead?"

I try not to roll my eyes at her. "I didn't seek him out. I told you he caught me in the act. I had to clue him in. He said he'd help me."

"In exchange for what?" she asks.

I think of something on the spot. "To pretend to date him in front of his family, to win him points with his grandfather."

She narrows her eyes at me. "Well, that's over with, so why did he sleep here last night? And what are you doing about Wes—are you guys going to be together or what?"

My god, I tell her the most unbelievable story, about murder no less, and all she wants to know is what my relationship status is.

"Asher stayed over because Miles pushed his way into my apartment and tried to . . ."

Dani gasps. "Oh my god, was he trying to kill you?"

"No, he was trying to . . . convince me to love him? He's obsessed. It's scary."

"Well then, it makes sense that he would be the killer," Annica says.

"That's what I thought at first too, but then why try to pin it on me? If I'm in jail we can't be together, so why would he be trying to send me there?"

"If he can't have you, no one can?" Dani suggests.

"Maybe. But then at the hotel, it was a woman who put the gun in our room. His ex-wife, Kate Holland. Either way, the police have all this information and should be looking into both of them. Especially after last night."

"I wonder who was taking pictures of you outside the station and sent them to the gossip page," Dani says. "How did they even know you'd be there?"

"It was probably Marissa," I say. "Get ready with me to go frame Sloane for murder!" I mock her annoying high-pitched tone. Though it could've also been Colton, as he made it crystal clear he was going to make sure I was branded as a killer all over social media.

"Sounds like something Asher would do," Annica mutters.

"It wasn't him, trust me."

She scoffs. "That's the problem, we can't trust you."

Dani was still scrolling through comments. "They're calling you murder slut."

I put my head in my hands. "That's not even creative."

"This one says the Pembroke Psycho," she continues.

"I think I like murder slut better."

"So what are you going to do, then, murder slut?" Dani asks.

"I'm going to let the police handle it now."

"And they really don't think it's you at all?" Annica asks.

"They might, but they don't have enough evidence to arrest me for it." No one says anything else as we all sip our coffees in awkward silence. "So am I forgiven?" I try.

"For keeping two giant lies from us?" Annica says. "Not really."

"But we'll work on it," Dani says. "Right, Annica? You said you would." Dani nudges her.

Annica shakes her off. "I said that about the Wes thing. This is a whole other thing. There's been nothing but lies coming out of your mouth since last summer. It's going to be pretty hard to trust you now. And would you have even told us about any of this had you not been caught? Twice?"

She has a point. Because no, I wouldn't have. "I'm sorry! Okay, I will make it up to you guys. I would've said something when the dust settled. You have to believe that I kept it from you because I thought that's what was best."

"Hm, well, I know one way you could start to make it up," Annica says. "You can let me read your short story."

"Fine, deal." What's the harm of it now that she knows about Wes? Plus this semester is when draft editing starts and I'm pretty sure by the end of it the whole class reads your story anyway. It is a small price to pay to have her back on my side.

"Friends again?" Dani says with a smile.

Annica rolls her eyes. "Yes, friends. Kind of."

"Friends," I repeat, holding up my mug as the other two clink theirs to mine.

ASHER DOESN'T STAY over the next two days, and I don't ask him to. Grange comes by on Wednesday to get a detailed account of the assault, which in the end starts to sound more like we assaulted Miles, not the other way around. I'm sure if Grange has seen Holland's face, he'd agree. I wonder if they called in Asher for questioning about any of this.

By Thursday I find myself standing on the boys' porch at dusk. The bare trees stand black against the gray sky like wavering skeletons, their branches creaking in the wind like bones. I knock on the front door, waiting for Asher to open it. But he doesn't; Wesley does.

"Sloane." He smiles, and it's warm in the bitter cold of winter. It almost knocks the breath from me to see him again, and I wonder how he managed to drift from my mind for even a moment, let alone a month.

"Wes, hey, you're back already." I smile, stepping inside.

"Yeah." He takes my coat. "I actually came back early to talk to you. Come upstairs. I want to show you something." I remember what Dani said about him and Marissa breaking up, and I wonder if that's what this is about. I wonder if he's seen the videos she's been making about me.

"Okay." I follow him up and see the attic door to Asher's room open a crack with the light on. I can talk to him after this.

When I walk into Wesley's room I almost don't recognize it. Large sheets of paper cover his bedroom walls. Some are photos of the beach house, and each room inside of it, next to a large, printed floor plan, all drawn on with pen and marker.

"You've redecorated," I say, looking around.

"Isn't it great?" Wes walks around. "I'm putting together the plans for the house, and a business proposal for my dad. I'm going to show him soon. I'm almost done. I worked on it all break."

"Wow."

"Margot's Bed-and-Breakfast." He smiles. "Named after my grandma."

I give him a close-lipped smile and click my tongue. "That's really sweet, Wes."

"I wanted you to see it first. If it wasn't for you I would've never even pursued it." He's looking at me like I'm the sun that rises each morning, and I can't help but wonder if he has no idea what everyone is saying about me these days. I open my mouth to bring it up, to tell him everything, but he closes the space between us and kisses me with a passion that I would've crawled for—no, *died for*—at the start of the school year. And now this, *this* is the Nicholas Sparks book scenario I've been wanting. So why does something still not feel right?

The kiss becomes deeper, and his hands move up my back, pulling me into him, and I realize where this is heading. I pull away from him.

"Sorry," he says. "Sorry, was that . . . I just got caught up in the moment."

"No, no, it's okay," I tell him. "I just wasn't expecting it." From outside in the hall I hear Asher's door slam and it makes me jump. Wes doesn't acknowledge it. "So I take it you and Marissa . . . ?"

"Yeah," he breathes. "I told her what happened, and we decided on a mutual breakup. I think we also just want different things after graduation."

I nod.

"What about you and Asher?" he asks. "Are you guys still together?" Wes had asked me that over winter break and I told him then that I wasn't sure. I guess I'm still not.

"I was actually going to talk to him tonight," I admit. I'm

shocked to know Annica hasn't told Wes about my and Asher's fake relationship yet. Or that I'm a murder suspect. Somehow he seems blissfully unaware of anything outside of his bed-and-breakfast.

"Oh." Wesley's smile quickly becomes a frown at the realization. "So you came here tonight for Asher."

"Well, yes, but to officially end things," I say, recovering. And that's not completely true because I don't even know why I came here. I thought maybe I'd see Asher again after I'd had a few days alone and I'd just know the answer.

Wes breathes what feels like a sigh of relief. "I know you obviously found something appealing about him . . . but I was honestly waiting for the day that you two called it off. The whole time I just felt like he didn't even really know what he had. Like he didn't even really want you . . ."

"Yeah," I sigh, knowing I have to go upstairs and find out exactly that.

I CLIMB THE stairs to Asher's room, half hoping he's not really up here. But he is. Standing in front of his dresser putting clothes away.

"What do you want?" he says with his back turned.

"It's me," I say.

He turns around and I notice the bruise on his cheek and another split lip. He must have seen his dad at some point this week. "What do you want?" he repeats.

I want you to be happy, is what I want to say.

"It worked," I say in a hushed tone, on the off chance anyone could be listening at the bottom of the stairs. "Wes has this whole plan drawn out for the beach house, and he's so excited about it.

He's going to bring the plans to his dad and I think this really might work. I think you're going to get the resort." I wait for the smirk, or for some type of positive emotion, but Asher doesn't say anything, just continues to put laundry away. "And he broke up with Marissa . . . and . . . then he kissed me."

He looks up then and raises a brow. "Then why are you up here with me and not down there with him? Isn't this what you wanted?"

"Yeah, I just . . ." I take a step or two closer, closing the space between us. "What you said the other night about *this*." I motion between the two of us. "I guess I just need to know if—"

He cuts me off. "There is nothing between us, there never was."

I huff a laugh. "Well, we both know that's not true."

"How is it not? I feel like I've been clear about my intentions."

I shake my head. He has been nothing short of confusing for months. "At the hotel, you said—"

"Guys will say anything for sex, Sawyer—you of all people should know that by now."

The insult feels like a slap in the face and my cheeks heat with embarrassment. "You're such an ass." My voice betrays me when it cracks and tears well up in my eyes.

"And I always have been. It's not my fault if you've forgotten that along the way." He looks up at me again. "What, are you really going to cry?"

I stare up at the ceiling trying to hold back the tears.

Asher rolls his eyes. "Go cry to Wes. I'm sure he'd love to hold your hand while you cry over me again."

I can't stop the words that come out next. The overwhelming urge to cut him back, cut him deeper. "Maybe he was right, maybe you will turn out just like your dad. Bitter, mean, and alone."

"Get. Out."

He doesn't need to tell me twice—I'm already going. I stomp down his stairs and slam the door behind me.

Wes comes out of his room at the commotion. "What's wrong, what happened?"

"Nothing, I just forgot who I was talking to, that's all."

"Ugh, don't tell me these characters are who I think they are," Annica says after reading through my story.

"You wanted to read it," I remind her as we sit in Renner's Tuesday-afternoon senior seminar. The first of the semester.

"I mean, it's an okay story, I guess," she says. "I just think the end is really obvious."

"How so?"

"She chooses the soldier, like you knew from the beginning that she would. There's no twist and there's just something about it that doesn't feel genuine. It feels like a lie." She looks up at me when she says the last part. "I have an idea for it, though. What if the letters that she's been getting, the ones that help her and the medic find the missing soldier, you find out that the medic had been writing them all along as some pathetic ploy to be with the main character longer. That's a twist."

Huh, it is a twist. A good one, I think to myself, making a note.

"I think I'll use that actually . . . thanks." I almost want to ask her what the catch is. Because I know I'm not forgiven yet, so giving me plot advice for nothing in return feels out of the norm for Annica Labrant. I take the papers from her and start to put them back in my bag. We stand and pack up before heading toward our next class, publishing.

"So have you heard anything from the detective? Did they catch Holland?" Annica asks as we make our way to the other end of the English building.

"Grange says he can't give me details on a case when I'm still technically a suspect. That or he just won't answer me at all. I'm starting to think I need to take matters into my own hands again."

"Because that worked out so well for you before," Annica mutters.

We pass a group of girls, and they move out of the way, whispering. That's what most people have done so far now that school has started back up.

"Tristan doesn't come back from Europe until the end of February, so I have a month before I really have to worry again," I say. But then mentally chastise myself because that's the kind of thinking I had about Graham, and look how that ended.

Graham.

His raspy breath and blood-soaked mouth pop into my head and I flinch.

"And what about Wes? Does he even know he's on some crazy broken-heart hit list?" she asks.

"No, and I'd like to keep it that way. There's no need to stress him out; he's got enough going on as it is."

"So more lies?"

"Are we all going out tonight for Ladies Night? Last first one of the semester," I say, trying to change the subject as we file into the row for our next class.

I HAVE ONLY six credits to complete before graduation, which means only three classes this semester: the other half of senior seminar, publishing, and sociolinguistics. I spend the rest of my free time at the gym, working on my short story, looking up jobs and internships for the summer, and going back through the murders. I bought a bigger corkboard than the one Asher stuck on my wall, because I ran out of room. I printed more names and photos, the cities where each murder happened, and the news articles from the web. I got more red yarn and put it all together, staring at it most nights waiting to find a connection. One that doesn't point to Miles Holland but rather to Kate Holland. I just can't find one that makes sense.

"Sloane?" Adrienne says in my doorway.

It makes me jump. I toss a blanket over the board as I stand up to face her. "Adrienne." I cross my arms. She's been MIA since the gallery.

"We should talk," she says.

"We should."

She stands in the doorway waiting for me to invite her into my room. But I don't.

"I didn't know who he was at first," she explains. "I never saw a picture of the professor you told me about last year. I met him at a bar in Ivy Gate and we hit it off. When I realized he was the same guy, I was too scared to tell you." I don't say anything; I just stare at her, jaw clenched. "I'm not seeing him anymore. And I'm sorry I ever did it in the first place."

"Why aren't you seeing him anymore?"

"I think he was only seeing me to get information about you, but I didn't realize it until it was too late." I just nod, not sure if I fully believe her story. "Do you think you can forgive me?"

I don't want to, but who am I to withhold forgiveness? "I'll consider it," I say, before shutting my bedroom door in her face. I look back at my suspect board for a while, before taking Adrienne's photo and name from the board.

I MEET EVERYONE at Water Street Tavern, and to my surprise, Asher is here. The bruises on his face have almost healed. I resist the urge to touch them when we're standing at the bar together.

"What?" he says, catching me looking at him from the corner of my eye.

"Nothing," I whisper, as the bartender hands him a beer and he walks away. Wes comes up beside me then.

"Still taking things slow, right?"

"Yes," I say, looking back at the group. "Definitely."

"So, I can't do this?" Wes inches closer to me so our shoulders are touching, and I have a flashback of last semester when Asher and I stood here like this watching Wes and Marissa from across the bar.

I give a nervous laugh. "Um, maybe just that, for now."

I feel like a virgin again with a boyfriend pressuring me for sex. Not that Wes is pressuring me, but I'm sure he found it off-putting the last two times he's tried, and I told him I was on my period, or I wasn't feeling good.

We aren't in a relationship; we're just . . . I don't even know what we are. Hanging out, I guess. I had to make it very clear that it can't look like we're rushing into anything, especially not in front of Annica. But what I really meant was not in front of Asher.

I get my drink and go back to the group, leaving Wes by the bar.

"I can't believe we're friends with the actual Pembroke Psycho,"

Jake says. Marissa's TikToks and the PC gossip page have finally made their way to the rest of my friend group. Wes still hasn't brought it up to me, though.

"None of what's on the gossip page is true," I say.

"Well, that's good," Charlie says. "Would really suck if you were murdering your exes. Asher would be a goner."

"Looks like she already tried to get to him," Jake teases about the bruises on Asher's face.

Asher doesn't say anything.

"Well, don't you guys know? Asher and Sloane were never really together. It was one big charade. Just a show for his family to win him some brownie points."

I stare daggers at Annica, though I never explicitly told her to keep that to herself. I just haven't had the chance to tell Wes that. I watch his face fall when he comes back to the table and hears it.

"Looks like it didn't work though," she says before taking a sip of her drink.

My mouth falls open. I don't ask how she knows about Ben. I assume Wes told her.

"You are *such* a cunt," Asher says to her.

"Takes one to know one," Annica says back.

"Okay, okay," I interrupt. "Let's not do this here."

"This is what happens when the balance of the group is ruined," she says to me. And I want to say that everything was fine before she opened her mouth and if anything is upsetting a balance right now it's her, but I'm on thin ice with everyone, so I stay quiet.

"I'm going to grab us all some shots," Jake says.

"Yeah, I'll go with you," Sam says, and follows.

"Oh, I love this song." Charlie looks at Dani. "Let's go dance."

Asher gets up and leaves the bar. Wes, Annica, and I are all that's left at the table.

"Happy?" Annica says to me.

Far from it.

AN HOUR LATER I'm lying in bed with Wes as he plants drunk kisses on my lips and neck, but I can't stop thinking about Asher.

I pause the kissing, pulling away to look at Wes. "Did you tell Annica that Asher's dad hits him?" I say.

"Hm? Oh, uh, like one time in high school I think I did. I'm surprised she even remembered."

I sit up. "High school? You've known about that since high school?"

Wes sighs, turning on his side and propping up his head on a hand. "Um, no, it's been going on for much longer than that."

My mouth hangs open, and Wes leans in to kiss it but I pull away. "Wes," I say. "How could you not tell anyone?"

He sighs again. "Sloane, you don't understand."

"I do understand, I saw it happen."

"No, I mean everyone knows. My dad says it's not our business."

"How could he say that? That's his nephew."

"It's complicated. My dad tried to offer to take in Asher and Kara when their mom passed but it started a huge fight so my dad told us to just stay out of it. He didn't tell you about that during your fake relationship?"

I was starting to think he wasn't going to bring it up. Like maybe it would just get swept under the rug. "I was going to tell you about that," I say.

"Well, if we're telling the truth, is there anything else you want to tell me?"

Your name is in that journal. Your name is in the journal and it'll be you that dies last if we can't catch who's behind this. "No."

When Wes falls asleep I text Asher.

I'm sorry.

He doesn't reply.

IT'S MID-FEBRUARY WHEN Grange comes back to Pembroke's campus to speak with me again.

"I told you everything I know, I gave you DNA samples, I don't know what else I can even say," I tell him when we sit down at the Bean.

"I just have a few more questions," he says, and I can tell he's tired.

"Well, I have questions for you too. Did you arrest Miles after he forced himself on me? Did you look into Kate?"

"You know I can't share that information, as I've told you almost every week now."

"Well, you must not have if you're still looking. Tristan comes back from Europe in two weeks—you have to make this go quicker."

"It's going as quick as it can. We've had to work with the departments in North Winwick and Pembroke to reopen these other cases, comb through security tapes, interview witnesses. This is not a speedy process."

"And you've talked to the Hollands?"

He sighs. "They're both clean."

"Did you search their homes?"

"Sloane." He doesn't have to say anything else: The tone in his voice is the one my mom uses when the conversation is over.

I go on anyway. "What about Marissa Wilder? Anything on her?"

"We have this covered. Now, the questions I have for you . . ."

I walk him back through everything that I can remember, which isn't much since I was blacked out almost every time someone died. The lack of progress makes me worry for Tristan and Wes. They aren't safe. Not yet.

CHAPTER 26

March

"Guess who's back!" Tristan Brent says as he walks through the doors of Cantine on a rainy evening in March, gift bags in hand.

Oh no.

"Hey!" I say. "How was your trip?" He was in Europe for a month longer than I thought he'd be. Which meant an extra month of peace for me.

"Oh, it was amazing. I wish I didn't have to come back," he says, plopping the bags on the bar counter.

Same, I think to myself.

"Well," I say. "Tell me all about it."

So Tristan tells me all about the Christmas markets in Germany, the way the Eiffel Tower sparkles at night in Paris, and the ruins of Rome. When we're not busy with customers we go through the millions of pictures on his phone. By the time he's gotten through all of it our shift is ending. I lock the door while we start cleaning up.

"What's been going on here while I've been gone?" he asks. "Did you ever figure out that weird note situation you were telling me about?"

"Funny you should ask, actually. I need to talk to you about something." I follow Tristan back to the freezer as he goes through the closing checklist. He checks the dates on the steak and chicken, writing new dates on what arrived today. I step in with him, letting the door close behind me. "So, um, let's see, how do I explain this . . ."

Tristan looks up at me, waiting.

"I have this journal, and every time someone breaks my heart, I write them a fake eulogy, like they died. And someone took my journal, and is murdering everyone in it, and leaving my journal page at the crime scene trying to frame me for it. And uh . . . you're in the journal. You're actually the next name so . . ."

He looks at me for a long moment in the white freezer light before laughing, his breath coming out like smoke in the chilly air. "Is this a joke? Are you trying to prank me right now or something? It's creative, I'll give you that."

"I wish," I say.

He blinks at me when I don't laugh with him. "Sloane, tell me this is a joke. Tell me you're kidding."

"I would love to do that, I really would, but . . ." Tristan walks past me to the freezer door and I go to follow him out, but he doesn't open it. "It's serious, Tristan—" He pushes against the door again, but it stays shut. "You have to push hard on that, sometimes it's stuck."

"I know," he says. "I am."

"Here, let me try." He moves and I give it a hard push like I usually do to get it open, but it still doesn't budge. "Okay, let's both try," I suggest. Tristan stands beside me and we both push as hard as we can on the freezer door.

"What the hell," he says.

"Call Jess and tell her to come back and open it," I say.

"My phone is behind the bar," he says. "You call."

"My phone is also behind the bar . . ."

"Fuck."

"Maybe try running at it?" I suggest. "Or maybe you could, like, kick it down?"

He looks at me in disbelief. "What do I look like, an Avenger?"

I shake my head. "A what?"

"Never mind, I'll try it," he says, backing up and taking a breath before running at the door and slamming into it with his shoulder. "Fuck!" He slides down the door holding his shoulder.

"Okay, um, maybe someone in the yogurt shop is still closing up and would hear us if we yell." I start pounding on the door, yelling for help. Tristan gets up from the floor and joins me. We yell for a few minutes and then wait to see if we can hear anyone.

I start to shiver.

Twenty or so minutes go by without anyone coming to our rescue. I pace around the freezer. "Worst-case scenario, we're just stuck in here until the morning crew comes in at what? Like seven in the morning?"

"That's eight hours from now," Tristan says with his back to the door.

"Okay, we'll just be a little cold."

"A little cold? This is a freezer!"

"People live in colder temperatures! I mean, there's, like, Eskimos and other people that live in the arctic—this can't be much worse. We'll be fine for eight hours."

"Sloane, this is a freezer."

"I heard you."

"There is not enough oxygen in here for both of us for eight hours."

"Oh."

We both sit with our backs to the freezer door, taking slow, shallow breaths. Eventually the motion sensor light goes out, leaving us in the dark. We don't move to turn it back on.

"Are we going to die in here?" I ask him in the frigid blackness.

"I don't know if we'll die, but we'll definitely get hypothermia and probably pass out."

"Lovely," I say, shivering. Tristan scoots closer to me so we're huddled together in the cold.

"I did make that bet," he admits.

I purse my lips and nod. "I know."

"I'm sorry."

"I know," I say again. "I forgive you."

"I didn't even know you or Alaina when I said it. I was just being a jerk. And when we started actually hanging out I realized I liked you. I wish I could take it back."

"I liked you too," I say.

"Is that why you wrote about me in your journal?"

"Yep."

"You have to admit we had fun, though. The concerts, the parties . . . the time you accidentally met my parents with no pants on."

I shake my head but my lips tug upward in the dark. "Or when

I had bronchitis for a whole month but we continued to see each other anyway. Your parents probably hated me."

"Nah, they were cool," he says. "Until I got bronchitis, and then so did they."

"Well, that's what you get."

He lets out a dry laugh. "If that was my karma then why am I trapped in a freezer right now?" Because this is *my* karma is what I want to tell him. When I don't say anything he talks again. "So what's going on exactly with these murders? Explain it to me again." But the thought of explaining this situation again makes my brain hurt. Or maybe that's from the lack of air. Or the below-thirty-degrees temperature.

"Aren't we supposed to be conserving air?"

A NOISE OUTSIDE the freezer thirty minutes later has me snapping up my head from Tristan's shoulder.

"Did you hear that?" I ask him.

"Hm?"

"Someone is in the restaurant." I turn and bang on the freezer again, but my arms move slower this time. It takes more effort. Tristan tries it too. There's more noise now directly in front of the freezer door until it swings open, revealing a police officer and our manager, Jess.

"Oh thank god," I say.

The officer helps us up, putting his coat around me. Jess gives hers to Tristan.

"What the hell happened?" Jess says, picking up the crowbar on the ground that must have been lodged in the handle.

"Miss, don't touch anything, please," the officer says, while on the phone with someone. "Yes . . . She was in there with him . . . Yes, it's taped onto the front of the freezer door . . . Yeah, I'll tell her." Tristan and I both look at the door, where Tristan's eulogy is. "Grange says not to touch that," the officer says to me.

Tristan starts to read it and I back away slowly.

"'We're here to mourn Tristan Brent,'" Tristan begins to read. "Died from poison? What the hell, Sloane."

"Sorry . . ."

"Detective Grange is on his way," the officer says.

GRANGE FINISHES QUESTIONING Jess and walks over to me. He has the eulogy page and the crowbar in evidence bags. Likely to try to get prints from.

"Do you believe I'm not a suspect now?" I say.

He sighs. "Are you sure you didn't see anyone come into the restaurant while you were closing up?"

"I'm sure," I say.

"All right," Grange says. "I'll follow you back to your apartment to make sure you get back okay and we'll put a police detail on you too."

"Like you didn't have one on me already." It's hard not to notice the black SUV that's parked outside the English building on campus whenever I have class, the same one that sometimes sits in front of my apartment.

"Observant."

BACK IN MY bed I lie awake in the dark. I pick up my phone and stare at Asher's number, desperate to tell him what just happened. He answers on the third ring.

"What's wrong?" He sounds groggy but concerned. I suddenly feel bad for calling him so late.

"Nothing's wrong . . . well, not anymore but—"

"Where are you?" he asks.

"I'm in bed."

"Oh."

I hear another voice on the line say, "Who is that?" A woman's voice. A knot forms in my stomach knowing he's in bed with someone else. But what did I expect?

"No one," I hear him say back to her.

"I just . . ." I suddenly feel foolish for calling. But at the same time I need him to know. Would he leave and come here to comfort me knowing I just nearly escaped the killer? "I wanted you to know I got locked in the freezer at work with Tristan. The police found us an hour later with Tristan's journal entry taped to the door. Whoever is doing this, they just tried to kill me too."

He's quiet for a while, and I can faintly hear him breathing. I close my eyes and listen to it until he says, "Well, I'm glad you made it out alive."

He hangs up.

AT THE BOYS' house the following week, we're all seated in the living room around Wesley, who stands in front of the TV. Jake and Charlie make a show of peering around Wes to continue watching March Madness.

"What's going on here?" Annica asks when we walk in.

"I'm practicing my proposal for my dad tomorrow," Wes says. "Ladies, please have a seat." We file into the room and Charlie moves over on the big couch to fit us all. In the corner on the recliner Asher sits with his feet up. The little dark-haired girl that I once saw leaving his room sits on the edge beside him.

Annica does a double take. "Who the hell is that?" she says to the group, motioning at the girl with her thumb, but not addressing her directly. And for once I agree with her unjustified rudeness, because who the hell is that?

"This is Erin," Asher says. The girl gives a snarky finger wave to Annica.

"Should we really be letting strangers in on a business proposal?" Annica says to Wes.

"She's not a stranger," Wesley says to her. "She's Asher's new . . . friend."

"And who are you?" Erin asks Annica.

Annica blinks at her. "The fact that you don't know that means you shouldn't be here."

"Okay," Wes says. "That's enough. Let's get on with the presentation." He starts to hook up his laptop to the TV.

Annica concedes, leaning back on the couch with her arms crossed, giving me a better view. Erin's long, pin-straight hair falls over her hooded Pembroke sweatshirt. She tucks a piece of it behind her ear, revealing at least six piercings going up to the top of it. She smiles down at Asher, crinkling her small button nose. I look over at him to find he's already looking at me. I turn my focus back to the presentation as Wes passes out a printed copy of it for us.

Wes presents the beach house, earning oohs and aahs from the group. He walks through the drawn-up plans and I start to flip through the pages of the presentation. Each room has a mock-up of what it will look like after renovation, the design details provided by Russel Interiors. And there's something familiar about that business, though I can't put my finger on it. Wes continues through the financials, the projected ROI, a marketing plan, and a bunch of other business-related material I don't understand. At the end he includes all the contact information for the contractors he's already received quotes and information for, and again there is Russel Interiors with the email below it listed as Katherine@RusselInteriors.com. It hits me then. Kate Holland's maiden name is Russel. Miles had mentioned it once before. Could this be her? Is Katherine Russel Kate Holland?

"Where did you find this interior design firm?" I ask after the presentation.

"The owner actually reached out to me. Her name is Kate," Wes says, and my stomach drops.

I try to school my features so no one can sense my unease. "Kate Russel reached out to you? How did she find you?"

"I've been posting some things on LinkedIn," Wes explains.

"I see." I look over at Asher but now he's whispering something to Erin.

The boys ask questions about how much money Wes is going to make, and if he's going to let them stay there for free. I google Russel Interiors, finding that it's located right in Bloomfield, down the street from Cantine. I make an appointment request for this weekend and hit send.

I'm going to talk to Kate Russel myself.

CHAPTER 27

I need your help

I text Asher when Russel Interiors approves my appointment request for Friday afternoon. He doesn't reply.

Kate Holland is Kate Russel. Wesley's interior designer. I made an appointment for Friday at noon, at her studio in Bloomfield. What do you say to one more investigation?

Still nothing. I partially don't blame him for still being upset with me after what I said to him, but he was just as hurtful to me.

FRIDAY MORNING I apply a coat of lip gloss in the car mirror and adjust my blouse before going into the studio. I tried to dress as professional as possible in a white button-down blouse, tucked into jeans so you can see the Gucci belt I took from Adrienne's closet.

"You didn't say there was a dress code," a voice says from down the sidewalk. Asher. He walks up in beige cargo pants and a navy long-sleeve, with a jean jacket over top. He looks like an H&M model.

"You came," I say, surprised.

"You called," he sighs.

"I texted actually. Which you could've replied to."

"I could've."

He opens the door to the studio and walks in, not bothering to hold it open for me. It swings back fast, causing me to stumble in my heels. A bubbly blonde who looks to be in her mid-twenties greets us when we walk in.

"We have an appointment with Kate Holland, I mean Russel. Kate Russel," I correct myself.

"Right," she says. "You must be Amy."

"Amy?" Asher says. I couldn't have made the appointment with my real name, obviously.

"Yes, that's me." I reach out a hand to shake hers.

"Caroline," she says. Then she turns to Asher to shake his hand as well.

"Vernon," Asher says, using his grandpa's name for his fake identity. Vernon and Amy, that's us.

"Nice to meet you both. Kate had to step out, so I'm going to help you today."

We follow her back to an office, Kate's office, I realize by the nameplate on the glass desk.

"So we won't be meeting with Kate at all? Or will she just be late?" I ask.

"Um, she may be coming back. I actually don't know." We sit in the two leather chairs in front of the desk as Caroline hands us both a folder. "These are just a showcase of some of our work, and details on the process. But let's get to know each other first and find out what you're looking for."

"Well, Caroline," Asher starts, "we just bought a gorgeous beachfront property on Nantucket."

"Oh wow." Caroline beams. "Good for you guys!"

"Yeah, well, I can't take the credit really. It was all thanks to Amy's OnlyFans account."

I gasp, choking on my own saliva, but try to turn it into a laugh. "Um, yeah, yes, my OnlyFans account. It's, like, super classy though, mostly feet stuff, nothing, like . . . too explicit."

Asher turns to me. "Babe, don't be modest, tell her about that shoot last week with the three other guys in it—"

I look at him wide-eyed. "Oh, no, that's okay, let's talk about decor!" I turn back toward Caroline.

"Honestly." Caroline reaches for my hand across the table. "Good for you for doing that."

Asher interrupts. "I'll tell you what we're looking for. First, curtains. We'll need large ones, and make sure they're thick so I don't have to watch my girlfriend fuck the neighbor out by the pool when they think I'm not home." I shoot another incredulous look at Asher.

"He's kidding." I laugh.

"And soundproof walls, is that something you can do? We sleep in separate bedrooms because she snores, and it sounds like someone trying to start up a lawn mower."

I kick him hard under the table.

"Ah!" He grabs his shin.

"Sorry, leg spasms," I say, smiling at Caroline.

"Side effect from all of the drinking," Asher explains. And I can't believe he's doing this. Why is he doing this?

"Well, maybe I wouldn't need to drink if I didn't have *you* as a boyfriend."

Caroline clears her throat uncomfortably. "Why don't I give you two a minute, and, um, I'll go see where Kate is!" Caroline shuffles out of the room and I glare at Asher.

"What the hell are you doing?!"

"I'm just having some fun." He shrugs.

"This is not fun. You're embarrassing me!"

"Am I?"

"My god." I rub my temples. "You are so frustrating."

"You're the one who asked me to be here."

Out of the corner of my eye I see someone walk back into the room, a very pregnant someone. "Sorry to keep you waiting," she says, walking around the desk. "Thought I was having contractions but we're good!" It's Kate, and she's pregnant. She settles into her chair and looks up at me. Her cheerful expression immediately sours. "You."

"I just need to talk to you—" I start.

"Get out," she says, standing back up. "Get out of my office. I don't want to hear anything you have to say."

I stand too. "Just five minutes, please, it's important."

"You think I don't know what this is about? I've talked to the police twice now. I have zero involvement with Miles, or you, or whatever is going on here. I am eight months pregnant and in a happy relationship. You're delusional if you think I'd even waste a second of my time thinking of you. Now get out or I'll call that detective."

Asher and I walk out of the office in defeat. When we're back in front of the building Asher says, "I'm starting to think it wasn't her in the hotel."

"I mean, Holland was at the gallery with Adrienne. Maybe he put her up to it." Maybe I was too quick to take her off my suspect board.

"Maybe," he says, walking back to his car.

"Wait, you're just leaving?" I ask after him.

"What else is there to discuss?"

"Maybe how you were a total jerk in there?"

Asher doesn't respond, only gets in the car and shuts the door, turning on the engine. I stand on the sidewalk with my arms crossed as he pulls out of the spot and drives away. But this conversation isn't done.

"WE WEREN'T DONE talking," I say, getting out of my car as he's about to walk into the house.

"When I got in the car and drove away, that meant the conversation was over." He walks in and I go after him. The lack of other cars in their driveway tells me none of the other boys are home. It's just me and him.

"What is your deal lately?" I say. "You're being so difficult, and don't even say this is usually how you are because it's not. I thought we were becoming friends at the very least."

"Well, you thought wrong." Asher turns to go up the stairs.

"And another thing," I yell, following after him.

"Look out, everyone, there's another thing!" he shouts from the top of the stairs.

"I think you're mad at me for being with Wes." I push open

the door to his room, which he shut in my face. "I think you're jealous!"

"Jealous?" He gives a dry laugh.

"Yeah, I think you are! I think that's why you're not speaking to me and bringing around that girl." I stand in his room with my arms crossed. He takes off the jacket, tossing it on his bed, and turns back to face me. There's something in his eyes that makes me want to push him further. I want to argue with him.

"Look who sounds jealous now." He walks over to his piano bench, sitting down and taking off his shoes.

"I'm not." I walk over to him. "I told you from the start that I wanted Wes. Now I have him, so what do I need to be jealous about?"

Asher stands and now we're face-to-face. "Then what are you doing in here trying to fight with me? Go fight with your boyfriend."

Wes isn't my boyfriend, but the point feels moot.

"I don't need to fight with him. He would never do the things you do. The way you blatantly embarrassed me in front of that girl for no reason. You're arrogant, and selfish," I say up at him, and I notice the way his eyes darken and how he looks at my mouth when I call him names. "And you're jealous."

He doesn't say anything, and the scent of his cologne is overwhelming, almost arousing. And the way he's looking at me right now . . .

"What if I am?"

My next breath feels caught in my chest. "Then . . . then—"

"Then what?" His eyes hold the same promiscuous gleam as the night in the hotel.

The hotel, and what he did to me there, comes to the forefront of my mind.

My fingers tremble slightly as I bring them up to the buttons on my blouse, undoing them one at a time. I have no explanation for my actions, as my heart rate picks up.

"What are you doing?" He watches as I finish unbuttoning my shirt and slide it over my shoulders, revealing the semi-see-through white lace bralette underneath.

"Making things even," I say.

I get down on my knees and look up at him from under my lashes. What *am* I doing? He looks down at me and I watch him swallow, before looking over at his open bedroom door. I reach up and start to unbutton his pants, then pull down the zipper. He doesn't stop me. He's already hard when I pull him from his briefs and stroke him once with my hand. I put the tip to my tongue, and close my mouth around him, swirling my tongue over him as he lets out a shallow breath. And I've committed to this now, I think to myself as I continue.

"Fuck, Sloane, fuck," he breathes.

I put a hand to his thigh, removing him from my mouth. "Sit back," I tell him. He does, sitting back on the piano bench, and I lean over him, slipping my other hand into his briefs while putting him back into my mouth.

"Fuck." He leans back, hitting the piano keys. He puts his hand in my hair again, yanking it back so I lift my head. "I want you to look at me," he says.

So I do.

"Good girl." And I roll my eyes at the *good girl*. He huffs a laugh, leaning back. "How do you still have an attitude while doing this?"

"Mm," I hum in acknowledgment, and his hips buck. I know he's close, so I work faster. His hand tightens in my hair as his other arm leans back on the piano.

"Fuck, I'm gonna—" he says, but doesn't finish—well, he does finish, just not the sentence. I sit back on my heels and wipe my mouth on my wrist. "Fuck," he says up to the ceiling before looking back to me, eyes half wild, half disbelieving.

We look at each other like that for a minute, his eyes dipping down to my chest, where he can no doubt see right through the lace fabric, and I have half a mind to slide off my jeans and fuck him on his piano bench. But I did what I set out to do, nothing more.

"Now we're even," I say, standing up to grab my blouse before leaving.

I almost get to the last button when I walk out onto the porch and Wes is getting out of his car. He's beaming from ear to ear and runs right to me.

"He approved it!" he yells. "My dad approved the proposal!" Wes scoops me up and spins me around.

"Oh my god! Wow," I say. "I'm so happy for you." He sets me down and goes in for a kiss, but I turn my face. "Cold sore," I say quickly. "Sorry, I have a cold sore coming in, I can feel it. I wouldn't want you to get one." More so I wouldn't want you to have to kiss the mouth that just went down on your cousin. He kisses my flushed cheeks instead, not even wondering why they're flushed, or why I'm leaving his house if he wasn't there. Asher comes down the stairs and sees us on the porch.

"Good news," Wes says to him. "The resort is all yours, man."

Asher walks up to the door and leans on the frame. "All mine, huh?" But he's looking at me as he says it. Wesley claps a hand to his shoulder before walking inside.

"I need to make a few calls, and then I'm making reservations at Lago for tonight to celebrate!" Wes calls out. "Everyone better be there!" He runs up the stairs to his room, leaving Asher and me alone on the porch.

Asher cocks his head to the side, raising his eyebrows at me. If he's looking for an explanation for what I did upstairs, he isn't going to get one.

"I'll see you at dinner," I say, turning to go.

"Dinner?" he says. "You're not already full?" I turn back around to see him smirking at me.

"That needs to stay—"

"A secret?" Asher finishes for me. "I know how we operate by now, Sawyer." I go to walk back down the stairs and to my car. "And by the way," he calls out, "we're not even. Far from it."

But aren't we? He went down on me, I went down on him, now our unfinished business is finished. I got it out of my system. Didn't I?

"WE'LL TAKE THREE bottles of your best champagne," Wes says to the waiter. "We're celebrating tonight." The waiter, in a white button-down and black bow tie, nods before walking away. Nine of us sit around the rectangular table with ivory linens and three lit candles down the center.

"I just can't believe he really is passing on the resort," Annica whispers to me and Dani while Wes talks to Sam. "I mean, it was practically set up for him. This bed-and-breakfast thing might not even work out."

"I think he's following his heart. That's what matters," Dani says.

Annica counters, "But leaving the family business in Asher's hands so his dad can siphon money through it? That place will have to shut down in a year, mark my words."

I look over at Asher where he's seated on the other end of the table with Erin. He says something that makes her laugh, and I wish I knew what it was. The waiter brings out the champagne with ice buckets and flutes, pouring us each a glass. Wes stands for a toast.

"I want to thank you all for helping me make Margot's Bed-and-Breakfast a reality. I couldn't have done it without you guys. Especially you, Sloane," Wes says, looking over at me, and I smile up sheepishly. "I'd also like to announce that renovations on the house start in May, so we have the house to ourselves for spring break and I'd like you all to be there, all expenses paid, of course."

"Wes!" Dani squeals. "I can't keep going on these free trips—I feel bad!"

"Me too," I say.

"Well, I don't!" Jake says over us. "Cheers to chasing your dreams, bro." Jake lifts his glass.

"And to Asher too," Wes says. "You wanted the resort, and you've earned it. You always worked harder there than I did, so I'm glad it's going to you."

"Thanks, man. And if it doesn't work out, you can always come back and be a partner at the resort. What's mine is yours," Asher says. "And what's yours is mine." He looks over at me and I quickly look away.

"Thanks for the vote of confidence." Wes laughs. "Cheers!"

Everyone sips their drinks, but I chug mine.

CHAPTER 28

April

I'm halfway through my shift, the last one before spring break,
when I get a text from Annica. It's a link to an article posted by a
Boston news station.

IVY GATE PROFESSOR ARRESTED FOR MULTIPLE HOMICIDES

I gasp, dropping the cup I was holding. It shatters on the floor.

"Shit, shit, shit." I step over the glass and run to the back. "Jess,
I have to make a quick call."

"Is everything okay?" she asks.

"Better than okay!" I run from her office and out the back door.

I dial Grange. "Pick up, pick up, pick up." He does on the last
ring.

"I take it you saw the news," he says.

"What happened?"

"All I can say is we found evidence that ties him to the homicides."

"My journal?" I say. "Did you find my journal?"

He's silent for a moment. "Not quite. It was a story, among other items." A story? The story he brought to me in his briefcase?

"A story about what?" I pry.

"I really can't give you any more details at this time—"

I cut him off. "I want to talk to him. Can you arrange that? I want to talk to Miles." This just doesn't seem right. There's no evidence for three months, and now there's a story among other items? What other items?

"I'm not sure if that's a good idea," Grange says.

"Please," I plead. "Can I just see him? He'll approve the visit: He'll want to talk to me."

Grange sighs on the other end of the line. "I'll see what I can do."

DETECTIVE GRANGE CALLS me two days later saying he was able to get an approved visitation for the following Thursday.

"But that's during spring break," I say.

"Do you want the visit or not?"

"Fine, yes. I'll be there."

He sends me the paperwork I have to fill out in order to visit the maximum-security prison just outside Boston. Our friends are supposed to go to the beach house Wednesday through Sunday. I tell them I'll get there Thursday night. When Wes asks why, I lie and say Adrienne needs me to drop her off at the airport for her spring break trip to Florida. No one needs to know what I'm really doing. Not even Asher.

ON THURSDAY I sit in a folding chair placed in front of thick glass, bouncing my leg nervously. I look around and think it's exactly like the movies and TV shows. I had to leave my phone and personal items with the officer when I arrived, but the clock on the wall says Miles is two minutes late. Grange got me a fifteen-minute visit, and now I have only thirteen.

Finally, a tired-looking man in an orange jumpsuit with his hands handcuffed in front of him is led out by an officer and sits on the other side of the glass. I pick up the phone on my left, the one we're supposed to communicate through. He does not pick up his.

"Pick it up," I say through the glass. We now have ten minutes. "Please," I add. He lifts his shackled hands and picks up the phone, holding it to his ear. "Tell me why you did it."

"Sloane," he says. "You came." He gives me a watery-eyed smile and it roils my gut.

"Please save the crazy for another time. Why did you kill all of these people and try to pin it on me?"

"I would never do that to you." He shakes his head. "I love you; you know that."

"No you don't. If you loved me you would not have done any of this. They said they found a story. Is it the one you tried to give to me? You murdered all of these guys, wrote it down, and then tried to give me the story? That is demented, Miles."

He's quiet for a minute, and I glance at the clock. Seven minutes. "I heard about it on campus," he says finally. "The Ryan kid, his name was familiar. Word got around about this strange eulogy type note that was in his pocket when he died, and I thought it was just a rumor going around the faculty. But it reminded me of that journal you kept, the one you showed me last year, and I realized he was in there. It was your journal page they found on him. It was brilliant, the whole idea. My next murder-mystery bestseller. I was going to ask for your permission to write it, your input even, but you wouldn't see me, so I wrote it anyway."

"You were going to *sell* this story? And you thought you'd get away with that?"

"Once again, as I've told you many times now, I am not the murderer."

"It doesn't look like that from here."

"I was set up," he says.

I give a disbelieving laugh. "That's rich coming from the person who tried to set me up."

"I'm telling the truth," he says. "Someone planted evidence in my office."

"In your locked drawer under your desk?"

"Yes," he says.

Our time is almost up. "Did you send Adrienne to the Four Seasons after the gallery shooting to drop the gun off to my room?"

"No." He looks me in the eyes when he answers and somehow I know he's telling the truth, but my mind refuses to believe it.

"I just don't know how you expect me to believe any of this."

"Read the story," he says. "I'm sure they have it in evidence. Read it." The officer comes to collect Miles from the phone.

"Wait," I say. "Wait!" But the visit is over.

"Read it," Miles says from the other side, before yelling, "I love you, Sloane!" He's ushered back into the prison where he belongs.

I GET IN my car to drive to Nantucket, thinking about my short thirteen-minute conversation with Miles and how it was the most confusing one yet. He's denied being the murderer this whole time, and even almost had me convinced that he isn't. I saw him in handcuffs myself, so why am I still not completely convinced? I call Grange from the car.

"Well, did you get what you were looking for?" he asks.

"No, I'm not sure he did this," I admit.

"You were once very adamant that he did."

"I know, I know what I said," I say quickly. "Can I read the story?"

"I cannot give you evidence before a trial, no."

"Well, did you read it?" I ask.

"No, not fully," he says.

"I need you to read it and tell me what happens."

"You want me to read this three-hundred-page, single-spaced book from a madman and give you the CliffsNotes?"

"Yes . . ."

"No."

"Can you at least tell me what happens at the very end? Tell me who he wrote that the killer was."

Grange sighs. "Enjoy your spring break, Miss Sawyer, you deserve to relax."

THE SUN SETS behind the McCavern beach house on Nantucket when I finally arrive, and it's even more stunning in person. Large white-trimmed windows cover gray slatted siding, with a double glass-paneled door welcoming you in the front of the house. As I walk down the stone driveway with my suitcase, I imagine the big sign in the front yard that'll say "Margot's Bed-and-Breakfast." I pretend I'm a guest there. I know when I enter, Wesley's face will be at the front desk to check me in, and I'll be drawn in by his smile and kind eyes, and I'll never want to leave.

It's half true when I walk in and Wes meets me at the door to take my bags. "Welcome to the soon-to-be Margot's," he says.

"Wow," I say back, taking in the open, airy layout of the first floor. The foyer opens up to a grand living room surrounded by floor-to-ceiling windows that look out into the backyard. Cream couches with light blue accents are placed on white stone floors. To the left is a white marble kitchen that looks like it's never seen a stain a day in its life.

"Wait until you see the back," Wes says, leading me to the sliding glass door. We walk out to a deck that overlooks an inground pool and hot tub surrounded by lush grass and an outdoor dining gazebo. Just past the grass is a trail to the beach. Our friends are all back there when we walk out, watching the sun set over the beach horizon. Dani and Annica come back up the beach path toward the house.

"Yay! You're here!" Dani calls out to me. I smile and wave.

"Sloane!" Jake yells from the pool. "Glad to know you weren't really the Pembroke Psycho after all!"

I look over to the hot tub, where Asher sits with Erin. She's drinking white wine right from the bottle. Real classy. Seeing them together makes me wonder how he treats the girls that he's actually seeing. Is he sweet to her? Does he hold her at night?

I'm not jealous, just curious.

"Glad you could make it," Asher says. "It really *sucked* without you here."

I give him a tight smile. "I'm sure it did." I look back at Wes standing with his arms crossed over his Cape Cod sweatshirt, and with a backward cap. He looks like he belongs here. "Why don't you show me to my room."

"*Our* room." He winks, placing a hand to the small of my back and leading me inside. We walk down the long hallway on the bottom floor and stop at the door at the end of the hall. "This is the master bedroom. We'll be in here until Saturday, when my family visits."

"Your family is coming?" No one said anything about the rest of them showing up. I'm not sure how I'd even go about seeing them all again, now being with Wes and not Asher.

"Yeah, we're having, like, a 'last party at the house' kind of situation before renovations start."

"Oh, okay."

The master room is huge, with white plush carpet and a bed on a two-step landing. It has its own sliding door to the patio as well as a bathroom with a claw-foot tub and a heated toilet seat. Wes drops my bags by the bed.

"There's another room I want to show you real quick. It's my favorite." I follow Wes out of the bedroom, back down the hall, and up the stairs leading to the second story of the house. We pass more bedrooms and bathrooms, even a small library, before getting to a ladder leading up to an opening in the ceiling.

"The attic?" I guess.

"Not quite," he says, grabbing on and hoisting himself up. He climbs to the top and I follow. The room is empty, aside from a few boxes and old containers of paint, but I know immediately why this is the best room in the house. The glass-paneled ceiling slants down to meet glass-paneled walls, like being in a bubble in the sky, which is now streaked with pink and orange. "Cool, huh?"

"Wow," I say. If I lived here I would die for this to be my room.

"You should see it during a storm. I'd come up here when I was younger to lie on the floor and watch the rain slide down the windows."

"What are you going to do with it?"

"Make it a room," Wes says. "Take out the ladder and put in stairs."

"I bet people would pay good money to stay in here," I say, walking out onto the small terrace, just outside the room. It's only big enough for two, but the view is breathtaking. You can see the entire beach. The salty breeze whips my hair around, and I tuck it behind my ears.

"I bet they would too. But it isn't about the money; it's about the experience. Me and my sisters have so many good memories here. I want that for other people. I want to give them that." Wes leans on the railing, looking out into the ocean before us, which stretches on and on, and I can't imagine a more perfect moment. We watch the sun dip below the horizon as the night sky darkens above us. And for the first time in a long time, I feel like everything is going to be okay.

CHAPTER 29

"So you'll have to, like, testify against him, right? Like, you'll be going to court?" Annica asks from the pool chair beside me.

"I mean, yeah, I guess so." I honestly hadn't even thought of that fact until right now. I'll be called as a witness, especially since it was my journal, and I was there for most of the deaths. They'll likely walk through them all and I'll have to relive them dying all over again. They might even read the pages aloud. The idea fills me with instant dread.

"What, did I say something wrong? Your face is, like, white right now," Annica says.

"No, I'm fine. Let's just try to not talk about it this week. I'm tired of talking about it."

"Talking about what?" Asher asks, walking out to the pool in swim trunks and no shirt. I look away, suddenly really admiring the outdoor umbrellas and the yellow-and-white-striped pattern on them.

"Wouldn't you like to know," Annica says.

Erin chimes in then from behind him. "You're the girl, right? The one everyone was calling the Pembroke Psycho? Bet you're glad that's over. Although I'm kind of jealous. I wish someone would go around killing *my* exes. That'd be nice."

I sit up and lower my sunglasses so she can see the glare I give her. "Well, sure, if you think holding a dying person in your arms and not being able to do anything to help, plus knowing that it's your fault they were shot in the first place, is *nice* . . . then yeah."

Erin blinks. "I just meant that, like, as a joke."

"Hilarious," Annica mutters.

I imagine pushing Asher's girlfriend into the pool. Erin shuts up, thankfully, and gets in the water. Without me having to push her.

"Someone's not playing nice today," Asher says, walking behind my chair to take a seat on the other side of me.

I turn to him, talking just above a whisper. "What I went through has been traumatic enough to send your Goth Barbie girlfriend into a spiral, so if she wants to make jokes, I'll gladly tell her why they aren't funny."

"Hm, so I take it I won't be able to talk you into an apology?"

"Apology? You want *me* to apologize to her?" I look at him incredulously.

"She was only trying to make conversation." He shrugs. "And you nearly bit her head off."

I think about pushing Asher into the pool as well.

"Who wants to play a game?" Jake yells from the patio, tossing a volleyball in the air.

Wes leaves for the market, and the rest of us make our way to a worn-down volleyball net on the beach. "All right, Dani and Charlie are team captains," Jake says. "Dani gets to pick first because she's a girl."

"Asher," she says immediately.

I scoff. "Dani, what the hell? You know I played in high school."

"I know, but we played the other day and Asher is really good. I'll pick you next, promise."

"Hey!" Annica whines.

"I pick Sam," Charlie says, which is also insulting because Sam is built like a toothpick. Surely I was still the better choice.

"Sloane," Dani counters.

"Jake."

"Great, now he has all the guys." I cross my arms. Asher rolls his eyes.

"Annica," Dani says.

"Then I'll take Erin." Charlie smiles. I smile too, because I'm going to spike it at Erin's face.

"If you target her you'll regret it," Asher says like he can read my mind, then looks at Annica. "That goes for both of you."

We take our spots in the sand, on either side of the net between us. Charlie serves first, and he floats an overhand serve to our side. Dani bumps it right in between Asher and me in the front.

"I got it!" I yell, going for a set.

"Mine," he says, jumping to tip it. We collide but he still manages to tap the ball over, earning us a point.

"I said I had it," I snap at him.

"So did I. If I call it, just back off."

"Okay, go team!" Dani says from the back. "Good start!"

We rotate so it's Asher's serve. He sends it over hard, and it smacks off Sam's arms and goes up to the net, where Jake spikes it down. It looks like it's going a little to my back left and I turn to dive for it when Asher dives for it as well. We run into each other again, this time with my arm landing under him.

I hiss in pain, bringing my arm close to my chest. "I had it, Asher."

"That was clearly my ball," he snaps back.

"You didn't call it!"

"Neither did you!"

"Guys?" Jake calls from the other side. "Is everyone ready? I'm going to serve."

"Just peachy," I mutter, getting up. Jake serves it far to our side and I run to the sand-drawn line to call it out.

"In," Sam says. And I guess it is, as the ball indent hits the line directly.

Asher lets out a long sigh, and I turn to him. "Why didn't you call it in, then?"

"Probably because you called it out?"

"This is going to be a long game," Dani mutters.

Jake serves again to Annica, and she returns it on one hit. Sam volleys it back and Asher bumps it from the back row, setting up the front. I call it and go for a set. Erin moves in on the other side of the net, leaving the front corner open, so I pretend to set up Annica but push the ball behind me so that it falls perfectly on the line. And now it's my serve.

"Good luck on the serve," Asher says as I walk past him. "Try not to *blow* it."

My fingers tighten on the ball. I toss it in the air with my left hand, and bring my right hand down hard, aiming at the back of his head. I hit my target, and he turns around rubbing his head. "What the fuck?"

"Sorry, accident," I say with a fake pity frown. He turns back around, and I toss the ball up again, bringing it down hard on his head a second time.

"Okay, what the hell is your problem today?" he says, stalking toward me until we're face-to-face.

"My problem?" I push my finger to his chest. "What is *your* problem?"

He grabs my wrist.

"Guys!" Dani yells.

I yank my arm from his grasp. "I can't be on a team with him," I say to her, pushing past Asher.

"Well, if I'm not on your team, then whose head will you serve the ball at?" Asher snarks.

"I said it was an accident."

"Seemed intentional to me. You know, when something happens multiple times, it's no longer an accident." He inclines his head, not talking about the serve.

"Ugh, screw this," Annica says. "I'm going back to the pool."

"And I need a drink," I say, following her inside.

EVERYONE GATHERS IN the living room waiting for the Ubers to pick us up. I can tell Asher is watching me from the corner of my eye but I don't acknowledge it. When the cars pull up, everyone goes to leave, and Wesley grabs my hand.

"You guys have fun," he calls out to the group.

Asher turns around. "What do you mean? Are you not coming?" He looks between Wes and me. I just stare at Wes, confused.

"No, Sloane and I have other plans," Wes says, eyeing me. I glance back at Asher, who is still standing there, like he might say that if we aren't going then neither is he. But he turns around to leave with the group. "Come with me." Wes takes my hand and leads me out to the backyard, down the beach path, and out to a spread of blankets on the beach.

"What is all this?" I ask when we get closer, seeing rose petals sprinkled around the blankets, two charcuterie boards, a pizza, and a bottle of white wine on ice.

"I wanted to surprise you."

"You did all of this yourself?" I sit on the blanket, wiping the sand from my feet before crawling farther in, plucking a piece of prosciutto from the board.

"Well, yes and no." Wes joins me, grabbing the bottle from the bucket and pouring us each a glass. "Dani helped me set it up." He hands me a glass and I take a sip.

"This is amazing, thank you," I say. "No one has ever set up a beach picnic for me. Or any picnic."

"Oh, I'm just trying to stay on your good side," he teases. "I wouldn't want to end up in that journal of yours."

I take a breath and let it out with a nervous laugh. "Right, wouldn't want that." I bring my wineglass back to my mouth for a big gulp, or two.

We talk and eat until the sky turns vibrant with the colors of the sunset.

"So I just thought," Wes starts, "we've been taking things slow lately, and I love slow, really I do. Some of my favorite things move slow, like . . . turtles and my grandpa—"

"Turtles and your grandpa?" I laugh.

"What I'm trying to say is, um, would you be my girlfriend?"

His girlfriend. This is what I've always wanted. So why do I have to remind myself of that before I answer? "Yes."

"Yeah?"

"Yeah."

Wes leans in to kiss me, and I kiss him back. His hands are light on my skin as his thumb brushes against my jaw and over my collarbone. Our mouths press together harder, the kisses deeper as his tongue slips into my mouth. He moves from my mouth, down my neck, to my collarbone and shoulders, slipping the straps of the dress down past my shoulders. I lean back on my elbows, tilting my head back as he explores. Wes positions himself over me and I lie down. His mouth is back on mine, and his hand starts to move up my thigh, under my dress. He traces his fingers over the thin line of my underwear.

We hear a loud splash in the pool up at the house, causing him to pause.

"I guess they're back," Wes says, sitting up. "We'll finish this later." He kisses my forehead and helps me up. I put the dress straps back over my shoulders. We clean up the picnic, carrying everything back up to the house.

"How was it?" Dani smirks from the pool, still in her dress she wore to dinner, with Charlie, who is also fully clothed.

"She said yes," Wes says.

"She said yes to what?" Asher asks from the patio with a bottle of wine in hand.

"To being his girlfriend!" Dani squeals.

We walk past Asher and Erin on our way into the house, where we put away the food. Wes leans in for another kiss but his phone starts to go off. I hear him sigh a few times on the line before saying, "I have to go pick up Jake, Sam, and Annica from a bar that's like thirty minutes away. Jake is apparently so drunk that no Uber will take them."

"Oh," I say, not surprised. Jake can get that way. "I'll take care of the blankets and the rest of the food."

"I'll be right back with the rest of our dumb friends," he says, grabbing his keys. Asher walks into the kitchen as I grab the blankets from the floor.

"Girlfriend, huh?" he says, following me down the other end of the hall toward the laundry room.

"Yeah, I guess so." I still can't believe it either.

"Looks like we both got everything we wanted, then," he says, but there's an edge in his voice. I start the washing machine and walk back out to where he stands in the hall. "Miles is in jail, and you're Wesley's girlfriend."

"We did," I say, standing in front of him with my arms crossed. "And you got your precious resort." He doesn't say anything. "Is there a problem?"

"Not at all. I couldn't wait for the whole thing to be over with."

I scoff. "Good, because neither could I."

"I hated every moment of it," he says.

"And I hated you." I didn't. I didn't hate him. I hated how frustrating and argumentative he could be. I hated how he'd leave me when I felt like I needed him. And I hated the way I wanted him despite it all.

His mouth twitches like he might laugh. "Is that so?" He takes a step toward me, and I step back. "*Hate* is a strong word."

"Well, it's true," I say, though it's not. "I hate you."

When he steps to me again, my back hits the wall. Asher leans in. "Say it again," he says. "Lie to me again."

"I hate you," I whisper.

He drags his thumb against my lip and down to my throat, before pulling me in and crashing his mouth into mine. And I don't stop him, I don't push him away. He picks me up, holding me against the wall of the dark hallway. I wrap my legs around him before he takes me into his room and shuts the door. He swipes everything off the dresser that he sets me on; whatever it is lands on the floor and shatters.

"Asher," I breathe his name, but more so as a reprimand. He kisses me wildly, down my neck and my chest.

"It's part of the remodel," he mutters, ripping down the front of my dress, his mouth on mine again, our teeth and tongues clashing. But then he's pulling me from the dresser, and I unbutton his pants, tugging them down along with his briefs. He's trying to find a way to get the dress off, but it's corseted in the back.

"Fuck it," he says, turning me around to the wall and lifting the dress. His one hand snakes up the front of me and grasps at my chest as he pushes himself inside me, igniting a fire throughout my body. This time I can't stop from crying out. He quickly brings his hand from my chest to my mouth to muffle the noise as he thrusts into me from behind, licking and biting at my neck, wild and uncaring. I'm grasping at anything, including the curtains over the window, which come down with a crash. I feel him start to rip at the corset in the back, desperately trying to get the dress off. He turns me around, pulling the dress down as I rip through the buttons on his shirt until we're both standing there completely naked together for the first time.

I push him down to the bed and climb on top of him, like I had intended to do in Boston. I slide down onto him, savoring the sound he makes when I do. I rock my hips over his, and when he groans it sends chills down my spine. Asher flips me onto my back, putting a leg over his shoulder, and rubbing at the sensitive bundle of nerves at the apex of my thighs with his other hand.

"You're mine," he says, breathless. "You're mine."

"I'm yours," I say without hesitation. In this moment I am his. Or perhaps I have been for a while now. His breathing becomes ragged in my ear and I know he's close. "I'm yours," I say again, my back arching and legs shaking as I tumble over the edge. And he thrusts hard a few more times as he finishes in me.

Asher remains on top of me while we catch our breath and the post-orgasm clarity rushes through us.

"Fuck," he says, before getting off me and stepping off the bed. "Fuck." He smacks the lamp right off the nightstand, causing me to flinch, and goes into his bathroom, shutting the door behind him.

I bring my knees to my chest, taking in the scene. The curtain rod is half on, tilting down with the curtain on the floor. The knickknacks from the dresser lay shattered on the floor. The lamp on the nightstand is now on the ground with the shade broken.

I get up, grabbing my dress from the floor before scurrying from his room and back to my own undetected. I shower and get into bed, letting silent tears fall down my cheeks over what I just did. What we just did. And whatever that means.

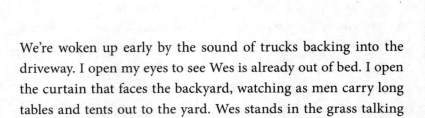

CHAPTER 30

We're woken up early by the sound of trucks backing into the driveway. I open my eyes to see Wes is already out of bed. I open the curtain that faces the backyard, watching as men carry long tables and tents out to the yard. Wes stands in the grass talking with his dad. Annica and Dani are in the kitchen when I walk out, still rubbing sleep from my eyes.

"What's going on?" I ask.

"They're setting up for the party," Annica says.

"The one with his family?"

"Well, it's not just his family. I think like half of this island was invited—we heard people talking about it at dinner last night."

Dani chimes in. "And some businessy people too, Charlie said. So it's very important that you stay away from Asher," Dani says to me.

"What? Why would you say that?"

"Because you two bickered all day yesterday. It really brought down the vibe."

"Oh, right."

"Did you guys see Erin left this morning?" Annica asks.

"No," Dani says. "What happened?"

"I don't know, but I saw her get in the car with her bags real early. Probably didn't want the riffraff here with all the important people."

"Good morning, girls." Wesley's mom walks in with a woman in a blue tweed blazer and matching skirt. She smiles at Annica and Dani, and I might just be paranoid, but I swear her eyes glaze right over me. "This is Helen, the best event planner on the East Coast. She'll be helping me with the setup today. Do you think you girls can wrangle up the boys and get them out of the house for a few hours so we can prepare for the party?"

"Shouldn't be too hard," Annica says with a smile. "We just have to promise them food and alcohol and they'll go anywhere."

"Perfect," Mrs. McCavern says, leading Helen to the backyard. "And this is where I'm thinking we have the caterer set up, and the dance floor should go here . . ." Her voice trails off from outside. The dance floor?

"I didn't pack anything for this kind of party," I say. "Can we shop and send the boys somewhere else?"

"Ooh yes! Let's shop!" Dani agrees.

"Yeah, I'll make them a tee time at the golf course," Annica says, picking up her phone.

"I'll go upstairs and start waking them up," Dani says.

That leaves Wes and Asher for me. I walk down the hall and stop in front of Asher's door, the same place I stood last night. I glance behind me at the wall he pushed me up against. I almost turn to leave, let someone else tell him they're golfing, but he opens the door and startles at me standing there. We stare at each other, both of us unsure why I'm at his door.

"Your aunt wants you all out of the house so they can prepare for the party. Annica is making you guys a tee time and we're going shopping."

He crosses his arms. "Shopping for what?" he asks.

"Something to wear for the party," I say in a matter-of-fact way. He goes to shut the door and I put my hand out before it can close. "Why did Erin leave?"

"I told her to leave," he says.

"Why?"

He steps aside, showing the room. "Why do you think?"

I look past him at the curtain rod still hanging off the wall, the broken pieces on the floor, all the reminders of what happened in this room. I turn back down the hall without another word.

I PURCHASED A beachy white two-piece outfit. The skirt is long, with a slit down the side of my leg, and the tube top ties together in the front, leaving ruffled white fabric hanging below. The whole thing cost me at least three shifts at Cantine, and all I could think about was whether Asher would like it. I stand in the bathroom applying a bit of blush to my sun-kissed cheeks. My hair is sporting a natural curl from the ocean water and salty air, so I let it be. I slip on cork-style wedges that I brought from home and step out onto the back patio from our bedroom.

It's hard to believe this was all put together in a few hours. The backyard glistens in the late afternoon with strung lights hanging above the crowd that's already starting to form. A DJ plays cocktail music from the deck, while people gather near the tables of hors d'oeuvres. A dance floor is staged in the middle of the grass, behind the pool. Two bartenders stand behind the bar in the pavilion, and that's where I find my friends. Asher stares at me from where he's leaning on the bar. I blush and look away from him quickly. Dani's yellow silk dress drapes over her tan shoulders, one piece of it sliding down as she does a twirl for Charlie. Annica stands beside them in a long light green dress that looks like it was meant for her and complements her hair color.

"You two should just date already," she says, watching Charlie twirl Dani around.

"Well, we weren't going to say anything until after Wesley's party, but we've decided to give it a shot!"

I smile. "Finally!"

"Well, what the hell, now I feel like I need to date someone in the group," Annica says, looking at Jake, Sam, and Asher.

"I'd rather die," Asher says. Jake and Sam turn around sipping their drinks.

I feel a hand wrap around my waist from behind. "You look so beautiful," Wes says in my ear.

"Thank you." I smile, taking a deep breath, but in my mind, I'm counting down the hours until I can be off this island and away from both McCavern boys. Or maybe just away from Asher. If he's gone, there's no one distracting me from the McCavern I should be with.

"Let's talk to my parents," he says, grabbing my hand, leading me into the crowd. We pass groups of influential men and women making idle chatter while Frank Sinatra plays in the background and I glance up at the sky as storm clouds form above. We come upon Mr. and Mrs. McCavern talking to a middle-aged man in a beige blazer.

"There he is," Wesley's dad says. "The man of the hour."

"You guys remember Sloane?" Wes says, stepping aside. His parents both give me tight-lipped smiles.

"You're Asher's girl, right?" his dad asks.

"Well," Wes starts. "Not anymore. I mean, she never actually was . . ." He trails off.

Wesley's mom looks between us. "So, are you two seeing each other now?"

"We are," Wes says, putting an arm around me.

"Mm." She takes a sip of her champagne and walks away, leaving us with Wesley's dad, who gives us a nod before following after his wife.

"Great," I say. "She hates me."

"She doesn't hate you," Wes says.

"Was she that way toward Marissa?"

"Speaking of Marissa," he says. "She's here."

"I'm sorry, what?" I start to look around, but I don't see her.

"Come on, let's dance." Wes takes my hand as a slow song starts. A few other couples join us on the dance floor. Wes pulls me close to him as we sway to the music but I'm searching the crowd for his ex. I find her by the bar, talking to Wesley's mom. Marissa introduces her to someone, and when he turns around it's . . . "Colton?" I say aloud.

Wes looks at me, confused. "What?"

"Colton Austi is Marissa's date? How do they even know each other?"

Wesley's dad interrupts us on the floor. "Wes, come meet the mayor real quick."

Wes looks over at his father. "The mayor?" We stop dancing,

but his hand is still around my waist. "Can it wait until after the song?"

A hand clasps onto Wesley's shoulder. "Don't worry about it, man," Asher says. "I can take over. Wouldn't want Sloane to be left alone on the dance floor."

"Great. Wesley, let's go." His dad puts a hand to his back. Wes opens his mouth to say something.

"Yeah, Wes, go on. I got this." Asher puts a hand around my waist and holds out the other for me to take.

I hesitate.

The girl who calls me a murderer online is talking to my boyfriend's mother, with my ex's brother as her date, who also calls me a murderer to anyone who will listen.

"Sloane?" Asher prompts. Wes glances over his shoulder, giving me a weary look as he's led into the crowd. I sigh, and give Asher my hand, placing my other one on his chest. "You seem anxious," Asher says.

"Marissa is here with Colton," I tell him. "Probably over there telling your aunt that I'm a serial killer. Just wait until I go over there. I'm gonna—"

"Come to Colorado with me," Asher interrupts. His voice rumbles through his chest. I feel it in my hand that rests there.

It catches me completely off guard. I look up at him. "What?" Small droplets of rain come down sporadically, like a warning.

"Come with me. Get away from all of this."

I can't help the laugh that escapes me. He's messing with me. He must be. "So we can what? Argue all the time?"

"If that's what you want to do." Asher looks down at me and

there's no amusement, no playfulness in his features. "I leave next week."

A light sprinkle falls around us, and people begin to walk to the nearest tent or the bar pavilion. "Next week? What about the rest of your classes?"

"I graduated in the fall semester; I've been done with school."

I didn't know that. He never said anything. "Then why have you been here all spring?" I ask him. He gives me another look, tilting his head to the side just slightly as if to say *come on, Sloane.*

I stop swaying with him and drop my hands. "You've got to be fucking kidding me, Asher."

He finally smirks at my tone. "Here we go."

"I asked you back in January how you felt. How could you let me go on with Wes and then turn around and ask me this?"

It's full-on raining now, and I turn to leave him on the dance floor, but I don't want to huddle underneath a crowded space with random people. I need to be alone. I walk through the yard to the front of the house, hoping to find a spot on the wraparound porch. Sheets of rain come down now as I run to the front of the house. A group of people stands on the porch, and one of them is a still-pregnant Kate Russel. Great, everyone really is here. I run to the detached garage, through the side door. It's spacious enough in here to be mistaken as a second home. I wring out my hair on the floor, wrapping my arms around myself as I pace the room. Colorado with Asher. I can't even imagine. It'd be a disaster.

"There you are." Asher walks in the side door after me.

"I want to be alone."

He ignores me. "I was wondering if they still had this," he says, walking up to the large structure covered in a tarp. He removes it and before us is a sailboat. *Of course* they have a sailboat. Asher climbs up the wheel of the tow it sits atop and over the silver railing. Then holds out his hand for me to join him. I look back at the door, where the rain and wind blow furiously outside. I slip off my heels and take his hand, climbing onto the boat with him. "Good memories on this thing."

I lean back on the railing with my arms crossed as he messes with the steering wheel. Thunder rumbles outside, shaking the structure.

"Tell me why," I say.

He clears his throat. "I think you know why."

"Then say it."

He looks at me for a while, before walking to the back part of the boat and disappearing down the stairs. And I should just leave. Go and find Wes. But the rain still comes down hard outside and I've never seen the inside of a boat. So I follow him down the stairs. Wood-paneled walls push in on me in the small space below the deck, and I think that boat living is definitely not for the claustrophobic.

"Asher?" I say his name when I don't see him. But then his hands are on my waist from behind, and I startle. He turns me around and lifts my chin up to him and puts his mouth on mine. I pull away. "Tell me why," I say again.

He grabs my hands and walks back, through a door that practically blends into the wall, and into a small bedroom. It's nearly pitch-black in here aside from the small porthole window that looks out into the garage. He sits on the edge of the bed, pulling me between his knees. "They say actions speak louder than words, don't they?" He starts to untie my top and I grab his hands to stop him. He stands again, leaning in so our foreheads are touching. "Let me show you why."

He kisses me softly, then kisses me again, and again. Each one sweeter than the last. And I'm waiting for the moment that his hands start grabbing me, pulling at my clothes. Waiting for his teeth on my skin. Waiting for him to take, like he usually does. Waiting to be fucked. But this time is different. When he reaches down to untie my top again, still wet from the rain, I let him. It falls to the floor, as he removes his blazer and unbuttons his shirt. I slide them down over his shoulders, running my hands over his chest, his shoulders, his arms. He lays me gently on the mattress and lies over top of me, planting these foreign soft lip kisses on my lips and my jaw. I reach down for his pants but he grabs my hand and threads his fingers through mine. He continues down my neck, over my chest, to my stomach. He lets go of my hand and starts to slide down my skirt, leaving me totally bare in front of him. His eyes roam over my body, really looking at me now, and usually I would want to shrink in on myself. But instead I open my legs for him. He unbuckles and unzips his pants, kicking them off and adding to the pile on the floor. We both inhale when he pushes into me, and I know in the way he holds me tight to his body and whispers my name that Asher Collins McCavern is in love.

He just won't say it.

We lie there, and for once, Asher holds me in his arms. He strokes my rain-soaked hair while my head rests on his chest.

"What are you thinking about?" I whisper.

"That we could do this in Colorado instead of arguing."

I sigh and shake my head as reality sets in. "I'm dating your cousin."

"Break up with him."

But how could I break up with Wes for Asher, who can't even admit that he loves me. How could I move across the country for something so fragile.

"We need to get back to the party," I say, getting up and walking over to my clothes.

He sits up in bed and leans forward, resting his arms on his knees. "Make sure you're packed to go by graduation. I'll be back that weekend."

I scoff. "What makes you so sure I'm going with you?"

He smiles that arrogant smile. "Because you're in love with me."

I finish tying on my top, shaking my head. I look over at him again and open my mouth . . . before closing it, and leaving the room.

Because he's right.

THE DIRT AND grass squish under my feet as I walk back to the yard holding my heels, to where the guests are huddled under the tents and pavilion.

"Where were you?" Dani says to me when I join them by the bar. "You're drenched. And I think . . . I think your top is on upside down?"

I fold my arms over my chest. "I got caught in the downpour. I had to take it off to wring it out," I say, shivering. "I'll probably go in and change. I just need to grab my phone. Have you seen Wes?"

Dani looks around. "No, I thought he was with you."

I unlock my phone to find multiple texts from Wesley.

Where are you?

Annica just told me you're sleeping
with Asher, is that true?

Sloane?

Followed by a missed call from Annica.

My stomach drops. "Oh my god."

I call her back, looking through the crowd again for her or Wes. She answers on the second ring. "Sloane," she sobs.

"Annica?"

"You have to get up here, hurry." Her words are a jumbled mess through the tears.

"What? What's wrong?"

"It's Wes," she cries. "He's hurt."

"Oh my god." I grab Dani. "Call 911, now!"

"What?!" Her eyes go wide.

"Where are you?" I ask Annica.

"Attic, hurry!" Her frantic cry sends a jolt through me as my worst fear seems to be coming true. "He's been stabbed."

CHAPTER 31

I ditch the heels as I run up the back deck, over broken glass and other items that blew away in the wind. I vaguely feel the stinging cuts on my feet but I keep running. I text Grange the address to the house with the word *hurry*.

Wes has been stabbed, in his own home no less, and it could've been any of them. Marissa, Kate, Colton, they're all here. Any one of them could've done it.

I climb the rungs of the ladder so fast, ignoring the burning sensation in my feet and arms from doing most of the work. When I'm eye level with the floor I see Wes slumped against the glass, red staining his white linen button-down. I get flashbacks of Graham, causing me to falter. Annica is bent over him with her hand pressed into his side.

"Oh my god. What happened—how did this happen?" I rush over to them, feeling for a pulse on his neck, and thank god when it's there. "Help! Somebody help us!" I yell from the attic. There's blood on his head, like someone knocked him out first.

"Wes told me to meet him here," Annica says through tears. "And when I got up here she just stabbed him."

"Who? Who stabbed him?" I look all around the room. Are we not alone up here? "Was it Marissa? Kate?"

She sniffles once before shoving something cold and hard into my hand. "It was you," she says.

I pull away and it clatters to the wooden floor. "What?"

Annica stands, looking down at Wes, and wiping away her tears with a bloody hand. A small smile spreads across her face and I can only stare at her, while firmly keeping a hand where I assume the stab wound is. The blood makes the shirt squelch under my fingers. I try to gather it up to apply more pressure. Annica turns and shuts the attic door, locking it. She grabs something from the corner of the room, crumples it up, and tosses it at me. It lands on the floor in front of me and I already know what it is. With my other hand, I shakily open it to confirm my suspicions, and there on the white paper is the printed copy of my journal page, the one for Wes, with just his name. I breathe in shallow breaths. "You?"

She grabs something else, something small and dark. The metal clinks against the rings on her hand. A gun. "I honestly can't believe you never figured it out."

I shake my head, trying to make sense of it. It can't be. It can't be her. This must be some kind of mistake.

"I found your journal Welcome Weekend, recognized all the names as your exes. Imagine my surprise when I got to the end and saw Wesley's name. God, I was furious. After I specifically asked you not to! I wanted just one thing from you and you couldn't even do that. You just take, and take, and take with no regard for anyone but yourself."

The way she talks to me now with such disgust in her tone, the same way she talks to Asher on a good day, I have no doubt in my mind. It is her. It has been her the entire time. I brought her to Ryan's apartment, I brought her to Marco's restaurant. I thought I was saving Bryce by keeping him around, but I only brought him closer to the killer.

She continues, because I am too stunned to speak. "Ryan was easy enough; he was already pretty drunk when I pushed him. And all I had to do to get him out there was tell him I had dirt on you. He really did *not* like you. Then we have Marco. I had been to his restaurant twice before we went as a group, so I could see what time he leaves and who all stays to close up. And wouldn't you know, he was always the last to leave. He'd play music and scrub that kitchen clean every night until long past midnight, with nothing but a bottle of wine to keep him company. The tricky part was making sure he'd be there until at least 3 a.m. So I had Dalton unknowingly suggest a bottle of wine to him that I put Rohypnol in. That's a whole other story, though." Annica shakes her head, waving a hand as if to say she'll tell me that story later.

But I have a feeling there won't be a later.

"None of you even noticed when I snuck out of Dalton's party to start the gas leak and plant a gasoline canister in your trunk. And let's see . . . who was next? Oh, Bryce." She laughs. "The sword was kind of crazy, wasn't it? I just really wanted to do something special for Halloween. Luckily, he was already drunk and coked out of his mind when I found him in the back room. I was in and out of there in under thirty minutes. Graham's was a real challenge. Pretending to be his manager and meeting with the building security, convincing them to have all cameras pointed to the most expensive gallery piece, creating the perfect blind spot, then shooting him and getting the gun into your hotel room all before you got back. I almost had Tristan too but you just had to go and get a police detail on him." Annica pauses like she's trying to remember if that was everyone. "And you know what really made this whole thing even better? You always let yourself get so fucking drunk that you black out almost every time. It was honestly amusing to watch you unravel each time that you couldn't remember what happened the night before, thinking that maybe it really *was* you. I know you thought that in the beginning, I could see it in your face."

"Why?" I say finally, when I think I have heard enough.

"To ruin your life. I wanted you to know what it feels like to have something taken from you, so I tried taking everything from you. I wanted you to rot in prison for crimes you didn't commit. And it was going so well. I really thought I had you when you went to the police. I thought surely you would not be walking back out of that station unless you were in handcuffs. But they let you go. They let you fucking go. So I had to redirect. You already thought it was Holland, and I couldn't let them find out it was me, so I was the one to put the evidence in his office."

"What about Jonah?" She didn't mention him, but I have to know.

"Jonah? No, I owe the whole idea to Jonah. He was my inspiration. I saw how his death affected you and I just knew this was how I'd get my revenge."

"All because I slept with Wesley?"

"It wasn't just Wes. I was so sick of you always getting your way. You don't even try and you still get everything handed to you.

Every boy I like likes you first. You fucked a professor, ruined his marriage, got him fired, and still got to continue on with no repercussions. You got a DUI and they expunged it from your record. All four years of school you hardly put in any work and you get better grades than me. I'll bet you would've even won this short-story competition . . . if you were still going to be around to submit it." She points the gun at me now.

"I already called 911; the police will be up here any moment." Though I didn't. I just told Dani to, in hopes that she would. There could be no one coming at all. That would explain why I haven't heard a single thing from downstairs.

"Then I guess I should make this quick. Walk to the balcony," she demands.

I look at Wes, unconscious. "I can't, I can't leave him," I cry with my hand still pressed to the wound.

She points the gun at him instead. "Oh, don't pretend to care about him now. Not when you're still sleeping with Asher. I could say I went to fire at you and missed, hitting him by accident. I wonder if he'd survive a stabbing and a gunshot—probably not." I stand up with my hands raised, and back up to the open door. "You were so guilt-ridden by all the lies and the murder that you couldn't take it anymore, so you jumped."

I make it onto the balcony and peer over the edge. The party is still going on below. I wonder if I scream for help if anyone would hear it. Did anyone hear it the first time? Did the people downstairs call anyone? Did Dani? Or will Annica get away with two more murders? "I thought we were friends," I say.

"I thought so too."

Finally, I can hear voices and stomping on the stairs growing louder, coming toward the attic. We both look at the locked door on the floor.

"You're just going to have to shoot me," I say. "I'm not going to jump. And then you'll be the one in prison for murder."

Annica laughs, and it's cold and maniacal. "Me? For using self-defense against the Pembroke Psycho? Your prints are on the knife now, and that is your journal page. I'll tell them all about how I saw you stab him, your final victim. I'll be a hero." There's banging on the locked attic door, as whoever it is tries to get in.

"Asher knows the truth."

"Asher?" She laughs, she actually laughs, like I just told her the funniest joke she's ever heard. But the door is about to bust open, and she knows she's out of time. I'm out of time. "Goodbye, Sloane."

The gun makes a clicking noise and I take a deep breath, closing my eyes. I play the song in my head, the one Asher played for me on the piano. There's shouting, other voices, but I can't bring myself to open my eyes. The gun fires with a crack and I wait for it to hit me but . . . when I open my eyes again, Annica is the one face down on the ground, a pool of red forming from under her green dress, and an officer by the attic entrance lowering his arm after firing the shot. The rest happens in a blur. Two officers are in the attic now: One is kneeling next to Wesley, the other is saying something to me. His mouth is moving but all I hear is the ringing in my ears after the gunshot, and "Clair de Lune."

It should have been me. The thought crosses my mind ever so briefly and is gone quicker than a blink. If she would have shot me, then I would no longer have to go to sleep feeling guilty over all the deaths. I would no longer have to feel guilty about lying to Wes, especially now if he doesn't make it.

Medics are here, getting Wes out of the room and pronouncing Annica dead. The other officer guides me to the ladder, where I climb down before him. He leads me down the stairs, to the living area, where people are gathered. Wes goes out on a stretcher, his parents following behind, his mother's face in anguish. She might be screaming, but I don't hear it over the melody in my head. Our friends are outside the front door when the officer leads me out to the other ambulance. I feel Dani's hand grab for me, and I see Asher's eyes. Terrified. I imagine that's what Wesley's eyes looked like while Annica stabbed him. While I was off cheating on him, again. The thought makes me physically ill. The medics look over me when we get to the truck and wrap me in a blanket when they realize none of the blood is mine, aside from what's coming from my torn-up feet. They shine lights in my eyes and ask me questions.

"She's in shock," one of them says to the officer.

Our friends stand off to the side of the truck, as the one transporting Wes drives away. When the small black bag is carried out of the house next, the crowd murmurs, looking around, wondering who is missing. If this were a movie, the scene would play in slow motion with a somber song. I suppose that's how I'm seeing it now.

"Who's in there?" I hear Dani yell. "Who is in there?"

I just stare ahead.

"Where's Annica?" Dani looks around. "Sloane, was she up there with you?"

Her voice sounds far away, like when you hear someone talking while you're asleep. The voice that wakes you from a dream. Or a nightmare. Because that's what this is, isn't it? When the medics don't get adequate responses from me, I am loaded into the back of the ambulance next. With Annica's body. I stare at the zipped-up black bag for the entire ride to the hospital, wondering how someone could hate someone else *that* much. And how I could be so blind to not see it. I thought about the look in her eyes when she held the gun up to me, and the way they looked wholly black in the low light of the attic. I didn't recognize those eyes. They weren't the same fiery, competitive eyes I met freshman year; they looked wild, scared, and even a little . . . relieved. She must have been tired—she had to be.

The ambulance pulls into Saint Ann's Hospital on the island, and I learn that Wes is being airlifted to another hospital in Boston. I hate hospitals with their all-white interiors and lights bright enough to make anyone look sickly. They put me in a room alone. Nurses come in to check my blood pressure and shine lights in my eyes. They clean up my feet and bandage them. They ask questions and I give them nods and shakes of my head, but I can't form the words to talk about what happened.

An hour or so later, Detective Grange shows up to the hospital. He stands at the doorway and knocks twice on the frame.

"Hello, Sloane," he says from the door. "Can I come in?"

I nod.

He sits in one of the visitors' chairs off to the side of the room and lets out a long sigh. "I spoke to a few of the officers at the house, but I think the only person who really knows what happened is you."

We sit in silence for a few minutes. I know he wants details but the whole memory feels jumbled in my head like the day after a blackout. I continue to stare down at my hands.

"Did you read the story?" I say finally.

"I did." More silence. "Holland . . . he wrote your friend as the murderer." I think of the photos Miles had in his apartment. Recent ones of me, and Annica. He was watching me. So in turn he was watching her. I let my head drop to my hands as more tears fall. I should've just read the goddamn story the night Miles showed up at my apartment. I would've known then. It wouldn't have saved everyone, but it would've saved Wes. "Do you think you could walk me through what happened tonight?"

I tell him what I can. He doesn't pry for answers like he usually does, only nods along. When my friends show up at the door, Grange stands to leave.

"I'm glad you're all right," he says before leaving. But I am not all right, not really.

The group doesn't stay long, and we don't say much. The uncomfortable silence paired with Dani's sniffling goes on for only a half hour before Asher tells them all to leave me be, and that he will stay here until my mom comes. I wish he wouldn't. When they're gone he continues to stand in the door frame.

"How are you feeling?" he finally asks.

"Like I should've been with him tonight, not you." I pull my feet back up to the bed and lie down again. I turn so I don't have to face him.

I hear him walk over to the bed and slip off his shoes. He sits down on the edge, before lying next to me. His hands start to rub my back, hesitantly, like he's not sure if this will help. I turn toward him and I want to tell him to leave, to just let me feel bad in peace, but when I open my mouth my voice cracks and I cry instead. He holds me to him like he did not even four hours ago now, but under completely different circumstances.

"I wish she would've just killed me," I cry into his shirt. "I do, then I wouldn't have to live with this anymore."

"Don't say that," he whispers.

I continue to cry, and from the uneven rise and fall of his chest, I think Asher is crying too.

CHAPTER 32

Wes will live.

We got the news days later, once we were all settled back in at Pembroke, dealing with the loss of almost two of our friends. Asher sent the text to the group, letting us all know. Wes suffered a lot of internal bleeding, but she didn't stab any major organs. He could be back at Pembroke as early as next week. The thought had me nearly chewing the insides of my cheeks raw. How could I face him again? I cheated on him three times with Asher and then got him almost stabbed to death. If he ever even wanted to see me again, I'd be lucky.

I haven't seen Asher, Dani, or anyone from the group since we've been back. Asher went to Colorado as planned. Dani has texted me every day since but I haven't replied. I know she has Charlie to console her, and maybe that's wrong of me to not respond. Annica was her best friend too. But my feelings on the matter are a little more complicated.

"I like your story," Claire says after reading through the final draft of my short story for Renner's class. She and my mom have been at my apartment since I left the hospital last weekend. I called my mom in tears and told her everything. But it's now Wednesday and they are packing up to leave.

"Thanks," I say. "But I'm changing the ending."

"Why?"

"Because she doesn't deserve the medic, and I'm not sure the soldier deserves her. So who does she choose?" I say, more so to myself.

"Maybe she chooses herself," Claire says.

"Maybe she does."

"We'll be back in two weeks for graduation," my mom says, coming into my room with her bags slung over her shoulder. "And I will be calling to check in every night."

"Okay," I say.

"And don't forget about your appointment with the therapist: It's Friday morning."

"Okay," I say again.

"And if you want to come home at any point, you can. I already spoke with the dean about you finishing your coursework from home."

"I'm going to finish out here, but okay."

The moment they leave, Dani texts in the group and says we should all get together, for a small memorial for Annica. The school wouldn't have a vigil for her like they did for Bryce. They wouldn't mourn a murderer. I wouldn't either. So I don't reply to the text.

Hours later I get a text from Charlie.

Please come over.

I know he's only asking on behalf of Dani. I leave in my pajama pants and a hoodie.

When I open the door to the house, everyone is in the living room. Sam, Charlie, Jake, and Dani. The group seems so much smaller without Wes, Asher, and Annica in the room. I stop in the frame and debate turning around. Dani gets up and walks to the door, wraps her arms around me, and cries. I hug her back, and I cry too.

We all sit in near silence in the living room, with the windows open, listening to the rain. But there's something about being together as a group that feels good. Even if no one talks, at least we aren't alone.

"I made a small memorial for her in the backyard, if you want to add anything to it," Dani whispers. "But don't feel like you have to."

I lift my head to look at her. "You think Wes is going to come back and want a memorial for someone who stabbed him in his backyard?" It comes out harsher than I meant it to.

"I know that what she did was wrong," Dani starts. "But she was obviously mentally unwell, and we didn't catch on soon enough to help her. She needed our help."

I stand to leave. "I will never forgive her, and I will never mourn her. I knew I shouldn't have even come over here."

"There were good memories too," she says quietly. And while that may be true, no amount of them could ever take away the bad from this year alone. "Just stay here with us for a while longer, please? You can sleep in Wesley's room."

Her pleading tone has me sitting back down, for another round of friendly silence. When everyone heads to their rooms for bed, I trudge up the stairs and stop between Wesley's door and Asher's. I go up the attic stairs to Asher's room to find it's exactly the way he left it. I climb into his bed and fall asleep.

HALF OF PEMBROKE still thinks I'm the Pembroke Psycho; the other half thinks I killed the Pembroke Psycho. Neither of these things is true. Though I guess the latter could be. It was me who drove Annica to this point, so it kind of was me who killed her.

I feel all the stares from my peers as I pick up my cap and gown for graduation. The whispers that accompany them. I can only grit my teeth as I scurry from the student center feeling robbed of the excitement that comes with graduation. I feel robbed of the entire year. And it makes me angry. The more I think about it, the angrier I become. How could she do this to me? Any normal person would just decide to no longer be friends after graduation. She could've just called off our whole friendship that very first weekend when she saw his name in my journal. Sure, I wouldn't have had friends for my entire senior year, but even that would've been better than this. My therapist says it's natural to be angry with her, that it's okay to let that anger out. I don't have to bottle it up.

Before I know where I'm heading, I'm on the front porch of the boys' house. I let myself in, past the empty living room, the kitchen, straight to the back door. And in the far end of the yard, propped up against the wooden fence, is the small memorial Dani made. It is a wooden cross, with a stuffed giraffe, a candle, flowers, and a bunch of photos of all of us.

So I let my anger out.

I pick up the cross and snap it over my knee, throwing the

pieces in the bonfire pit. I kick the giraffe over their fence and pop the heads off the flowers, rip apart the petals, and start to tear up the photos.

"I thought about doing that too."

I turn to see Wesley standing by the back door.

"Oh my god, you're back." I run to him, and he grunts when I hug him. "Sorry." I release him, remembering the stab wound on his side. "Are you okay?"

"Mentally, no. Physically . . . also no."

"When did you get back?"

"Monday," he says. But it's Thursday, and he never said anything.

"Oh. You never texted, or called, or . . ."

"Yeah," he says. "I just needed some time." He grabs the lighter fluid from the cement steps, pouring it over the wood and pieces of Annica's memorial, and lights it. We both sit in the chairs around the small fire. "I need you to tell me everything, and I need it to be the truth."

I don't want to cause him any more harm, but I am tired of lying, and I don't think I could do it if I tried. "I'm so sorry," I say.

"The truth, Sloane."

So I tell him about the journal, about working with Asher to catch Miles. I tell him how Asher caught me trying to hide evidence, and about the agreement we made in order for him to help me. Then I tell him what happened that night when I found him upstairs. The whole story feels rehearsed for how many times I've said it by now. To Grange, to my friends, to the therapist, and now to Wes.

His mouth forms a hard line, taking it all in.

"Where were you? Where were you when she took me upstairs?"

"I was with Asher," I admit.

"Doing what exactly?"

I couldn't say it. "I think you already know," I whisper.

We watch the flames crack and hiss. The photos now nothing but ash in the wind. I don't want to ask him what this means for us, or if I even want there to be an us. Can I even ever really be with Wes if half my heart belongs to someone else?

"I'm sorry," I say again.

"I know this year was hard for you, and I was so caught up with Marissa and the house for most of it that I didn't even realize what was going on. You had to make tough choices and do difficult things. And I don't even blame you for falling for my cousin because it seems like he was the only one there for you through it all. I just wish you told me."

"I wish I did too." How different would things be if I had just confided in him from the start? "Are we breaking up?" I ask.

He takes a deep breath. "Yeah, I think we are. As a couple, but not as friends."

Friends. That word again. But this time, I feel relieved to hear it. He should hate me; he should never want to see me ever again. I look over at him in the orange glow of the fire before standing up and walking over to him. He looks up at me, unsure of what I'm doing as I sit on his lap, curl in my knees, and lean onto his chest. He lets out a breath and brings his arms around me, holding me that way until the last embers go out.

"ALMOST READY?" ADRIENNE says from my door.

I stand in the mirror of my bedroom with my cap and gown on over my white dress.

"Yeah, I'm ready."

When we leave the apartment for the ceremony I almost trip when my foot collides with the small package sitting on our door-mat. Ripping it open, and looking inside, I see what looks like a large stack of paper. I pull it from the packaging and read the sticky note on the front.

This was never my story to tell.
MH

"What is that?" she asks.

"Um, one second," I say, going back inside.

It's the story he wrote about the murders. I take it to my bedroom and set it on my bed. I'll come back to it later. Maybe I'll read it. But I look at it again, then at the small trash can in my room.

I toss it in.

THOUSANDS OF CHAIRS are placed in the middle of the field and the stands are full of everyone's families. We walk out sorted by college, and in alphabetical order. I can only hope the ceremony goes quick as the sun beats down on us. The dean briefly glosses over the deaths of the would-be graduates this year and I can't help but look down the row at where Annica would be sitting. Did she not even care about graduating? Did she even think she would? We turn our tassels and some people toss their caps into the air, but I don't.

I go out to eat with my family after commencement and my mother talks about moving me back home until I find a job. I nod along, but I think about Asher. What if I did move out to Colorado with him? Would he even still want me to? We haven't spoken in the two weeks since he left. He could be with Brandy now for all I know.

After a lot of convincing, my mom and Don drop me off at the boys' house after dinner, where everyone is already outside drinking. Wes sits on the railing of the porch, and I take a mental note, because this is the last time I'll ever see it. If senior year was a book, then this would be the last chapter. This is where the main character would realize that everything she went through made her better in the end. She would have a job lined up or an internship, and she would walk up onto that porch and kiss her boyfriend, the one she worked so hard to win over. Her friends would cheer, someone would pop champagne. In a Netflix series, some indie pop song would play in the background as the camera zooms out away from the house. The credits would roll.

But instead, Jake throws up in the bushes by the porch.

I sigh, walking past him and up the porch steps. Wes brings me in for a long hug and kisses my cheek. Dani comes out holding a bottle of champagne. So there's that at least. She shakes it up and holds it out over the railing.

"To graduation!" Dani yells, more like half slurs, and I know she's already drunk. She pops the bottle, and it sprays into the yard. Dani hands it to me and I take a sip. She does too, before pouring some out into the yard. "And one for Annica."

Maybe she'll be able to taste it in hell.

I walk inside, looking for Asher. People are all around the living room, jumping on the couches, smoking, spilling champagne everywhere. He said he'd be here. I walk up the stairs toward his room and stop at the door.

I know my answer.

I open the door, looking at the boxes all over his floor. His bed is gone, his piano is gone. I hear the sink running in the bathroom and give a sigh of relief knowing he's here. I take a deep breath, preparing to see him. But before he comes out, something catches my eye. A half-packed box lies open where his bar cart used to be, and inside is a small brown leather book. But those are common, right?

I walk over to the box, bending down to get a closer look.

"Sloane?" Asher comes from the bathroom and spots me crouched over the box.

And I don't have to open it to know what it is. I've carried this journal around for four years: I know how the leather cover feels on my fingertips. The exact weight of it in my bookbag. The way the bottom left corner has started to wear away.

"Sloane, wait." This time there's worry in his voice. I untie the side and open it to find Ryan's eulogy, with the torn-out page that was once Jonah's overlapping it. "I can explain."

My hands shake and my shoulders slump. "Why do you have this?" I look at him now, and Asher is pale under my gaze, likely deciding if he should lie or tell the truth. "Answer the question."

"Can we go back to your place and talk about this?"

"Tell me why you have it." I stand with the journal in hand.

"I didn't know she was going to kill anyone," he says quietly, and I almost don't hear it over the music blaring downstairs.

My breath hitches in my throat at his words, his admission. That he had any part in this. "You knew? You knew this whole time it was her?"

"You have to understand, everything I did, I did to protect you.

She asked me to take the journal, scan the pages, and help her distribute them. She said it was a prank, something to just throw you off. She said she wanted to win that stupid essay competition and she needed you to spiral. And in return she'd talk Wes out of the resort—"

"You let people die, for your *resort*? Oh my god, Asher." I put my hand to my mouth, shaking my head in disbelief.

"When she told me she killed Ryan I told her I wasn't going to help her with whatever this was, and she said if I turned her in I would go down with her. You have to understand, Sloane, I was going to go to jail with her if I said anything. I was trying to help you the best I could."

I suddenly think of how Annica laughed when I mentioned Asher's name before she died. And how she gave me plot advice for my story, saying . . . the main character should find out that the character based off Asher had been deceiving her the whole time.

God, she basically told me.

"Help me? You let me run around for *months* trying to pin murders on an innocent man! We broke into his car and his house, for *nothing*! You let people die, over and over again, instead of just going to the police after Ryan!" I feel the panic rising in my throat as my breathing becomes shallow again. It all makes sense. How much Annica had hated him this year, questioning everything he ever did or said to me. She thought he would tell me the truth, that he'd turn her in. She never believed for a moment that he had any feelings toward me, because he never did. He can't say he loves me because he doesn't. He just needed to distract me long enough for him to get off scot-free. I feel myself start to hyperventilate now, the room growing smaller. "I can't, I can't believe this."

"I didn't care at the start. I just wanted what she promised me, but I really did fall for you—you have to believe that. I love you, and I'm so sorry."

I cut him a look, one that makes him shut his mouth.

"I trusted you," I say. "I trusted both of you."

"I love you," he says again, like it'll take it all away. Like the words will wash it all away. He steps toward me.

I shake my head and back away. "Don't." He stops. "I should turn you in. I should call Grange and tell him you helped her."

"But you won't," Asher says. "Because you love me too, I know you do."

"No," I say. "No."

"Yes, you do. And I would spend the rest of my life trying to make it up to you if you could forgive me somehow—"

"You were never going to tell me, were you? You were going to whisk me away to Vail and just wait for it to all blow over." Again, he doesn't say anything. I just shake my head at him as tear after tear slips down my cheeks. Genuinely surprised that I even have any left. "I never want to see you again." I move past him, still with the journal in hand, and stop. "You know what, keep this." I throw the journal at his chest. "I would only fill the remaining pages with your name anyway."

I leave the house without another word to anyone. I don't stop when Dani calls after me, or when Wes tries to follow me down the street while I walk somewhere to call for a ride.

Alone in my apartment I stare at Grange's number on my phone. I should call and say Asher was an accessory. There will be no trial now that Annica is dead. There would be if I did this. Could I stand up there and condemn him to possible jail time for printing the pages of the journal, for agreeing to initially help her, then standing by while she did it? Can people even get jail time for that? My thumb hovers over the call button, then away. He manipulated me, he used me, he lied to me. I wonder what Ben would do to him if Asher was going to go to prison. And deep down, in some sick twisted part of me, I can't hurt him. I can't do it.

Frustrated, I throw my phone at the wall. It leaves a small hole in the plaster before falling into the suitcase that I had started to pack. The one I would have taken with me to Colorado.

I let out a frustrated scream, then another, until my throat is raw. Then I lie down in the dark, still in my graduation dress, and go through the names of the dead again. Jonah, Ryan, Marco, Bryce, Graham. Jonah, Ryan, Marco, Bryce, Graham.

Asher. Asher. Asher.

THE FOLLOWING DAY, I don't leave my bed. I'm supposed to be packing up my things. Our lease is up at the end of next week.

There's a small knock on my door before Adrienne opens it. "Hey, were the cookie sheets yours or mine? I don't remember."

I lie facing the wall. "Just take them. I don't care."

"Are you okay?" she asks.

"No."

"Do you want to talk about it?"

With another person who has lied to me this year? "No."

"Okay," she whispers, shutting the door.

My phone buzzes periodically. They're texts from my family, texts from Dani, texts from Asher.

I shut my phone off.

CHAPTER 33

Annica wins the short-story competition.

After two days in bed I turn my phone back on to a whole host of messages, including an email from Renner to the class breaking the news. She must have submitted her final story before spring break. But since she's dead, and a murderer, the second-place story will get the prize.

Whoever that is, because it isn't me.

I almost laugh at the irony. She wanted so badly to win, to beat me in something, and she finally did. But she'll never know. Or maybe she will. Maybe she's looking down—or looking up, rather—at my life now, smug as the hell I hope she's now an occupant of.

I sit up, watching the small specks of dust float around in the morning sun before I make eye contact with the small trash bin in my room. Miles Holland's story sticks out at the top of it. He was right about one thing; it is not his story to tell. I look over at my goals still taped to my mirror. The only one not crossed out: *Write your first book.*

It's not Holland's story to tell, because it's mine.

I take my laptop from my bag and open it up. I won't write a eulogy for everyone who broke my heart this year. I will write a whole damn book.

I let it all sink in. Adrienne smiling at me while seeing Miles behind my back. Annica's soothing words after every murder, the ones *she* committed. And Asher. I can't even think of him without wanting to hyperventilate and crawl back under the covers.

I scroll through what has to now be hundreds of text messages and voicemails he's left me in the past few days begging for forgiveness. He says he loves me, but it won't be enough. It will never be enough. He was the biggest liar of them all.

So here I sit at the final chapter of my senior year, the last ten minutes of the series, and I've decided for once, I will choose myself. I didn't get a love story, or even a happy ending, but I won't close the book empty-handed.

After all, every ending is a new beginning, right?

My fingers hover over the keyboard as I take a deep breath. When I start to type, I imagine in the limited-series version of my life, the camera would zoom into the screen as the letters began to appear one by one on the page, the blinking cursor pausing at the end.

`Here Lie All the Boys Who Broke My Heart`

CHAPTER 34

Asher

"Let me guess," Wesley says from behind me. "It's your fault that Sloane just stormed out of the house crying?"

I drop her journal back into the box that I carelessly left out and quickly wipe away the water welling up in my own eyes before I turn to face my cousin. I want to tell him to fuck off. I want to tell him it's not his business, but when he steps forward and flinches slightly at the pain still in his side, I realize it is his business. What would he say if I told him the truth? That it wasn't just Annica that betrayed him, but his own flesh and blood.

"Yes, it's my fault," I say, locking my hands together on my head and taking a breath. I stare up at the ceiling and Wes stands in the doorway waiting for an explanation. "I have to tell you something."

"Shoot," Wes says.

"I . . ." I choke on the words as my future flashes before me. Wesley would tell the family, and would they be shocked to find out that Ben's son almost let his cousin die in order to take over the business? No, probably not. But that would be it. That would be the nail in the coffin. I wouldn't have the resort, and I wouldn't have Sloane, and after all that happened just to get to this point . . . "I think she would've been better off with you. I'm sorry that I got in between that."

I watch as Wes tries not to roll his eyes, pushing off the frame. "Right," he says, turning to leave.

"Wes," I call after him. "I really am sorry for everything that happened this year. I'm sorry."

His eyes narrow slightly, and I can tell he's trying to figure out if this is a genuine apology. It makes me hate myself even more than I already do. "Whatever, man."

He turns to go back to the party, and I let out the breath I was holding. The one that should've contained the truth. But again, just like everything else in my life, I fucked it all up.

I finish packing up my things in silence, the whole time picturing Sloane's face when she found out the truth, and how I wish I could go back in time and never put the journal in that box. No, fuck, I wish I could go back to the moment Annica stormed into my bedroom with that journal in hand. When I close my eyes I can still hear the way she raged over Sloane and Wesley. And dammit, I should've known better. I truly made a deal with the devil that day.

I PICK UP my phone, the only thing not packed away, as I lie in bed and try calling Sloane. It rings five times before going to voicemail. I text her with another useless apology and watch as it says delivered. She hasn't blocked my number. Not yet anyway.

I HAND THE last box off to the moving company that's driving my stuff back to Colorado and check my phone again. By now I've called and texted Sloane a handful of times, even leaving her a voicemail. I can't remember the last time I ever left someone a voicemail. But it's been almost twenty-four hours since she left my room and I still haven't gotten a reply. A loud thump catches my attention as the two movers lifting my piano into the truck drop one end of it.

"Dude, I said be careful with the fucking piano!" I yell.

"I wouldn't be so rude to the people moving your most prized possessions across the country for you," I hear Danielle say from beside me.

I only shake my head, putting away my phone so she can't see the embarrassing amount of texts and calls I've left Sloane.

"Still haven't heard from her?" she asks.

"No," I sigh. "Have you?"

"No," she says. "I think she just needs some alone time. That's usually how she is after a breakup."

"I asked her to come with me," I tell Danielle. Her raised eyebrows tell me that Sloane didn't tell her that. Perhaps because she never intended to go.

"When is your flight?" she asks me.

"Tomorrow at two."

"Then there's still plenty of time to fix it." She pats my arm before walking into the house.

By 6 p.m. my room is as empty as the day we moved in and my time at Pembroke is officially over. I say my final goodbyes to the boys, who all promise to come up to ski next season. Though we all know that if Wes doesn't go, Jake, Sam, and Charlie won't either. They were always his friends more than mine.

Danielle gives me a hug and starts to cry. "It's really over," she sniffs. "We're all leaving."

"It's not goodbye," Charlie tells her. "It's just . . . 'see you later.'"

I nod in agreement at that. I was never good at consoling anyone. I never seem to have the right words.

"Maybe for us," she whispers to herself, hinting at Annica. I swallow hard as I feel the guilt creeping in again. A reminder that *everyone* got hurt. Maybe not physically, but everyone lost someone they thought was a friend. And I had a hand in that.

The room starts to feel suffocating, and I find myself backing toward the door before giving a brief wave of my hand and exiting the house. I get into the back of the Uber with my carry-on luggage, checking my phone one more time for a response from Sloane.

"To the Holiday Inn by the airport?" the driver asks. I consider changing the drop-off point to her apartment. Would she even want to see me? Is she still there?

"Yes," I say. "The Holiday Inn by the airport."

I TEXT SLOANE again, and again. I leave another desperate voicemail. I order a bottle of wine to my room and leave her five more voicemails. I send one more text after I've finished the bottle. I can barely read it at this point, but it doesn't deliver. Sloane has finally blocked me.

THE SUNGLASSES DO little to nothing to help with the hangover I have today as I trudge through the airport. I grab a coffee and get settled at my gate before going back through the messages I sent last night, each one sounding more desperate and embarrassing than the last. Part of me is glad she finally blocked me, as if it could've gotten any worse.

"We are now boarding flight 1371 with service to Vail, Colorado," the airport worker announces on the speaker. "Please have your boarding pass and identification ready."

Although I have a first-class seat, I wait out the boarding process until the very end to minimize the amount of time I have to stand in line with this bad of a hangover. I've never been sick on a flight, but I'm starting to think today might be the day. When the line begins to dwindle and the last group is boarding, I stand and grab my carry-on. I look down at my phone for a moment, thinking of Sloane, like I have been nonstop for the past three days. Hell, the past nine months really. I have thought of her every single day of this school year. At first just to wonder what would make her tick and how best to manipulate her into getting what I wanted . . . until I began to wonder what made her laugh, and how in the world I was going to keep her safe from all of this. Every. Single. Day.

I dial her number one more time knowing it won't ring now that I'm blocked, but it does. It rings three times, and I'm hopeful that I can at least leave her one last pathetic voicemail before I fly home, but then the line stops ringing and there is no voicemail prompt. Because she answers the phone.

My breath is caught in my throat as we both sit silently on each end of the phone. "Sloane?" I say finally. She doesn't answer, but I hear her take a long breath and sigh on the other end. "Sloane, please—"

"I need to know everything," she says in such a small voice that I have to practically press the phone into my ear to hear it.

The airport speaker turns on again: "Last call for boarding

flight 1371 with service to Vail, Colorado." I look back at the gate and the attendants getting ready to close the door to the terminal, but my mind was made up the moment she answered the phone.

"I'm on my way."

ACKNOWLEDGMENTS

Where to begin? No, really—I had to start pulling books from my shelves, looking at other acknowledgment pages to see how this usually goes, because I didn't know where to begin! How do I possibly give a meaningful, heartfelt thank-you to everyone who made this possible?

To my super wonderful and amazing literary agent, Kristen Bertoloni—you took a chance on me and look where we are now! I'll never forget getting that first email from you; I was in my car, and I literally screamed, probably almost causing a collision (but it would have been worth it). Since then, you've been my guide into the publishing world, answering any and all of my constant questions. You're my sounding board when I'm second-guessing things and my favorite person to squeal in excitement with on the phone every time we get good news. Thank you, thank you, thank you!!! When it's all said and done, we didn't flop—we ate.

To my editing team—Allie Roche, Charlotte Osment, and Alex Bessette—you three have been nothing short of a dream. From our very first conversations about this story and how genuinely excited you all were about the characters, my face would hurt after every call from smiling so much. You made the editing process effortless! Thank you for believing in this story—and in me. Alex and Charlotte, I can't wait to continue this journey with you both on the next one. Allie, we still have a date on the Staten Island Ferry with a pack of High Noons—I won't forget!

To everyone at Avon/HarperCollins—Liate Stehlik, Jennifer Hart, Tessa Woodward, May Chen, DJ DeSmyter, Andrea Molitor, Mary Interdonati, Marie Rossi, Hope Breeman, Paul Miele-Herndon—as well as the team at Simon & Schuster UK—thank you all SO MUCH. From the stunning cover designs to the meticulous copy and production edits to the brilliant marketing strategies in the US and the UK, your talent and hard work have touched every part of this process. Everything has felt seamless because of you, and I truly couldn't imagine better teams to bring this story to life.

To everyone at Trident Media Group working with foreign markets to make this book available around the world—thank you for all that you do!

To my sister, Chloe—AKA my little plot monkey. You've spent years of your life listening to me ramble on about books and ideas for books, and it has been one of the greatest joys of my life having someone to share a love for reading and stories with. I hope you know you've signed up for many years to come of proofreading and in-depth voice memos about people who aren't real.

To Ann Marie, Allison, and Amy (who I just now realized all have names that start with A—the A Team!)—thank you for reading the earliest versions of *Here Lie* and providing valuable feedback. It wouldn't be what it is today without your honesty and support.

To my parents, my other siblings, and my grandparents—thank you for all that you do/have done for me. A heavenly thank-you to my grandpa, who sadly won't get to see this come to fruition, but who always encouraged every whim I had growing up. He was the first family member—aside from Chloe—to know I was thinking about writing a book in the first place. I know he's proud of me, and if he were here, he'd be telling me how to invest my earnings.

To my friends—Taylor, Jake, Kyleigh, Natalie, and Brian—the humans I talk to daily (often on multiple social media platforms, while also texting, calling, and voice memoing): thank you for your unwavering support. Thank you for telling me I could do this even when I felt like I couldn't. Thank you for bragging about me to literally anyone who will listen and for promoting this book like you're on commission. It's your voices and your hearts in these characters.

To my husband, Nick—you may have thought I was crazy when I came home one day and said, "I think I'm going to try writing a book" and then spent countless nights holed up in the spare room doing just that, with no guarantee of ever being published. You supported me then just as you do now. You've eased my anxiety when I couldn't sleep, made me tea every night while I wrote, and given me more foot and back rubs than I can count. I once told you I wanted everything in life, to which you said, *Then I'll make sure you have it.* I'm eternally grateful for you. I can't believe we get to do this together.

ABOUT THE AUTHOR

Emma Simmerman is a debut author with an advertising degree from Kent State University. She is a Youngstown, Ohio, native who now resides in Cleveland with her husband, Nick, and her two cats, Kitty and Cleo. When she's not writing, she enjoys reading, crocheting, and drinking overpriced cocktails with her friends.